The
Jazz
Sutra

THE JAZZ BUYER

Short Fiction

Hal Howland

**The New
Atlantian Library**

THE NEW ATLANTIAN LIBRARY
is an imprint of
ABSOLUTELY AMAZING eBOOKS

Published by Whiz Bang LLC, 926 Truman Avenue, Key West, Florida 33040, USA.

For information contact:
Publisher@AbsolutelyAmazingEbooks.com
ISBN-13: 978-0692313428
ISBN-10: 0692313427

For Lisa Marderosian,
the most musical name in my repertoire

Also by Hal Howland

Fiction
Cities & Women: Short Fiction
After Jerusalem: A Story and Two Novellas
Landini Cadence and Other Stories: A Rich Castillo
Threesome
Murder in Key West (anthology) Volumes I and II

Nonfiction
The Human Drummer: Thoughts on the Life Percussive

Jazz Recordings
The Howland Ensemble
Reiko
10 Years in 5 Days

The Jazz Stoyer

TABLE OF CONTENTS

ACROPHOBIA AND THE PROFESSOR

FOR AS LONG AS SHE COULD REMEMBER, Sasha Mayakovski had been drawn to the water. She dipped her toes in the Mediterranean for the first time as an infant in Tel Aviv and loved splashing in the gentle waves. Her parents insisted that she and her little sister, Irina, take swimming lessons when Sasha was eight, but by then the girl needed no encouragement. She had taught herself to get around in any body of water, natural or artificial; the lessons merely gave her the science of it. Sasha took up scuba diving as soon as she was big enough to support the gear and learned to navigate the spectacular coral reefs in the Gulf of Aqaba. She majored in marine biology at Hebrew University, and her graduate studies at Stanford took her to the great reefs of Australia and the Florida Keys. Dr. Sasha Mayakovski became one of the leaders in her field, heading the department at the University of Miami and lecturing on conservation throughout the world. She remained utterly fearless in the water, swimming with the shark and the barracuda as if strolling a neighborhood street with a friend. She admired and envied these creatures the way the first aviators viewed the birds of the sky.

But the sky itself was another matter.

As a child Sasha had loved diving from rocky cliffs or

high boards, and she had wondered why her mother would cringe and shut her eyes during the family's day trips via narrow mountain ledges above the Negev. This innocent enjoyment of high places disappeared suddenly one unforgettable summer afternoon.

Sasha's father was a diplomat. When the modern State of Israel was new, he attended several meetings and conferences in Washington, D.C. He brought the family with him the year that Sasha turned twelve. They celebrated her birthday on the National Mall, as lovely a place as any she had seen on dry land. The next day, the family drove out to the Virginia piedmont and toured Skyline Drive. Sasha noticed that her mom seemed less nervous on this manicured highway, bordered as it was by lush vegetation and sturdy stone barriers. They stopped at practically every overlook so everyone could take in the breathtaking Shenandoah Valley. When they broke for lunch, a park ranger invited the family to accompany him to the top of his fire tower. Mrs. Mayakovski declined the invitation, but the girls and their father followed the uniformed young man with excitement.

That was the event that changed everything for Sasha. She was fine climbing the first few levels, laughing with Irina and savoring the fragrant summer humidity, so different from the parched landscapes of home. But when they reached the point where they could see over the treetops, where birds flew past them at eye level, where the endless blue universe opened like a swallowing chasm, Sasha froze. She gripped the rail with both hands and felt her legs turn to jelly. No one noticed her reaction until Irina and their dad had continued on to the next level.

When they did notice, they returned to her and tried to calm her unforeseen fear. Irina was eager to reach the summit, and the ranger could not allow anyone to climb unaccompanied. Once it became clear that Sasha was unable to go on, they agreed that she should wait there: the guardhouse at the top was only a few levels higher, after all, and Irina and the men would return for her in a few minutes.

To Sasha those minutes were a blur. She stood at the rail unable to move in any direction, blind to the verdant beauty that surrounded her, praying for the moment when her father would gently pry her sweating hands from the cold steel and usher her back down to safety.

After that day, Sasha was glad to miss the scenery from any high, open place. She had no problem flying in airplanes, but rooftops, balconies, and her once beloved lakeside cliffs were off limits. It occurred to Sasha a few years later that her sudden acrophobia had arrived precisely at the onset of puberty, but at the time the two events seemed unconnected.

Sasha did enjoy one brief respite from her fear. She spent her sixteenth birthday with the family in Paris. None of the others, not even Mrs. Mayakovski, was willing to forego the view from the top of the Eiffel Tower. With her mom's encouragement, Sasha agreed to give it a try. Indeed, she was able to stand at the rail as Paris spread before her like a huge, three-dimensional map. *It must be a magic city after all,* she thought. But that was the last time Sasha was able to withstand a roofless place so far from terra firma.

During college, Sasha took basic psychology as an

elective. At one point she entertained a theory that her fear of heights was related to her sexuality. Sasha had gravitated toward other girls from the beginning and had never felt the slightest curiosity about the opposite sex. The thought of lying there while some hairy, powerful beast penetrated her repeatedly seemed at best ridiculous. She began to wonder whether encountering the phallic Virginia fire tower at the dawn of adolescence had sealed some biological pact that she would never want to dissolve.

Many years later, Dr. Sasha Mayakovski found herself traveling at least once a year from her office in Miami to Key West to speak at events sponsored by Reef Relief and other environmental organizations. Usually she drove her own car, an economical sedan. One brilliant spring morning after a particularly stressful week of classes and meetings, she decided to rent a convertible for the three-hour spectacle that was U.S. 1.

Sasha had traveled that stretch of road so many times in a closed car that it had never occurred to her how different it would feel with the top down. When she reached the apex of the Jewfish Creek Bridge just above Key Largo, the vastness of space opened before her like the yawning canopy high above the Shenandoah. Her neck and shoulders tightened like a straitjacket, and she gripped the steering wheel as if it might come off in her hands. A panorama that a filmmaker would have treasured was for Sasha an infinite vortex of pure terror. She concentrated all her energy on the bumper of the car a quarter mile ahead of her and counted the seconds until she descended to the mostly flat roadbed of the Keys. She was tempted to stop at the first of many tiki bars and order a double vodka, but it was only eight in the morning. She cruised Key Largo sucking in deep breaths and stretching her upper body back into shape.

Sasha knew that two more high bridge spans lay between her and Key West: the Channel Five Bridge below Islamorada and the Seven Mile Bridge below Marathon, both of which afforded world-renowned views of the very sort of fantastic turquoise liquid that had embraced Sasha as a child. *All right, damn it,* she told herself, *you're a big girl now. This is ridiculous. Let's try to enjoy what everyone else thinks is so fucking great.*

The Channel Five Bridge was relatively stress-free, perhaps because of the gracefully curving approach and the opportunity to steal brief glimpses of particularly inviting water. *OK, that wasn't so bad. See? You can do this.*

Sasha drove the long segment between Islamorada and Marathon feeling confident that her intellect could subdue the subconscious monster. She watched her speed in Marathon, where the cops were apt to pounce on any vehicle that did not bear a Monroe County plate.

As she climbed the gentle hill toward the Seven Mile Bridge, Sasha breathed, loosened her shoulders, flexed her fingers, invented ephemeral mantras, and vowed to prove herself to the indifferent forces of nature. From the flat approach to Pigeon Key, the dizzying span above Moser Channel was a mere bump in the road. *Just take it, you pussy. You'll be fine.*

As Sasha finished her last silent incantation and began to ascend the span, two young men in a black pickup truck began tailgating her. There was fast-moving traffic in both directions, and Sasha's usual strategy of slowing down until the fools gave up and passed her was not going to work. She had no choice but to maintain her speed, keep that next bumper in her sights as if she were being towed across the bridge, and ignore the gale-force winds that conspired to unhook her seat belt and release her screaming into the ether. Sasha had not felt such paralyzing fear since *that* afternoon. When finally she reached the gas station between the bridge and Bahia Honda State Park, Sasha pulled over and burst into tears.

After that humiliating experience, the Bahia Honda and Niles Channel bridges were a breeze. Sasha traveled the rest of the way to Key West in relative peace.

Sasha checked into her guesthouse and took a brief nap before lunch. In the afternoon she walked down to the corner of Duval and Greene Streets, where Reef Relief had set up the stage from which Sasha and several other panelists would address the annual gathering of environmentalists fighting to undo decades of damage by unregulated polluters. The stage was roughly shoulder height, no big deal, and the podium was positioned safely in the middle of the platform. But the chairs on which the panelists would await their turns to speak were perched precariously close to the back edge, with no hard wall, tenting, or even a comforting plastic banner waving in the breeze. Sasha approached the executive director of Reef Relief and asked him to have the chairs moved up a few feet. Still, when the program began, Sasha found herself leaning ahead as if she were being dragged backward off the stage and onto the bone-crushing pavement.

When the program was over, Reef Relief treated the

panelists to a sumptuous Cuban dinner. Sasha gulped two *mojitos,* went back to her room, and slept through the night.

The next morning, Sasha considered dropping off her rental car at the airport and flying back to Miami. But she knew she would feel safe if she drove with the top up, and if she flew she would have to rent another car to get from the Miami airport to her home in Coral Gables. On the way back up the Keys, Sasha was amazed at what a difference a thin layer of canvas made: she was able to play the radio and enjoy the view like a regular person.

A ninety-minute massage and two trips to the chiropractor that week did little to unlock Sasha's traumatized neck and shoulders.

The following year, Sasha was invited to speak at another marine-conservation meeting on Miami Beach. The event took place in a high-rise hotel conference room, followed by a reception in the penthouse. Sasha looked comfortably out over her city from well behind the floor-to-ceiling windows, but she could not get too close; nor could she join those of her colleagues who had ventured out onto the vertiginous balcony.

After the reception, Sasha took the elevator down, exited the building, and stood gazing up at it. *You don't look anything like a penis,* she smiled. *You're just another monument to greed and arrogance.*

Dr. Sasha Mayakovski drove home, took off all her clothes, and jumped in the pool.

AMERICAN ORATORIO

GEOFFREY FRANCIS HANSEN DESCENDED the gangplank, steadied himself against a barrel of horseshoes that was the first immobile object he had seen in two months, and took several deep breaths to settle his stomach. The crisp, clean Plymouth autumn air was little help.

Mrs. Greta Hansen was already seated on her trunk, fanning herself with a secessionist pamphlet that a teenage boy had thrust at her before being ushered out of the way by an overburdened British tea merchant.

Geoffrey hobbled over to his wife and placed a hand on her shoulder to haul himself upright. Having seen a contraband draft of the pamphlet aboard the ship, he smiled grimly. "My dear, I shall be glad never again to set foot on another seagoing vessel so long as I may live."

Greta placed her gloved hand on her husband's and patted it a few times. A practical woman of sturdy constitution, she customarily humored Geoffrey's delicate sensibilities.

The two were obliged to wait on the windblown dock until the rest of their luggage, furniture, and, most important, Geoffrey's harpsichord could be unloaded and placed in the wagon. Greta glanced back curiously at the old black driver who waited patiently, caressing his reins and singing softly to his master's horses. Just ahead of the wagon waited the small covered carriage that would transport the Hansens to their rented cottage near the town square.

Several hours passed before the little convoy pulled into the gate and the two house servants, Estelle and her husband, Marcus, helped bring in the couple's belongings. Neither Geoffrey nor Greta had much appetite for the light meal Estelle had prepared, but they sampled the tasty provisions out of politeness. They did appreciate the roaring fire Marcus had going in the open kitchen hearth. The wet, frigid air that had descended on the dock to accompany the setting sun was all too reminiscent of London.

Geoffrey's bold adventure, forsaking his bustling native city for a new life in the American colonies, was Greta's idea. Geoffrey's writing had fallen into a rut—like most contemporary composers, he had begun recycling his early works and had resorted to safe formulas to appease his aristocratic patrons—and, no matter where they lived, he could expect to supplement his income by teaching lessons. When Geoffrey's restless former school chum Jean-Baptiste Cousineau wrote and invited Geoffrey to head the theory and composition department of the small conservatory Cousineau had established in Plymouth, Greta would not allow her husband to refuse. "It will be all to the good," she assured him. "You will see."

Indeed, as their first winter settled over the icy Massachusetts hills, Geoffrey surrendered to the quieter pace of life and learned the bright side of simplicity. When spring crocuses finally poked through the melting snow, he helped Greta plant the large vegetable garden she could never have realized back home. The rest of his time was spent composing chamber pieces for a few local musicians, teaching those players' children, and acquainting himself with the wealthy importers and bankers who might underwrite his larger-scale compositions.

Nearly all the Hansens' neighbors were Protestants whose musical knowledge was confined to folk tunes from the old country and to the hymns they sang on Sunday mornings. The small semiprofessional choir Jean-Baptiste Cousineau had assembled from local churches was growing, but Geoffrey had few resources to call on as he patched together an orchestra composed of teachers, students, and amateurs. Rehearsals were rough going, and their first concerts were met with bewilderment and begrudging applause. But with Greta's unfailing encouragement, Geoffrey remained committed to promoting good music in his strange new homeland.

After several years of slow but steady improvement, Geoffrey began to feel that the time was right to try out a new musical form that had taken hold in England a year before the Hansens' departure. The undisputed star of the London scene was an older German immigrant whose name was annoyingly similar to Geoffrey's own. Having succumbed to the financial difficulties of producing opera, this George Frideric Handel had begun experimenting with something called *oratorio*. Musically the form was new only in terminology—three or four solo singers, a chorus, and an orchestra, as in opera—but it dispensed with sets and special effects and therefore could be performed on any stage, or lack thereof. Handel's early oratorios favored historical or biblical themes and turned out to be wildly successful. This popularity, combined with the irksome name problem and Greta's optimism, sealed Geoffrey's decision to seek greener pastures.

As he began sketching his big new score, Geoffrey struggled with the slim pickings at his disposal. As in Europe, he would have to borrow two trumpeters and a kettledrummer from the local militia. He would also have to keep a tight leash on these soldiers in rehearsal to prevent their drowning out his undersize string section. Geoffrey managed to recruit a handful of flute, oboe, bassoon, and horn players, but he relied on unconventional doubling to cover the parts. He would never lead the full orchestra he had enjoyed in London, and he would learn to forgive a variety of problems not only with balance but also with pitch, rhythm, dynamics, reading ability, and scheduling.

To concentrate on his new composition, Geoffrey had cut back slightly on his teaching, doubled his fund-raising efforts, and spent every available moment in ascetic solitude. For months he refused to read newspapers or to engage in idle talk. Those townsfolk who had grown accustomed to hoisting an occasional tankard with Geoffrey down at the pub began to wonder what had become of the crusading musician.

Always Geoffrey's loyal champion, Greta had agreed not to discuss her husband's unfinished masterpiece with the servants or with the town wives who visited their home to purchase the bounty that overflowed her garden. In private Greta could not stop humming the graceful Italianate melodies she heard coming from Geoffrey's locked music room, but she promised not to share anything she knew about the rising mountain of manuscript paper atop the harpsichord.

As the deep reds and oranges of autumn began to accumulate beside the muddy streets and the harvest consumed most people's time, the necessity for long and repeated rehearsal allowed word of Geoffrey's groundbreaking work to filter through the community. The oratorio would require the efforts of every singer and every instrumentalist within a hundred miles, but the quality of Geoffrey's writing and the spirit of newness not only in the music itself but also in the patriotic possibilities it represented—the best of Europe transformed in the New World—compelled the participants to suffer every indignity to see the piece's fruition.

Typically, Geoffrey was still composing, revising, rejecting, and rewriting during the rehearsal process, and the continual changes tried everyone's patience. Those less gifted performers who occasionally provoked the composer's ire reminded themselves that the end would justify the means. Teamwork and camaraderie forged friendships and even a few love affairs that would endure for years to come.

Finally one November evening Geoffrey emerged from his inner sanctum, joined Greta at the supper table, and smiled with deep satisfaction. "It is finished," he told his wife as she fought her tears of joy. His placed the heavy score on the table at her elbow.

In observance of the coming holiday season, Geoffrey had drawn his text from predictions in the Old Testament. His oratorio would be a glorious Christmas gift to a young nation. He fished through the stack of loose leaves and pulled out the title page. Holding it before Greta's eyes,

Geoffrey announced, "I call it *The Saviour*."

Greta studied the page and recalled the months of lovely music she had heard through Geoffrey's door. Inspired by colonial independence and by her hope for a new spiritual openness among an enlightened citizenry, Greta concluded that the title should be less restrictive. "Geoffrey, my dear," she smiled, "methinks you should call it simply *Saviour*."

Geoffrey liked the clean sound of it, so he dipped a forefinger in his brown gravy and made a great show of deleting the definite article.

Opening-night jitters combined with cold drafts permeating the wooden church to produce a shaky but warmly received premiere performance of *Saviour* on Christmas Eve. An exuberant "Hosanna" chorus midway through inspired such a rousing response that it had to be repeated immediately, and each of six successive performances throughout the season strengthened proportionately. The local newspaper declared Geoffrey's innovation an unqualified success—an opinion that was widely shared, since the audience for each performance consisted of exactly the same friends, relatives, neighbors, and curious admirers of the composer, his performers, and his supportive spouse.

Geoffrey had cleverly arranged *Saviour* as a smorgasbord of recitatives, arias, choruses, and instrumental interludes that could be performed in various combinations, thereby rendering it equally suitable for the Easter season. The following spring Geoffrey reassembled his massive ensemble to celebrate the spirit of annual rebirth.

Geoffrey was about to depart for dress rehearsal on Maundy Thursday when a lone rider sped through the square and tied up at the composer's gate. He handed Geoffrey an ornately engraved letter sealed with blood-red wax. Geoffrey felt immense gratitude for his performers' dedication and hated the thought of arriving late for this crucial run-through, but the expensive gold-bordered paper in his hand was intriguing. He decided to read it in the carriage. Geoffrey took his seat, told his driver to set out, and cracked the seal.

My Dear Well-Intentioned But Unfortunately Misguided Young Master Hansen,

Word has reached me regarding the charming village rendition, by a motley assortment of peasants and dilettantes, of your overreaching composition entitled, I believe, Ye Saviour. *It is entirely understandable, given your state of complete isolation and frontier ignorance, that you might not be aware of my own thematically identical oratorio, premiered recently in Dublin to deafening acclaim, called* Messiah *(please inform your uncultured compatriots that there is no* The*). It is your very great fortune, Master Hansen, that I am here in the civilised world and that you are there, labouring in colonial obscurity and, I would imagine, wallowing in detestable filth and suffering deprivation of every kind. For were that not the case, my dear sir, I should be obliged to kick your lowly American arse from one end of your reeking pigsty to the other. You shall kindly refrain from any future performances of your pale imitation of my genius. Failure to obey this directive shall be* *prosecuted to the full extent of Royal Jurisprudence and very well may deprive your illiterate hamlet of its unworthy musical hero.*

Please accept my best wishes for the joyous Easter season.

With all glad tidings,
I remain yours faithfully,
George Frideric Handel
London

Geoffrey sat in the carriage struggling to contain his rage. He subdued the impulse to tear up Handel's letter by recognizing its value as a souvenir. Geoffrey rode on to the church considering a variety of implausible reasons for cancelling the costly performance. Ultimately he decided simply to tell everyone the truth about his monumental coincidence.

Given the short notice, Geoffrey and his forces had no choice but to replace *Saviour* with traditional Easter hymns and pastoral symphonies. Fortunately, the huge ensemble packed such a wallop that without a hastily reprinted program the audience might hardly have noticed the difference.

By the time the slow summer season arrived, Geoffrey had recovered from Handel's demoralizing reprimand and, true to form, had begun recycling the individual sections of *Saviour*. He recast the work as a grand opera based on Greek mythology, complete with sets, costumes, and *deus ex machina* created by his faithful team of farmhands and their loving wives.

The Wrath of Poseidon is still performed today in opera houses around the world, a fitting tribute to American ingenuity.

AN ARMY OF BEGGARS

I LIKE TO SMOKE A BOWL BEFORE MOWING the lawn. It helps keep my mind off the drudgery of the work itself and allows me to notice little natural beauties I might otherwise overlook. Lizards are more colorful, stephanotis exhales twice as sweetly, and simple mowing patterns resemble crop circles. The trees and shrubs on my half-acre have grown considerably in my twelve years here, but there remains a lot of grass to cut. My first local boss used to say farewell on Friday afternoons with a reference to "the tyranny of the lawn." Until I can afford to have someone plow up all the grass and xeriscape the place, I must own a reliable mower.

The most common grass in the Florida Keys is a spiky, vinelike variety called Saint Augustine. It grows fast and high, requires minimal water, and tolerates salt. It goes to sleep between Thanksgiving and Easter and for those months needs little or no attention. Tight, soft zoysia does well here too, and is a lot more pleasant on bare feet; but its fine leaves can clog a mower in no time.

The Keys are hard on a mower. I have gone through several, gas and electric, in my time here. The twenty-minute bluegrass lawn I left up north was so gentle that my little cordless machine seemed indestructible. Down here, the limestone caprock is only a few inches below the surface. Whatever grass and soil one can claim rides on a layer of steel-bending stones and roots, not to mention the odd fallen coconut crouching in the tall weeds. Add in punishing heat and humidity and the need to store the machine outdoors, under the house—the building itself sits on stilts because I live in a flood zone—and one learns not to spend too much money on yard equipment.

This past Saturday I had to tighten the blade of my newest mower twice. The first time, I thought I could get away with using a big wrench. When the blade worked its way loose again about half an hour later, I trudged back upstairs for the socket kit. To my amazement, the first socket I tried fit the bolt.

I learned shortly after moving here that mowing the lawn in shorts, with or without a T-shirt, was asking for trouble. Small rocks and twigs flew out from under the machine and assaulted my shins and higher targets, often causing cuts and bruises that looked pathetic in polite company. And spraying mosquito repellant directly onto the skin is not healthy. So I accepted the discomfort of long jeans and long sleeves; applying the smelly chemicals to the clothing solves the bug problem. The end result is that a few minutes into the job I am completely soaked in sweat and covered in black dirt, white coral dust, leaves, and burrs.

I was still stoned when finally I made my way up the stairs for almost the last time that day to reward myself with a cold beer. My next chore, washing the car, could wait a little while. As I entered the air-conditioned living room, I remarked to no one and for no particular reason that my clothes felt like an army of beggars. Whatever role the influence of marijuana played in this imagery I do not know, but I liked the sound of it. *An army of beggars.* I went to the kitchen, opened the fridge, and popped a bottle. Sweat streamed off of me wherever I stood, and I did not want to stain the tile kitchen floor. Nor was I ready to go back outside into the thick heat. So I walked to the carpeted music room and stared out the back window. The satisfaction of a job well done does not last long in this weather-beaten environment, so I hardly noticed the difference I had made in the yard. I just stood there imagining that my wet, filthy garments were the arthritic hands and emaciated arms of a thousand stinking refugees. The pitiable supplicants clung to me, their sunken eyes burning into my memory like accusations.

I had seen such people up close as a child in Israel: impoverished Palestinian mothers and their diseased children covered in flies, literally dying in the streets as Western tourists ambled by with their cameras. The situation was worse in the neighboring Arab states, which lacked medical supplies and American dollars. Gulping my ice-cold brew at the window, I remembered the twisted bodies, the agony in the fading voices. I then flashed on the homeless wastrels I had seen shivering on steaming grates a few blocks from the White House.

Pot tends also to have an aphrodisiac effect on me. The accompanying erection can come and go depending on my thoughts, or it can last as long as necessary. The presence of cannabis in my system has enabled some of the greatest sex of my life. But the hard-on I was experiencing in my soaked jeans while standing at the window envisioning the world's poor sliding off my legs was less well timed. It led to the inevitable image of a particular dark woman in the crowd whose desperation compelled her to reach for me there just as our eyes met. Her literal hunger and my lust bespoke the shame of the whole human race. In my reverie I gave her everything in my pockets and kept walking.

The good news is that the little car with which I replaced my old van takes less time to wash than the old lawn took to mow.

Eventually I cooled down, but I was still hard when I stepped into the shower. I resolved to increase my annual donation to UNICEF.

The rest of the day passed without controversy.

Dad Fakes His Death And Goes West

MY FATHER, A CIA AGENT by a circuitous route, had a weak heart. This was only in the physical sense: Dad embodied the Hemingwayesque machismo of his generation. His warmth showed more in his relations with large populations (the poor, underfunded sports organizations, minorities in general) rather than with individuals, but he could be tender in quiet family settings when no outsiders were looking.

Dad suffered two more or less minor heart attacks in the 1960s before the one that finally killed him, at sixty-seven, in 1980. In all those years, doctors constantly reminded Dad that his condition was no laughing matter and urged him to improve his eating habits. He had been quite athletic as a youth and, after high school, had coached various baseball teams and track-and-field aspirants. Dad counted among his close friends Olympic champions and heroes of the World Series. Still, he enjoyed the standard diet of his day, rich in red meat and hard liquor—though he never missed an opportunity to point out that none of us kids had ever seen him drunk. Mom was a chain smoker and a closet alcoholic as well as a gourmet cook and so did little to discourage Dad's self-destruction.

Whenever one of us misbehaved to the point of

inflaming Dad's volatile temper, he would say, "Do you really want to send your old man to the electric chair?" This was his subtle way of proclaiming a not infrequent temptation to murder his own undeserving offspring. But as a consequence I heard the term *electric chair* long before I had any knowledge of that diabolical instrument or of capital punishment in general. Once I did understand Dad's meaning, not only did I become terrified of his occasional dark moods, I developed a morbid fascination with the various methods humankind had invented with which to dispose of its less obedient representatives.

What does the sweating, wrongly convicted inmate feel at the precise moment when the switch is thrown? Is it all over in a merciful flash, as the authorities would have us believe, or does the prisoner sit there suffering in indescribable agony as the relatives of the real killer's victims luxuriate in their Pyrrhic victory? As we turn our faces away from the shuddering, smoking body in the chair, we are free to catalog the variety of other ways in which governments have committed state-sanctioned homicide. Recall our royal ancestors' twisted cruelties: the unspeakable horror of burning at the stake, breaking on the wheel, the rack, the bizarre ritual of drawing and quartering, the shiny flourishes of swords and axes wielded by sometimes inaccurate executioners (lament the grisly demise of Mary, Queen of Scots). What did the French aristocrat's momentarily sentient severed head see and feel as it tumbled into the bloodstained basket at the base of the humanely designed guillotine? How does it feel, and how long does one feel it, when a rush of sickening vertigo ends with the strangling grip of the hangman's noose? Does one hear the snapping of the spinal column? Are those grotesque contortions involuntary, or the manifestations of living hell? (Dubious Lincoln conspirator Mary Surratt's fall from grace apparently failed to break her neck, and it is said that she struggled for a full five minutes before her larynx was crushed.) What searing pain is the final reward of the prisoner who stands bound to a splintered post several yards from a dutiful firing squad? It probably matters little whether three or a dozen bullets rip simultaneously through the poor bastard's heart; the time between that event and the brain's instructions to turn out the lights cannot be less than excruciating. How often do the missiles fired from several rifles aimed at the same small target accidentally strike one another and fly off course to cause some unforeseen damage? That information probably does not appear in the institutional press release. Those who have witnessed the terror and torment of slow asphyxiation in the gas chamber do not generally recount deep feelings of moral satisfaction. And our current enlightened peaceful exit, lethal injection, has earned more than enough critics in the medical and legal professions to confirm that it is just our most sanitized brand of torture. How can we call ourselves a civilized society so long as we continue to allow these barbaric practices?

I have never bought the absurd notion that the death penalty has anything to do with justice. It is about *revenge,* and revenge is just as base and unworthy of our species as the urge to commit murder. One would expect the wealth-obsessed Republicans to seize the argument that condemning someone to death, guaranteed to result in years of appeals and delays, is far more expensive than sentencing him or her to life in prison. But apparently greed is less glamorous than bogus patriotism and Christian hypocrisy.

I digress.

Over the years Dad went out of his way to prepare us kids for the day when suddenly he would not be there. We were all out of school and on our own when the big one hit in 1980. But of course none of Dad's morbid jokes on the subject could have spared us the shock and grief of his actual death.

I was so devastated and so deep in denial during the funeral that I refused to see Dad in his coffin. Mom and my older sister did likewise, preferring to remember him as the jolly picture of vitality. My younger brother did ask that the lid be lifted, for him alone, and it was solely on his good word that I relied for the awful truth that Dad was gone. Yes, there were the death certificates and the cold reports of the military personnel who attended to Dad in his final moments. He collapsed in the terminal of an air-force base while on his way to visit my brother: as a penny-pinching retired officer Dad was entitled to travel for free on military transport.

But what if Dad and his younger son had made some private pact? What if my brother's last-minute return to the funeral home for one final glimpse was just a clever diversion?

As often as Dad would remind us that we could lose him at any time to his faulty ticker, in moments of family frustration he would announce facetiously that he was fed up and was moving to Jackson Hole, Wyoming. Dad had spent happy years as a young archaeologist roaming the American West—he had unearthed dinosaurs, Native American artifacts, even the ancient bones of stillborn infants—and had cherished those memories as an antidote to the realities of domestic and professional life.

One night recently I dreamed that Dad had indeed faked his death and had slipped out the back door for Jackson. In my dream I succumb to my curiosity and pay him a surprise visit.

Never one for facial hair, Dad probably has grown a full beard and mustache as his token disguise. Jackson, like most other once unspoiled natural places, is today a pale imitation of the rugged outpost Dad remembered. But as I wander its gentrified streets looking for my perhaps transformed father, I figure, *Yes, but it still beats the smelly, congested metropolis in which he raised us and from which he urged us one day to escape.*

In the dream I turn a corner and enter a laundry. There in the shadows, folding his twin sheets before shoving them into a weathered duffle bag, is the man I refused to see dead. Our eyes meet, the shock of recognition battling the acceptance of our individual aging. Dad's full head of hair, which I never saw fully gray, has gone completely white; I have inherited my maternal grandfather's thin, receding frontier. Except for a slightly stooped posture, Dad shows vestiges of his old athletic prowess.

I walk over and say, "I thought I might find you here."

We embrace, awkwardly. For the first time ever, Dad looks embarrassed. Given our location, I try to break the ice with a funny reminiscence.

During one of my rare visits home during college, I was downstairs washing my clothes while giving Dad the obligatory progress report. Before transferring my things from the washer to the dryer, I pulled out the lint trap and cleaned it. Dad had no use for the mechanics of any activity he considered "women's work," so he pointed to the object in my hands and asked, "What the hell is that?" I explained that it was the lint trap and that one should clean it before every load. Dad looked into my eyes and asked, "Does your mother know about this?"

On our childhood camping trips Dad often observed that in life a man needs very little beyond a tent, a fishing pole, and a Coleman stove. (A reporter from an earlier time would have replaced this last item with a simple hardwood fire, lighted without matches.) In my dream, judging by Dad's minimal laundry, I assume his digs must be something similar; or maybe the brutal Wyoming winters have required the luxury of a climate-controlled trailer. In any case, he does not invite me to his home, and I do not ask to see it. As I turn to go, he says something I will always treasure:

"Son, your secret is safe with me."

I spend the night in a local motel and catch the first flight home. The day after tomorrow is an important one at the penitentiary, and it is my turn to press the button.

The Fine Art Of Professional Suicide

THE TOOTHLESS, TREMBLING OLD MAN approached the circulation desk and struggled to speak. Normally he would have been dismissed as one of a hundred lazy vagrants who spent their days in the public library to soak up air-conditioning, surf the Web, harass patrons and employees, or catch a few winks before the county cop on duty ran them off or hauled them to jail. But the staff respected Albert "Papa" Feldstein and held him up as a reminder that one should never judge a book by its cover. Feldstein's nickname recalled his days as one of America's foremost Hemingway scholars at Columbia University. He had fled New York in the 1970s and come to Key West to write what promised to be his hero's definitive biography. As a new Key Wester he had rubbed shoulders with Jim Harrison, Tom McGuane, Robert Stone, Hunter S. Thompson, and Tennessee Williams. But associating also with notorious local drunks and drug smugglers, who served ostensibly as source material, exposed Feldstein's personal weaknesses and caused his eventual dissolution. He was a sad example of Key West's large and largely misunderstood homeless population. Still, reeking though he was of alcohol, sweat, and urine, Feldstein commanded the librarian's attention.

Zelda Prentice happened to be standing behind the circulation desk to hand an envelope to the county courier; her regular post was the small office from which she administered the Monroe County Public Library system's computer network. The shapely, fortyish blonde happened also to be the only attractive woman on the staff—most of her colleagues, male and female, displayed the obesity that had become an American epidemic—and she was not surprised that the one intelligible word in Feldstein's gummy, slurred message was *body*. Prepared to feign appreciation for the old man's remark, Prentice made a move toward her office when Feldstein's trembling became so severe that she feared he might collapse. He raised his emaciated right arm and pointed toward the fiction section. Prentice had no desire to follow Feldstein into a confined space and hoped to release him into the care of the regular circulation staff, but the pathetic creature's urgency compelled her.

When the two entered the narrow aisle between the last stack of bookshelves and the windows facing Fleming Street, Prentice jumped back and screamed. A fit man about her age with light-brown hair lay supine on the floor, bleeding from a small but well-placed chest wound. After a moment Prentice recognized the man as Henry Rivers, who three years before had traded a career as the most popular English teacher at Key West High School for the relative peace and quiet of the library's cataloging department. The high school's academic mediocrity, student and parent misbehavior, bureaucratic nonsense, the opportunity to concentrate on his own writing, and the naive expectation that at the library he would be working with qualified personnel had precipitated Rivers's unexpected move. Rivers had learned immediately thereafter that in exchange for the security of government employment he was surrounded by the same inbred Conchs and rednecks who ran practically every other institution in the Florida Keys. He later joked to a friend that the county's employment application for any position from the top down should consist of a business card on which is printed the question, *Do you have a pulse?* After two decades of introducing teenagers to the greatest writers in history, Rivers found himself taking direction from peasants who did not know Ernest Hemingway from James Joyce.

Zelda Prentice ran back to the circulation desk and dialed 911. Detective Lieutenant Rich Castillo and his partner, Sergeant Alvin Varela, arrived in a few minutes, followed immediately by an ambulance crew. They loaded Rivers's body in the vehicle and wound their way out of town to the morgue at Lower Keys Medical Center on adjacent Stock Island.

The forensics team reported that Henry Rivers had died of a stab wound, but the murder weapon did not appear to be a metal blade. Within Rivers's heart the technicians found tiny splinters of lignum vitae, a hard and increasingly rare wood once used for ship's bearings and tools; now the small, slow-growing trees were found mostly in the Middle and Upper Keys.

Rich Castillo and Alvin Varela had interviewed Henry Rivers several years before in connection with the stalking of local Irish novelist Brice Miller. Rivers and Miller were casual lovers at the time, and the teacher had seen his friend through an ordeal that ended with the suicide of a deranged real-estate salesman and religious fanatic named Paul Ihlström.

Rivers had made no secret of his disappointment with the library's inefficient operation, which included unnecessary positions and procedures, incompetence, fraud, cronyism, and negligent leadership, the last of which coasted in pleasant denial because the county commission considered the library system untouchable. Rivers got along well with the few staffers he deemed fit for their jobs, but he had earned more than a few enemies among the rest. His supervisor was an illiterate fool who had no more business working in a library than she did running for congress; she spent most of her workday waddling around socializing with other products of the local Bubba system. Chief among those freeloaders was the children's librarian, who had wrested her job from a far superior applicant because the lesbian branch manager had a crush on her. She was responsible for wasting thousands of tax dollars each month on worthless comic books, teenage vampire novels, and videodiscs of lowbrow movies, most of which materials she ordered for her own personal use. She oversaw a so-called parenting section that consisted mostly of books on coping with a behavioral disorder that the more obnoxious of her two sons happened to possess. Henry Rivers had wanted to ask the woman why in her weekly programs in the auditorium she was not teaching kids to read real books by real writers, but he suspected that she regarded names like Faulkner, Steinbeck, and Twain as traumatic childhood memories. Rivers's one trusted ally, the head of the cataloging department, had long before given up on improving the situation and was about to retire after putting in his twenty-five years. Rivers had learned that the only way to get through the day there was to keep quiet and treat his colleagues with basic civility. Those who considered Rivers to be passive-aggressive preferred that impression to an airing of his opinions. Few of these drones knew that Henry Rivers the writer was on a first-name basis with influential columnists at the *Miami Herald* and other major periodicals, National Public Radio commentators, and every journalist in Monroe County. The only reason Rivers had not blown the whistle on the dysfunctional library system was that he had hoped to change things when his boss's job became vacant.

Irene Lennon was a respected sculptor whose small White Street gallery was a necessary stop on any tour of the thriving Key West art scene. Lennon's specialty was wood, and many of her pieces had become local and national icons. On the morning that she read the news of Henry Rivers's murder, she notified police that several years before she had sold Rivers a beautiful letter opener made of recycled lignum vitae; she remembered the sale particularly because more than once Rivers had promised but forgotten to return the object so Lennon could repair a small split in its tip. A search of Rivers's Margaret Street cottage failed to produce the letter opener.

Sergeant Alvin Varela interviewed a number of Henry Rivers's friends and acquaintances. No one who had visited Rivers's home remembered seeing any unusual objects on his desk, but those who knew him well opined that Rivers was not the type to misplace or discard something of artistic value.

Lieutenant Rich Castillo's girlfriend, Victoria Landini, was one of Key West's best and busiest massage therapists. She had counted Henry Rivers among her regular clients and was saddened to learn of his demise. A voracious reader, Landini had enjoyed Rivers's anecdotes of life in the literary trenches. She knew no one in her predominantly upscale clientele who might have wanted to see Rivers dead.

Victoria Landini honored the professional code that what was said in the massage room stayed there. But one night over an uncharacteristic second glass of wine, she felt compelled to mention to Rich Castillo that Henry Rivers and Brice Miller had fallen out about the time Rivers had left his teaching post. Landini had facetiously asked Rivers whether Miller disapproved of the writer's questionable career move and was met with a surprising admission. It seemed that Rivers had used a sexually overrated version of Miller for a fictional character in one of his recently published short stories. Feeling secure in their friendship, Rivers had made the mistake of telling Miller confidentially that the character was based on her. He assured her that no reader could be familiar enough with their intermittent relationship to recognize Miller as the character's model. Miller read the piece and, instead of the bemused, flattered reaction Rivers had expected, she flew into a rage. Miller called Rivers an invasive creep, threw him out of her apartment, and ordered him never to acknowledge or contact her again—an order that, given Miller's shocking tirade, Rivers was only too glad to obey.

Lieutenant Rich Castillo telephoned Brice Miller and

asked her to visit his office. Her lilting brogue on the line gave no indication that Castillo's call was disconcerting or unexpected.

The interview was uneventful until Castillo introduced the subject of Henry Rivers's lignum vitae letter opener. Miller denied ever seeing it, but her inability to sustain eye contact at that point in the conversation confirmed Castillo's suspicion. After dismissing Miller he requested a warrant to search her apartment on Elizabeth Street.

That search turned up nothing, but Rich Castillo had already conferred with Waste Management regarding the single trash pickup the company had performed in Miller's neighborhood the morning following their interview. He assigned a pair of rookie cops the unenviable task of sifting through a truckload of garbage that was about to be hauled to a landfill on the mainland. The senior of the two smelly sleuths returned to Castillo's office and placed a ziplock plastic bag on his desk. In it was a twelve-inch lignum vitae letter opener with a sharp and slightly chipped point. Analysis revealed traces of Henry Rivers's blood.

The thick, bulbous handle of the letter opener turned out to be covered not only with Brice Miller's fingerprints but also with vaginal residue. Interrogation by a female detective revealed that the latter evidence had resulted from an evening when Henry Rivers and Brice Miller were making love standing at Rivers's desk. The novelist had bent over the table as her lover entered her from behind. Spotting the gracefully carved letter opener had inspired Miller to massage herself with its handle to enhance Rivers's contribution. She had woken the next morning to find the thing under her pillow. Rivers had told Miller about his unrealized intention to return the letter opener so Irene Lennon could file and polish the rough tip. Having noted how thoroughly Miller had enjoyed the tool's alternative purpose, Rivers had presented it to his friend as a gift. It had spent most of its time in Miller's nightstand until the day of Lieutenant Rich Castillo's phone call. Miller cited embarrassment as the reason for her earlier denial.

But under further intense questioning, Brice Miller conceded that her gnawing anger over Henry Rivers's unwelcome short story had paralleled Rivers's increasing book sales—which had begun to outpace her own. Finally one day she had taken the versatile device to the library, approached Rivers with a forced smile, and asked, "Is it too late to apologize?" Rivers had ushered her into the concealed aisle in the fiction stacks that was the closest thing to privacy the library could offer. Miller's swift and ferocious attack as she pretended to invite Rivers's forgiving kiss had literally taken her former lover's breath away. Henry Rivers was dead before he hit the moldy linoleum floor.

Brice Miller's arrest provided lively discussion in the Southernmost City's relaxed literary community. Local authors had been cranking out implausible Key West murder mysteries for so long that a real slaying involving two of their own was considered a tragedy too good to be true.

Miller's unsupervised confession compelled her lawyer to enter a plea of not guilty by reason of insanity.

Among the prosecution's witnesses was Victoria Landini, who recalled a conversation in which she and her best friend, fellow massage therapist Eileen O'Connor, had discussed the contested subject of fictional source material. O'Connor and Brice Miller had been casual friends for years, and the two had run into each other—at the library, coincidentally—during a period when Miller was struggling with an erotic manuscript she feared could be interpreted autobiographically. In the conversation with Eileen O'Connor, Victoria Landini had taken the position that a writer's choice of subject matter was no one else's business and that in any case Brice Miller had been established long enough to write whatever she pleased.

Police seized Miller's unfinished manuscript and determined that the moderately endowed Henry Rivers could not have inspired anything in Miller's steamy fantasy, which she had never permitted her old friend to read.

Judge Hayley Sterling's jury did not buy Brice Miller's plea, and she was sentenced to life in prison with the possibility of parole. She was sent to a state women's facility on the mainland.

One morning in the prison dining hall, Brice Miller met Darlene Guzmán, who was serving eight years for embezzling half a million dollars from the Monroe County School Board. Guzmán's husband, the disgraced former schools superintendent and his wife's onetime unapologetic employer, had narrowly avoided incarceration himself and was currently selling appliances at Sears. Mrs. Guzmán's colorful conspiracy theories amused Brice Miller and sent her back to her cell brimming with ideas.

The following year, as part of her rehabilitation

program, Brice Miller pseudonymously self-published a thick novel about an impotent, psychotic librarian who chooses the wrong subject for the lackluster pornographic fiction that occupies his lonely evenings. The profits from Miller's sensational bestseller were used to establish the Henry Rivers Memorial Scholarship for Young Writers at Key West High School.

THE
JAZZ BUYER

FORTY-THREE-YEAR-OLD ISAAC IRETON, whose friends called him Ike, had chosen to specialize in the two least profitable forms of Western music: classical and jazz. Ike played principal clarinet in the second-best orchestra in Baltimore and as a saxophonist and flutist led the most innovative jazz group south of New York. That is, he was not in the Baltimore Symphony, and a real jazzer who lived anywhere except New York had better be famous; Ike was not. He therefore was destined for the life of obscurity that he shared with thousands of other gifted freelance musicians across the country. Ike's excuse for his particular predicament was that while enrolled at the Peabody Conservatory of Music he had inherited his parents' paid-off house after they were killed in a plane crash and that the sudden onset of comfort and manageable responsibility had prevented his moving to Los Angeles, where he might have earned a handsome income as a studio player and film composer. Ike hated teaching, but he coached half a dozen promising private students on Tuesday and Thursday evenings.

Ike's sporadic schedule of concerts, club dates, and events to support local nonprofits left a huge but not especially frightening hole in his week. He had endured a long line of disposable day jobs to sustain his muse, and he could not justify taking a job that required a serious mental or emotional investment. The forty-hour grind into which Ike fell in 1994 was as the jazz buyer at the city's main branch of Radius Records.

Ike's comprehensive musical knowledge made him instantly indispensable to his co-workers, most of whom did not know Vivaldi from Coltrane. Typically, Radius gave most of its retail real estate to rock and pop, with the other genres dividing up the remaining third of the sprawling space. But because the Radius philosophy was to offer a vast selection in exchange for high prices, practically every type of music was fully and fairly represented. The classical section enjoyed its own soundproof enclosure and a handful of educated part-timers. Their loyal customers' only running complaint was that, since the classical room was toward the back of the building, they had to endure whatever unlistenable crap was playing on the main floor as they made their way toward musical paradise. Ike's large jazz section was situated just outside the classical room, so he could wear both hats when necessary. To get jazz CDs played on the house audio system Ike had to prevail on a sympathetic cashier at the front registers, and for the customers' sake he erred toward the mainstream.

The starting pay at Radius Records was five dollars an hour, whether one was a Ph.D. or a year shy of a high-school diploma. This "level playing field," along with a litany of paranoid security measures, was management's way of keeping the elitists in their place. One could ascend the pay scale quickly; but the most one could ever earn, even as a store manager, was a joke. The only person in the multinational corporation who was moderately well off was the CEO, whose Malibu villa was slowly sliding into the Pacific just as the brick-and-mortar record business was about to sink under the weight of the Internet. The stingy compensation did allow overqualified personnel like Ike to keep their priorities in perspective. Ike did not have to respect his young bosses or their juvenile policies, and he could enjoy the goofy cast of characters who made up the staff.

Kyle Eccles, the general manager, was a thirty-something dullard whose long, thinning brown ponytail was his sole concession to hipness. He dressed like a professional golfer. He did a good job of juggling a bewildering assortment of personalities and behaviors, and the head office in L.A. appreciated Kyle's tightfisted style. He knew just enough about several genres of music to hold a five-minute conversation on each, but one would have been hard pressed to guess his favorite. He was one of those retail lifers who would have been just as happy managing a hardware store. Kyle's most disturbing characteristic for Ike Ireton was that the two of them looked so much alike in the face that when talking with the manager Ike often felt that he was gazing into some creepy funhouse mirror. Ike was amazed that no one else seemed to notice the resemblance, and he was relieved that Kyle himself either had not seen it or had chosen not to draw attention to it. By tacit agreement, their civil relationship was strictly business.

As the record manager, Aidan Bishop was responsible for maintaining the overall inventory and coordinating the various store buyers who oversaw individual sections or combinations thereof: classical, jazz, rock, folk, world, new age (which the classical guys pronounced like *sewage*), books, and accessories. At twenty-six, Aidan was good-looking in a delicate way, with impeccable shoulder-length sandy hair and a gauzy wardrobe that showed off his thin rock-star physique. He was attractive to both women and men and seemed equally flattered by their attention. Aidan had a live-in girlfriend, but he gave the impression that the two were sometimes joined by an unnamed third party. He had an irreverent sense of humor that helped him bond with his mostly young staff while appeasing Kyle's neurotic tendencies. Aidan's eclectic musical tastes emanated from sincere enthusiasm. He knew when to correct a rude teenager and when to listen to an older subordinate whose experience ran beyond stacks of catalogs and a neglected Stratocaster.

The only truly insufferable member of the staff was Tilden Fechner, the head of the classical department. He referred to himself as the classical *manager,* a position that did not exist in the corporate hierarchy. Til, self-nicknamed perhaps for Richard Strauss's *Til Eulenspiegel's Merry Pranks* (though no one ever cared to ask), was a paunchy semiretired lawyer whose impressive-sounding spiel was lifted verbatim from liner notes and from the *Penguin Guide to Recorded Classical Music.* Til could tell a customer everything some critic had ever wanted him or her to know about a particular recording of *La Bohème* without giving the slightest impression that Til had ever set foot in an opera house. Til sensed that Ike Ireton saw through his facade, and Til took his revenge on the musician by playing the most saccharine pops repertoire he could find whenever Ike was forced to spell one of Til's part-timers in the classical room. Til and Kyle Eccles did not get along, mostly because as control freaks they were too much alike. Til's idea of being one of the guys was to use the F-word in the lunch room while it was filled with staffers young enough to be his children.

The most highly valued store employee was Bill Katz, the rock buyer. Bill commanded a deep knowledge of American pop, from its roots in blues, country, gospel, and folk to its latest ephemera. Since Bill was responsible for the store's financial bread and butter, management gave him wide latitude. So did everyone else, because Bill suffered from chronic flatulence. The computer terminal where Bill managed his inventory was perpetually shrouded in foul air that was doubly offensive because it was located on the sales floor within range of defenseless customers. His breath was equally nauseating. No one who ever got near Bill found his digestive difficulties to be the least bit amusing. Almost as obnoxious was Bill's penchant for so-called progressive rock and its ugly subgenres. He was of that generation born too late for the British Invasion and too early for punk. He had no use for the Beatles except to the extent that their innovations had paved the way for the pretentious nonsense he adored. Bill's favorite of the seminal quartet's albums was *Let It Be,* which the group and its fans recognized as the closest thing there was to a bad Beatles record.

The kid who managed the small but interesting book department was a recent high-school graduate with long, greasy black hair, multiple tattoos, and multiple piercings. He dressed exclusively in black, starting with jackboots and finished with a long coat. Only management knew the kid's real name; the handle to which he answered was *Vlad the Impaler.* It was OK to drop the last two words once one had acknowledged Vlad's menacing aura. He stocked small quantities of everything from Jane Austen to James Patterson, but his own fetishes were peculiar. Vlad made sure that in addition to novels, reference books, and the usual periodicals like *Rolling Stone* and *Guitar Player* were ample selections of soft porn, socialist manifestos, and self-published manuals on bomb-making and interrogation techniques. In one private chat with Ike Ireton while the latter was trying to reorganize his Dexter Gordon bin, Vlad offered an unsolicited commentary on the future of genital plastic surgery. Vlad would fly into a First Amendment tirade whenever management questioned his literary judgment.

Vlad, who actually was quite handsome beneath his Bram Stoker veneer, had several young female fans on the staff who mimicked his gothic look and who missed no opportunity to annoy everyone else by playing nonstop death-metal music during their register shifts. Behind the scenes, these kids tended to be the quietest, sweetest people in the building.

Each branch of Radius Records boasted an in-store art department that produced bin cards, decals, posters advertising store events, oversize reproductions of album covers, and other visual materials. The fluid nature of the pop music business kept the artists hopping year round. Most of them were talented painters and sculptors who, like Ike Ireton, felt that a humbling day gig in one's own field was better than no electricity. The head artist at Ike's branch, Stephen Guilder, did a remarkable job on the wall display announcing the saxophonist's second self-produced CD of world-class obscure jazz. Ike released the

CD just in time for the holidays, but he gave away as gifts to staffers more copies than the store would ever sell to customers.

Each Radius branch also employed half a dozen supposedly anonymous loss-prevention geeks, muscular young men who might have flunked out of the police academy. They walked around in their paramilitary T-shirts pretending to be customers, busting the occasional shoplifter and making the staff itself feel unwelcome. Ike lodged a formal complaint with Kyle after one skinhead ordered the jazz buyer to open his briefcase on a crowded holiday evening as he was leaving the store. Ike pointlessly described the mortifying incident while Kyle sat behind his desk wearing his carnival grin.

The store was so big and, on the main floor, so noisy that to reach another employee one would grab one of many telephone receivers mounted on the walls and say, for example, *"Aidan Bishop, please pick up the com."* The workday was an eight-hour medley of bad music punctuated by people saying, *"Aidan Bishop, please pick up the com."* Sometimes, late at night or when the store was closed for inventory, staffers would give in to mischief. Bill Katz was notorious for assuming various accents or channeling black-and-white movie stars for his on-air appeals. An urgent Charlton Heston would appear out of the clouds with, *"Aidan Bishop, for the love of God, man, pick up the com!"* Or a twinkly leprechaun would intone, *"Aye, Aidan Bishop, by the blood of the martyrs, laddie, could ye find it in yer heart to pick oop the bleedin' com!"* These moments of levity would be among Ike Ireton's few fond memories of his Radius tenure.

Ike did appreciate the education he received there in world music, an area that had attracted him as steadily as American fare had devolved. Practically the only recordings he heard at Radius that were not either old news or something too terrible to withstand were made in far-flung studios around the globe. In addition to now familiar sounds like the Gipsy Kings and Serge Gainsbourg's eccentric "Bonnie and Clyde" duet with Brigitte Bardot were haunting, invigorating, unclassifiable albums from Africa, Asia, the Middle East, the former Soviet Union, and elsewhere. One could give up on stateside music entirely and still find plenty of great stuff.

Ike was less grateful to have inherited a small but momentarily significant selection of "bachelor-pad music," a genre that celebrated the sights, sounds, and smells of the Rat Pack era. Young moderns who normally deafened themselves to Pearl Jam or Metallica would don tuxedos and flared cocktail dresses, gather in rooms decorated in the style of Ike's parents, sip martinis, and snap their fingers to a sonic backdrop as cheesy as a molded pink plastic chair. The suave mastery of Sinatra mingled with the absurdity of Combustible Edison. The jazz buyer was able to pay lip service to this embarrassing appendix to his section, for, like all dress-up games, the bachelor-pad phase would be mercifully brief.

A few weeks after hiring Ike, Kyle Eccles considered the wealth of musical knowledge at his disposal and decided to publish a free monthly newsletter. Each buyer would write a column, and other staffers could contribute short articles as the spirit moved them. Kyle acted as editor, but except for deleting profanities and correcting the worst grammatical errors he was refreshingly hands-off. From the inaugural issue, Ike's jazz column was the best written and most widely read item in the newsletter and actually boosted sales in his underdog department. Ike avoided jargon and went out of his way to invite wary customers into his world. By contrast, Tilden Fechner's classical column was as tedious as its author. Til's unmusical prose, combined with the need to avoid plagiarism, betrayed the cracks in his expertise. Most of Til's customers knew more about music than he did anyway and were the least likely of any listeners to consult or be influenced by junk mail. The popularity of Ike's column was a thorn in Til's side, and Til did not improve his position by adding a hand-drawn self-portrait to his byline. Eventually Kyle decided that the newsletter was a fun but unjustifiable use of paper. The publication died a natural death after a year of tepid numbers and ecological guilt.

In a renewed effort to saturate the shoppers' senses, Kyle made a short-lived deal with a local perfume distributor to display its new unisex cologne just inside the front door. Within days, the whole store and nearly everyone in it bore this treacly scent. Ike was relieved when after a few weeks a city councilman's wife complained of an allergic reaction and the display was dismantled.

Radius's reputation as America's premier chain of record stores brought in a steady stream of regionally famous customers. It was common to see the conductor of the Symphony, television newscasters, or sports heroes browsing the aisles, pausing now and then to chat or to sign an autograph. Ike enjoyed assisting these luminaries and gently broadening their musical horizons.

One of Ike's favorite regulars made up in entertainment value what he lacked in celebrity. Tilden Fechner always ran for cover when he saw this ancient Holocaust survivor coming, for the man would spend hours hunched over the classical bins looking for anti-Semitic messages embedded in German and Slavic record labels. He threatened to sue the head office over a variant spelling of Prokofiev's name.

To celebrate the release of the Beatles' long-awaited *Anthology* multimedia collection, Kyle hired one of those awful Beatles tribute bands to perform in the store on a Saturday afternoon. About the only thing the four cheeky mop-tops did right was to make their way uneventfully from the storage room to the front window in their matching black suits. Their singing and playing were so undistinguished, their accents so lame, their instruments so inauthentic, and the very notion of their existence so pathetic that Ike wanted to strangle them in alphabetical order. Everyone else thought they were great, and the store sold a truckload of Liverpudlian product.

Ike Ireton enjoyed an intermittent love affair with a prominent local songwriter, but it was not going anywhere. Although Ike's "real life" occurred outside Radius Records, the fact that he was spending forty hours a week there drew him into its quirky culture. Try as he might to dismiss the Radius gang as a collection of poseurs whose love of music was stronger than their need to make money, Ike occasionally felt attracted to one of the charming young women who relied on him for an intelligent answer to a customer's question. Ike looked at least ten years younger than he was and appreciated the staff's tendency to treat him as a kind of older brother. Most of the girls who worked there were either far too young for him or were already attached to someone. But Ike did indulge in a couple of platonic dinner dates. The first was with an outspoken Scottish rocker whose long hair was black on the left and fuchsia on the right. She was several years older than Vlad the Impaler but was among his sartorial comrades. Ike loved the girl's brogue and her frank appraisals of her generation's mediocre repertoire. Her thin nose ring had Ike wondering what other adornments her black minidress concealed, but the nonsmoker lost his curiosity when her first question to him after dinner was whether she might light up in his car. Ike's only other date with a Radius employee was with a gorgeous little Argentinean with lustrous olive skin and full, beckoning lips who spent their entire evening telling him about her pet scorpions, tarantulas, and venomous snakes.

Two years into Ike Ireton's visit to Planet Radius, he was offered the position of concert manager at his alma mater, the Peabody Conservatory. The job was a good deal more substantial than his present one, but so was the salary. Ike had worked on the Peabody stage crew throughout college and was comfortable with life on both sides of the footlights. That the conductor of the orchestra in which Ike performed also led the Peabody student orchestra meant not only that Ike would have a friendly guide to campus politics but also that the one man's schedule conflicts would match the other's. Ike's agreeable relations with his own students and with the young oddballs at Radius Records promised an easy transition to the twenty-member undergraduate workforce he would supervise at Peabody.

On Ike's last day at Radius, the managers and a few other buyers treated Ike to a farewell lunch. After their drinks were served, the pseudointellectual who oversaw the folk and world sections asked Ike what exactly a concert manager did. Ike did not feel like describing the mountainous paperwork, scheduling, orchestra management, musician contracting, program typesetting and printing, marquee lettering, prop location, set and costume rental, lighting, promotion, box-office management, travel booking, instrument repair, faculty babysitting, administrative confrontation, and other unpleasant duty the job entailed, so he replied, "Well, among other things you make sure that a nervous voice major has a tuned piano in place for her senior recital." The kid took a sip of his soft drink and said, "So basically you're gonna be a roadie?" A brief but meaningful snicker went around the table. Ike looked at the gathering of untested cubs and smiled. "Yeah," he said. "I'm gonna be a roadie."

In 2006, seven years after Ike Ireton had realized that the joke was indeed on him and he took yet another insulting but less stressful day job, Radius Records went out of business, closed all its stores, and laid off thousands of mostly lovable misfits whose entire music collections now reside in a plastic wafer in their shirt pockets.

MURDER IN THE IVORY TOWER

OLIVIER JACQUARD MOUNTED THE PODIUM and smiled at the eighty-seven young musicians arrayed before him, comfortable in the knowledge that nearly every one of them hated his guts. It was only the second orchestra rehearsal of the term, but Jacquard's reputation was firmly established throughout the music school and across the campus. Jacquard had earned the permanent enmity of the college maintenance crew during several years when the outdated concert hall was being renovated and the orchestra was forced to perform in various unsuitable spaces throughout the crumbling institution.

Jacquard's philosophy was *Reach them young.* In his career both as a second-rate oboist and as a third-rate conductor, he had met few musicians whose opinions of conductors were not rooted in fear, disrespect, mistrust, unvarnished hatred, or all of these. By acting the part of the fire-breathing despot of cartoon fame, Jacquard was merely preparing his tender charges for the real world.

Typically, Jacquard chose to begin the season's rehearsals with the most difficult and least programmable piece in his ever-growing repertoire of unlistenable modern scores. These works invariably required a large battery of esoteric percussion instruments that no student musician could be expected to possess, which gave

Jacquard sufficient opportunity to humiliate the bottom-dwelling drummers for their reliable ignorance. "Ze composer calls here for ze *tambourin de Provençe* to be played *fortissimo* on ze shell with ze *rute du bois,* and you give me a tom-tom tapped with wire brushes?" he seethed at a cute freshman. "Does a violinist arrive without his bow? A clarinetist without his reed?"

The shivering girl was determined not to weep, but her knees would not stop knocking together.

"Go back to ze storage room, and do not return here without ze proper equipage!"

It would not have occurred to Jacquard that neither this nor any other average American college would have owned a *tambourin de Provençe* or the crude fistful of twigs that a German romanticist might have observed slapping the side of a marching bass drum during a village festival. Jacquard saw himself as the modernist equivalent of those self-satisfied historians who spend their careers replicating the music of Haydn and Mozart with the fetishistic conviction that sound quality and intonation must never interfere with authenticity. And Jacquard failed to notice the student's return several minutes later, armed with a disintegrating swing-era field drum whose bottom head was missing, or to appreciate the ingenuity with which the girl had raided a janitor's closet for a whisk broom.

At rehearsal's end, having effectively dashed his young players' hopes of finding anything in the piece that resembled melody, harmony, or natural rhythm, Jacquard smiled to himself and returned the heavily annotated score to his flaking leather satchel. Luxuriating in eighty-seven visual daggers as he stepped down from the podium, the maestro exited the room just as a high-pitched scream emanated from backstage.

Being closest to the alarming sound, the percussionists interrupted the tedious disassembly of their sprawling gear and rushed to the source.

On the floor at the foot of the darkened spiral staircase leading to the lighting booth lay the impeccably dressed and profusely bleeding supine body of the one person in the music school held in lower universal esteem than Jacquard himself: dean Ineke Maarten. Dr. Maarten had apparently been struck or perhaps even shot in the back of the head, and the warped floorboards were angled such that a great deal of blood had pooled under her shoulders and was seeping into one of a dozen Chanel suits Dr. Maarten wore like uniforms. Dark red liquid soaked the pink wool tufts. The immaculate condition of Dr. Maarten's smart new black pumps—the once-pretty administrator's physical attributes remained two sculpted calves that looked incapable of supporting a figure of some considerable bulk—disabused any theory that Dr. Maarten might have fallen down a precarious flight of metal stairs she would never have climbed in a hundred years.

Olivier Jacquard was already enjoying a decadent lunch of fried chicken, buttered garlic mashed potatoes, collards, and espresso in the faculty dining hall up the hill by the time a small contingent of police descended on the music building, strung up yards of yellow tape, and fanned out to interview students, faculty, and staff.

Ineke Maarten's murder was especially unwelcome news to Dr. Angela Fiorello, the assistant dean of music who had hoped she would never face the possibility of taking over the department and who was as popular as Dr. Maarten was not. The still trim, attractive blonde had long ago discredited stereotypes of the massive warrior soprano in a dazzling career that had charmed audiences in every European opera house. Dr. Fiorello enjoyed administrating even less than she had enjoyed teaching, but it was the logical academic trajectory. Effervescent in small gatherings, she had a mortal fear of public speaking and a healthy distaste for fund-raising, two chores that now would dominate her schedule. She hoped the emotional cost of these despised activities would not erode the joy she had derived from the company of students and the less neurotic members of the faculty.

The police would find no shortage of institutional suspects in the case of Dr. Maarten's demise. In addition to her image as a caustic, high-strung bitch who would have sold her mother's wedding ring for a photo opportunity with some potential donor, Dr. Maarten presided over a hornet's nest of dysfunctional geniuses whose daily lives were a litany of numbing repetition and unrealized potential. Aside from a few legitimate virtuosi whose commitment to the arts compelled them to pass on to future generations what they had learned in their distinguished if unaffordable performing careers, the faculty contained more than a few mediocre pedants who had collected their undergraduate *and* graduate degrees from this same institution and simply had hung around long enough to have been offered an office as a means of clearing the hallways. These hacks taught private lessons on their chosen instruments and moderated annual seminars on a variety of minor topics, recycling the notes they had taken not so many years before as students, ensuring a perpetual supply of overwritten dissertations on subjects as riveting as an examination of the atypical viola part in the second movement of some forgotten string quartet. One could hear in these individuals' conversation the years of boiling resentment aimed at a dystopian machine that had stripped away their brilliance and reduced them to ivy-crowned ridicule. Those in this population who led credit-earning ensembles behaved like petulant teenagers whenever the school production manager was obliged to point out the technical impossibility of realizing their aesthetic delusions. Witnessing their twitchy demeanor before and during a performance applied a refreshing comic balm to an otherwise excruciating musical experience. The semifamous director of the wind ensemble actually referred to his unseasoned players as "my people," as though they too were a force to be reckoned with.

The U-shaped, two-story music building, including a dank basement filled with priceless instruments, had begun its existence in the nineteenth century as a convent, complete with Inquisition decor. This design proved ideal for a conservatory: dormitory cells became practice rooms and offices, offices became classrooms, the dining room was transformed into an ample but acoustically infuriating rehearsal hall, the mother superior's quarters provided adequate space for a respectable music library, and the chapel remained just that, a necessary refuge.

Many of the pupils earned pocket money with work-study jobs on the stage crew, in offices, or as teachers' aides and therefore could be found in various semiprofessional capacities throughout the school. But on their own the students ganged together in the cliques of their concentrations and rarely commingled: the fruity voice majors and music-theater extroverts hung out upstairs, not far from the austere organ majors whose extra pairs of shiny shoes were seen more often dangling from their backpacks than dancing across the maple pedal board; downstairs roamed the jive-talking hipsters whose membership in the jazz ensemble distinguished them from the mere mortals who made up the bulk of the instrumental program and whose inability to improvise pointed them straight down the path of self-perpetuating academic failure; the loud brass jocks' goofy behavior had many a string and woodwind player fantasizing about life beyond the proscribed universe of inside harmonies, upbeats, and brief, terrorizing solos; similarly, the guitar majors and piano majors consorted mostly with their own kind, the former identified by their instrument cases, the latter by their stacks of books with bent pages. These kids had emerged from doting families whose own fantasies prevented their ever warning the little darlings that they had entered a field in which most of them stood practically no chance of making a living. Full of themselves as only college students can be, the poor fools trudged on, repeating their futile scales and arpeggios in euphoric denial while the law and engineering majors up the hill were already playing the stock market. The unreality of their pursuit notwithstanding, however, any one of the music students might have greeted the news of Dr. Maarten's death with something other than sadness.

The first day of autumn announced itself with uncharacteristic certainty: a morning that might simply have represented a colorful and slightly cooler version of summer began with a crunchy layer of frost on the grass. People left their homes, saw their breath in the air, and felt cheated.

Cynthia Gérard, a pretty, fortyish brunette professor of piano whose full schedule of private students spared her from classroom teaching, walked toward the music building a bit too close to Dorian Fielding, the pretty, fortyish brunet music librarian—not in any hope of converting the presumably gay scholar, but simply for warmth. "Have you ever noticed that culture and good weather are mutually exclusive?" she asked her colleague.

Dorian had never given the issue much thought, though he was looking forward to his annual winter holiday in Key West. "Hmm. How do you mean?"

"Well," Cynthia continued, "think of the great cultural centers in Europe, and even here: every one of them has seasons, and at least one of those seasons is unbearable. Maybe all art is born of suffering after all. Name a single city that has both nice weather year-round and a decent orchestra, or a serious museum."

Dorian smirked. "Ah. How about Florence? Or Tel Aviv?" His eyes, stinging in the uncustomarily cold air, scanned an imaginary globe. "Madrid? Miami—but their orchestra went broke years ago. Los Angeles!"

"All those places get cold at least part of the year," Cynthia persisted.

"Yeah," Dorian replied. "I guess you're right."

"Let's have lunch sometime this week," Cynthia said.

"I want to pick your brain about Key West. Surely a piano teacher can make a go of it in a town that size. This place is really starting to creep me out."

Dorian looked at her with the familiar grimace that had crossed just about everyone's face in the weeks following Ineke Maarten's unsolved murder. "Sure," he said. "How about today?"

"Can't today," Cynthia replied. "My student Becky Gleischmann is giving her first recital of the term, and I told her I'd hold her hand right up to the downbeat. She's a nervous wreck."

When they reached the door of the music building, Dorian bent down and kissed Cynthia lightly on the cheek. The dry outdoor air produced a static-electric shock that caused both of them to jump.

"Ow!" he said, rubbing his lips.

"*Ow* is right!" she laughed. "Counting the days! Later, dude."

Dorian turned right toward the library, and Cynthia descended the moldy stairs to her studio. Her first task was to flip on the dehumidifier beneath her two nested grand pianos.

Rebecca Gleischmann's recital would begin without promise. Even though her good grades and cheerful personality had endeared her to the faculty, Becky sometimes failed to take to heart the etiquette of classical music. The blonde beauty had been advised to dress appropriately for her term debut, preferably in all black. The midday performance was considered less formal than an evening affair, but Cynthia Gérard had warned Becky not to walk out there looking like Tori Amos.

Cynthia's heart sank when Becky arrived at the studio door wearing a low-cut, midriff-baring sweater and hip-hugging jeans that indeed would reveal too much information when the shapely sophomore sat down at the keyboard. At least both garments were black. And the terrified look on the girl's face led Cynthia to give Becky the benefit of the doubt. She hugged her student, told her she would be great, and put her through her warm-up exercises.

The generalized hiss of faculty disapproval that greeted Becky when she strutted onstage was countered somewhat by her peers' lascivious whispers. The unspoken consensus was that she had better play flawlessly and then offer an apology to Dean Fiorello for her racy attire.

Becky bowed, not too deeply, and took her place at the long black Steinway. Tradition aside, one could not deny the girl's splendid presence.

Becky kept her cool when a freshman's cell phone began ringing during the opening Schubert sonata: that rude occurrence was common enough during concerts by visiting celebrities. (Violinist Itzhak Perlman had delayed a recent performance of the Mendelssohn concerto not only to admonish a listener whose phone had begun playing a Bach two-part invention just before the introduction but also to point out the incorrect composer, genre, and key.) But disaster struck during Debussy's gorgeous prelude *La cathédrale engloutie,* when Becky nailed the thunderous low C and broke the string—an occurrence most pianists live their entire lives without having to experience. The cataclysm that is a snapped low C on a nine-foot concert grand, the present performer's horrified reaction, and the mostly young audience's involuntary laughter brought Rebecca Gleischmann's first recital of the term to a sudden and undignified close. The girl burst into tears, leapt from the instrument, and ran (beautifully) off the stage.

Cynthia rose from her seat, scanned the audience with revulsion, and went up to console her student. As she held Becky in her arms and reminded her never to let a roomful of idiots ruin a performance, Cynthia glanced at her watch and wondered whether she might be able to save lunch with Dorian after all.

The pin-cushion effigy of Ineke Maarten that the cops found hanging in Becky Gleischmann's dorm room turned out to be just one of a number of such treatments discovered throughout the campus, proved nothing, and in fact went some distance toward restoring the impertinent girl's credibility following her aborted recital. That event was rescheduled, Becky showed up in a stunning floor-length black gown and turned in a magnificent performance, and the school's full-time piano technician was given six months in which to overhaul a fleet of neglected Steinways.

Lunch with Dorian Fielding had sent Cynthia Gérard straight to her computer to begin plotting her escape to Key West. Continued darkness, cold, pavement, pollution, and perpetual gridlock were no match for the prospect of gliding through the tropical breeze in minimal clothing twelve months a year. She could handle the beautiful three-hour oversea drive from Key West to Miami for the occasional cultural fix that a town of twenty-five thousand dropouts could not be expected to provide. Cynthia would wait until near the end of the semester to submit her resignation. But when she told Becky Gleischmann confidentially of her plans, the mischievous blonde surprised her teacher with a thorough knowledge of the Southernmost City's comprehensive menu of lesbian and bisexual recreation.

"I'll e-mail you some links," Becky smiled. "Let me know if you ever need to see a familiar face." The women embraced, and Becky paused at the door to confirm that her blushing mentor had got the message.

Olivier Jacquard acceded to the new dean's polite request to offer an audience-friendly program for the fall orchestra concert. He reluctantly tabled the cacophonous epic with which he had opened the semester and presented a well-balanced compromise consisting of Beethoven's Third *Leonore* Overture, Mozart's Piano Concerto no. 21, featuring the celebrated Rebecca Gleischmann, and, after some administrative arm-twisting and several marathon rehearsals, Bartók's *Music for Strings, Percussion, and Celesta*. (Jacquard's case for the once-daunting Bartók included the work's prominent role in the hit films *Being John Malkovich* and *The Shining*.) Becky was in the dressing room changing back into street clothes when Jacquard pointed to the adorable Korean freshman timpanist Seung-Eun Lee for a solo bow that only briefly would have dampened Becky's moment in the sun.

Weeks became months. As inescapable snow filled gutters, melted and refroze on worn campus paths, and became sooty gray slush at splashing crosswalks, the police were no closer to discovering Ineke Maarten's killer.

The former dean of music had been a lifelong opera

buff, and the school's international reputation rested almost solely on its lavish devotion to that expensive genre. Much of Dr. Maarten's ceaseless fund-raising was a by-product of an obsession that nearly had bankrupted the institution on more than one occasion. The season before the dean's murder had marked one hundred years since the nuns had vacated the premises, and to recognize that milestone Dr. Maarten had mounted a chilling production of Poulenc's *Les Dialogues des Carmélites*. The city newspaper had praised "world-class" performances by several student singers and an "unforgettable" depiction of the final guillotine scene. The offstage device the production office had rigged up to produce the sound effect of the heavy blade severing the praying women's heads was simple enough—a long steel pipe held at a forty-five-degree angle as an oiled gym weight slid down the pipe to a wooden block bolted to a resonating chamber—but it had sent the audience home with visions that indeed would haunt their dreams. The dean of the athletic department, jealous of Dr. Maarten's fiscal acumen, had refused to loan the pampered music school any of his equipment; so the gym weight used for that scene was the sole contribution of the conspicuously fit music librarian, Dorian Fielding.

Some weeks before, after sleepless hours trying to remember some minor detail without which the opera surely would have been a dismal failure, Ineke Maarten had dragged herself from bed and driven to the school at one o'clock on a Sunday morning. For all its gaps and eccentricities, the school boasted one of the best music libraries in the eastern United States; the answer to Dr.

Maarten's query was certain to be found on its shelves.

When the dean put her key in the lock and entered the darkened library, she had the vague impression that she was not alone. She could have confirmed this impression without embarrassment by allowing her eyes to adjust to the filtered moonlight and backing out the way she had come in. Instead she switched on the lights—and was astonished to discover Dorian Fielding, math professor Efrem Kuntzler, and freshman piano major Rebecca Gleischmann, all naked, intertwined on the floor near an audio-visual console stacked with pornographic videos. Rarely at a loss for words, the dean merely excused herself, saying, "Dorian, we need to talk," and beat a hasty retreat to the neighborhood bar.

At the emergency meeting in her office the following Monday morning, the dean and the guilty trio had agreed that the incident would remain their secret so long as nothing of the sort ever again took place on school grounds. Fears of a scandal persuaded Dr. Maarten not to fire Dorian, expel Becky, or out Dr. Kuntzler. Having been somewhat adventurous herself as an undergraduate, the dean managed a discreet smirk as the three nervous participants shuffled back out to the courtyard.

But Dorian could not shake the humiliation of being discovered by his boss in such a state, involved not only with an eighteen-year-old student but also with a respected, widely published, married mathematician. He and Becky promised to keep the blunder to themselves, but Dr. Kuntzler did not trust the dean to behave likewise: Dr. Maarten had distinguished herself at more than one cocktail party by broadcasting intimate faculty details that her listeners could easily have done without. Every time Dorian and the dean passed each other in the halls following that unfortunate night, the forced professionalism and the administrator's knowing chuckle reverberated in the librarian's head like a jury's echoing verdict. Dr. Maarten was easy enough to dislike on a good day, but now Dorian could barely stand the sight of her.

Dorian Fielding's eclectic tastes in music ran the gamut from Gregorian chant to the most radical experiments of the avant-garde. He was among a handful of people on campus who appreciated Olivier Jacquard's self-imposed mandate to expose his students to contemporary works they might never hear anywhere else. When Dorian learned that Jacquard was considering the world premiere of local composer Yuri Ulyanovsky's outrageous tone poem *The Martyrs of Tiananmen Square,* which called for not one but three anvils to be struck simultaneously with ball-peen hammers, Dorian realized he had found the solution to his problem.

Dorian approached Jacquard one morning, expressed his fascination with Ulyanovsky's score, and asked permission to make a study copy of it for the library. He promised not to circulate it, and the conductor agreed not to mention the transaction to the somewhat paranoid composer. (Ulyanovsky was wont to stamp his copyright notice on every page of his creations, as though the average listener might find any sanitary use for them.) Score in hand, Dorian attended the first of two rehearsals at which Jacquard would subject his defenseless orchestra to *The Martyrs* and made careful note of the anvils' ear-splitting entrances. On the day of the second rehearsal, he called Dr. Maarten on his cell phone and asked her to meet him backstage for a private chat to ameliorate the uncomfortable atmosphere that had developed between them.

One morning early in March, Cynthia Gérard was finishing her workout at the Island Gym in Key West. The glowing pianist was looking forward to a peaceful walk along Higgs Beach before the first of several afternoon students would arrive at her rented William Street cottage. She had just tossed her towel into the tote bag and was turning toward the door when Dorian Fielding walked in, grinning.

"Well!" she exclaimed. Soaked in sweat, Cynthia shrank slightly from Dorian's easy embrace.

"*Well,* yourself!" he smiled. "Your landlord said I'd find you here. Guess who just moved to town! You are looking at the new music librarian at world-renowned Florida Keys Community College. Brunch?"

Cynthia laughed. "Like this?"

Dorian thought his colleague looked smashing in her tight black leotard, but he did not want to misstep; they had not spoken in months. He just stood there, beaming.

Cynthia reached into the bag for her gray running shorts. "At least let me put these on," she said, blushing.

"I hear Camille's has amazing waffles," the archivist suggested. As the two left the gym, Dorian glanced over at the racks of free weights and smiled to himself.

Once they were seated and their coffee was served, Dorian looked at his watch and said, "I have another surprise for you."

In the next moment, Becky Gleischmann strutted in

the door wearing a minuscule red tank top, the smallest white shorts either of them had ever seen, and sea-green flip-flops. She came to the table and placed a hand on Cynthia's shoulder. "Spring break!" she laughed.

THE PERMANENT RESIDENT

All the beautiful sounds of the world in a single word . . .
-Stephen Sondheim

I GUESS I HAVE ALWAYS TALKED to myself. Mostly in private, of course, at home or in the car or in some other reasonable seclusion. Today's technological prodigies appear to be talking to themselves all the time, when they might actually be conversing with someone's disembodied voice mail. But I am a loner, so there has always been some unseen companion appreciating my perceptive observations. I bought a cell phone several years ago because my neurotic boss needed access to me on the road, but after hours I turned the thing off; I still do.

As a child I had the usual imaginary friends, mostly prepubescent crushes from fifties television: Annette from *Mickey Mouse,* Penny from *Sky King.* When I was six, the blonde classmate across the street would invite me over to play doctor. We satisfied our interest in each other's nakedness with the same ephemeral curiosity we applied to an autumn leaf or a weathered piece of glass. She set the pattern for my social and romantic life: one girlfriend rotating in a loose orbit of lesser acquaintances, a few lifelong buddies. I have always gotten on better with females than with those of my own sex, but I have made a few enemies on both sides of the aisle. People distrust you if you do not keep them entertained.

As a military brat I got used to this arrangement. Dad was an officer, so we lived in nice houses on base. But it was a new one every two years, with another whole set of acquaintances. I never had much use for the dysfunctional rednecks who crave military life and usually found myself in the company of city kids from the embassy. Usually, though, it was I and someone who remained visible only to his or her creator.

I have had several vivid recurring dreams about houses we lived in all over the world. Usually in the dreams the houses are larger than they were and feature numerous hidden rooms and passageways. In one dream there is a whole wing no one else knows about in which some other family lives in complete isolation; I never recognize their faces as they lounge in long hallways and ornate bedrooms. In another dream our house occupies a steep blue-green canyon surrounded by dark, fantastic mountains that can change in a moment from arid desolation to lush fertility. In another the house sits fully exposed in the middle of a huge urban square whose worn red cobblestones are forever steaming with fragrant summer rain. In none of these dreams is there ever another known person, only I, wandering, harmonizing.

The innocent sprites of childhood became the erotic sirens of adolescence, gentle voices on my pillow savoring my solitary aftermaths. I created long, detailed conversations with these carnal passengers. One morning my visiting cousin admitted that she had hidden in my closet the night before and had witnessed everything. I started locking my door.

Over time I talked also to adversaries, real and imagined, venting the words I could never have said in person. Stupid, belligerent schoolmates, incompetent colleagues, old flames whose last spiteful words went unanswered. One time I lost my voice for four days because of a solitary shouting match that coincided with a sudden influx of winter germs.

Years ago at a party a young woman brought in a chart that foretold people's sexual destinies based on their astrological signs. I, the sole Virgo at this gathering, learned that I likely would discover my most satisfying sex partner in myself. At the time I was embarrassed and slightly insulted, especially since the hostess of the party, my girlfriend, was the prettiest woman in the room and a wildcat in bed. But in later years I began to wonder whether there was something to astrology. After numerous relationships that ran the gamut from the numbingly routine to the spiritually transcendent, I realized I had become a virtuoso masturbator. With or without the encouragement of marijuana, I had developed an astounding repertoire of skills and techniques that only the most intuitive of my lovers had matched. Whether alone with my fantasies or on the sofa with an imaginary goddess at my side and a naughty film on the screen, I was achieving orgasms of unprecedented intensity. Usually these eruptions would be followed by automatic laughter of surprise and amazement. Only rarely was I tempted to say to my absent co-conspirator, *You should have been here for that!* Self-pleasuring had evolved beyond lonely substitution to an art form all its own. If I was really stoned I sometimes would drift off to sleep afterward, waking much later with the crusty towel lying across my chest.

Among my creepier recurring dreams is one in which I am half conscious and acutely aware of a sinister male presence in the room, usually older than I, positioned at the side of the bed. This person may or may not be armed with some long implement such as a spear or a pitchfork. But I am either paralyzed or unable to reach the shadowy form, using hands or feet. Sometimes I wake myself screaming impotently at the motionless attacker. I experienced this dream once in the company of an actual lover, who in the morning informed me that I had called out and kicked her twice, without injury, before she reached over and rocked me back to peaceful silence.

One night last year I woke in the light of the full moon to see a petite female silhouette standing at the foot of my bed. Without the lunar assurance I might have reacted with alarm. I could not make out any details except that she had shoulder-length hair of an undetermined color and that she was naked. Instinctively I knew that the woman was both benign and quite real. She whispered my full name in an aristocratic British accent.

I moved over and pulled back the covers. She padded to my side, ran her fingers through my hair, and climbed in. I turned to her, and we embraced. She was as warm as if she had lain there for hours. In the silver moonlight her face was a gauzy countenance, cute, perhaps beautiful, the sort of endearing face that would be equally at ease in the tousled Sunday-paper living room and in pampered glory at the dining table.

"I am here," she whispered. "I am here, now, always, but only like this, in the night."

I lay in silent wonder caressing her silken hair. I was too astonished by her presence to notice my Pavlovian erection.

She pressed herself against it and whispered, "Shsh." She pushed gently on my shoulder so that I lay on my back. She sat up and began touching me with feathery fingertips until we could no longer endure the yearning. She went down, took me in her mouth and hands, and used the merest motion of each for several minutes. She moaned softly at the arrival of my salty anticipation. Then she rose, climbed over, and placed me inside her. She pushed down all the way and leaned forward, her hair around us like the tropical breeze. "This is our time, our place," she whispered. "In the day, in the world, you may do as you wish. But here in your home, at night, you are ours. I will be visible by the light of the moon or by candlelight. I will disappear at the touch of any lamp switch or at the rising of the sun. Will you receive and cherish me in this way?"

I could not speak. I held her hips and pushed up into her warmth.

"Good," she whispered. "You may call me Maria. Everything we do will be for the first time." She began to move slowly. "I am your first friend, first love, first kiss, first touch, first climax, first colleague, first partner, first prostitute. I will speak like a queen, a scholar, a waif; I will speak not at all."

I took Maria firmly by the shoulders to confirm her reality. I could not help laughing aloud at the absurdity of her arrival. I considered which of my mischievous pals might have arranged this fantasy. The last person to possess a key to my home, the woman who most closely had resembled a partner, had returned it, and other keepsakes, some months before: the only thing *we* had in common was the best sex either of us had ever known. We even had discussed the possibility that sex was enough to sustain us, but in the end what we shared lost out to everything we lacked.

The increased aggression of Maria's motions validated her claim. "Shsh," she repeated. "I am going to come." She buried me deep and slowed down. She wrapped herself around me and trembled for several seconds as her moans reached a soft crescendo against my neck. Her contractions coursed through us like hot waves, and then she was still. "Now, you," she said.

In the morning, no evidence remained of Maria's existence except a long black hair on my pillow. I went about my day in euphoria, occasionally glancing over my shoulder. I felt bonded to Maria. Although she had not added to her simple rules, I did not even consider telling anyone about our strange experience. I would not be writing about her now if it were still practical to read by candlelight.

The next night I took extra pains to prepare myself for bed. Clean and shaven, I extinguished the lights and slipped into crisp new sheets. I lay in silence for what seemed an eternity. I did not realize I had fallen asleep until I felt Maria next to me, massaging my scalp and kissing my cheek.

Everything was new all over again, as she had

promised, with variations on untried themes. And in the morning, Maria was gone for another day.

Maria has accompanied me every night for nearly a year. She has vowed to leave me only if I reject her. I cannot explain her appearance or how it is that I deserve her. Nor can I offer any apology to those friends whose late-night invitations I must decline. Of course I wonder what would happen if one of them paid me an unannounced visit: whether Maria would be visible to anyone else. But Virgo's orderly subjects appreciate the cyclical nature of the universe.

PUBLIC SEX

"HELLO. MY NAME IS MAGGIE, and I am a sex addict."

"Hello, Maggie," came the cheerful semicircular chorus.

I stood there, a fraud, assuming, *hoping* my listeners knew it. "I began masturbating at age nine, had my first orgasm at ten, gave my first hand job at eleven, gave my first blow job at twelve, had my first intercourse with a boy at thirteen, and had my first lesbian sex at fourteen." Most of the listeners' attire was comfortably prudent, but I had made a point of showing up in black heels, tight black jeans, and a thin pink cotton V-neck sweater with no bra. "One night, out of curiosity, I wrote a list of my sex partners—by which I mean people with whom I had enjoyed any sort of sexual activity that was orgasmic for one or both of us—and came up with fifty-three males and twenty-seven females. I have participated in half a dozen threesomes and a few episodes of group sex." I paused and smiled at the six men and three women in the room, not counting Dr. Byron McNulty, the balding, avuncular therapist seated on my far right. "I am twenty-eight years old."

Maggie is short for *Magdalena,* which, paired with *Delacroix,* makes for a damn-near perfect name for me. Both my parents are Catholic, and the story goes that Mom chose my handle with care, as it were. She answered all my childhood sex questions with unembarrassed candor, to the point of reassuring me about the moaning sounds I heard nearly every night from their bedroom. Hearing similar sounds from the living room late one evening in my twelfth year led me to spy on my older sister and her boyfriend. I crept down the stairs just far enough to see what they were doing on the sofa and sat watching for several minutes. The guy's eyes were slits as he grimaced absurdly. My sister spotted me just as he was about to come. She took his thing out of her mouth and placed a finger before her lips. Whether this was timed strategically I do not know, but I got to see the first big spurt fly up into her shiny brown hair before she went back down and drank the rest, eyeing me. When he stopped convulsing she looked up toward my room, and I returned quietly to bed. The next morning she scolded me for invading their privacy, but not for watching them. From such experiences, practice, and avid reading, I gained what I consider to be a healthy sexual education.

My listeners, ranging in age from about my own to their forties, shifted in their seats. The woman second from my right, whom I recognized as one of my high-school science teachers, discreetly relocated the hand she perhaps unconsciously had clenched between her thighs and viewed me with studied indifference. The cute guy closest to me on the left was obviously hard and smiled when he saw that I had noticed. The musty air in the social hall was similarly thick, and I relished the setting: St. Michael's, where I had been confirmed, where I had attended grades one through eight, and where, like all good Catholics, I had entertained a continual stream of sexual fantasies involving priests, nuns, altar servers, statues, holy objects, and selected iconography. Back then everyone moved on to the high school at Our Lady of

Sorrows, but I continued attending mass at St. Mike's. In my sophomore year we got a young, handsome new pastor, and one Sunday morning I fantasized that I had jacked him off into his chalice just before communion. I could swear he looked right at me as he raised it to his lips. One could not have chosen a better spot for the weekly meeting of Sex Addicts Anonymous than the local headquarters of the second-most neurotic institution on the planet. I can only imagine what a Jewish branch of SAA would be like.

"Maggie," Dr. McNulty smiled, "thank you for joining us. What do you hope to gain from these sessions?"

I could not very well admit that I was there merely for a turn-on or that I had no desire to be "cured." Dr. McNulty evidently misinterpreted my hesitation.

"There's no need to be nervous, Maggie," he smiled. "We're all friends here."

I had been a theater major at Georgetown and was anything but nervous, at least in the way Dr. McNulty meant. I remembered the old advice that an inexperienced public speaker should picture his or her listeners naked or seated on the toilet. I certainly was picturing this gang naked, cavorting on a huge mattress fitted with black satin sheets. "I hope to learn more about myself and my condition," I replied.

The fact is that I had always been fascinated by public sex; I considered it a form of performance art. This bullshit meeting was just a variation on blowing a guy in a supermarket parking lot. I watched the goofball on my left gently stroke his bulge a couple of times.

"Why do you feel that you are a sex addict?" Dr.

McNulty asked.

Given the background I had offered, which I was certain represented at least an obsession if not a bona fide addiction, I wanted to believe he was kidding. "Well," I smiled, "most people come home from work, eat dinner, and enjoy family time or generic television. My idea of a relaxing evening is a glass of wine, a joint, a vibrator, and a dirty movie. I can masturbate to porn for hours and then go out on a date and have sex until dawn. I get wet at the mere sound of words like *clit, cock, ejaculation,* and *vagina*." More gluteal shifting permeated the audience as the soft pink yarn caressed my nipples. "I don't feel complete unless I have an orgasm at least every couple of days."

Dr. McNulty looked over his notes. "I take it sex and love are not necessarily corollary for you?"

"Of course not," I smiled. "I mean, it's nice when they are, but you know how it is."

Low giggles confirmed that my listeners did. It was time for the next speaker, and I took my seat. After the meeting, the guy with the hard-on and I sneaked up to the sanctuary and he took me from behind as I knelt on a prie-dieu. The following week my old science teacher admitted that she had followed us and watched from the choir loft. I think the guy's name was Larry.

The SAA meetings grew tiresome after a few weeks, but they yielded a couple of other adventures. One of the older guys and I did it in his car one night, and I accepted an invitation from the youngest of the three women to join her and her butch roommate in their apartment. We all agreed that as addictions go ours was relatively benign.

My performance art occasionally has placed me in risky situations, but of course danger is part of the thrill. I masturbated unnoticed on a crowded city bus one winter afternoon while seated next to an adorable teenager on her way home from swim practice. Amazing what one can hide in a down parka. I did the same, but openly and for the benefit of a middle-aged naval officer pretending to check her lipstick, beside a garden path at Dumbarton Oaks. I had gone there in a short skirt sans underwear specifically to see what I could get away with. I jacked off a guy under the table at a congressman's dinner party. I have had sex of every kind in an airplane seat, a beach cabana, a campsite, a canoe, a concert hall, a convention center, a firing range, home movies, a hospital (I masturbated a recuperating friend who complained that the nurses were immune to his charms), hot tubs, a library, a museum, nightclubs, oceans, offices, public restrooms, a Pullman car, a rehearsal studio, a restaurant, a river, swimming pools, a tiki bar, uncounted movie theaters, an unlocked motel room, a vacant classroom, a wildlife preserve, a YMCA (two drag queens spirited me up the fire escape), a youth hostel, and in every other imaginable situation. The only familiar place I have not performed sexually is on stage, and I am sorely tempted to try it; a Dutch diplomat told me I could be a star in Amsterdam. In college I did work briefly in an erotic massage parlor, but too many of the clients were unclean or grossly out of shape. I have cruised online sex-chat rooms and pretended to be a guy or an underage girl. I have enjoyed Skype sex on several occasions, both alone and with another person in the room with me. I was sexting before it was cool. With my experience I would make an excellent call girl, but I am not sure the money justifies *that* level of danger. I like to think that I am recklessly in control of my body.

My best friend, a gay poet, once asked me, "How much semen *have* you summoned?" I imagined it would fill the crystal vase on his coffee table.

I cherish a number of unrealized sexual fantasies, some of which will remain as such because I would not want to have my portrait displayed at the post office. I want to jack off a boy in front of a group of students at a girls' boarding school; I would focus on a particular girl, make the kid squirt all over her smart uniform, and forbid her to disturb the evidence as she attended the rest of her day's classes. I want to do the same in a busy shopping mall, following the chick around afterward to observe the shoppers' reactions. I want to spank the tight little butts of a girls' gymnastics team. I want to make love atop the world's tallest building and in one of those glassed-in undersea resorts. I want to make love skydiving. I want to join the Mile High Club and make sure the pilot can see us in the mirror. I want to fuck in a weightless environment and culminate with an explosive hand job. I want to attend a *bukkake* party and see how many guys I can accommodate in one sitting. I want to make a professional porn film and show it to my old acting coach. I want to give lap dances in a sorority house. I want to go down on a bride at her bachelorette party. I want to narrate erotic audiobooks while all the studio personnel are naked. I want to revisit every person with whom I ever had bad sex. I want to do everything, everywhere, with every good-looking human being.

An appropriate ending to this story fell in my lap late one night when I was proofreading. My cell rang. I normally do not answer an unknown number, but I was feeling spontaneous. There was heavy breathing on the line, followed by a series of quite specific descriptions of things my caller wished to do to me; they ranged from the sublime to the ridiculous. At one point the guy held the phone such that I could hear the wet, patient rhythm of his other hand. I recognized the voice just before he came.

"Thank you, Dr. McNulty," I smiled. "Please tell everyone I said hi."

THE SOUTHERNMOST ERECTION

ONE DAY EARLY IN THE TWENTY-FIRST century, Key West mayor Jimmy Yearley received a letter from an anonymous donor who offered the Southernmost City three million dollars to commission a full-sized replica of Michelangelo's *David*. The statue would be placed in Mallory Square and would be surrounded by a circle of benches. The donor intended the work as a gift to the city's large population of gay men, its (in the donor's words) "underserved minority" of straight women, and art lovers in general. Any funds remaining after unveiling the statue would go to the municipal Art in Public Places Committee.

Mayor Yearley took the proposal to the city commission and won approval to release an international call to artists. The APPC received hundreds of applications and selected a prominent Italian sculptor whose Michelangelo reproductions had fooled more than one historian.

The unveiling took place on the first day of spring, and representatives of the arts and public-service communities throughout Monroe County attended it. Everyone agreed that the statue was spot on and that it added a touch of classical sophistication to the city's funky image.

Miranda Perez and Berthe Liadov, both eighteen, were new servers at El Meson de Pepe, the Cuban restaurant and dance hall located at the edge of Mallory Square (and home of the best *mojito* on the island). On the afternoon following the unveiling, Miranda and Berthe were walking to work in dazzling sunshine.

The girls were recent graduates of the Key West Prep School Culinary Institute, created to provide a perpetual supply of personnel for the city's hospitality industry. The institution did not necessarily explain to its graduates how they might hope to afford Key West's punitive cost of living.

Arriving early for their shifts, Miranda and Berthe walked slowly around *David,* avoiding eye contact with each other. Without a word they found themselves seated close together on the bench directly in front of the looming replica. They looked him up and down for a few minutes.

"It's kind of small, isn't it?" Berthe suggested, looking at scattered groups of cruise-ship passengers fanning themselves with city maps.

"Are you kidding?" Miranda replied.

"Not him, *it,*" Berthe clarified.

"What?"

"You know precisely what," Berthe said, giggling.

"Oh," Miranda said. She looked at her friend. "And how would you know? I thought you'd only seen two guys, one of whom was your brother."

"Exactly," Berthe said.

Miranda straightened up seriously. "Well, he's supposed to be sort of this man-child, the first *David* who wasn't just a boy, but also a powerful warrior. Look at those huge hands."

"Right."

Miranda studied the object. "Michelangelo was queer, you know."

"OK, whatever," Berthe said.

There was a long silence as half a dozen French tourists approached the statue, sniffed, and continued across the scorching plaza.

Miranda looked at her watch. "Well," she said, slapping Berthe softly on the thigh, "we'd better get in there. This goofy shirt is sticking to me already."

The next afternoon, the mayor opened a second envelope from the anonymous donor. This one contained a check for six million dollars, to sponsor an annual jazz festival. It would be held at the beautiful new concert hall on the former Navy pier and would feature both international and local artists. "I want real jazz," the donor wrote, "not the polite cocktail music one hears in Key West. That stuff has been giving jazz a bad name for fifty years."

The visual-arts community's reaction to *David*'s appearance was mixed. Some artists felt the piece was too austere for the island's predominantly tropical themes, some gallery owners lamented its location amid the city's gaudiest tourist attractions, others were simply glad whenever a serious artwork, however derivative, appeared within the city limits.

The next afternoon, Miranda and Berthe were seated at *David*'s feet while awaiting their shifts. They both had felt drawn to the bench as if by appointment.

No sooner had they taken up their places than Berthe

sucked in her breath. "Oh my God!" she exclaimed between clenched teeth. "Look!"

Miranda did not need to guess where Berthe's eyes were directed, and, when hers focused on the object, she concurred: *"Oh my God!"*

The organ had thickened slightly, and an unmistakable glans was peeking out. The girls stared for several seconds, looked at each other, and simultaneously rose from the bench. The statue had been altered in no other way, and the creamy Italian marble of the area in question seemed to have been carved exactly as it now appeared.

"This is too weird, Berthe," Miranda said. "Maybe we're, like, being filmed or something. Let's go in before someone recognizes us."

As the girls walked toward the restaurant they agreed to meet earlier the next afternoon to study the development more closely.

But the coconut telegraph could not wait. By sunset, rumors had spread throughout Old Town, and groups of locals and tourists had revisited the statue.

One of the bystanders was the flamboyant city commissioner and ubiquitous theater patron Tom Easterhouse, who not only had attended the unveiling but also had angled his way into every photograph taken of the event. Immediately on seeing the transformation, he whipped out his cell phone and pried Mayor Yearley away from the dinner table. The two agreed that an emergency session of the city commission was in order.

At that meeting, Easterhouse suggested that the change in the statue was the work of a talented vandal. Key

West was home to more than a few sculptors who theoretically could have pulled off such a stunt. But everyone agreed that not only would none of these individuals have had the effrontery to desecrate a famous artwork, however derivative, but also that none would have had the time to render the deed to such a polished level (and quietly). Each commissioner examined the unit as closely as possible and concluded that it looked exactly like a Michelangelo, perhaps following a dip in the hot tub.

The next morning, Mayor Yearley arrived at his office to find an overnight letter on his desk. The envelope contained a check for nine million dollars, to which was attached a small yellow note that read, "I know what you're thinking. *David* stays. Await further instructions."

Later that morning, the mayor's e-mail contained a message: "The check you received today is to launch an annual early-music festival, to be held throughout the city, to which only the best ensembles from the mainland and abroad are to be invited. I want to see your list before you book anyone. I expect authentic medieval and Renaissance music, none of this new-age crossover crap."

By the afternoon, Miranda and Berthe were not surprised to find a larger group gaping at their discovery. But the girls now felt a proprietary relationship with *David* and muscled their way to the bench like two Nordic bus passengers.

"Christ!" Berthe exclaimed, then buried her face in her hands.

"I don't believe it!" replied Miranda.

In the space of twenty-four hours, the phallus had grown tumescent.

The girls did not hear the illiterate commentary going on around them. They simply stared until it was time to get up and go in to work.

The following day, having witnessed not only this latest development but also the two girls' reverence, Tom Easterhouse volunteered to lead a vigil to determine who was behind the enhancements. Mayor Yearley and the other commissioners agreed that Easterhouse's unofficial presence could do no harm, but, on the advice of commissioner, lawyer, and radio personality Ed Finz, they balked at financing Easterhouse's plan to supply participants with hors d'oeuvres and beverages. Commissioner Carmen Turlington suggested that provisions might be solicited from the conveniently located and unfortunately named restaurant Crabby Dick's.

But the vigil was for naught. No guerilla sculptor appeared in the night, and the several prominent citizens who positioned themselves in shaded areas around the square observed no further change in *David*'s anatomy.

Easterhouse suggested posting a group of different watchers on consecutive nights, but everyone he approached for the strange duty pleaded sleep deprivation and other excuses. The vigil was canceled.

"For God's sake, Tom," said Mark Hoyle, senior writer of the weekly *Solares Hill,* "this is Key West, old boy. Strange things happen here every day. You know that better than anyone."

David remained exactly as Miranda and Berthe had last seen him until the phenomenon had become just another tired subject in the "Citizens' Voice" column of the daily *Key West Citizen.*

But on the afternoon of the summer solstice, the girls arrived to find that their man had rejoined the cause of artistic freedom. The item had expanded and now pointed straight ahead. (Only those familiar with the original commission knew that *straight ahead* meant in the honorary direction of Florence.)

"God, it's beautiful," they said.

By now, word had reached the highest levels of international society. Professional and amateur photographs, some digitally augmented, were traveling the Web faster than Paris Hilton's flexible jaws. Every morning talk show in America sent its perky female host to cover the site as discreetly as possible. The most endearing treatment featured a red-faced Katie Couric, artfully positioned so that nothing of the semierect johnson could be seen except in the instant that a sunrise breeze tossed the host's blonde hair a bit too far to the west.

Inevitably, a growing number of residents, visitors, and public officials complained that the phenomenon, however noteworthy, was offensive to many and harmful to the city's crucial tourist trade. Except for dwindling groups of adolescents, visitors to Mallory Square were avoiding *David* like the plague.

One person who did not fail to seize upon the organ's conveniently horizontal posture was Sugar Walls, a petite Cambodian dancer appearing through the month of June at Teasers, the strip club a few blocks up Duval Street. She arranged a late-night photo session with *Citizen* staffer Rob O'Brien, during which the naked sprite managed harmlessly to straddle the shaft in several imaginative poses. The best of these made their way into Ms. Walls's press kit and onto the marquee at Teasers.

The following morning, Mayor Yearley was almost disappointed at the sight of a familiar envelope. Sighing as he slit the opening, the mayor removed a check for twelve million dollars and a brief note: "Please present this to Monica Hassler at the Florida Keys Council of the Arts. Tell her to bag the minigrants and to start offering local artists some serious bucks. I want real art, not a bunch of rug rats butchering Beethoven on steel drums. Of course, *David* remains in place."

Hoping to avoid a public-relations nightmare, city officials began seeking ways to cover the object without losing the mysterious donor's patronage.

The entire staff of a popular Duval Street gay bar, One After 909, offered to take turns tying rainbow flags around the offending schlong.

A local sailmaker suggested draping the whole statue with canvas, but officials feared that (1) the protrusion would show anyway, and (2) the patron might retaliate in some outrageous fashion.

This latter possibility had lesbian organizations fantasizing about the arrival of a titanic *Sappho* in full color. These thoughts fermented down to speculation that the donor was just a petty schmuck with money and a sick sense of humor.

In fact the donor's gender would never be established, and no one could dispute a refreshing intolerance for mediocrity.

But the damage was beginning to look serious. Reservations for Fantasy Fest, the overabundance of unclothed living flesh that descended on Key West every October, had drooped well below annual norms. Other seasonal events hung similarly. Even traditional Keys activities such as dive tours and charter-fishing excursions appeared a bit flaccid.

On the first afternoon of autumn, Miranda and Berthe approached *David* from behind, as usual. But, guided by an ineffable sense of cosmic alignment, the girls parted a few yards from the taut buttocks and went separately around to opposite flanks. When they were directly facing each other, they froze.

David had achieved a full, yearning erection. The object of the girls' months of study was now nearly vertical, perfected by a graceful upward curve.

Miranda and Berthe looked into each other's eyes and walked to their place. They sat down, holding hands.

"My God," Berthe whispered.

"Yes," Miranda agreed.

Standing unnoticed a few feet behind the girls' bench were Sugar Walls and her bodyguard.

"*Damn,*" said Sugar. "Get that Rob O'Brien on the phone."

A pair of seagulls chattered above them in the cloudless blue sky.

"I've heard that size doesn't matter," Berthe offered, "except in your mind."

"That's what they say," Miranda concurred. "Like, *ouch,* right? But it's pretty impressive to look at."

"Yes, it is."

Of course it was entirely too impressive for community leaders, the media, the right-wing corporations that now controlled American politics, and the international tourism industry. Cruise-ship lines dropped Key West from their itineraries, bus tours and hotel reservations were canceled, the ferry from Fort Myers suspended operations, the few major carriers that serviced the city's little airport prepared to pull out, and the state governor placed a tollbooth where U.S. 1 joined the mainland. Every commercial entity on the planet having anything to do with Key West accused the city of unforgivable bad taste. The lifeblood of the island seemed to be draining into the polluted sea.

Jimmy Yearley could barely contain his anger at the sight of the predictable envelope. Inside this one was a check for fifteen million dollars and another curt note: "Use this to replace your countrified songwriter festival with a *real* songwriter festival, featuring talent not just from Nashville but also from all over America. I want *original* music, no Jimmy Buffett clones, no Caribbean platitudes. Show me your lineup by e-mail."

At the same time that an emergency session of the Key West City Commission was taking place at the Harvey Government Center on Truman Avenue, an emergency session of the Monroe County Board of County Commissioners was convening at the Key Largo Public Library.

A moment after county mayor Dixie Speerhardt called that meeting to order, courtly commissioner Charles "Sonny" McAllister, whose architectural contributions to the city of Key West had included the mausolean post office on Whitehead Street, pushed back his chair and leapt to his feet. "Dad *gum* it, people!" he drawled. "We cannot have, in the middle of Mallory Square, a statue of a fellow with his pecker pointing to Jesus and the angels!"

Laughter filled the room, but, all in attendance having noted the commissioner's unsmiling face, ceased as abruptly as it had begun.

Mayor Speerhardt tapped lightly on the table. "Commissioner McAllister," she said softly, "please sit down."

Appearing suddenly aware of the silence, McAllister took his seat and leaned forward. "Ladies and gentlemen," he said quietly, "this is not just about money. Today we in the Florida Keys are the laughingstock of the civilized world. Something *must* be done."

Nodding ensued on both sides of the dais.

Commissioner George Neuwerth of Marathon, hoping to lighten the mood, chuckled and said, "But you've got to admit, it's pretty amazing."

People shifted in their seats.

Mayor Speerhardt leaned in. "Fellow commissioners, ladies and gentlemen, we all know that, as repulsive as this thing is, from a legal standpoint it is out of county hands. It is Key West's problem. I assure you that Mayor Yearley is as outraged as any one of us."

Meanwhile, in Key West itself, life had taken on the placid rhythm and alert intimacy felt by those who remain behind during a hurricane evacuation. Residents simply ignored *David* and enjoyed the sudden season of peace and quiet. The controversy even inspired moments of levity and creative thinking.

Over lunch with theatrical colleagues at Mangoes, actor Tom "Pierrot" Lunaire recalled a chestnut:

"At Charles de Gaulle's retirement party, an American journalist approached Madame de Gaulle and asked, 'What are you most looking forward to in your husband's retirement?'

"Madame de Gaulle smiled and exclaimed, 'A penis!'

"President de Gaulle, having overheard his wife's unfortunate response, leaned over to her and said, 'I believe zey pronounce it *happiness.*'"

At the next meeting of the Key West Writers Guild at Kelly's Caribbean Bar, Grill, and Brewery, director Ann Galerius was pleased to introduce a new member. The elderly woman seated to the speaker's right, Mrs. Margaret Dunstable, told the group of about twenty that she had recently moved down from Vermont, that her poetry had been published in various New England journals, and that she had signed up that morning to read her new work, entitled "Ode to You Know What."

After Galerius dispensed with official business, Mrs. Dunstable was invited to read. She rose somewhat awkwardly and stepped to the podium.

Bad acoustics aside, the reader did not at least have to compete with the powerboat races that normally would have been roaring a few blocks north in the Gulf.

Mrs. Dunstable's poem, a bit longer than guild rules normally permitted, managed to incorporate nearly every phallic euphemism in the English language and a number of graphic descriptions of phallic behavior. By the final couplet, there was clearly more than the usual amount of perspiration above the assembled upper lips. When Mrs. Dunstable turned to the gentleman seated closest to her and asked him to pass her a glass of water, the gentleman, noting to himself that complying would require rising from his seat, tapped Galerius on the forearm. The director reached for the pitcher.

The next morning, following mass at St. Mary Star of the Sea Church on Windsor Lane, a group of twelve nuns from rural Paris, Virginia, in town to help dedicate a new shelter for the homeless, convened in front of the Lourdes grotto that graced the churchyard.

Even in their piedmont seclusion, the sisters had heard about the abomination at Mallory Square. One of them suggested they visit the site, proposing that their presence would cause at least a few gawkers to reevaluate their base impulses. After halfhearted protests within the group, the ladies mounted their rented bicycles and rode downtown.

Once assembled before *David,* the nuns reacted with disgust, dismay, and delight. Before long the women were giggling and forgetting that they were wearing suffocating habits under a noonday sun.

Sister Caroline of the Ascension, the young woman who had suggested their detour, looked around and said, "But seriously: if this isn't proof of God's mysterious power, what is?"

At the next meeting of the Art in Public Places Committee, chairperson and gallery owner Nance Frankfurter opened by saying, "I suppose if things get any weirder around here we'll have to start calling ourselves the Art in *Pubic* Places Committee."

County sheriff Rick "Ace" Rothstein and Key West police chief Bill Maddning, freed from managing hordes of tourists, appeared before both the county and city commissions with joint proposals to crack down on speeding, tailgating, rolling stops, nonexistent turn signals, and other typical Keys driving habits, and to raise the fines for each of these offenses to at least three hundred dollars. "These measures apply to our own as well," Rothstein said. "I want to hear from any citizen who observes one of my officers driving foolishly."

The chamber erupted in the loudest applause anyone could remember in that space.

Maddning went further to propose that motorcycles and motor scooters be banned within the city limits. "Regarding the former," he said, "the handful of businesses that benefit from the bikers' deafening presence surely would survive without them, and these oafs who use charity events to justify their clownish exhibitionism do nothing for our damaged reputation."

A smattering of mostly female applause.

"As for the latter," Maddning continued, "we simply don't need the stinking, screaming, beeping, creeping scooters that clog our roads, often in the hands of kids who cannot operate them safely. There is no destination on this island that cannot be reached in minutes on foot or by bicycle."

Commissioner Turlington agreed. "I say we offer businesses that rent motorized two-wheelers a choice: switch to bicycles or get out of town."

More applause.

"Little electric cars must remain available for the elderly and disabled," she continued. "I'd insist on that. But everyone else could use the exercise."

The energy public officials were feeling because of the

city's new quality of life introduced proposals to raise taxes on snowbirds, to ban motorized personal watercraft and recreational vehicles, to enforce the noise laws applied to musicians and deejays, to close fraudulent businesses whose window displays made *David* look like a choirboy, and to ban chain stores.

It was with somewhat less enthusiasm that the county commission admitted that there was no need to retain the Tourist Development Council, its umbrella committees, or its advertising agency in Miami. TDC director Harold Axelrod took the news with characteristic dignity and told his employees that, where possible, they would be considered for positions within regular county government.

Key West's involuntary moratorium on greed, corruption, and cancerous growth prompted the private sector toward creative acts of its own.

First to move into play were the Spottswood Companies, which financed the relocation of twenty core members of the all-imported Key West Symphony Orchestra, to fill the gaps in the orchestra's regular season.

Ann Henlopen, a former State Department official and now president of the dynamic Rodel Foundation, relocated three teachers from the Washington Ballet, to collaborate with Key West's CoffeeMill Cultural Centre in developing a permanent dance conservatory with a climate-controlled studio.

Similarly unselfish gestures began taking place throughout the happily isolated community.

The least expected occurrence was the phone call placed by the Keys' most famous real-estate developer,

Edwin O'Quick III, to the Keys' second most famous real-estate developer, Pritam Chanté, inviting the latter to lunch in a private room at the Casa Marina.

After the two men sat down, O'Quick leaned forward and said, "All this has me doing some soul-searching."

As the self-described world's only Buddhist-Sikh-Christian, Chanté was no mere hitchhiker on the metaphysical highway. He viewed his companion nervously and said nothing.

"Obviously, this maniac has Jimmy by the balls," O'Quick said. "The only way he's going to remove that statue is if guys like you and me make him an offer he can't refuse."

"Uh huh?" Chanté replied as their iced tea arrived.

When the waiter left, O'Quick resumed: "And there's something else." He looked around as though spotting microphones. "I really like the way the place feels these days."

Chanté took a sip.

"Listen," O'Quick continued, "I think it's time we did the right thing."

Chanté grimaced. "Where are you going with this, man?"

O'Quick sat up straight and put his palms on the table. "I've decided, in exchange for the removal of the statue to a private gallery, to halt all new construction in Key West. I'm going to donate my remaining lots to the city, provided they are developed only as green space." O'Quick took some tea and waited for a reaction.

Chanté's fingers were clenched on the outer edges of the table.

"I suggest you do the same with those cheesy townhouses you're building in Marathon," O'Quick smiled. "Just give them away. Our colleagues are welcome to follow suit."

"Ed, do you know what you're saying?" Chanté asked before draining his glass.

O'Quick looked out at the turquoise water. "I've never been so sure of anything in my life. I'm getting out of this racket."

Indeed Edwin O'Quick III stunned the community when he announced that he was closing the Key West branch of his company, Historic Tours of Armenia, over the objections of his lawyer, city commissioner and radio personality Ed Finz. This act, besides removing from the city's narrow streets the Conch Trains and Old Town Trolleys whose hyperbolic narrators had been assaulting quaint neighborhoods for decades, freed O'Quick's mind for further introspection. He donated three million dollars each to the Audubon House and Tropical Gardens, Clean Florida Keys, Fort Zachary Taylor Historic State Park, the Key West Botanical Gardens, Last Stand, the Nature Conservancy, Reef Relief, Save a Turtle, and the World Wildlife Fund. Ed O'Quick relocated to his Washington, D.C., office, settled his affairs there, and applied for a position with the National Park Service.

In tribute to O'Quick's generosity, Pritam Chanté gave modest sums of money to environmental groups in the Middle Keys. He continued building his cheesy townhouses in Marathon.

Faith Sizemore, the beautiful new president of America Online, headquartered near Dulles Airport in

Northern Virginia, was carrying on a clandestine affair with her office manager, Nicole Braggadocio. Over Chinese takeout one evening at a Middleburg bed-and-breakfast, Faith invited her partner to spend a few days with her at Pearl's Rainbow in Key West. Naturally the pair had learned more than enough about the misbehaving *David* and the resultant calm. Faith had vacationed in Key West during noisier times and was eager to show off the town to Nicole.

The women arrived and enjoyed a blissful evening on the island and in each other's arms. The next morning at the Banana Café, Faith took Nicole's hand and looked into her eyes. "I know we're both sick of freezing our asses off in D.C., fighting that traffic," she purred. "What would you say if I asked you to move down here, find us a little cottage, and open an AOL field office in Key West?"

Nicole's eyes welled with tears. Both women had been stealing glances at the gorgeous blonde behind the bar, but neither noticed her startled smile when Nicole jumped up and kissed Faith hard on the mouth.

Within months, every major information-technology company in the world would have a Key West branch.

And so it was that Key West's days as a dirty, disappointing tourist town were over, and that its days as a clean, cultured community that could take care of itself had finally begun.

The Southernmost Erection, as *David*'s unembarrassed member had become known, remained poised throughout the holidays and into the new year.

On the first afternoon of spring, Miranda Perez and

Berthe Liadov arrived at the bench and turned toward their hero.

Little *David* had returned to its original state.

"Oh my God," said Berthe softly.

The girls stared wistfully for a minute.

"You know," Berthe said finally, "I think I like him better this way."

Miranda turned to her friend. "Yeah, right."

The girls laughed and embraced.

Miranda took Berthe's hand. "Let's go, Missy."

News of *David*'s priapic resolution was greeted throughout the town with sadness, soon to be replaced by hope. Some wondered whether the SE would be an annual cycle, like the ever-shifting sunset. Others feared the international tourist trade would declare that the coast was clear and the town would go straight back to hell. Most were simply glad that something had happened to save the citizens from themselves.

Mayor Jimmy Yearley entered his office the next morning whistling an old blues tune that stopped abruptly at the sight of another envelope. He ripped it open so violently that he almost destroyed a check for eighteen million dollars. The attached note read, "Perhaps now they understand. Use this money however you see fit."

Toward the end of the spring theater season, Michael Manners, technical director of the Waterfront Playhouse, was having lunch at El Meson de Pepe with his former boss, Rebecca Templeton, director of the Tennessee Williams Theatre (known among acoustical engineers as TWIT). Manners's dismissal several years earlier because of departmental downsizing had caused some ill will in

Key West's congenial arts community, but the two professionals had long since mended their fences. They were meeting to discuss next season's joint production of *The Tempest,* for which local composer and former Washingtonian Horst Heimlich had written twelve-tone music to be performed on Elizabethan instruments. Members of the Folger Consort would travel from their residence at the Folger Shakespeare Library to perform the score. Manners and Templeton had looked over the composer's sketches and declared them "groovy." The two finished lunch and strolled to the quiet plaza.

Without a word they found themselves seated next to each other on the bench in front of *David.*

Templeton was feeling her midday *mojito.* "You know, Mike, I don't care what anyone says. Small can be really nice."

Manners followed her gaze and smiled. "Sure, darlin'," he said, patting her hand. "But talk about *potential.*"

STRAY

DÉSEAN UNDERWOOD WOKE in the middle of the night realizing he had dreamed that he and Orla Quinn had made a suicide pact. He lay freezing in sweat, staring at the palm fronds dancing in the moonlight outside his open window. He saw Orla's ruddy face, the watery melancholic blue eyes, the shoulder-length hair, a deeper red than it really was. In the dream they were college students on a generic leafy campus, embracing on the sidewalk outside her dorm. They had agreed to lie down together one last time that night and drink a tea made from an herb called *Seneca's daughter*. They would ease back holding hands and drift away. "Stay," he whispered in her ear on the sidewalk. "Please stay." *No,* she said. *Not like this.*

DéSean and Orla had been briefly and intermittently intimate: sweet, easy, not without imagination. Orla had in fact been DéSean's first date since his move to Key West from Los Angeles in 1998. They met at a writers' conference. Days, weeks, or months would pass between encounters. Disappointed with masculinity in general, Orla occasionally teased him with threats to go lesbian. She actually tried it with a girl a few times before realizing she was turning asexual. She said she thought the need for physical contact was silly. Since record labels were not exactly fighting over her Gaelic folk songs, Orla carried this thinking to its logical conclusion and became a stripper at the Red Garter on Duval Street. DéSean heard the news cheerfully, caught her act once, and e-mailed her a perceptive review. Orla tolerated his lascivious follow-ups, but they never touched that way again. DéSean accepted their platonic friendship and enjoyed her feminist paranoia whenever she felt like airing it over a cup of coffee.

They hardly had spoken in years. Why DéSean had dreamed the suicide pact was a mystery to him. He lay in his cold sweat and saw her too-red hair under the dripping oaks. He thought of her tight little swimmer's body but could not arouse himself. He squirmed in the disgusting puddle and threw off the covers. He sprang up, turned on the lamp, and stripped the bed. He carried the linens to the hamper feeling the damp tropical breeze as he walked naked through the cottage. He would let the mattress dry before putting on clean sheets. He could not have slept anyway. He threw a beach towel over his reading chair and sat down with the infernal stunted manuscript and the dull red pencil with its hardened eraser.

When the sun was well up, DéSean called Orla and told her about the dream. She was surprised to hear his voice. He knew he was bothering her. She volunteered that she was alone, not that he would have asked. Her only insight was that the term *Seneca's daughter* was overdramatic and historically dubious. Even his subconscious was a waste of time. He smiled at her halfhearted offer to get together sometime and hung up. *Bitch.* The soft curls against his neck, the watery unseeing eyes, the sound of sparse raindrops hitting pavement.

The two foul-mouthed white cops who came to DéSean Underwood's Bahama Village address that night acted as if they owned the place. No *Sir, we have a warrant,* no Miranda: the fat thugs just walked in, pushed DéSean against the wall, and cuffed him. Only then did he realize that white cops with guns drawn surrounded the little building.

Orla Quinn had slit her wrists in her bathtub that afternoon. On the floor beside the toilet were printouts of all their e-mails.

Several hours later, the police realized that DéSean Underwood had ceased to amuse and let him go. He watched the sunrise from the hot tub on his back porch, sweating out the humiliation, soothing his bruises with a joint and a glass of Scotch. He mourned his friend and wondered what she could have been thinking.

At seven o'clock DéSean climbed into his taxi and drove to the airport. The sun was already high enough to vibrate the tarmac. His first fare was a beautiful young Middle Eastern woman who said she was staying at the nearby Casa Marina but asked him first to drive her around the island. "Take your time," she smiled. He showed her through Old Town, negotiated his favorite narrow lanes, drove slowly past lush gardens, responded succinctly to her fluent English. She was Persian, she explained, not Arab. The people of Iran did not necessarily endorse their government's views. "Neither do we ours," DéSean laughed. The woman introduced herself as Nahid Parvaneh and said she was in Key West to interview for the position of head chef at a bold new hotel restaurant. DéSean wished her well and promised to sample her cuisine. He dropped her off and returned to the terminal.

Late that night Ms. Parvaneh was found at the bottom

of the Casa Marina's main swimming pool. Her throat was cut, and there was no sign of a struggle or of foul play. A small knife from the Casa's kitchen was found near the body. When DéSean Underwood read about it in the next morning's *Key West Citizen,* a chill ran through him. He lay in bed that night afraid to sleep. When finally he did, he dreamed of the sleek jet-black hair swaying behind him in the taxi. The police did not know that Ms. Parvaneh had been DéSean's fare, and he saw no reason that they should.

Orla Quinn's funeral was attended by a small gathering of the Key West arts community. Resident musicians respected Orla's unsalable tunes, a few of which had found occasional performances at Finnegan's Wake and Irish Kevin's. Those locals who knew of Orla's "day job" were more likely to admire than to condemn her creative choices. DéSean watched the placement of the urn and paced the old cemetery long after the other mourners had left. The suicide dream returned to his bed that night, and he woke in tears.

DéSean was not a heavy drinker, but he enjoyed an occasional *mojito* at El Meson de Pepe. With the Orla dream now haunting his daylight hours as well, the next evening found him seated at the outdoor bar listening to the salsa band and chatting with a pair of wealthy young Venezuelan tourists. Having confessed his trade opened him to a flurry of questions regarding local attractions.

Late that night Umberto Morales discovered his wife's body hanging from the balcony of their rented luxury condominium at Trumbo Point. She had used a length of rope a charter-boat captain had left on the dock behind the

Waterfront Market. No note was found, and an inconsolable Morales was unable to tell police what could have motivated the sudden end to his happy marriage.

DéSean Underwood finished reading about it and set aside the newspaper. He waited until after noon to call Kaira Fallingwater. The two had been friends and occasional lovers for a decade and had walked each other through a number of personal crises. Obscure little publishers had brought out several books of Kaira's award-winning poetry: free verse expressing an appealing mixture of Native American religions, kabbalah, Santeria, Sufism, and every other mystic thread that caught her fancy. Anywhere else Kaira would have been dismissed as a hippie dilettante, but Key Westers had embraced her as a holy vessel. "I believe in everything," she would say in her breathy alto as her nimble fingers undid DéSean's belt buckle. Kaira could actually make herself come without lifting a finger, simply by imagining the Virgin Mary's immaculate initiation. Whether this present encounter would as usual end in a mutual hand job, DéSean knew he had to see Kaira.

It turned out that Kaira had been thinking of her old friend anyway, and the predictable hungry act took place almost immediately on DéSean's entry into Kaira's incensed apartment. She lay back on the sofa and stretched full length, emitting the deep, satisfied moan he had always associated only with her. She cupped her warm hand over him and listened to his story.

Finally she said, "Your aura is wounded. It begins with someone you know and continues with people you just met. They might have been flirting with suicide for years, or the idea might never have occurred to them. Your arrival in their lives is the catalyst. It's like you've become a cooler, the guy a casino owner hires to spoil a winner's luck. Whether you yourself have ever considered killing yourself is irrelevant. But that's the only way to end the cycle. Unless."

"Unless?" DéSean asked.

"Show me exactly where these suicides occurred," Kaira replied.

At three o'clock the following morning, Kaira rode her bicycle to each of the sites and erected a little altar composed of items from her collection. The casual observer would never have discerned a meaning in their placement or in the varied selections of bones, feathers, beads, statuettes, stones, and drops of holy water mixed with Kaira's own blood. Each altar would stay in place until the next full moon. Even in a town full of eccentrics it was remarkable that no one thought to disturb any of the memorials.

A week before dismantling the first altar, Kaira called DéSean and issued her instructions. "On the night of the next three full moons I will drink your semen and pray for your victims. Then it will be over."

The two marked their calendars and met at Kaira's apartment on the appointed evenings for their ritual. No further suicides occurred in Key West during that period. The one person who months later would shoot himself in an abandoned boat near the Cow Key Channel bridge was a New Hampshire snowbird whose ill-conceived Jet Ski business had failed and who had never met DéSean Underwood.

DéSean and Kaira stopped meeting regularly after the coast was clear, despite the pleasant nature of their exorcism. The young man applied for and won a grant to establish a twenty-four-hour suicide hotline staffed by local psychologists.

On a cold, rainy night seven months later, Kaira Fallingwater was pedaling home with a basketful of groceries when she was killed by a hit-and-run driver at the corner of Margaret and Southard Streets.

DéSean Underwood had been distracted by the pretty fare in his rearview mirror and did not realize he had driven past Kaira's bloody corpse until he read about it the next day. He got in his cab, drove to the long-term lot at the airport, and finished his bottle of Scotch. He left the keys in the ignition and ran across the road. He jumped over the seawall and unzipped his backpack. He filled it with rocks, strapped it to his shoulders, and walked toward a distant light on the horizon.

A Whole
New Leonard

LEONARD GROSSMAN JR. USUALLY WOKE with an erection. Since that affirming tightness first thing in the morning often accompanied an acute need to pee, Leonard's routine was to throw back the covers, swing his legs over, stand, take a moment to admire himself in the full-length mirror, pad the few steps around the corner to the bathroom, bend his morning glory down as far as it would go without hurting, sit on the toilet, and relieve himself. In a real emergency he could pee standing with a hard-on, but it meant assuming an awkward position and holding the impertinent organ at a briefly painful angle. In either case, the act of urinating would resolve the erection to a handsome tumescence that he would pause to appreciate on his way back to bed. On most mornings he could doze a few minutes or longer before heading downstairs for breakfast. Leonard worked a flexible schedule as a lifestyle columnist at the city newspaper and enjoyed the luxury of waking in bright sunshine. He recently had turned fifty.

The morning of Wednesday, March 18, 2009, was like no other. Leonard woke with his familiar problem and prepared to remedy it. As he threw back the covers, he felt an increased pressure down there. When he stood before the mirror, what Leonard saw made him question his sanity. In the space of six hours, Leonard's penis had nearly doubled in size. Leonard stood at the mirror beholding a situation for which most men would sell their souls. Leonard's respectable five-inch erection had suddenly taken on dimensions witnessed only in pornography. The transformation was so astounding that Leonard forgot he had to pee. He stood there a moment to confirm that he was not back in bed dreaming. Then he ran to his desk and picked up the ruler. Leonard's fingers trembled as he held the clear plastic device alongside his cock. He had to reexamine the ruler to be sure it was not turned around to the metric side.

The dream of postpubescent males the world over had come true. Leonard's cock was a thick nine inches long. A full minute of staring passed before this blessed truth could sink in. Leonard ran back to the mirror. His reflection did not lie: there it was, a whole new Leonard. He turned and beheld the miracle from every angle. He positioned the ruler next to it and reconfirmed the magic number. He looked into his eyes. "My God," he said aloud.

Suddenly Leonard remembered his full bladder. He ran in, bent down the massive appendage, took his seat, and came to grips with new laws of physics. It was all Leonard could do to keep the thing from touching the side of the bowl or dipping into the water. He got back up and assumed a radical version of his awkward stance and watched as the mighty wand gave way to a radical version of his handsome tumescence. Once finished, he returned to the mirror and stared. The thing reminded him of copies of *Playgirl* magazine he had seen in the apartment that an old flame had shared with a self-proclaimed nymphomaniac. "This is unbelievable," Leonard said. He twisted from side to side and luxuriated in gravity as the cock swung like a pendulum.

Leonard's knees began to shake, and he sat back on the bed. In the mirror the penis extended comfortably over the edge of the mattress instead of just touching the top surface. Leonard held it up and saw the tip reach above his navel, a signpost he normally could not have passed in any condition. Leonard watched himself make the thing hard again and sat back in wonder. "God in heaven."

Leonard lived alone and normally did not wear clothes at home. He had moved from Chicago to Miami specifically so he could wear as little as possible throughout the year. On the morning of March 18, Leonard could not take his eyes off his new pal as he stepped slowly downstairs to pour water in the teakettle. Like someone trying to use his cell phone while driving, Leonard attended to his breakfast ritual completely distracted by this other presence. He performed most of his familiar tasks with one hand so he could fondle and study the thing.

Leonard was not religious. He had been raised Jewish, but by the time of his bar mitzvah he had decided that religion was bullshit. No omniscient God, especially not the pissed-off patriarch of the Old Testament, could allow what humanity had become. In college Leonard had fallen in love with a Catholic girl, attended mass with her a few times, decided to take instruction, joined the church, and worshipped regularly for several years until one day he realized that the loving, forgiving God of an organization run by misogynistic pedophiles was no less an illusion.

There was something out there smarter than people, Leonard knew; there had to be. What superior being had invented the universe, and what had invented its inventor? Science could not explain. God, or whatever you wanted to call it, was that unknowable entity. But Leonard felt that whether you subscribed to the Christian fairy tale, the Judaic fairy tale, or any of the other fairy tales human beings had created to assuage their cosmic ignorance, that was all it was: reassuring nonsense whose most notable gift to Earth's population was an abundance of great art. At its best, religion was a superstitious attempt to feel a sense of belonging: to one's family, friends, community, the world at large, that slippery universe. At its worst, it was organized hypocrisy. Still, here was this awesome reality between Leonard's legs that had not existed the night before.

One of the few fun characteristics Leonard had inherited during his brief Catholic phase was an affinity with the number three. He would perform daily tasks in increments of three or of numbers divisible by three. Leonard decided that if his penis had not resumed its former dimensions in three days he would make an appointment with his urologist. He did not expect the man to offer a rational explanation, but at least Leonard would receive a specialist's opinion.

Indeed the urologist, an amiable neighbor of roughly Leonard's age, could do no more than sit back in predictable astonishment and shake his head with an envious grin on his face. "Lenny," the doctor said, "I don't think I need to tell you that this is unprecedented. Truly a miracle, something for the record books." He smiled at his patient. "For now, let's keep this between you and me. I want to do some research. But if this hasn't changed in, say, a week, I'd like your permission to publish what surely will be a groundbreaking article for *The Journal of the American Medical Association*."

Leonard smiled at his friend and thought about the unwieldy number seven. "Let's give it nine days, just to be safe," he said.

Leonard went home, undressed, and stood before the mirror. He would have to streamline his habits if he was going to get anything done while this fantastic new feature demanded his attention. Leonard found himself seeking his reflection in whatever surface was before him: the door of the microwave oven, the glass of a bookcase, the television screen. Everywhere he looked, what he saw was his new penis. In its flaccid state it was nearly as big as his former erection. And the new boner was so impressive that he could not help achieving one at every opportunity. He walked around the house with the thing in his hand like a child who cannot stop playing with a new puppy.

Whether and, if so, how to break the news to a female acquaintance bedeviled Leonard. His latest relationship had ended months earlier in mutual frustration: typically, a once rapturous love affair had cooled to a friendship with benefits, those benefits occurring less and less frequently until she was simply a companion. Myra Bloom, svelte at forty-nine and happily widowed, had wanted more of Leonard's attention than he could spare: most of his free time away from the newspaper was spent writing books and articles on a variety of subjects too complex for the time and space constraints of journalism. But Leonard knew he had to ring Myra and at least show her what had happened to him.

Like some other women, Myra had found an opportunity early in their relationship to say that size was not important to her. Leonard had assumed that women felt the need to make this pronouncement to any lover whose endowment was average or below. In Leonard's youth, a few girls had made a point of telling him that his firm, smooth penis was unusually attractive. "It's so pretty!" one of them was wont to sing. Only two women in his life, one in high school and one in his thirties, had been so unkind as to suggest that Leonard's five-inch member was inadequate: one had had little experience and was just repeating misinformation, and the other had not recovered well from an episiotomy and simply needed a thicker object to stimulate her. Leonard had written off the first and relinquished the second, but he could not help wishing he could revisit both women in his present state.

Meanwhile, Leonard was curious to see whether women on the street, customarily subtler than their male observers, would notice. He had always looked young for his age and kept himself in good shape. He therefore felt no embarrassment in squeezing into a pair of tight jeans he had not worn in a few years and tucking in his usually loose T-shirt. This experiment precluded underwear. Again he paused before the mirror and smiled. He drove to the Beach and found a parking space on Ocean Drive. He got out and strolled several blocks on the seaside path before doubling back on the opposite sidewalk lined with cafés and hotels. Throughout his brief essay he felt immense gratification in the glances and smiles of women of all ages. He listened for giggles and quiet comments from bikini-clad girls passing in pairs or groups. Leonard was less enthusiastic about the knowing grins of natty young men. But he ended his promenade assured that he now inhabited a new world.

Leonard called Myra and asked her out to dinner and a movie. She was pleasantly surprised to hear his voice, and Leonard felt slightly guilty about the vain purpose for his call. He knew that, size notwithstanding, Myra would welcome him back if he appeared willing to put more effort into the relationship.

Leonard dressed conservatively for their date and, since the air was cool, wore a sweater that covered his new state of being. Throughout the evening Myra seemed content with catching up and did not appear to perceive any difference. She did remark that there was a certain glow about him, but Leonard took this as lighthearted assurance that she was ready for whatever the night might bring. The two had enjoyed great sex at their peak and good sex in their waning days. On this particular evening they had shared a single chaste hug at Myra's door as they prepared to leave for the restaurant. Leonard could barely contain his curiosity.

"You have to promise me something," he said as they reentered Myra's condominium close to midnight. He gently backed her against the living-room wall.

She smiled provocatively and unbuttoned her jacket. "Something about what?"

"Something I'm going to show you," he said seriously.

Myra removed the jacket and let it fall to the floor behind her. Except for a bouquet of flowers, Leonard did not appear to have brought a gift. Myra appreciated his forward behavior but had promised herself not to expect sex. Still, she allowed a soft moan.

"Don't move," Leonard said.

Myra smiled broadly.

Leonard quickly removed his sweater and pulled out his shirttail. Myra was still looking into his eyes. His unsteady fingers as he fumbled with the belt buckle quickened Myra's breathing, but Leonard was determined to make this presentation as clinical as possible: it was too significant to devalue with bawdy humor. He undid his trousers and let them fall. Remembering how ludicrous a man looks with his pants around his ankles, Leonard made quick work of removing his shoes. He kicked aside the trousers and underwear and paused. "You must keep this our secret, for now," he smiled. He could already feel the blood rushing into the organ. But he thought it best to get Myra's uncolored opinion, so, to delay the inevitable, he pictured the title page of his unfinished manuscript on the future of Cuban tourism. Leonard unbuttoned his shirt, tossed it onto the reading chair, and stood naked before her.

Myra looked down and gasped. "Oh, my God, Leonard!" She flattened herself against the wall and stared.

Leonard studied her body language and said nothing.

Myra shifted her position and viewed the penis from different angles. "Um," she began, "I don't mean to be rude, but what happened?"

"Happened?" he repeated.

"Did you have an operation? This is amazing!"

"Nope," Leonard smiled.

Both of them were aware that penile-enlargement surgery was in its infancy and that the results generally ranged from disappointing to disastrous.

Myra looked into his eyes for a second and then back at exhibit A. "Well, but, I mean—"

"I just woke up this way several days ago," he said. "I felt like a heel calling you, but you're my dearest friend and I have to know what you think of it."

Myra stared at Leonard's tumescent cock. "Your dearest friend," she smiled.

"Well," Leonard said blushing, "you know what I mean. Whatever else we are, we'll always be friends. But you're the last woman who saw me undressed, and I had to—"

"You definitely made the correct decision," Myra smiled, stepping forward. She reached out and caressed the thing, cooing as it rose. She could not believe what she was seeing. She got on her knees and examined the result. She cupped her hand under Leonard's balls and sat back against the wainscoting. "Jesus Christ, man!"

Leonard smiled down at her and stretched at full height. "You like?"

Myra wrapped both hands around the shaft. "My God, Len." She savored the feel of it. "But how? How is this possible?"

Leonard simply stood there in her grasp.

"Well, I don't know what to say, but—" Myra stood and undressed as quickly as she could. She pulled him to her, the massive hardness hot against her abdomen. "Here, or in there?" she pleaded. She looked at the chair and considered bending over it. She entertained the same thought about the dining-room table. But she had to watch the thing go in, had to see it in action. She took Leonard's hand and led him to her bedroom. She sat on the edge of the bed where she could watch the two of them in her dresser mirror. She inched back on her elbows and put her heels on the mattress. "Come here," she said.

Leonard had not expected to place his new organ inside Myra, or anyone else, without some considerable foreplay. But Myra's invitation was obviously sincere. She, like he, had to experience the thing. He reached down to confirm that she was wet and inserted the tip.

Myra winced. "Take your time, there, cowboy."

He did, and when finally the whole cock was inside her he embraced her and held her still. They shivered together in the fullness of it.

The next morning Leonard woke hard, needing to pee, and realizing that Myra was lying at his side staring. She had pulled back the covers and was gently touching herself.

"I still can't believe it," she whispered.

"Neither can I," Leonard replied. He went to the bathroom and returned especially handsome.

With a few taps of her fingertips Myra brought back the erection and spent the rest of the morning kissing, stroking, and riding it. She had more orgasms that morning than she had enjoyed in weeks of solitary masturbation. She promised for the time being not to tell a soul about Leonard's metamorphosis, but she could not wait for his blessing to confide in someone, anyone. She even fantasized about doing a ménage à trois with Leonard and her best friend, just to get her feedback. She envisioned a photomontage, a Facebook page, a book deal, a bloody talk show. "I just want you to understand," she said later over brunch, "that I'd still love you as you were."

Leonard grinned.

"But this is fucking amazing," she said.

Leonard drove home wondering whether he had created a monster. He felt no more committed to Myra than he had when they drifted apart, and he feared that once the novelty of his new size wore off they would fall back into their comfortable patterns. He worried more about Myra's reaction should it turn out that he simply had contracted some glorious but short-lived disease. He sensed that Myra shared his concerns.

Leonard and Myra resumed dating and enjoyed their enhanced passion, each on guard for signs of complacence.

Accepting that Myra wanted to be his partner to whatever extent was possible, Leonard could not resist occasionally testing the waters elsewhere. He sometimes strolled Lincoln Road in the perfumed evenings wearing jeans or thin dress pants, watching women's eyes.

One night Leonard decided to get the perspective of someone accustomed to seeing cocks of all sizes on a daily basis, so he presented himself at an Asian massage parlor in a strip mall. "Wow!" was the petite woman's immediate reaction. After she got him hard, she retreated in awe. "*Wow!*" She took another step back. "Excuse me just a moment," she said. She left the room and returned seconds later with the three other girls Leonard had met in the lobby. They took turns examining and petting the cock, and the visiting trio watched as the first girl brought

Leonard to a volcanic finish. There was general applause as the happy client lay on the table laughing.

Finally one day Leonard succumbed to his gnawing memory and looked up the girl who had insulted him in high school. It took seconds to locate her on Facebook. He read her profile, scoffing at her academic and professional achievements, dismissing her right-wing bromides, and recalling that night in the back of his dad's car when she had informed Leonard that he had a small penis. With a click of the mouse he requested her friendship.

She responded the next day with an e-mail. She filled in the basic facts of her life and asked about his. She did not mention that night, nor did Leonard expect her to. She probably had discovered for herself that Leonard's cock had been perfectly normal. Even if she remembered hurting his feelings, it was too early in their renewed acquaintance for her to apologize.

Leonard examined the message as dispassionately as possible. The editor in him bristled at typical American errors in grammar, spelling, and syntax. He wondered whether the sexy blonde bitch was now a fat, lonely divorcée. He really did not care a thing about her except what she would say if she saw his new cock. He was dying to send her a photograph of it and wondered how to broach the subject.

The former sexy blonde admitted to being a slightly overweight but not at all lonely executive at a Hollywood studio specializing in artsy, low-budget independent films. Several increasingly frank e-mails later, she boasted that among the semifamous men she had dated in the past thirty years were two porn stars and a mainstream actor whose most memorable talent was likewise in his pants.

Still, Leonard was curious.

The woman agreed to share a full-length naked photo of herself if Leonard would do the same. "You first," she insisted.

Leonard waited several minutes after clicking *Send*. Then a single word appeared in his inbox: "Wow!" He opened the e-mail and saw the same word repeated three more times. There was no attachment.

The woman explained that Leonard's surprising growth, in addition to his boyish physique after all this time, was intimidating. She had made an online promise, but she prepared Leonard for disappointment.

Many more minutes passed before another e-mail appeared in the inbox. Leonard saw the virtual paper clip and opened the message.

"Please be kind," it read.

Leonard downloaded the attachment and opened it. The matronly person who smiled at him over the miles and decades resembled the mothers who had served refreshments to him and his friends after school. He would never have looked twice at one of those women then, nor could he imagine being aroused by the image now before him. He looked down at his huge cock, hanging limp between his thighs, and smiled. He sent a complimentary reply.

A few minutes later she wrote, "I want you to know that I have never forgotten what I said to you in the car that night. I am so sorry, Leonard. Can you forgive me?"

Of course he could.

The next day Leonard received a call from his

urologist. He wanted an *after* photograph to accompany the stock *before* photograph that would illustrate his article in the AMA journal.

Three months later, after global reaction to the doctor's metaphysical piece had made him a celebrity in his field, Leonard's urologist was tapped as the keynote speaker at the next AMA convention in Los Angeles. Leonard sat in the audience comfortably aware of peeks and whispers from professionals of all genders and hoped that he would not be called up to the stage for a demonstration. He remembered how things had turned out for King Kong. Fortunately, the urologist simply finished his account with a joke: "Now everybody's going to want one, and there's not a damn thing any of us can do about it!"

Leonard went back to his hotel and undressed. As he stood before the mirror, he heard a gentle knock at the door. He walked over and opened it, showing only his face.

It was the teenage tormentor turned studio chief. She said that she was dating a semifamous neurosurgeon who was awaiting her in the lobby, that they had attended the convention, and that she had tried and failed to find Leonard before he left the building. She stood there waiting.

"Come in," Leonard smiled.

She looked down and gasped. "You do realize that you have the body of a man half your age, right?"

Leonard smiled at her and felt the organ thicken.

"And you know that in porn films they rarely show anything above the man's waist?"

The johnson was halfway up and rising.

"I promise you the perfect stage name," she continued.

Leonard was now hard as a rock, but the former classmate did not touch him. She circled him several times, saying "Wow!" each time she paused. She arranged to send over her beautiful young assistant with some paperwork. She also assigned Leonard a specially trained makeup girl who would shave off all his body hair and maintain his ageless appearance. A star was born.

Leonard quit the newspaper, moved to Santa Monica, and devoted his free time to serious writing. The rest of his hours were spent in the gym or before the camera in the company of girls young enough to be his daughters, had he ever considered marriage. One of them had been a novice in a convent and in their most widely anticipated scene together played the part with pious devotion. Leonard of course began the scene dressed as a masked priest. Afterward, in the sacristy of the abandoned Mexican cathedral where they had filmed, the girl asked Leonard if the story of his transformation was real or just a clever hoax. He assured her of the truth. "Almost makes you want to believe in God," she smiled, touching him through his pants. "I just hope it doesn't get any bigger. See you next time!" She kissed Leonard's cheek and walked carefully out to her waiting limousine.

Leonard returned home to half a dozen messages on his voice mail. One was from Myra, who said she had just bought a house in Laurel Canyon and that she would arrive in time to invite him to Thanksgiving dinner. The second message was from an unknown woman who claimed she and Leonard had gone to graduate school together, the crackly third was from a Buddhist monk calling from Laos, the fourth was from the imam of the largest mosque in Düsseldorf, the fifth was from the Church of Scientology, and the sixth was from the French ambassador to the Vatican. Leonard erased all the messages except the first and checked in with his agent.

Nine months later, Leonard Grossman Jr. learned that the last article he had written in Miami had won the Pulitzer prize and that his latest novel was short-listed for the National Book Award. The first person he wanted to tell was Myra. To be safe, he waited three days.

THE YOUNGER WOMAN'S WORDPLAY

WHEN I WAS THIRTY-THREE, I fell in love with a nineteen-year-old girl. It was not planned, of course. She was a friend of a music student who assisted the orchestra in which I performed. She showed up with her friend at a concert, we exchanged glances, we talked during the greenroom reception, and we went to lunch a few days thereafter. She turned out to be highly intelligent, witty, and socially responsible: she interned in an environmental-law office near her university and volunteered at an animal-rescue facility. She was Chinese-American, with long blue-black hair, mysterious dark eyes, a delicious little mouth, and a firm, petite figure. She was left-handed, which presented (and would fulfill) interesting possibilities. She spoke without an accent, and her first name was neither Chinese nor American.

Her most endearing trait was her love of wordplay. A prodigy at the computer keyboard, she sometimes talked in typographical errors: *The Wizard of Oz* became *The Wizrad of Zo*. She enjoyed emphasizing the wrong syllable of certain words: the name of the trio Sting fronted was pronounced *Pollis*. Having picked up other bits of musical terminology, she observed that I used an *acoustic* razor. She felt that people would drive more civilly if speed-limit signs were replaced by traditional tempo markings: the speed in an urban school zone would be *largo;* neighborhood streets would be marked *adagio* or *andante;* a two-lane country road could accommodate *allegro;* and no state trooper would harass a motorist travelling an interstate highway at *presto*—but pity the fool who got caught doing *prestissimo* in a *vivace ma non troppo* zone. She was forever inventing parody titles, as in Paul Simon's imaginary self-pleasuring manual *Fifty Ways to Love Your Lever*. She would separate two synonyms with the word *yet:* a new painting was *modern yet contemporary*. The adjective *various* often preceded a singular noun, as in *"Welcome to our various home."* She missed no opportunity to satirize political correctness: she decided that the term *shark-infested waters* used in a newscast was deeply offensive to the squalus community and that a more appropriate alternative might be *shark-rich waters, copiously sharked waters,* or *nonshark-challenged waters*. Similarly, a female alligator was an *alligatrix*. Anything really gross was *disgustible*. Our hometown football team had won the Super Bowl more than once. During the brief season that we found ourselves watching their games on television (neither of us cared about the sport or understood its rules), she would wait eagerly for the announcer to exclaim, *"And there's a flag on the field!"* so she could answer, *"And there's a fag on the field!"*—which was my cue to assume an effeminate voice and cry, *"Oh, yoo-hoo, you guys: do you have to play so rough?"* We justified this private bigotry by our linguistic fascination. When she took me out for *dim sum,* she suggested that most Yanks thought the term described what you got when your calculator needed a new battery. Her slightly older sister, a medical student, was even shorter than she but had larger tits and therefore was known as *Chest.* In months to come I would wish I had met the sister first, not because I like big tits, which I do not, but for other reasons that I will discuss.

The girl's only annoying habit early on was an unapologetic crush on Steve Perry, the handsome singer of the arena-rock band Journey. I had acknowledged the group's well-crafted hits myself and had appreciated Perry's virtuosity, which by his own admission he owed mostly to Sam Cooke. But I would endure more than my share of the band's overwrought repertoire.

She owned several cats and coveted all the other cats in her neighborhood. Her actual philosophy of life was *You can never have too many cats or pictures of cats.* Her felines had conventional names but were known collectively as *boohoppers, furrakits,* and *fuzzybutts.* They had free reign of her and, later, our environment.

At first, our age difference mattered remarkably little to either of us, owing primarily to her precocious intellect. It mattered even less to her girlfriends, who envied her having captured the heart of a worldly classical musician. Inevitably, though, she began to tease me in mostly benign ways. One day I was listening to an old record by the Byrds, and, after using her adorable ass to block the right-hand speaker for several seconds, she remarked, *"It sounds like they're wearing sandals!"* On those rare occasions when we disagreed on something cultural or political, she would declare that I had *a decade problem.*

She was a virgin, my first in many years. Her only admitted sexual experience prior to our meeting was a forced hand job in the dark at a party. She had complied with the guy's demand only to keep him from raising his voice and drawing attention to their hiding place behind a sofa. (The young jerk did not offer to reciprocate, nor would she have let him.) This episode had deepened her profound discomfort with all things erotic. Our own sexual courtship was a yearlong lesson in patience, gentleness, and frustration on both sides, with tears aplenty.

Once we did become acquainted with each other's body, she blossomed into an adventuress, eager to realize fantasies she secretly had cultivated from romance novels. She said she found pornography repulsive, but, having discovered an extremely graphic magazine in her sister's dresser, she became fascinated by it. She could turn herself on watching videos that depicted activities she would never have performed herself. She was unimpressed by the huge cocks on the screen and made a show of pretending to enjoy mine, despite her inexperience and her lack of natural talent in this area. Not only did she insist that we try every position and every possible location—an old couple discovered us making love on a park bench in broad daylight, and all she did was slow down and smile back at them—but one evening she visited the porn shop at which her face had become perhaps a bit too familiar and brought home several interesting toys. Her favorite, to look at as it lay idle on the nightstand, was a vibrating, squirting dildo modeled on a famous "actor."

She never tried to use it because our own intercourse was difficult enough for her and she could never have accommodated the thing without wasting half the night easing it in (she said it resembled a forearm). She did like how I looked in my jeans while wearing various rings and straps that she had bought. She loved to feather me with an ermine mitten, but she hated giving or receiving direct masturbation. Oral sex was generally inconclusive. As our intimacy continued to stagnate, she began collecting handcuffs and leather lingerie that we never used and that she never wore. I had always found such accessories to be silly and unnecessary (and still do), but I would gladly have shared them had they pleased her.

The missing pieces of our relationship fell into place when finally she introduced me to her parents. Her sweet, cosmopolitan mother was overjoyed to have a fellow arts conversationalist at the table, but her older dad was morose and taciturn. It turned out that Mom slept downstairs in a former walk-in closet off the living room and that *Buh* (a pejorative take on *Boy*) occupied a sparsely furnished garret above the girls' room. The only time we ever made love in her room we did so quietly on the floor, near the opposite wall. Her sister walked in on us and, before exiting, told us to tap on the door when it was safe to reenter. Her shadow as she stood guard in the hallway was distracting in more ways than one.

I never got my sweetheart to confirm or deny that her father had violated her and her sister as children, but all three women's behavior toward the man pointed in that direction. On the few occasions when the four or five of us were together for dinner or some event, it was all politeness and good cheer; but there was a palpable tension in the air. That *Buh* was an administrator at the exclusive university where the girls were enrolled and therefore was responsible for their free tuition perhaps explained their continuing to live under the same roof.

Over time she became insanely jealous, not only of other women on the street—she would watch me for the slightest nod in their direction as we walked—but also of former girlfriends, none of whom she had ever met or with whom I was still in contact. I came home from a rehearsal one night to discover that she had gone through my things and had destroyed old photographs and had cut pages out of books containing harmless handwritten dedications. She sat weeping on the sofa surrounded by these mutilated symbols of her pain. I buried my anger and begged her to see a psychiatrist.

Not surprisingly, the shrink suggested that she stop seeing me, and that she step back and exorcise her demons before attempting to date someone closer to her in age. I was so concerned for her mental health that I agreed to withdraw. She sat dry-eyed through our brief but melancholy farewell. She had been so much fun in our early weeks that I half expected us one day to reunite as platonic friends, but we never did.

I bumped into her sister months after the breakup. We confessed our secret attraction to each other, and we agreed not to make things worse by acting on it.

Recently I read online that the taller girl is now an executive with a major financial institution. There was no mention of a husband or family. I hope she is happy and well.

There are several feral cats of varying colors and personalities that roam my neighborhood. One of them, a Maine coon similar to one that my younger woman brought home one day from the animal shelter, likes to observe me from a safe distance as I work in the yard or relax in the hot tub. So far as I know, none of these creatures has a name. But I cannot help greeting each mysterious visitor as a *fuzzybutt,* a *furrakit,* or a *boohopper.*

AFTER

JERUSALEM

1 May 1993
Dear Minister LeFebvre:
By summer's end, you will be dead. We know you understand it's not personal.

Friends of New Palestine

X

Paris

ANAT ARAD STOOD NAKED before the vanity and surveyed her reflection in the mirror. It was a reflection as hard, smooth, and elegant as the old beveled glass itself, but not as fragile. Four years in camp outside Tel Aviv and patrolling the hot Gaza streets had combined with a merciless commander to produce the sleek leonine body of a professional athlete. She watched herself lean forward and pick up the darkened silver hand mirror that on the morning of her bas mitzvah she had admired on her grandmother's dressing table, an inlaid Austrian treasure not unlike the delicate piece now before her. Without looking away, she turned slowly until she met the limit of her long slender neck, tanned the color of milk chocolate; then with a deft pirouette she turned to the hand mirror and admired herself from behind. She transferred her weight from one foot to the other, stood on tiptoe, and leaned from the waist until she needed her left hand to steady herself against the foot of the bed. She returned her attention to the gently sculpted small of the back, the firm little bottom—she turned slightly to hide the small welt her commander had delivered with a riding crop while directing maneuvers in the Negev, a false disciplinary action administered during the last of those forced private moments when Corporal Arad finally admitted she just did not find the older woman attractive—the graceful golden legs. From toe to shoulder, she watched herself slowly flex and more slowly relax. She stayed with the hand mirror as she turned back to face the vanity, shifting her eyes at the last instant and savoring the sight, pleasing even to her own worst critic. She repeated the leisurely flexing routine, taking stock of the cliff-proven thighs, the tiny waist—she smiled at the thin gold navel ring she had earned in a wager with her bunkmate, Rachel—the lean ribcage, the proud cup-shaped little breasts, the wine-colored nipples that now responded to the spring-morning breeze gliding over the red rooftops and into her room.

Perfect, she realized, stepping back. As she viewed the whole package, she traced curved fingertips up the outsides of her legs and drew them together in the warm hairless triangle.

Corporal Arad leaned to her left and retrieved the vanity chair she had set aside. She glanced toward the darkened bathroom and the plush towel she had arranged neatly over the old brass rod that still showed beads of condensation. She remembered the long hot bath in which on every morning that week she had lingered, unapologetically running the hot water until it dared her like the desert sun she had left only days ago.

Paris was already beginning to feel familiar, yet she would not forget the punishing beauty of her homeland. She twirled the chair backward in front of the vanity, spread her legs, and sat before the mirror.

She had not seen her face that morning. She had risen and gone straight to the bath, sitting without preparation on the cold porcelain and opening the faucet full blast. She had not seen plumbing in six months. Now she sat in the reversed vanity chair with her elbows on the backrest, and she faced herself.

Anat Arad had never fully appreciated her beauty. Aggressive and fiercely competitive as a child, she had grown up on dust-blown ball fields and asphalt tracks in the company of curious but cautious boys. Well into her teens she had begun to recognize the feminine grace of her body, but she had never loved the angular ethereal face. She had never seen the nobility of the high aristocratic forehead, the mystery of the wide-set hieroglyphic eyes, the long stern thin nose, the full rich mouth, the strong cleft chin.

She had never worn makeup in public, and the few times she had tried to apply it she had done so clumsily and had disapproved of the result. One night she softened and asked Rachel to teach her how, but the fair bunkmate grew impatient with Arad's twitching. Finally Rachel put down her pencil and wiped away the streaked effort. "Don't you know how lovely you are?" she asked softly, and an uneasy silence ensued in their corner of the barracks before Rachel darted forward and kissed her friend on the cheek.

Corporal Arad looked long into the black depths of her own eyes, letting her mind wander. She imagined she was someone else, anyone else: Olympic runners who had inspired her; less likely models like stateswomen, though she could think of none less bulbous than their male colleagues; film stars, though her own screenworthiness seemed little consolation; even the pretty men she had seen in American magazines. She reached back and unsnapped the simple brass barrette holding her hair in its customary tight denial and shook her head back, letting the shiny onyx profusion cascade over her shoulders. She closed her eyes and swayed as the silken tresses glided across her back and forward across her nipples.

Corporal Arad sat back and smiled. She even began to laugh but caught herself.

She had made no sound that week save the running of bath water, had appeared outside the hotel only to jog and for brief light meals in shaded cafés.

She leaned forward and bore into the immovable black eyes as her left hand descended slowly.

You touch me, you bastard, and I'll kill you.

Falls Church, Virginia
AARON WOOD SAT ON THE BACK PATIO in the
weightless May breeze, leaned back in his forest-green
hardwood chaise and stared up into the big silver maple
that loomed not five feet from the low stone patio wall.
You can't plant one of these just anywhere, he said silently
to his father, dead now thirteen years, selfless provider,
gregarious, diplomatic, optimistic. *They grow like
wildfire, fat and shapeless, without logic, gnarled and
groping for the sky.* He studied the jagged ungraceful
branches that sniffed in all directions and crisscrossed one
another like myriad blind serpents, tempering the beauty
in the single symmetrical leaf and in the flaxen winged
seeds that twirled with insidious procreativity. He listened
as the seeds clicked and scurried across the darkened
flagstones, watched as they gathered in the thick carpet of
English ivy that he had cultivated, or rather that had
proliferated quite effortlessly from the dozen seedlings he
had laid in twelve years before when he had inherited the
house. He looked around and admired his red, purple, and
pink azaleas and musky boxwood, at home in the acidic
Virginia clay, the last few pink magnolia petals whose
clean perfume trembled through the garden, the spindly
white dogwoods that had spawned several offspring in the
shadow of the towering silver maple, the little redbuds, the
miraculous new oaks that a year ago had landed exactly
where he would have planted them—the yard was

overpopulated with unfettered maples, which he hoped
someday to replace with oak, weeping willow, mimosa,
crape myrtle—and the beautifully incongruous yellow rain
tree that flourished between the magnolia and the big
maple, grown now in twenty years to as many feet, a merry
apparition, impossible in its cascading shawl of hyacinth-
shaped blossoms suspended like the tear-glistened blonde
curls of a thousand prom queens.

He surveyed the narrow band along his back
neighbor's ugly chain-link fence where he piled the sawed
remains of felled dead pines and the stack of maple
trimmings that had never made it to the fireplace. Two
dozen unused bricks were left from the patio project that
had been his father's final attempt to draw the spiteful
mother out of the glaucomalike reclusive ritual into which
she had retreated to endure her Victorian marriage. This
was also the place where just after graduation he had
helped his father bury Caramel, the greyhound that had
been their pet since Camelot, whose Egyptian beauty and
acceptance of the family's patriarchal makeup had
endeared her especially to the father. The graceful runner
had spurned all suitors and reigned in virgin splendor
until well past her prime, when finally she was
overpowered by a neighborhood lout and gave unloving
birth to a basketful of amorphous vermin, cast out at the
earliest opportunity so as not to deepen her humiliation.
She never outgrew the mean streak that kept even the
father at a distance during mealtime and that once cost the
teenage brother a sizable chunk of nasal cartilage; the
dog's name was inspired not by any perceived sweetness
but rather by a contemporary racehorse.

He looked with resignation at the aluminum tool shed cowering between the fattened girths of twin-sister maples that had been allowed to take root too close to blind male vanity. He knew he could not continue to delay the arduous process of dragging a family's accumulated jetsam out of the precarious little structure and deciding what to keep: the British kerosene heaters, still in their original plywood boxes, they had used in Israel; the empty wooden crate the father had built to bring back the infant-burial pot he had unearthed beneath the ruins of Har Megiddo, the biblical Armageddon; the cumbersome chunks of granite and marble they had taken as guilty souvenirs from Caesarea, Baalbek, and Luxor; the old cages and aquaria from the brother's fascination with small pets that soon became insatiable monsters destined for local parks; the broken antique pinball machine the brother had bought at a Dutch flea market; the broken pots and wickets of abandoned garden schemes; the Egyptian horsehair flyswatters and Peruvian Indian headdresses, now just recognizable in the poisonous air generated in darkness, heat, humidity, and the fumes of peat moss; the bent wire hubcap he himself had rescued from an Amsterdam gutter; the hundreds of other items he would discover in the dismal bunker backed up to the fence at the edge of the yard behind the modest four-bedroom house—a "shack," his father had disdainfully called it after his renovations had failed to budge the wife from her steadfast self-destruction—that he had always called home and that now was his by default and that, long since paid off, was manageable on his musician's wages.

He had come out onto his patio for breakfast, briefly to

throw off tomorrow's mail and telephone chores, before he would shower, dress, and drive to the pleasant outdoor concert site whose charms would nearly mitigate inadequate rehearsal and insulting money.

Were it not for money, there would be no dishonesty nor greed nor crime nor war, no hunger, no corporate espionage; everyone would be well educated, the arts would flourish—

The pointless fantasy exploded in his mind, and he returned to the blazing azaleas, the sweet magnolia, the inconsolable yellow rain; he swept across the verdant cushion of his ivy, the little dogwoods and oaks, and the redbuds. He closed his eyes and surveyed in his mind the familiar beauties around the side, ivy that finally had begun to climb the patio walls, and in the front yard: the old black walnut that dominated his quiet cul-de-sac and called attention not only for its late-summer thumping hail of green fragrant fruit nearly the size of tennis balls—he left these for the squirrels—but also for being the last to green in spring and the first to shed in fall, the luxuriant Japanese cherry his father had planted long before realizing the wife would never revisit Jefferson's lonely vigil, and the other incorrigible maples that redeemed their undistinguished appearance by providing abundant shade against the August sun and by giving the house the illusion of sitting apart from the mediocrity that surrounded it.

But he could not prevent his eyes' focusing on the hoary embattled maple just beyond his patio. At one time the tree had been allowed to expel its profusion in all directions, huge branches growing parallel with the ground and hovering above the upper tier of the patio; these, and their impatient tributaries, he had removed. Every few years the foliage would brush against the roof, filling the gutters with springtime seeds and the wet matted yellow leaves of autumn.

It was with a sense of celebration that he allowed grass to grow in the sidewalk cracks, merely mowed rather than annihilated dandelions and clover, and observed the gothic dignity of his patio walls as slowly they were adorned with dark water stains and moss. *Everyone is meticulous about something,* he theorized as he scanned his neighbors' surgically sustained landscapes.

But he knew he would always have to assert control over that maple, whose trunk was now too obese to put a man's arms around, but whose roots the tree experts had assured him posed no threat to his nearby foundation. As he stared at the knurled swollen bark, raised in ungainly stumps and dark recesses, his eyes came to rest, as often they did, on the long pursing vertical slit about halfway up the trunk. It was where lightning had struck the tree some fifteen years before, shearing off a thick appendage. In the intervening years, the healing crevice had grown back first as a smoothening oval; but now the raised outer lips had grown closer together and the old receding injury had darkened so that the whole feature's appearance was absolutely vaginal. He had never voiced this observation, nor had anyone else; but no one looking more than briefly at that slit could fail to recognize its female insistence. If he softened his focus, the labia would undulate in postcoital repose. In his mind he formed a swollen clitoris from the hooded remains of the cauterized crotch. From wrenching emasculation had emerged the poetic justice of female superiority, the lips drawing closer together with the passing seasons until one day they would form the dispassionate kiss of self-satisfaction while back against the fence rotted the hacked segments of encrusted phallic resignation. As he narrowed his field of vision, the gray bark became soft pink flesh and, projected onto the veined pulsation of his eyelids, Elise.

He knew then that the primeval misogyny he had allowed to invade his thoughts this morning grew not from cause but from effect, not jealousy but envy, speculation rather than remorse, unregret beyond any remembrance as he wondered how different things might be if he had exchanged restless diversity for the perfect flower who had been the first to take him in her hand, the joyous gift of whose virginity had consecrated a luminous June meadow, who at eighteen in a darkening wood had shimmered above him in unembarrassed ecstasy. He pictured her reclining on her parents' living-room sofa after school still dressed above the waist, long chestnut waves adorning her shoulders, teasing him with soft motions as he leaned back and stared with fascination at her welcoming blossom. He took in the scent of lingering magnolia girlhood and opened his eyes to confirm that it came only from fallen petals the color of cream from which the last berry has been drawn. But he did not follow Elise to bittersweet conclusion this time. He would, as he had over the years learned to do, transfer the memory and longing to the work.

The work had attained a life of its own, as ephemeral rituals and covenants declared in the delusions of their creators. He had devoted his life to the work despite its utter refusal to grant him the peace he knew he could expect from no other endeavor. He sometimes yearned to disappear in remote pastoral seclusion.

But the work was better than the hypocrisy of retreat. He knew the presence of God, a power beyond human understanding in whose design people are but the most arrogant of myriad varieties. But he could not honor the superstitions of a species that had shown such systematic disregard for its host and its neighbors. So the monastery was out, he thought, speculating as to how many go there for reasons beyond peaceful surroundings, simple work, sweet ancient music—and even monks survive by selling.

If he had wed Elise, what then? His devoted perfect angel, a Midwestern medley of possessiveness and mistrust of the unpredictable, probably would have made him happy enough. She would studiously have forsaken all others—he knew this at the time, and he would have proof ten years on, when Elise, divorced, indiscriminately seasoned, fat, and stripped of the tender intuition of her teens, would for five strange and courageous days reappear before rejoining her quest to become the genderless embodiment of her parents.

And of course he would never have known Tatiana, the mad impulsive affair that destroyed a marriage as ill-founded as the one it saved him from entering—nor any of the others before Elise's vain comet-flash without whose acquaintance he might have shared in Elise's low expectations.

He reopened his eyes and found them automatically fixed on the cruel gray wooden vulva that even in the space of one morning seemed to have healed closer together in vengeful denial and forgotten purpose, one day to be recognized not as the dew-kissed flower of youth but as what it was: a scab. He gathered his things and went inside. He did not wait to see the last magnolia petal drift slowly to earth.

Aaron Wood was a single, successful pianist, gifted on several instruments and as a composer and critic, congenitally hungry for change, gazing wistfully with kind hazel eyes down roads not taken, impelled to start each day with an exhilarating physical workout, the brow having recently begun creeping back in pursuit of the umber mane he had allowed both as recreation and as a symbol of his undiminished contempt for the establishment that had swallowed his generation not quite so dyspeptically as their parents had said it would. He was trapped in a joyless and increasingly temporary relationship with a fellow artist whose extended family consisted of numberless manic-depressives. If the few remaining toys on his wish list were acquired and his property aligned with his formally casual vision, Aaron Wood would have liked nothing so much as the sudden onset of amnesia.

Cairo

THE GOLD WAS THE RICHEST, most inviting smooth yellow he had ever seen. *No wonder they had so many deities. One god could not alone inspire such beauty.* Khaled al-Malik turned from the glass case and looked out the window at the heavy brown shroud of poison that hung over Cairo and slowly dissolved the fragile monuments their ancestors had erected to divine kings who could not save them from themselves. Feeling sick, al-Malik turned back toward the burial mask. *Pigs. The best of us are pigs.* He went down to the street and took a long drag from the pocketed remains of his last unfiltered cigarette and threw it to the pavement. He twisted the toe of his worn cordovan loafer until the butt was a generic gray stain that could have come from one of the ravens cruising overhead. With admiration he watched the dozen or so circling birds. He became so engrossed in the chattering acrobatics that he actually forgot that Muhammad Kadir was half an hour late, not that there was anything unusual about that. Al-Malik went back inside the museum and did not even see his comrade when he shuffled up and leaned on the rail about six feet to his right.

"Alertness and punctuality are twin gifts, as you would say," Kadir spoke softly to the transcendent black eyes in the case.

Without turning, al-Malik replied, "As are beauty and wisdom."

"Love and imagination."

"Sovereignty and justice."

"God and woman."

"Is there a difference?"

"One makes one bold, the other glad."

"You need one to deserve the other."

"But which is the vessel and which the shore?"

"You have been too long in America, Muhammad. Your harlots are rotting your brain."

"I have been rotten, I admit, but my brain has remained unaffected."

"Then get a prescription for your diseased parts. You will need them."

"I aim to serve."

"We are counting on your aim. And your alertness, and especially your punctuality. Where the hell were you?"

"And you have perhaps been softened by comfort. The bus service has not achieved the magnificence of your dead mentor here."

"Nor has the culmination of our labor been ever so close at hand. Look out there: each bird dives for its individual sustenance, but only after the weak fall in behind their leader can peace prevail."

"So you are now both assassin and philosopher, and condescending as well, Khaled? Whence your zeal? Sometimes I wonder but that we should fall behind the leader we already have and let him do the talking, or the killing."

"Don't be a fool, Muhammad. Arafat has lost his way, did a long time ago. It is he who has grown soft and comfortable. We function to nip at his chair-fattened behind and keep him marching forward."

"We are indeed the shrill lapdogs of a grateful and nonexistent nation. And as for the close-at-hand, are not the Zionists readier than ever to negotiate with Arafat?"

"With the PLO, perhaps, tacitly, after Jerusalem and her American pimp erase the semen tracks of their latest fornication. The American no sooner spills his seed in one infected womb than he is seen on the evening news thrusting the great Phallus of Freedom into the sister-in-law next door."

"Has some parasite invaded the water at the British embassy, al-Malik? I cannot believe we are having this conversation."

Al-Malik finally shifted, but without facing the younger man. He removed an envelope from his jacket and held it out. "Here's that Olympia Xenakis CD you were looking for."

"Ah." Kadir slipped the envelope into his canvas book bag.

"We should not be seen here. I will walk north and turn left at the taxi stand. Take another route, and try to keep your jeans fastened. Incidentally: it is good to see you, my friend."

"And you, Khaled, crucifix and all."

"It may save your reckless ass, Muhammad. Do not forget that." Al-Malik shot a quick grin to his right, turned, and walked purposefully toward the stairs, thumbing pages in his worn copy of *Fodor's Egypt*.

"Al-Malik!" Kadir called softly without turning from the rail.

The older man stopped and cast an impatient frown

behind him.

"Arafat will not live forever, Khaled. Nor will Rabin and his generation."

"Nor will you, my friend. Nor I. God helps those who help themselves."

Khaled al-Malik went to the corner and bought a copy of *Egyptian Gazette*. He was about to cross the street when he caught Kadir in the corner of his eye, coming toward him with a confident smirk on his face. *I told the idiot to go the other way.* He paused at the curb, opened the paper, and scanned it until Kadir was within earshot.

"*I obscenity in the milk of thy father,*" the younger man said under his breath.

"*Thou never hadst one,*" replied al-Malik. "Your Hemingway."

"Correctamundo, dude."

"Miss that plane, my worthless friend, and the bell tolls for thee."

Paris

ANAT ARAD STARED INTO THE INTENSE, dilated black eyes in the mirror. The long dark hair had curled and matted on top, and beads of sweat still gathered among her lashes, stung her eyes, and ran down her cheeks; she tasted the hot salty fluid. She acknowledged the warm completion emanating from the center of her body.

You pathetic son of a whore. I warned you. Laugh? Laugh at me after you have surrendered all your strength? Look at you now, dead and irrelevant.

Corporal Arad held herself up with the shaking left hand pressed down onto the wet needlepoint seat cushion and felt the diminishing waves course through her like electric shocks. She maintained this posture for several minutes and listened to her heart. As finally she regained a sense of time and place, she tried to straighten up. When she put some weight on the unsteady balls of her feet, she lost her balance and fell backward onto the bed. Seized by the maddening needles shooting up from her feet and forearms, she looked back at herself, teetering on the edge of the bed with the tipped vanity chair between her legs, and she began to laugh. She centered herself on the edge of the bed and let the chair fall forward. Tapping her toes on the carpet only sharpened the needles, so she inched her way to the headboard, stacked the pillows, and waited.

When it stopped, she looked down between her legs into the mirror. She was shocked by the unaccustomed sight of herself in this position, but she did not lower her knees. She exhaled on the beads of sweat running down her breasts and ran her fingertips across her cold wet brows. When her skin was dry, Corporal Arad lifted her head, pulled away the top pillow, and laid it down beside her. She leaned back and stretched. As the sounds of voices and vehicles in the street below began to register, she fell asleep.

Anat Arad slept for nearly an hour. When she awoke, she had turned on her right side away from the window and was clutching the pillow against her body. Instinctively she reached behind the headboard for her pistol. Thus assured, she relaxed, stretched, and swung her left leg over the cool side of the pillow. She pressed her smooth body against it and surrendered to comfort and solitude. She surveyed the rows of white orchids on the wallpaper and imagined them as a parade of young beautiful nuns. They emerged from a sunny meadow, slipped back into their rooms, and savored the warm resolution in their loins. She imagined herself among them, silently closing the heavy wood door and turning to Sister Rachel. She plucked blades of grass from her fragrant white habit, embraced her, slowly undressed her, guided her hands, held her warm body against hers, ran fingertips up and down her back.

After several minutes, Corporal Arad became aware of the cooling breeze drifting through the window. Slowly she turned onto her back and spent a few minutes looking at the molded white ceiling. Then she rose and padded across the room. For a moment she stood at the window and looked out over the rooftops, down to the rows of windows, the painted shop signs, the street, the people walking, riding, and sitting there. She did not notice whether anyone saw her. She stepped into the bathroom and into the empty tub, sat on the cold porcelain, and turned on the water.

She lingered until she had lost interest in replenishing the warmth. With a familiar motion, she curled a toe around the chain and gently removed the stopper, lifting it from the water and replacing it on the left edge of the tub against the wall. She lay back and watched her reddened mound emerge below. She rose, dried off, and stepped back into the bedroom. She flipped the vanity chair around, draped a dry towel over it, and sat before the mirror. Patiently she brushed out her long black hair and returned it to its barrette. She rose and went to the bureau. In a few moments she was dressed in her genderless fatigues. She grabbed her black leather wallet, pocketed the room key, and went down to the street for dinner.

When Corporal Arad returned, the sun was disappearing over the rooftops in the distance. The furniture cast long shadows that skirted across the carpet and climbed perceptibly up the wall. She put down her things, sat on the bed, and watched the horizon turn slowly from yellow to orange to purple. Finally she pulled down the shade and switched on the lamp. She sat down in the big armchair, picked up her book, and read a few pages without retaining any of the words. Closing it in her lap, she looked across the room and studied her orchids on the wall.

Falls Church, Virginia

AARON WOOD'S TELEPHONE RANG about ten o'clock on the morning after the outdoor concert he had already consigned to that storehouse of professional memories that receded in proportion to the size of the paycheck that was their only tangible result. He had been awake three hours, having brought a mug of coffee to his desk to finish the business matters he had interrupted the day before to take advantage of the perfect late-spring morning. The person on the other end of the line probably was the parent of one of his students, hoping to reschedule a lesson; or maybe it was one of his editors with a new assignment, which would be more or less indistinguishable from the previous assignment; maybe it was one of the arts councils to which he had applied to fund his unsalable projects, on which occasions he at least could pay his colleagues what they were worth; maybe it was one of those booking agents to whom he nearly always said yes despite his better judgment, yesterday's bucolic train wreck being typical; maybe it was one of those few peers who still played music for the right reasons, that is, they were not trying to make a living at it; or maybe it was Tatiana, deliciously penitent Catholic Tatiana, who several years ago had been transferred back to Washington and had bought an elegant house ten minutes away, who like himself was complacently settled in a boring relationship, and who called about once every two months and invited him over for dinner, a dip in the hot tub, the same conversation they had been having on every such occasion since college, and an hour of the greatest sex either of them had ever known.

"Aaron Wood," he said.

"Mr. Wood, please," came the young, senatorial tone.

"This is he." It amused him to be treated, or patronized, as though he presided over a large office with actual employees.

"Mr. Wood? You probably don't remember me, but this is Arnie Vogel. I worked for your father in Amsterdam."

"Yes!"

"You and I first met at one of your dad's parties. I remember he kept calling you downstairs until finally you agreed to play the piano."

Wood had suffered that ordeal on more than one occasion, of course, but he did remember the friendly black-haired junior consulate staffer who had taken him aside and confessed his appreciation for jazz and the Beatles. "Sure! How are you? Are you back in Washington?"

"I've been with the U.S. Information Agency for some time now. We send American artists overseas and bring foreign artists here—pretty much what your dad did in Israel."

"Great!"

"That's actually why I'm calling. Katie and I caught your concert last month at the Corcoran. I must say, I thought you and your group were superb."

"Thank you!"

"Not only did I enjoy your performance and your music, but I very much appreciated what you had to say just before the intermission, about the pieces and the people who inspired them. I loved that gentle tune you wrote in memory of your father—I think he'd be damned proud, Aaron. May I call you Aaron?"

"Please do."

"You made your point without shoving it down our throats, and I admired that."

"Thank you," Wood repeated self-consciously.

"So I got to thinking maybe you had inherited some of your dad's gift for building bridges with just the right casual phrase—you even reminded me a little of him—and I thought you might be interested in doing something with our program."

"Yes, of course, I'd be delighted." Wood's mind was already skirting through the circuitous game of phone tag, forms, unreliable transportation, hotels, rentals, equipment failures, and the other details of touring. He knew that USIA tours often placed musicians in less than ideal performing situations. But Wood knew also that this particular caller was real and had been one of his father's most trusted aides, despite being a young Democrat who had sympathized more with the Dutch antiwar protesters camped outside the consulate than with the Nixon administration he had been sworn to serve. Wood felt strongly about promoting international peace through the goodwill that artists had always shared regardless of their nations' lamentable politics. And Wood felt especially good, as he suspected Vogel did, about representing in some small way their embattled new president, Bill

Clinton.

"Wonderful," Vogel replied. "You know, I've worked with so many brilliant performers over the years. And it never ceases to amaze me that jazz musicians, perhaps our purest ambassadors, get such shabby treatment in their own country."

"Well—"

"But we're trying to do something about that, and I guess you know that our artists suffer no such indignities overseas."

"Yes."

"Well, so how are things? How is Carl? And you have a sister who visited Amsterdam one Christmas?"

"Cheryl."

"Yes!" Vogel laughed nervously before allowing an uncomfortable silence. "Her husband, nice guy—"

"Mark. They're great. Mark was a true brother to Carl and me when Dad died, always has been."

"And your mom—"

"She passed away."

"Yes. I'm very sorry."

Both men were growing uneasy with the downward-spiraling conversation. Wood was resisting the temptation to acknowledge that his mother had hated Amsterdam and her role as a diplomatic wife, had spent most of their five years there soaking in alcohol, had never let her husband forget how miserable his job had made her, had halfheartedly attempted suicide after his death by taking not even a full bottle of innocuous painkillers, had spent her last nine years in a nursing home sitting on the edge of her bed holding onto her walker and watching an old black-and-white television, chain-smoking and doubling over in convulsions of coughing, and had died in her sleep one night years after Cheryl's lawyer had tried to get the woman to sign her will. And Vogel was hoping he would not have to acknowledge that he knew some of these things and had imagined the rest.

"Say," Vogel continued, "why don't you and I have lunch?"

"I'd like that. Someplace near the State Department?"

"Or I could take off and come out—"

"My schedule's pretty flexible," Wood understated. "I can take the Metro to Foggy Bottom, meet at your office." Wood suddenly remembered the pride he used to feel on those occasions when his father would take the family through the Department and show off his office before leading them downstairs for their physicals, their shots, and their unquestionable diplomatic passports, all the details of their lives taken care of by a benevolent Uncle Sam who kept his loving eye on the world and gently prodded his loyal charges out into it to preach the gospel of democracy. And he remembered the only other time he had stepped inside that building, the day he played a Mozart concerto in the auditorium, the last time his father would see him play: Before the musicians could set up, they were subjected to a long security check. While they were waiting in the lobby, a rising tabloid-television star named Geraldo Rivera had breezed in to conduct an interview and had made a smart-aleck remark to the receptionist about carrying a bomb and was left indignantly cooling his heels until after the subversive-looking instrument cases had disappeared down the hall.

"You know the Four Seasons, where Pennsylvania meets M Street?" Vogel offered.

"Sure," Wood replied, having played the hotel many times.

"I was going to suggest Le Gaulois, just up the street from here, but the other place will be quieter. Next Thursday?"

"What time?"

"One o'clock?"

"I'll look forward to it," Wood said—a lie, not because he was to meet with one of the few of his father's associates with whom as a youth he had had anything in common, but simply because he rarely spent time in establishments where as a musician he was instructed to enter and leave by the kitchen door.

"It's good to talk with you, Aaron."

"And with you, Arnie."

"Right on. Goodbye for now."

"Bye." *Right on?*

Cairo

MUHAMMAD KADIR OPENED THE DOOR to his room and tossed the book bag onto the bed. He went to the dresser, opened the top drawer, retrieved his laptop, laid it on the little round table, and switched it on. He pulled the compact disc out of the book bag, inserted it, and clicked an icon:

PRIME MINISTER'S ITINERARY 1 & 2 JULY
7/1
10:30 a.m., arrive U.S. ambassador's residence
Noon, speech on Israeli-Palestinian teacher exchange, Tel Aviv University
12:30 p.m., lunch, university chancellor's residence
2:00 p.m., arrive U.S. embassy, brief remarks, auditorium
2:30 p.m., helicopter from embassy roof to Jerusalem
4:00 p.m., same speech, Hebrew University
7:30 p.m., limousine to Damascus Gate
8:00 p.m., same speech to invited Israeli-Palestinian audience, telecast live in Egypt, Israel, Jordan, Lebanon, Syria
8:30 p.m., limousine back to helicopter
9:00 p.m., return to Tel Aviv
7/2
8:30 a.m., limousine to Ben-Gurion Airport
9:26 a.m., depart Tel Aviv for Amman

Kadir studied the screen for a few minutes; then he ejected the CD and returned it to the book bag. He walked to the door.

Kadir took a taxi downtown. At the small painted *Orfeo Records* sign he stopped, entered, and strolled to the jazz section in the rear of the shop. He stood before the Miles Davis bin, glanced quickly toward the counter, and began flipping through CDs until he came to *In a Silent Way*.

"A misunderstood and seminal recording, yes?" came the gentle old voice behind his shoulder.

"A brilliant reflection of restless times," Kadir responded.

"Jazz, under attack, turning itself inside out—but for evolution or for prosperity?"

"You need one to deserve the other," Kadir mused.

"But which is the vessel and which the shore?"

"To an American, there is only one shore; the vessel matters not."

"Fortunately I know you better than that, Muhammad."

"You doubt my sincerity?"

"Your sincerity is well known, son. It is your poor attempt at cynicism that betrays you."

"Then to your till, old one. I have this only on LP."

Nick Xenakis grinned and turned toward the counter. Kadir followed him without speaking. Once behind his machine, Xenakis took the CD box, entered its code, and paused. He looked kindly at Kadir. "Cash or check, sir?" Xenakis grinned at his protégé.

"Plastic." Kadir removed the itinerary CD from his bag and handed it across the counter.

Xenakis slipped it through the check slot in his cash register. "Thank you, sir," he smiled patiently. As Kadir looked among the new releases and accessories, Xenakis pulled out a brown paper Orfeo Records bag—the logo featured Eurydice's eyes glistening in the distance through the strings of a kithara—and slipped Kadir's purchase into it. "Enjoy."

"And thank you," Kadir replied. He turned for the door.

"Sir!" Xenakis called. "My niece, Olympia, is a fine jazz singer. Her new CD is just out, and she has authorized me to give away a few copies to customers of discriminating taste. Would you care to hear it?" he smiled, pointing to a short stack behind the counter.

"No, thanks. Jazz is an instrumental music, old one. It abhors words. It seeks peace in a world free of the pain caused by words."

"Some words are less threatening than others. These are love songs."

"Shallow propositions and domestic insurance. Wayne Shorter's saxophone, Tony Williams's big cymbal: those are the sounds of love."

"You are a fine piece of work, Muhammad. Keep your edge, and you will achieve."

"And you are a forgiving uncle whose pretty niece can do many things well, but singing is not among them."

"I am not as old as I look, Muhammad. Perhaps I should test your reflexes prematurely."

"Olympia has told me what you do prematurely. They

make a balm for that."

"And you should apply some to your impertinent tongue."

"My tongue is too versatile to be desensitized. It performs tasks other men attempt with clumsier tools."

"Yes, your gym coach spoke well of your technique."

"I had the best teacher."

The two men laughed heartily and shook hands.

"Go with God, Muhammad."

"That I shall. Good to see you, Nick."

"Say hello for me."

Falls Church, Virginia

AARON WOOD WAS TYING HIS TIE when the phone
rang. He lived less than a mile from a Metro station, and
since it was another perfect May day he had decided to
walk. Usually he did not answer the telephone if he was
preparing to leave, but there was always that moment
when he knew it might be the person he was leaving to
meet.

"Aaron Wood."

"Ah, Aaron. Arnie Vogel here. It suddenly occurred to
me that the Four Seasons is not very near the Foggy
Bottom Metro, and it's such a nice day—why don't we meet
at One Step Down instead? We can sit outside if you like."

Wood welcomed the news: his memories of the city's
coziest jazz club were more pleasant. "Great." He removed
the tie, grabbed his jacket, and stepped into the brilliant
sun.

A gentle breeze washed him with residual magnolia
fragrance, triggering the automatic visions of Elise.

He took the long escalator up to the intersection of
Twenty-third and I Streets, teeming as it usually was with
George Washington University students. By their
animated behavior, he recognized the heady atmosphere
of final exams and bittersweet farewells. He drifted into
his fantasy of having switched majors, straightening up his
office desk and preparing for the semester's last American
Lit session, opening the door to find the beautiful brunette

164

senior standing there, the one who had given him no peace that year with her perceptive questions and her florid but promising prose and her made-up reasons to stay after class, being torn between the impossible and the unthinkable. And how would it be now in that life with fat hard cynical Elise, who would not have relinquished what she regarded as an intellectual responsibility to have career-stunting children just as he had considered it his ecological responsibility not to? He watched the groups of bright laughing girls in their tight jeans and tank tops, and not one of them was young Elise. In the windows above he saw no disconsolate herringbone poetry teacher praying that the insatiable boyfriend was not waiting around the corner—and how long could the bearded watcher hope to continue his guilty liaisons and to block out the reality of his pathetic slow decline until he was no longer the alluring man of experience but simply the cute doddering old fool? So Wood called up his essence of magnolia and walked up the hill away from the campus and toward the verdant avenue.

"Aaron!" came the familiar voice as Wood approached the sooty white awning outside One Step Down. Noting the grayed temples and resolved to enjoy these perhaps wonderful possibilities that had fallen in his lap despite his refusal to trade on his father's associations, he walked to the rail and extended his hand.

"Arnie! It's good to see you."

"And you. You've hardly changed! Do you care for a drink?"

Wood glanced at the iced tea sitting on the table and ordered the same.

"Amsterdam, 1967," Vogel reminisced. "The Summer of Love."

"An amazing time." Wood looked around. "I wonder whether we appreciate D.C. more because we've lived elsewhere, or less because we weren't here in '68, during the riots." *What?*

"Exactly. Those old neighborhoods along Fourteenth Street will never be the same."

"And the situation that led to all that hasn't much improved." *Do I hope to be perceived as more than just another liberal dilettante?*

Vogel laughed. "Listen to us! The most beautiful day of the year, and the first thing we do is dredge up the old guilt trips."

"And so many to choose from."

"Well, I think we inherited more problems than we created."

"Right on." Wood felt suddenly comfortable with the archaic expression. Both men knew that whatever criticism they might heap on the previous generation was somehow directed at everyone except Aaron Senior.

"So," Vogel offered confessionally, "how many copies of *Sergeant Pepper* did you go through before they brought out the CDs?"

"That one always reminds me of Holland."

They glanced over the menu and ordered sandwiches.

"You're basically doing Dad's old job?" Wood asked, surprised at Vogel's frivolity.

"My area has been more performing artists, whereas he sent writers on lecture tours."

"I still have these great letters Dad received: Faulkner

wondering what to wear in Japan, professing his ignorance of foreign affairs, then opining that the Germans didn't really want unification—and many would say history has borne him out."

"It's a privilege to work with people of that magnitude—and it seems the greater they are, the more down-to-earth they are."

"Exactly—again, jazzers being a good example."

"Well, speaking of jazz: We're preparing to send a few groups to various locations that happen also to be near summer jazz festivals. The main performances on our behalf will be in schools and community centers. It's short notice, but this minitour, two weeks, made me think of you. What would you say to an opportunity to revisit the Middle East?"

Wood was astounded. "Arnie, I'd love to! I've always dreamed of going back there." He paused. "Of course, when we left, they had taken a little break from shooting at one another."

"Well, you wouldn't be anywhere near the unrest in Gaza or the West Bank. You wouldn't even go to Jerusalem, where there are occasional incidents—though I could arrange an escort if you wanted to visit there. No, I'm thinking of some schools and kibbutzim near Tiberias, and then there's a second festival down in Eilat, on the Red Sea."

"I've probably romanticized those places all out of proportion."

"They've taken good care of their country."

With the help of a few billion U.S. dollars, and on the backs of their stateless Palestinian neighbors.

167

"Then it gets a bit more exotic," Vogel continued, "with a week in Egypt."

"Man. I'm flattered you thought of me."

"We'll handle your transportation over and back and in the field. It won't be first class, but you'll stay in clean, modern hotels. We'll also store and watch over your gear."

"Will we be teaching too?"

"The festivals will of course be straight concerts. The other presentations will be clinics, where between tunes you might discuss jazz history or improvisation. It's up to you whether a master class pops up here or there."

"Overseas, it seems people assume that Americans mirror our government's views on everything, and they vent their anger at us as though we had the president's ear. Should we avoid discussing politics altogether?"

"Except in a general way, yes. It's easy to create controversy with an innocent remark that gets misinterpreted. But people aren't likely to approach you about anything beyond music."

Vogel produced a small stack of forms and talked of an appointment in his office, but there would be quiet solitude for paperwork. The two men ate and eased back into small talk.

On his way to the subway, Wood found himself peering between buildings to catch glimpses of the Capitol in the distance, the White House a few blocks east, the great Egyptian obelisk on the Mall. He nearly tripped over an old homeless woman as he stepped onto the escalator. *God bless America.*

Cairo

KHALED AL-MALIK SAT IN HIS FADED navy-blue sedan and watched the door. The high midmorning sun beat fiercely onto the torn black upholstery. *He has less than an hour. The fool knows how tight the security is here now.*

Finally the dusty gray subcompact pulled into the rental lot. After fiddling with his things, Muhammad Kadir got out, slung the book bag over his shoulder, and shuffled toward the terminal.

Nice of you to drop by.

Al-Malik waited fifteen minutes. He walked to the far corner of the lot and doubled back near the fence, entering the terminal by the left wing. He stopped at a pay phone from which he could view the distant counter and spotted Kadir sitting in the lounge. When Kadir's flight was called, al-Malik watched him rise and move into line. Al-Malik shifted enough to see the line of passengers inch toward the gate, and he watched Kadir hand over his boarding pass and enter the dark corridor. He followed the shape of the walkway out of the building and through the large windows and saw it meet the forward hatch of the white jet adorned with the blue Star of David. He waited until the plane backed onto the taxiway, turned, moved away, and finally lifted its inconceivable bulk into the air. He went to the window and watched the plane disappear into the shimmering white sky.

Al-Malik looked at his watch. With hours to kill, he strolled to the airport shop and bought *Egyptian Gazette*. He ordered tea and read his paper cover to cover. Long before necessary, he began slowly pacing the terminal, walking the perimeter in one direction, then in the other, and then across at even intervals as if marking off an athletic field. When finally his flight was called, he hurried to the gate, his rumpled tweed jacket in one hand and his little carry-on in the other. He thrust his boarding pass at the attendant even as she was processing the woman ahead of him. He hurried down the corridor and stepped onto the plane, sought out his aisle seat as though it were an article of lost furniture from his home, and did not look at the young Scandinavian mother sitting by the window or at the curious flaxen daughter positioned between them. He waited impatiently for the other passengers to file aboard and for the temporary liberation from smog and charades.

As soon as the plane was clear of the mainland, he inserted earplugs, reclined his seat, and closed his eyes. He did not sleep.

He reopened his eyes when the attendant touched him lightly on the left shoulder. He removed the earplugs as the plane descended but did not look out the window. Khaled al-Malik sat rigidly against the back of his seat until the plane came to a complete stop. He shifted only slightly when the child began jumping up and down in front of her seat. When the forward door was opened, Khaled al-Malik immediately stood, grabbed his bag, and forced his way into line. He ignored the cheerful attendant at the door.

"Au revoir, Monsieur."

Falls Church, Virginia
"AARON WOOD."

"Aaron. Arnie here. How's it going?"

"Fine. And you?"

"Fine. Thanks for getting everything back to me so promptly. Listen, have you talked to your guys yet?"

"Actually, no. I wanted to get the word from you before—"

"Well, because I have good news and bad news. The good news is the director very much liked what we presented, and your tour is on. The bad news is there's been a shifting of funds, and he's wondering how you would feel about going over solo."

The line was silent for a moment.

"It's an interesting idea, Arnie. I'm glad I didn't go running to the group with this."

"Indeed. I was afraid you might back out."

The two chuckled uncomfortably.

"Of course," Vogel continued, "the same model instrument your contract calls for will be there at each site, and I'm ready to go to bat for you regarding repertoire, format, whatever you need."

Even if Vogel were standing by him only from personal loyalty, both recognized the vindication of Wood's music bestowed by retaining it after stripping away three-fourths of its texture—not to mention the logistical and social simplicity of touring solo.

"The festivals as well as the State presenters are amenable to this?"

"Absolutely. I'll get back to you with final details. Thanks for the open mind, Aaron."

Thus inspired, Wood went straight to the piano and improvised for three hours. If he felt guilty, it was because he felt no guilt. The regular guys probably were all booked anyway.

The next day's mail contained his itinerary, which he studied and reconciled with his other obligations: he would find substitutes for a few club dates, he would reschedule his lessons, and on the road he would finish his one outstanding journal article. As he had expected, the tour was busy, with just enough time to fit the geographical pieces together. But he welcomed the activity, because it promised minimal discomfort in classrooms and at dining tables endeavoring not to be misinterpreted. He did hope to take the promised side trip. In the coming weeks, he thought of silent dunes, voluptuous orange groves, humbling ruins and tombs, pungent earthy smells and dark flavors, bell-tinkling street markets, and the cacophony of mingled ancient languages. It occurred to him that he might meet some interesting people.

10

Paris

ANAT ARAD MADE A SECOND PASS at the opening chapter, but she could not concentrate. She laid the book aside and switched off the lamp. For the next hour, she sat in the big armchair and listened to the street below, the rising and falling voices, the bee-buzzing mopeds, the impatient taxi horns. She watched the sensuous red, blue, and green reflections and gauzy shadows on the wall as the evening breeze tickled the old curtains. It was too early to retire, so she resolved to sit in the colored shadows and let Paris drift into her room and fill her last hours of peace with its unforgettable energy. Perhaps she would go down to the sidewalk and linger over one more cup of chocolate and watch the laughing students ride by or eavesdrop on an American tourist and her harmless Gypsy.

Corporal Arad suddenly heard quiet footsteps in the carpeted hallway. She reached behind the headboard. As she crouched on the floor beside the bed with the pistol pointed at the door, she slipped her left foot under the bed and gently pulled out the carbine. The footsteps had stopped.

It is too early for this. He is due tomorrow.

The silence continued several more seconds. She began thinking the footsteps belonged to one of the other guests, though she had heard no keys and no door. She began once again to sense the street when the light Morse-code rhythm she had been in no hurry to hear was played out on her door.

So typical, she smiled. *"Zion."*

She slipped around the bed and backed up to the opposite wall beside the door with the pistol held aloft. She released the deadbolt but not the chain. She said quietly, "It's open." The door jerked open, and a man's oily forehead appeared in the dark opening as the chain arrested his motion. Corporal Arad pressed the muzzle against the skull. "Who the f—"

"Put that down, little fool," the man whispered, not backing away. "Let me in."

"What do you want? It is a bit late to be soliciting contributions."

"Your contribution thusfar has been appreciated, Anatoliy. Now put down that Yankee pea shooter and open the door."

"Where is Muhammad?"

"Open the Godforsaken door, girl. There has been a change."

"I can see that. Does this change have a name?"

"It will have a name your mother never taught you if you persist in this nonsense." He paused. "It is Khaled."

Corporal Arad lowered the pistol, and Khaled al-Malik stood upright as Arad gently pushed the door home and slipped off the chain. She took a step backward and again raised the gun to eye level.

Al-Malik entered and flashed a patronizing smile. "I commend your caution, but I assure you it is for the moment unnecessary. Your puckish twin has begun to worry me. He is reckless and sloppy. I gave him the false itinerary and sent him on to Tel Aviv. You are to go there tomorrow and keep an eye on him. You will be assigned to guard detail outside the U.S. embassy."

"Guard detail! Tel Aviv!"

"Lower your voice. This is temporary, to keep the idiot out of the way until we need him. Would you prefer to return to the Negev and your fat sweaty mistress?"

"I would prefer to do the job for which I am trained."

"You are a soldier, Anatoliy, and you will do whatever soldier's work you are told to do. Here is your ticket. Goldstein's man will meet you on the other end and provide further details. Goldstein knows nothing."

"What about LeFebvre, and Jerusalem?"

"I will take care of him, and when it is appropriate I will call for you from Jerusalem. You may tell Muhammad all of this if he asks—all except the false itinerary, of course. He likes a surprise."

"Anyone likes a *pleasant* surprise, but such your news cannot be called. Is that everything? Sir?"

"Everything that matters. Now, if you will loan me one of your pillows, it has been a very long day. Is there an extra blan—"

"Surely you do not expect—"

"Hush, girl. The hotel is full. You have earned your soft bed. I am not one of those boastful youths who would make a natural woman of you."

Arad was astonished. "A lucky thing, as you would leave the room somewhat lighter."

"Yes, Anatoliy: you are good entertainment."

"Stop calling me that. And as to my nature, you have neither the right to speak of it nor the knowledge even to rationalize your bigotry. Our business together is the future of Palestine; my personal life is none of your concern."

"Exactly. Now hand me a pillow and get some sleep. Your flight leaves at 7:02."

"Why did you bring Muhammad into this in the first place if your opinion of him is so low?"

"It is because I love him too well that I have taken him briefly out of commission. You forget that I have known him nearly as long as you have. He has a good eye, but it is too often pointed at the wrong target. His time will come; so will yours. Good night. And put that thing away before you fall asleep, in case you begin dreaming of your desert camel."

"She never touched me, bastard. Good night."

Anat Arad walked back through the colored shadows to the other side of the bed and sat down in the big armchair. She struggled to regain her street sounds, watched the wall, and tried to block out the deep snoring of Khaled al-Malik. She did not remove the pistol from her lap, and she did not sleep. When the sky began to lighten, she took a change of uniform and both firearms into the bathroom and locked the door. She bathed quickly, dressed, packed her things, stepped over the foul-smelling lump on the floor, tossed the key onto the bed, and left.

As she breezed past the front desk with her bags, the old clerk gave her a puzzled look.

"Ah, bonjour, Monsieur. My father came last night to tell me that Mama has fallen ill, and I must return at once to Madrid. Papa will pay the bill. Au revoir!"

"So sorry, Mademoiselle."

Outside the hotel, Corporal Arad summoned a taxi.

"De Gaulle Airport, s'il vous plait." She arrived, checked in, and took a seat in the large waiting room.

In a few minutes, Muhammad Kadir shuffled up from behind and gave her a nudge on the arm.

"Christ Jesus!" she exclaimed. "I thought—"

"Hi, Ani," Kadir replied calmly. "You're looking fit."

"Damn right. What the hell are you—"

"There's been a little change in plans," Kadir whispered.

"So I'm told. But unless I'm mistaken, Tel Aviv is somewhat southeast of here."

"Paris is so much more inviting in May, don't you agree? I couldn't see postponing my holiday over a little glitch in the software."

"So you know about the bogus itinerary."

"I wrote it. I merely checked it in Cairo to confirm that Khaled thinks he slipped it to me. See, he is under the impression that I am, shall we say, less than absolutely reliable."

"I can't imagine how he ever got such an idea."

"Nor can I. Have I ever let him down? Or you?"

"Speaking for myself, twin, of course not. Khaled doesn't understand you as I do. I doubt he is capable of understanding anything that didn't originate in his fanatic delusions."

"Don't be too hard on him, Ani. He believes with all his heart, as do we. But it's true he has gone too far. This whole thing was insane from the start, and it is much more so now that the Israeli and American governments have changed over and the negotiations are at least still being attended. Nothing is to be gained by it. Soon people who were born during our lifetime will sit down and redraw the map. There will be peace."

"Yes, and Japan will slaughter no more whales, and we all will drink from the formerly radioactive lakes of Siberia. I'm not sure I share your flower-power optimism, Muhammad, but it is part of why I love you. Come here, fool, and kiss me."

The two indulged in a long embrace.

"The main thing," Kadir whispered in his sister's ear, "is that Khaled has the real itinerary but thinks I don't. That gives us a chance to put a stop to this madness."

"I'm scared, Muhammad. If we fail—"

"We must not. We risk everything either way. Incidentally, Nick says hi."

"How is the Nose, after all?" Arad smiled.

"Scrappy as ever."

"God, remember that summer, Nick's new boat, that pristine water? Now, that was a holiday."

"Sure was. You were just starting to look good in a bathing suit."

"I'd say the same of you, but I don't recall noticing."

"Too bad; it might have turned your life around."

"Dog!"

"Tease!"

"Never!" she laughed. "Honestly, did I ever act provocatively around boys?"

"You never had to."

She smiled. "Thank you, Muhammad. You are my truest friend."

"It is because we are more than friends that I must get you off this runaway train."

"But how? Goldstein waits for me in Tel Aviv. Khaled and God knows who else thinks you're already there. We may be fugitives for the rest of—"

"Would that be so bad? New names, waiting tables at Club Med?"

"Don't be ridiculous. Al-Malik's hominids would hunt us down like—"

"Why? He knows I don't give a damn for his paranoia, and as far as he's concerned neither of us knows anything worth silencing. It would be cost-effective to write us off. Sheikh Hadid's money won't last forever."

"But you know al-Malik doesn't think that way; no zealot thinks that way. There is only the shore, and the vessel matters not."

"You're right. But one of us could be sacrificed, and I shall not let it be you."

Arad hugged her brother. "You are a good man, Muhammad." She lingered in his arms. "A rare thing, yes?"

"I wouldn't know. They all seem rather crude to me."

"Yes, they do." She paused. "Why is that? Is it nature? Must the male strut his laughable uncivilized display, and if it fails to impress the demurring female, must he stomp and seize by force? Must he treat his neighboring nations the same, as chattel, meat from the harem? Can not these primitive impulses be bred out of the only species capable of recognizing them for the folly they are?"

"You know, al-Malik recently made a similar analogy, about Uncle Sam as international rapist. But coming from him it was merely comical, because to his generation those honorable considerations do not apply to actual women."

"May I ask you something?" Arad whispered, leaning over and resting her head on Kadir's shoulder. "Something personal?"

"Are you going to embarrass me in public? I was not prepared for this conversation."

"Then perhaps I should ask another time. I guess I feel that time may be all we have."

"Time is all anyone has, Ani. We must make the best of it. What key to the universe can I impart this day before the sky falls on us?"

"If you're going to be that way—"

"I'm sorry."

"What's it like? You know, being inside a woman? How does that make you feel?"

"Oh. Ani. Well, it's, I suppose it's the inverse, or the obverse, really, of what it must be like for, but you haven't, I mean, it's wonderful, a feeling of being joined in a profound oneness with another soul, an intimacy so close and so consuming that you just lose all sense of reality. It's a kind of impelling journey you take together that, with the right person and love and rhythm and intuition—are you really just curious, or do you feel you're missing something?"

"Mostly the former, I suppose."

"Do you, when you, um—"

"Well, I don't normally have anything inside me. Sometimes I use this little vibrator. I was just wondering what it's like for you as a man, with all that equipment and control and need to—"

"Sometimes you want to be in control, sometimes you release control to your partner, sometimes you share it equally. It's not necessarily this attack mentality."

"Don't get defensive; I'm not holding up coitus as a social ill. Every girl probably wonders what it's like to have a penis." She paused. "Someday, if we're ever truly equal and all the sociopolitical aspects of sex can be cast aside, we may know whether this curiosity is natural or just a reaction to centuries of powerlessness."

"I too will look forward to that day. There is too much competition in the world, and I guess we've established that it all starts in the bedroom. What made you think of this, anyway?"

"I had the strangest fantasy yesterday, very disturbing."

"About anyone I know?"

"I'll never tell! No, it was hateful, and at the same time incredibly erotic."

"That sounds familiar."

"Yes? Not just making up after a fight, but lust fueled by total revulsion?"

"I don't know about revulsion, particularly—I like to be at least somewhat attracted to her—but love and hate are powerfully magnetic."

"Well, that's just it: for the first time in my life I found myself fantasizing about a man. A beautiful, sensitive man, and I *was* attracted to him, ached all over for him."

"There's nothing wrong with being bisexual, you know."

"Do you ever have such feelings, wonder what it's like to be female, or gay?"

"I wonder about the female half of the equation, as I guess any man does: what it is to be the receiver, to have the space that wants filling rather than the means to fill it."

"Perhaps it was just that this imaginary person is everything I would want in a man, yet I can never have him—so I had to destroy him."

Kadir looked long and silently into Arad's dilated black eyes. "Perhaps," he said.

XX

Chantilly, Virginia

AARON WOOD DROVE HIS DARK-GREEN convertible into the long-term lot at Dulles and parked. He got out, gathered two bags, and headed for the terminal.

He never tired of seeing the bold tentlike building with its world's-fair tower, looking yet like an extraterrestrial colony scattered across the green Virginia countryside. When it was first built, his father used to joke that someday the concave roof would fill up with snow and collapse; as a child, Aaron had wondered occasionally why it had not.

Once inside, he walked the broad expanse and checked in. In that morning's *Post* he had scanned a piece about a Zionist French cabinet minister's murder outside his home the night before, and he hoped he would have no trouble making his connection in Paris. He sat down in the waiting area and took out the draft he had printed out just before leaving the house.

He loved surrendering to that editorial nirvana that could be aroused only in the presence of paper and a red pen. He was just getting to some delicious foreplay when his flight was called.

When the airborne cabin had settled into low talking and long periods of silence, Wood resumed work on his manuscript. He normally disliked editing in a location where someone could read over his shoulder—his neighbors, a pleasant old couple apparently on their way to a scrapbook full of Versailles, seemed likely to produce thought-splintering interruptions—but quiet moments at his destinations would be rare. And even if his suburban seatmates did grow inquisitive, a brief discourse on his present subject, a comparison of French and Italian practices for improvising harpsichord accompaniments in baroque opera, should guarantee his undisturbed productivity for the rest of the flight. He was halfway through his third pass when the captain began showing off the Eiffel Tower.

The terminal at Charles de Gaulle was refreshing chaos recalling the sheer wonder that societies manage to function on any level.

The sight of Europeans was nourishing. He picked out pretty women, surveyed their unfaddish attire, read their lips. He discreetly looked them up and down, not as a hunter, he told himself, but as an art student. He imagined their whispering in his ear or calling his name from the sunny garden, kissed them goodbye as they scurried out the door late for work lamenting in irresistible fractured English the injustice of leaving his warm bed, lapsing into soft obscenities in their native tongues as they fumbled with their keys, turning in the doorway and washing him with one last pouting look of promised ecstasy. He shuddered at the thought of ever growing immune to their divine music.

Wood's reverie was broken by the sight of a middle-aged Arab man pacing along the wall of windows. It occurred to Wood that this was the man's second pass in that direction. For a few moments he watched as the man reached the far wall, turned, and paced back the opposite way. The distraction reminded Wood that his long connection had only just begun, so he reached for his manuscript.

It was rough going this time. He could not block out the seductive voices, not the least alluring of which was that of the unseen siren who every few minutes leaned into some hidden microphone and filled the air with sensuous reverberations about this or that flight, speaking first *en français* and then crisply repeating herself in several other languages. Eventually she was lying next to him and softly announcing his rising tide in multilingual eloquence as the warm spring breeze drifted over them and her long dark hair caressed his body with trembling magnolia fragrance.

"Monsieur? Monsieur?"

Wood looked up to see a young woman standing in front of his seat.

"Tel Aviv, oui?"

Suddenly Wood remembered her sitting across from him and realized that their flight had been called. "Oui!" he exclaimed. "Merci!" He gathered his things and followed the young woman across the floor.

They exchanged pleasant smiles. As the line began to move, he noticed that one of the first passengers was the curious Arab man, tucking a misshapen tweed jacket under his arm as he thrust his boarding pass at the gate attendant.

Wood was slightly disappointed when the forthcoming citizen found her seat several rows ahead of his. His editing was down to the finishing touches. Instead, he was placed next to a pair of talkative Israeli businessmen. Across from him on the aisle sat the fidgety Arab, periodically checking his watch and tapping his toe against the base of the seat in front of him.

Later, as the big jet eased down over the shimmering Mediterranean and began its approach, Wood's pulse quickened. How would it all have changed? Tel Aviv, Haifa, the floating seaside cafés, Mount Carmel, the Dead Sea, Beersheba, Jericho, holy Jerusalem? He did not expect to see much of the territory he had clambered over as a child, but he was overwhelmed with the realization that it was once again so near. Would he be able to find their old house, or had its labyrinthine garden paths yielded to high-rise apartments or a shopping center? He reminded himself that many communities in the region had changed little in thousands of years; he would try not to weep for those that had gone the way of their stateside sponsors. Then, after Israel, Egypt: surely no chrome diner was guarding the pharaohs' tombs.

Long after the eccentric Arab had pushed ahead and disappeared into the crowd, Wood entered the terminal and looked above the heads of those awaiting passengers on his flight. He soon located the small white sign held aloft with his name on it. He made eye contact, approached the young man, and shook his hand.

"Mr. Wood? Alan Reiger, U.S. Embassy. Welcome to Tel Aviv. I hope your trip was good."

"Excellent, thank you."

"I understand you've been to Israel before."

"As a young child: my father was cultural attaché here for three years."

"Yes, Arnie had wonderful things to say about him. We're very glad you could come, and we look forward to your performances. Let's get you settled at the hotel, and then you can meet the gang over dinner."

They walked out into the blazing dry air, and Wood smiled as date palms leaned into the breeze.

Reiger called for him at four-thirty and took him to the embassy. On the way, Wood watched the passing city, which had been modern before and was much more so now. He remembered how the family had gone over to the embassy on Friday evenings to watch American movies, how when the night was warm the projector would be set up on the roof and the families would assemble on lawn chairs and share refreshments. The films themselves were safe items like *The Glenn Miller Story* or *Journey to the Center of the Earth,* but it was mostly the communal event, the conclave of visitors in a new and alien state, that he remembered. He remembered sitting heaven-bound at Mann Auditorium, listening to the Philharmonic or trembling as Butterfly plunged her dagger. He remembered old Mrs. Kravitz, his intimidating first piano teacher—would her stylish house in the woods still stand?—and he remembered his pretty schoolteachers and their fragrant skin. Finally, he remembered that nearly everyone he had known in the Middle East had been American.

"Aaron Wood?" Reiger announced as they entered the distinguished office. "Ambassador Nichols."

"Thank you for coming, Mr. Wood. Arnie sent me your recordings. We're very glad to have you with us."

"Thank you, sir. I'm honored to be here."

"Al has arranged a welcome dinner for you down at Succa Levana; it's quite delightful at sunset. I wish I could join you, but perhaps later during your stay. I look forward to hearing you tomorrow evening."

The men said goodbye, and Reiger escorted Wood back out to the black sedan. Wood had not recognized any feature of the embassy but had not expected to. Perhaps after tomorrow's concert in the auditorium he would sneak up to the roof. They drove a few miles south to Old Jaffa, parked, and walked a block to the restaurant. They entered the glass-walled patio and approached a corner table already occupied by three men, one of whom wore a military uniform.

"Mr. Wood?" Reiger began. "This is Bernie Lederman from USIA; he'll be your site liaison and interpreter. Idris Fatool here will be your driver. And this is Major Hiram Goldstein, who will be glad to assign an escort for you should you care to visit any sites not on your itinerary. I invited Major Goldstein this evening because he happens to be quite the jazz fan; in fact, he knows more about it than most Americans here."

Wood smiled and took each hand in turn.

"Yes," Goldstein said in a grandfatherly wheeze, "I hev tried to keep your colonists vell informed, but zey are mostly hopeless, I'm afred."

Unnecessarily loud laughter erupted around the table.

"Well," Reiger said, taking a seat. "What are you drinking, Mr. Wood?"

"Aaron, please. Red wine."

"Let's order a bottle," said Reiger. "I see we have some catching up to do."

Goldstein leaned in. "Mr. Vood?" he began malodorously.

"Aaron, sir."

"Ehron. You know, Ehron, lest year ve hed Herbie Hencock here et ze festivel in Eilat—ze zem one you vill play on ze veekend. Ze gret Herbie Hencock! Und do you know zat I alone amonk zeze distingvished gendlemen undershtoot vat ze hell he vas talkink about?"

More laughter ensued, this time including Wood and Reiger.

"It's true," Lederman broke in. "Those two were in the corner discussing Sonny Rollins this and Coleman Hawkins that and who played bass on some old Fletcher Harrison rec—"

"Hendershon!" Goldstein corrected harshly. "Fledger Hendershon, fool! Zee vat I mean?"

The wine arrived. The waiter patiently removed the cork, poured a small amount in Reiger's glass, and waited.

"Oy, fill ze demn ting!" Goldstein bellowed. "Zat one vouldn't know a goot vintage iv it bit him on ze ess!"

The waiter filled both glasses and retreated.

Reiger held up his glass. "To our guest, Aaron Wood, who we hope has not by now developed second thoughts."

The five clinked their glasses and drank.

Wood stepped in. "To my gracious hosts, and a week of adventure."

"To jezz, ze music of ze dispossessed," Goldstein offered.

Finally young Fatool spoke. "To peace!"

"Hear, hear," replied Wood as the table fell briefly silent. He alone clinked Fatool's glass.

"Well, gentlemen," Reiger said cheerfully. "Perhaps we should order."

"Ze fish is outshtandink here," Goldstein exhaled.

Wood looked out toward the sea. He ordered soup and a salad.

The next morning, Lederman and Fatool picked up Wood at his hotel and drove him to that day's uneventful clinics, two before noon at nearby high schools and one at the university, returning before dinnertime so Wood could rest and prepare for the evening concert. That performance went smoothly as well and was something of a relief, since it involved talking only afterward, at the reception. Wood did manage to slip away momentarily and take in the sparkling view from the roof, but, again, he failed to recognize anything.

The following morning began the tightly scheduled trip north to several kibbutzim before the Galilee festival appearance. Lederman knocked on Wood's door at the appointed hour, but this time they stopped by the embassy on the way out of town.

Lederman got out and opened Wood's door. "Major Goldstein asked us to bring you to see him before we left. This way, please."

The two left Fatool in the car and went around the corner to a separate two-story building, in the courtyard of which flew only the Israeli flag. Lederman led Wood inside and up the stairs to Goldstein's paneled office.

"Ah, gendlemen. Hello. Mr. V—Ehron, come in, please."

Wood entered, and Lederman stepped out into the hallway.

"Ehron," Goldstein said, "I vas tinking. Since today you vill be heading tovard zome of your olt shtumping grounds und you may vell be tempted to visit zome shpots vere ze zecurity might perheps be less den guerunteed, I tought it might be vize to zend alonk en ezcort. I zertainly dun't expect you'll encounter any problems, but bedder zeff den zorry, yes?"

"Well, I don't want to cause you any headaches," Wood smiled knowingly, "but of course I'd love to see a bit of the countryside."

"No headache at all zis mornink," Goldstein smiled back. "I just vant zomeone to be nearby." He stepped toward the door and called out something in Hebrew.

In the next moment, a petite, athletic young woman in fatigues entered the room, snapped to attention, and saluted Goldstein, who stood behind his desk looking not at the woman but at Wood.

Aaron Wood looked at the woman and strained not to show a reaction. *Holy Mother of God,* he thought as he pretended she was the unshaven lackey he was expecting.

"Ehron Vood?" Goldstein announced watchfully. "Zis is Corporal Arad."

The woman turned automatically to face Wood without smiling. "Pleased to meet you," she said in a clear, cosmopolitan voice.

"And you," replied Wood.

"Corporal Arad shpiks good English und vill be most helpvul iv necessary—but again, I expect she is merely goink alonk for ze ride."

Wood tried looking through Corporal Arad as though she did not exist. "Thank you, sir."

Goldstein said something in Hebrew, and Corporal Arad returned to face him. Again she saluted, turned in one crisp motion, and left the room. As the sound of her boots on the stairs began to fade, Goldstein went to the door and quietly closed it before returning to his desk. "Ehron," he said.

"Yes?" Wood summoned.

"Ehron, zis is a most hendsome young voman, yes?" Goldstein smiled mischievously.

Wood was determined not to misstep. "Uh, yes, sir, I suppose she is. I remember seeing many female soldiers when we were here in—"

"Und you are a hendsome young men, yes?" Goldstein continued.

"That's kind of you to say, sir, but—"

"Vell, Ehron, let me tell you zometing. On ze one hend, I vant to look efter my flock und zay zat iv you are tinking vat I vould hope a hendsome young men vould be tinking et ze moment, vorget it already, yes? On ze other hend, I must tell you zat zis young voman is very special, und part of vy I hev given her zis assignment is zat she hes been letly under a gret deal of pressure und could use a chenge of scenery. She vas sent to me temporarily from an elite commando training mission—she is perheps ze finest marksman, or marksperson, or vatever ze hell, I hev ever met—und she really does not belonk here. She hes med few contects amonk her teammates since her arrival, und I tink she might appreciate a few days in ze company of someone who hes read a book in ze lest year or two, iv you know vat I mean. Indeed she likes music: she knows Palestrina und Beethoven ze vay I know Coltrane. Zo vat I em zaying, Ehron, is, feel free to talk to her; she may open up to a fresh, foreign ettitude. It vill probably do her good, und it cannot do harm." He paused and smiled. "Zat is all I vill say about Corporal Arad."

Wood viewed the officer carefully. *What, if anything, is going on here?* Corporal Arad's appearance was a welcome diversion, to be sure, though Wood was not looking forward to sharing the backseat of the sedan with quite possibly the most beautiful woman he had ever seen while Lederman and Fatool grinned into the rearview mirror. *I have enough to think about this week without being prevailed on to play big brother to some lonely sniper. Does Goldstein suspect something about Arad that he hopes she might reveal to a visiting American musician? Is he trying to get rid of her, hoping she'll defect over the border to Jordan? Is he a relative trying to marry off the last burden of his old age?* "I appreciate your confidence, sir, and I shall not betray it. If Corporal Arad wishes to talk with me, she will find a good listener."

"Zat is excellent, Ehron, more den I should hope vor. Ze army is not en easy life, und one vonders vy zome people seek it out. I vould be most pleased zomeday to zee a zmile on Corporal Arad's face." He paused. "Oy, listen to me, en olt men: I should perheps not hev brought you here today—"

"Nonsense, Major Goldstein. If Corporal Arad has not smiled before we return to Tel Aviv, the next bottle of wine is on me."

"Und iv she is zmilink when next she appears in zat doorway, I vill zend you home vit ze whole demn case!"

The two men laughed and shook hands. Goldstein held open the door. Wood walked out and down the stairs, not noticing until he had reached the small foyer that

Lederman was absent. When he returned to the curb, he encountered a covered jeep parked where the sedan had been. Corporal Arad was seated behind the wheel.

"Mr. Lederman was concerned that we were running behind schedule," she called as Wood approached, "so they went on ahead to smooth any ruffled feathers until you arrive. We'll be back on track by lunchtime. Please hop in, Mr. Wood."

12

Cairo

"ORFEO RECORDS. MAY I HELP YOU?"

"To the shore, comrade."

"Ah, Paul Revere himself. What alarm are you sounding this day?"

"Very funny. I must see you at once."

"You are local?"

"I am across the street."

"Then you see me already. What do you want?"

"Your Caliban has bolted."

"What?"

"I will be right over."

In a few moments, Khaled al-Malik burst unsmiling into the shop.

"Ah, Militiaman Revere," mused Nick Xenakis. "You look a bit frayed. Perhaps some Otis Redding would—"

"Shut up, Nick. Are we alone?" al-Malik spat, casting suspicious eyes over the rows of CD bins.

"It is early. Sting's disciples will begin arriving during lunch hour."

"Look, this is serious. Muhammad has disappeared."

"Disappeared? Then I have trained him better than I thought."

"Exactly. I knew he was irresponsible, but apparently he is also very stupid."

"Or very smart."

"Which brings me to your door, guru. Which is your

inclination?"

"If I know you as I fear I do, I suspect that some weeks back you sat in your car and watched the young man enter the terminal."

"Yes."

"Whereupon you enacted a circuitous obstacle course and posted your righteous ass where you could observe his embarkation."

"Of course."

"And finally you stood at the window as the aircraft imitated the noble flight of the martyrs."

"As the boy's commander, I of course did all these things, Nick."

"Then, my dear Khaled, I suggest that you seek young Muhammad in the wrong city. Tel Aviv is somewhat northeast of here."

"I have been to Tel Aviv, whoreson. He is not there."

"Were not your eunuchs awaiting his arrival?"

"Of course. He was not on the plane."

"He was not on the plane, or he did not get off it? Perhaps he was preoccupied in the loo. The boy has a healthy libido, yes?"

"Don't be ridiculous. I tell you I watched him embark here in Cairo, and I have confirmed that he did not disembark in Tel Aviv."

"Well, I assure you, Khaled, all rancor aside, I have not seen him here. You are welcome to check my stockroom."

"As well I should."

"Look: did it ever occur to you that perhaps Muhammad simply came to his senses and decided to abandon your absurd scheme? Perhaps you only think you saw him embark here."

"I watched him present his boarding pass, walk down the hall, and get on the plane."

"Really? Do your estimable talents now also include X-ray vision? Are not those gate extensions opaque? Do they not bend and fold like accordions? Unless you strapped Muhammad into his seat, I suggest that you did not in fact watch him get on the plane."

Al-Malik looked puzzled. "Would not an alarm have sounded? An attendant rushed into the terminal?"

"Apparently not. I suspect such defections are rather uncommon among visitors. Perhaps he let a penniless college student take his place. Where was he in line?"

"Last, as usual."

"Well, then: he simply waited till he was out of sight of the terminal, lagged behind in the corridor, and either hugged the wall as it was withdrawn or escaped through a door."

"The gate was probably twenty feet off the ground, Nick."

"Muhammad has scaled more than his parcel of granite walls."

"The little bastard. I should have taken care of him a long time ago. I could tell he was losing it."

"Muhammad can take care of himself. It is you who has careened round the bend, al-Malik. I suggest you follow your young mutineer's lead and vanish."

"And if you did hear of his whereabouts—"

"You would be the last to know, yes. This turn of events is perhaps the best thing that could have happened for any of us."

"Are you insane, hagseed? What if the boy has forged on alone? What if he is captured, and interrogated? He would sing louder than your bleating niece!"

"These impotent insults are laughable. Muhammad Kadir has more character than every branch of your family tree. Nothing in the Zionists' toolbox could break him. And as for me, I am old. I have regretted and paid for my mistakes—not the least of which is having made your acquaintance—and I am at peace with my God. If your flimsy machinery be about to fly apart, I suggest you do everyone a favor and get out of the way. If Muhammad or Anat or even one of your illiterates is offered up in this madness, it will be you who has signed the death warrant. I can only hope that the young man and his angel of a sister have seen through your veil of poison and are now as far from you as the love of the Virgin can take them. Would that their high school had not settled for the first soccer coach it found."

"You may live to eat these hurtful words, old man."

"Your ability to amuse has waned, al-Malik. It is your stench now that lingers. Get out of my shop."

Khaled al-Malik looked at Nick Xenakis as though peering through the scope of his rifle. He smirked, turned, and left.

Tel Aviv

THEY HAD DRIVEN ALMOST COMPLETELY out of town without speaking a word.

Finally, as the urban distractions and the predictability of the outskirts began giving way to rolling countryside, Anat Arad shifted uncomfortably in her seat. "So," she said a bit loudly over the roar of the jeep engine, "you play the piano."

Aaron Wood looked at her, immediately looked away, and smiled. "Yes."

"And you are here on behalf of your State Department."

"Yes, the U.S. Information Agency. They send American artists abroad and host foreign artists in the States."

"Ah."

"My counterpart Israeli pianist is probably holding forth in some Bethesda gymnasium as we speak," he ventured.

"And you are teaching here as well as performing?" Arad asked sincerely.

"A bit: mostly just answering questions." He paused. "I guess you'll have memorized my answers by the end of the day."

Still no reaction.

"Do you teach in America? The piano?"

"Yes. It's my livelihood, actually. Few musicians there

make a living solely as performers."

"So I have heard. It is too bad your government is not more actively involved in promoting the arts."

Now we're getting somewhere. "Absolutely. The average American's appreci—"

"I studied a bit of piano as a child," Arad revealed in a full voice. "I got rather good at it."

Wood glanced at her elegant hands. "Oh? Do you still play?"

"I would, but I was moved around a lot, and there has not been an instrument in a long time."

"Do you have room for a piano where you live?"

"Well, there is an old upright in the NCO club, but they never tune it."

"Perhaps I can suggest to Major Goldstein that it be looked at. Sometimes an outside influence—"

"So, what do you think of the major?" Arad asked.

Wood looked at her, searching for a manifestation of the lighter tone her voice had taken on. Instead, he found himself again having to shake off the impact of her beauty. "He's quite a character, isn't he? He must be fun to work for."

"Well," Arad replied, "*fun* is not a word I would use to describe the work I am doing there. But yes, the major is eccentric. And kind."

"Yes, he is."

"I know perfectly well, for instance, that he sent me on this little field trip—no offense, Mr. Wood—to get me away from there for a while, give me a breath of air."

"Oh?"

"And I have a feeling he knows that I know this, and

201

that I am grateful to him for it."

"Perhaps."

"I was not meant to be a traffic cop."

Wood turned slightly toward her. "Was there a mix-up somewhere, or is embassy duty some sort of punish—"

"Well, it is a joke, is it not? Babysitting American secretaries?"

"I can understand that."

"What are your marines there for, anyway?"

"Decoration, perhaps," Wood smiled. "You know, ambiance."

That did it.

"Yes, it would be a shame if those wooden soldiers ever had to get their uniforms dirty," Arad said cheerfully. Then suddenly her smile evaporated. "I am so sorry. That was unfair and untrue. I know what those men have given to their country and to the world, and what they are capable of."

The two rode in silence for a few minutes.

"I suppose it's different for you," Wood said, "growing up here. In America, we became very suspicious and intolerant of the military during and after Vietnam: it wasn't the blind patriotism, or the just cause, of our parents' generation. Even today, we tend to typecast soldiers as dim-witted killing machines that can't wait for the next Panama or Iraq. And in our hearts, we know those perceptions are cruel and ungrateful. Actually, to tell you the truth, I was never so proud to be an American as on the day of my father's funeral at Arlington. But—"

"Your father is buried at Arlington? With the Kennedys?"

"Well, along with a few thousand others."

"Was he a career officer?"

"No, he served five years in the medical corps. After that he was a teacher, later a diplomat. That's how—"

"Did he see action at the front?"

"No. I don't think he ever left the States until after his discharge, when a former colleague recommended him to supervise a student-exchange program in Austria."

"Austria?"

"Yes. That's what I mean: Even those who were shipped out and maimed were fighting mostly on someone else's behalf. But here, you've seen warfare on your own shores during your lifetime, and many perceive you to be surrounded by ancient enemies who would drive you out of exis—"

"And who says we are not?" Arad snapped.

Wood looked at her strong profile. "No one, Corporal. I was merely pointing out that it's easy for a young American to take the military for granted, but that a young Israeli couldn't even if he or she wanted to."

"Yes, that is how it is," Arad replied quietly. "I am sor—"

"And stop apologizing," Wood smiled.

Corporal Arad smiled back. "Here I am, assigned to keep you safe from a nonexistent danger, and the first thing I do is insult you. My personal angst is not your concern."

"Well, someone of your intelligence won't be allowed to languish in a position below your potential." He paused. "It's hard to imagine the connection, but I don't get a big thrill out of schlepping a truckload of gear on a Saturday night and playing Top 40 songs to afford the serious side of *my* career."

Corporal Arad covered her mouth and giggled.

Fantastic.

"Yes, we each must bear our cross," she said brightly as she stepped a bit harder on the accelerator.

"I know," Wood continued, "listening to some brat reel off the same excuses week after week for botching a lesson is not exactly dodging bullets in—" He started. "Have you yourself been shot at?"

"No. But I have undergone a most rigorous training program, out in the desert, just recently. And I spent some time on patrol in Gaza, but that was not really so dangerous for m—" Suddenly Arad became quiet and looked around at the countryside.

"Not so dangerous?" Wood persisted. "How so? Our news reports portray your relations with the Palestinians as especially tense since the *intifada.*"

Arad was quiet for another long moment, then looked at Wood with serious black eyes.

"I'm sorry," Wood said. "That is undoubtedly a delicate subject. My State adviser even told me to avoid discussing politics while I'm over here. Consider it dropped, OK?"

Corporal Arad looked back at Wood with a softened expression he had not yet seen. "Mr. Wood?"

"Please call me Aaron, if that's all right."

"Aaron." She paused. "My name is Anat, by the way."

Anat Arad. Scarcely musical. But practice makes—

"May I ask you something, Aaron?" she continued, her voice perceptibly lower and more modulated. "After all, we have already broached the subject and therefore cannot turn back. I promise not to run to your adviser with the shocking details."

Wood was beginning to like everything about this girl.

"Tell me," Arad pursued in a provocative tone, "how do you feel—you personally, not as a representative of your government—about the Palestinians?"

Wood stared straight ahead. *Why is everyone trying to get me to say something stupid? I did not come over here to die in a Lebanese detention camp. But that's absurd. She's just an angry young woman. Goldstein was right. She'll probably turn away from me altogether if I refuse to answer. Haven't you always suspected that the people here would make peace with one another if their aged rulers got out of the way? You're sitting right next to the real story.* "Well," Wood began, searching her face for clues, "I can speak only as a foreigner who can't possibly understand the day-to-day dynamics of the situation, much less the centuries of bitterness, but I feel that the Palestinians have a legitimate right to a Palestinian homeland." He paused, but she did not react. "These people have long shared this region with you, the place was called Palestine long before the creation of the State of Israel, they're clearly not going to get up and move away, and at the very least nothing is being accomplished by the two societies' continuing to hammer at each other." He watched the high forehead, the serious brow. "I mean, look at America: it's taken over two centuries for African Americans to begin feeling welcome in their own country, and the *Native* Americans have been all but rubbed off the map. It's the same guilt trip wherever you are, Anat."

Finally Corporal Arad looked again in his direction, and her face fairly blossomed. "Thank you," she smiled.

"*Thank you?* I passed the quiz? Does this mean you're not going to kick me out at sixty miles per hour after all?" *Jesus Christ, you are beautiful.*

"No, I have decided to let you live for now. Besides, we have established that you are not the only one of us capable of a diplomatic faux pas."

"Yes."

"You see, Aaron, I was born in Gaza. My mother is a Palestinian."

"Ah. You could have said—"

"I can walk the streets there in or out of uniform."

"And your father?"

"He was Israeli. He was killed three months before I was born."

"Oh. I'm sorry."

"Do you want to know how he was killed, by whom, and why?" She did not wait for an answer, but paused to steady her voice. "My father was stabbed by an off-duty officer of the Israeli secret police. He was stabbed in broad daylight in front of his own home by his own countryman for the crime of marrying my mother."

Wood was transfixed.

They drove on for several minutes without speaking.

"Anat," Wood said finally, "I don't know whether this will make any sense to you, but let me try to say it anyway. You have been tested in ways the average Westerner might find impossible to comprehend. You have lived in the crossfire of an ancient and maybe irresolvable conflict. Your parents came together because nothing could keep them apart, and as a result they were denied the fulfillment of their life. My own parents probably had no business being in the same room with each other, yet they stayed together forty years, raised three children, and appeared for all the world to be the model of unimpeachable normalcy. We who grew up in their house felt their anger, pride, and denial, and ultimately the horror of slow death. You exist, Anat, because of the noblest kind of love. I exist, most probably, because someone forgot to reach into a drawer. Please don't get me wrong: I'm not trying to make one situation seem more or less horrific than the other. I just have the feeling that you and I have some things in common."

Arad turned and smiled, and her beautiful eyes were wet. "Yes."

He looked at her a long time. "It's a bit surprising, isn't it?"

"Yes, it is, and perhaps not. I certainly was happier, well, not happier, but better protected, when we were discussing the piano. But I am glad I do not feel so safe now." She paused. "I do find it terribly easy to talk to you. And I assure you that that is not normally the case."

"Nor with me."

Another long silence.

Arad stole several curious looks at Wood and then smiled exuberantly. "Aaron, do you believe in—ah, I am being foolish."

"No, go on. Please."

Arad merely giggled slightly.

"Let me guess, then. You were going to ask whether I believe in fate."

"Perhaps," she said cheerfully.

"And we both know that neither of us believes in fate."

"What makes you so sure?"

"You would not have grown so strong if you believed your future was sealed that day in Gaza."

"Right again, Father Wood," she smiled.

It was then he noticed the tiny gold cross hanging from a threadlike chain around her neck.

She saw his eyes. "This? More decoration than devotion, I am afraid. Ambiance, as you would say," she laughed slyly. "I was—are you ready for this?—I was raised a Catholic. You are looking at a one-woman spiritual upheaval, Aaron."

I am looking at the most magnificent example of God's creation I have ever seen. Surely you know this. "Something about you *seems* Catholic."

"What? The guilt?"

"Yes, the fierce repression of your true feelings." He threw up his hands. "Ugh! I sound like a shrink."

"No, you're absolutely right."

"Were you raised a Catholic in Gaza? Who wouldn't be confused! And where did you learn such natural English?"

"Well, now, you're really going to laugh: I learned English in California."

"Really!"

"You see, I have a twin brother: Muhammad. Our mother was very poor; she didn't think she would be able to care for us. One of the inspectors who investigated our father's murder knew a couple at the American embassy who had been trying to conceive. Our mother simply could not function at that point, so the couple adopted us—and then they were relocated. Muhammad and I went through grade school in L.A. It's crazy, isn't it? I can't believe I'm telling you all this."

"Wow. A twin." He paused thoughtfully. "How did you end up back in Israel?"

"By the time we had finished grade school, our mother had got back on her feet. She had never stopped writing, of course; we exchanged photographs and so on. She had a Greek friend in Cairo, a former historian at the Antiquities Museum, whom we would visit during the summers, and Mother would join us. In fact Nick—Nick Xenakis is our friend's name—will be at your festival in Eilat! He is a fountain of musical knowledge, and great fun; you will like him." She paused. "Anyway, when we were eleven, our foster parents were killed in a car accident."

"Jesus."

"So we returned. Our paternal grandmother had grown very old and had immigrated from Austria, to be buried in Israel. We lived with her and Mother and enrolled in school here. I took back my father's name and, for Grandmother's sake, had my bas mitzvah. Muhammad took our mother's maiden name, Kadir. He still lives in Gaza. We're very close."

Suddenly the jeep slowed, and Wood turned forward to see that they had arrived at their first destination.

"Well," he said. "The gig. I hope Lederman knows how to tap dance or something. Are we very late?"

"Not terribly." She looked at him and smiled warmly. "I have enjoyed talking with you, Aaron."

"And I with you. After this stop, I expect to find out how you got from the bas mitzvah to the grand tour and that pistol on your hip."

"I'll think about it. But first you must get in there and play your piano."

Cairo

"ORFEO RECORDS. MAY I HELP YOU?"

"To the shore, old one."

"Icarus!"

"The corona is too hot?"

"Raging."

"Perhaps I should fly to the moon instead."

"You must."

At five o'clock, Nick Xenakis closed his shop and went home. When it grew dark, he filled his CD changer and programmed it. He left on the usual number of lights and slipped out by the basement door, hugging the alley walls and fences until he was clear of the neighborhood and could move in the shadows to the place where he had taught Muhammad Kadir to meet him when there was trouble. He picked the lock just off the employees' driveway, passed through the dark social hall, and ascended the stairs. Candles were burning. He passed silently along the wall, opened the old oak door, and entered. Within the hour, he heard the rustling of the curtain.

"Bless me, Father, for I have Zen," whispered the young voice.

"That's what I hear. You should know better than to skip soccer practice."

"But Coach has begun making up the rules as he goes along."

"And that ball he carries around has developed an ominous ticking sound."

"I have quit the team, Padre."

"A wise move. But surely you have not abandoned your goaltender."

"Of course not. I knew that after supposedly feeding me the false itinerary Khaled would send Ani to spy on me, so I went to Paris and hung out till she showed up."

"Well, Muhammad, as usual, your luck was equal to your skill. Someday that may not be the case. Where is your sister, and al-Malik?"

"She's been temporarily assigned to guard detail outside the U.S. embassy: surrounded night and day by armed soldiers and plainclothes Mossad geeks—not to mention however many marines work up the courage to walk over and ask for her phone number. He wouldn't dare make a move on her there."

"We don't know that, Muhammad. He may not be the pariah he would like us to think he is. God, how I rue the day you two fell under his spell."

"Let's not go over that again, Nick. It was the times. We were young and idealistic, and along came an activist with all the answers."

"But I knew the sickness in his eyes then. Had we not been separated so much of the time, I could have got the two of you away from him."

"Well, it just didn't work out that way. The more controversy he stirred up, the more we revered him. Eventually he took you in as well."

"He took me not, Muhammad. I allowed myself to become involved in this because it was the only way to watch over you and Ani, and because I am old and dispensable. It was a foolish mistake."

"It's too late for regrets. And whereas you have walked these streets a long time, you are hardly dispensable. Damn it, Nick, you are the father Ani and I never had. We will not let you down."

"You cannot. It is I who has disappointed."

"Nonsense." He paused. "But tell me: why do you so hate al-Malik? We all know now that he's crazy—but you, who are never quick to judge, despised him from the start."

Xenakis was silent for a moment. "Sometimes I forget that you are now a man, Muhammad," he said, nearly sounding his years. "If I tell you, you must promise to *be* a man and never tell your sister, or anyone else."

"It would hardly be the first of our secrets, Padre."

"Do you remember that while you and Ani lived in Los Angeles your mother worked as a custodian at the new high school across the line in Israel?"

"Of course."

"Well, for a short time, Khaled al-Malik, who in those days was calling himself Eliahu Goodman, taught gym at that school. One day after class he offered to coach one of his tennis pupils. When they were through, he followed her into the locker room and forced himself on her. Do you know who found them?"

Kadir gasped. "O, vile—"

"And do you know why your mother could not report what she saw? Just before you returned, she had begun writing me about a fabulous new man in her life, who had given her back her heart, who had enabled her once again to fall in love—and she wanted my blessing and my advice on how to break the wonderful news to you and Ani. Well, he saved her the trouble that afternoon in the girls' locker room."

"You lie!"

"You know I would not, Muhammad. They had been seeing each other less than a month. Your mother went into shock, and the pig managed to talk her out of turning him in. The girl reported it to the authorities the next day but refused to go through a trial. Al-Malik was allowed to resign quietly and disappear. The next time he surfaced— well, you know the rest."

"The cur. With these two hands I will—"

"And I wish I could help you. But first you must get to Tel Aviv, make your excuses, and not let Ani out of your sight. There isn't much time now, and he is sure to call for her soon."

"And you, Padre? What will you do?"

"I will do what I have always done: slip out the back and create a little diversion."

"Will I see you before Eilat?"

"Only if something goes wrong."

"When this is over, music will never have sounded sweeter."

"When this is over, I hope we will all be alive to hear it."

Plain of Sharon, Israel

AARON WOOD SHOOK THE LAST HAND and stepped toward the door. He could feel her watching him, but he stayed comfortably within his professional shell. He smiled and waved goodbye to his hosts.

Throughout Wood's performance, Corporal Arad had stood against the back wall by the door. During the playing and throughout the question-and-answer period, her eyes had never left him. As he approached the door, he smiled and waited for her to exit. But she did not move. Her eyes had taken on a dark intensity.

She did not return his smile. Finally, she pushed herself away from the wall and motioned for him to go ahead.

Wood hesitated, then stepped out into the sun. As Wood followed Lederman and Fatool toward the parking lot, Corporal Arad quickly caught up and walked beside him without speaking. He looked at her and smiled, but her expression had not changed. When they reached the cars, there was a moment of shuffling feet and averted eyes.

"Say, if you guys don't mind," Wood said, "I think I'll continue riding with Corporal Arad here. She was in the middle of a great story."

Lederman and Fatool smiled respectfully, nodded, and moved toward the sedan. Without looking at each other, Wood and Arad turned and walked in silence to the jeep.

Before closing his door, Lederman leaned back and called, "There's a nice little café down in the village. Why don't we meet there?"

Wood answered, "That sounds fine." He smiled politely at Corporal Arad and watched as she climbed with feline grace into the vehicle.

Once inside, he shifted uncomfortably. Finally, as they pulled away from the compound, he asked, "Do you think those two are feeling a bit superfluous today?"

"How so?" Corporal Arad answered tersely.

"Well, you seem innocently to have usurped Fatool's job, and we know you could do Lederman's."

"I could hardly be perceived as a representative of your government, though, could I?"

"No, I suppose not, at least not in that outfit. And the guys are enjoying a few days in the country. But I suppose they'll be pretty sick of my playing by week's end."

Corporal Arad's face darkened again. "I don't see how that would be possible," she said in a low voice.

Wood looked at her and smiled warmly. "Why, thank you, Anat. You liked it?"

Arad looked out the window, softened her grip on the wheel, and took a deep breath. "Yes," she said in her businesslike tone.

They rode in silence for a while.

"So," Wood offered, "where were we? Ah, the bas mitz—Anat? Are you all right?"

Corporal Arad was gripping the wheel again with bloodless knuckles and struggling to relax her jaw. Her eyes were wet.

Wood gave her the hand towel he had retained after

his performance.

"Thank you," she said softly.

Another long silence ensued as they descended the bumpy road toward the village.

"I suppose I didn't know quite what to expect," Corporal Arad said finally, still touching her face periodically with the towel.

"Of—"

"Of your playing. Aaron."

"Thank you," he repeated softly.

"I mean, you're not just good. It's as though you take on another spirit or dimension, you're so totally involved. You breathe every nuance as though your life depended on it. And I know these, what did you call them, clinics, they probably aren't as important to you as a formal concert, yet you just—well, I must say, Aaron, I'm impressed."

"Thank you, Anat."

"More than impressed."

They looked briefly at each other and rode on. He wanted to reach for her hand.

"May I tell you something?" she said sonorously.

He smiled back at her.

"I hope this doesn't embarrass you, but watching and listening to you in there caressing those sinuous melodies and exotic chords, I couldn't escape the feeling that you were far beyond mere playing. It was as though you were, you know, making love."

Wood shifted nervously. "Oh! Really?"

"Come on, now. You know that most musicians don't throw themselves into it like that. Many don't even get the notes. You *owned* them."

"Well," he responded, clearing his throat, "I suppose it is a similar state of mind, artistic rapture and, um, sex, if the music really means something to you. And even when it doesn't, it's hard to distance yourself entirely from the drive to create, to become one with it, to ennoble the collective spirit. That's why art is so essential. Maybe if our politicians were as attuned to these things as you are—"

Corporal Arad's official repose returned as she flexed her thigh and stepped on the brake. Wood saw low buildings, curbside tables, and Lederman and Fatool stepping out of their black sedan. He smiled at Corporal Arad and watched her hop out of the jeep.

The group took a shaded table and made small talk, ordered, and ate. Throughout the meal, Wood and Arad avoided making eye contact and went out of their way to entertain their companions. After lunch, the four repaired to their separate vehicles and pulled away from the curb without speaking.

"Well," Arad said finally as they were once again on the open road, "that was interesting."

"Interesting?"

"Well. The tension. You didn't feel it?"

"I felt a bit inhibited, yes."

"More than inhibited, I'm afraid, speaking for myself," she said softly, looking away. "Why do I suddenly feel so uncomfortable?"

Wood watched her a moment and smiled. "Well, first, I had to go and suggest that those two were the ones feeling uncomfortable. And then, just before stopping, we got onto a rather personal subject—it's understandable. We're probably reading too much into it," he said gently.

"You think?"

"Yes, perhaps."

"Then why do I still hear that piano ringing in my head? Why do I feel that I made a terrible mistake by saying what I said, or by being here at all?"

Wood turned toward her. "Look. If you're afraid you put me on the spot, forget it, OK? You only confirmed my intuition that you're a deeply sensitive person. If you're afraid you let down your defenses, well, maybe that's not such a bad thing to do now and then. And if you're afraid that an interesting bond may be forming between us, nothing could be more natural than that: I'm here for now less than a week, we've had a sort of meeting of the minds, and the desire to explore that is more urgent than it might otherwise be."

"Are you always this cool and analytical, Aaron?"

Wood smiled. "I'm sorry. No, I'm not. And I'm sure you'd behave similarly if I were the one feeling a bit out of control."

"Yes, I probably would." She paused. "I grew up very competitive, always having to prove I could support that chip on my shoulder. I guess I'm not used to some of these feelings."

"Well, Anat, on the one hand, I'm moved that I was able to reach you through my playing—that's what performing is all about. On the other hand, I do not want to make you feel uneasy or vulnerable if you do not wish to feel that way. We can drop this altogether if—"

"But it's not so simple. In just one morning I grew to like you rather more than I have a right to, and then suddenly your music just sort of washed over me—back there at the table I felt like a kid with a couple of chaperones." She paused and checked her speedometer. "I'm sorry, Aaron. I shouldn't be saying these things."

"Let's just consider this week a gift," he said. "We can agree that we like each other, we can enjoy each other's company, and perhaps we can exchange addresses. Or we can pretend that none of these feelings exists, you can resume being a beautiful soldier, and I can resume being a confused piano player touring Israel beside you—I can even resume riding with Simon and Garfunkel up there, for that matter—and we'll both feel cowardly and unfulfilled."

"Do you really think I'm beautiful?" she asked seriously.

Wood looked at her in astonishment. "You're joking, right? This is another quiz: let's find the longest route to the nose on one's face?"

"Don't tease me, man," she said cheerfully.

"I'm supposed to convince you that you're beautiful? Do you not have every man in Tel Aviv knocking on your door?"

"Oh, Aaron," she sighed. "There is much you do not know about me."

"I do know that you must have suffered even more profoundly than I thought if every day you are not absolutely stunned by your reflection in the mirror."

Arad was quiet for a while. "That's very kind of you to say. Thank you."

There was a long silence.

"Normally I have an easy answer for this," she said almost to herself.

Wood did not take her cue. He knew by now that if she had something to tell him, eventually she would. "No answers we can give each other in this short week will be easy."

"No." She tightened her grip on the wheel.

"So let's back up: do the chip on the shoulder and the uniform and the unnecessary job dissatisfaction all—"

"Unnecessary?" she said coyly.

"Are you going to make me tell you again that, if you wanted to, you could be on the cover of any magazine in America?"

"Those women are doing very little for their country."

"Oh, come now. First of all, as a matter of fact, they are pumping millions of dollars into their country's economy— though I agree that that probably is not their prime motivation. And whereas you could say that they are only contributing to the objectification of women, no less are they exploiting the shallowness of men. In the artistic sense, they are at least bringing beauty to a world badly in need of it. Some of them probably can carry on an intelligent conversation. I don't know how many of them can shoot straight." He paused and savored her laughter. "In any event, I think the sexiest magazines are those aimed at women—because they portray you the way you see yourselves."

"You're pretty comfortable with women, aren't you?" she insisted, smiling.

"Well, yes, actually. My closest friends over the years have been women."

"Ooh-la-la!"

"Society's treatment of women has been cruel and

ignorant, and has denied all of us the fullness of human potential. Maybe someday we'll learn to relax."

"Yes. I too will look forward to that day."

Wood looked out the window a long time, feeling at once Arad's increasing pull on him and the certainty that they both were wondering the same thing. He turned and caught her watching him.

She arched her left eyebrow, smiled elegantly, and faced the front.

The long silence continued.

"So," Arad said, "we've established you're comfortable with women. Are you especially comfortable with a particular woman at the moment?"

He returned her conspiratorial grin. "At this very moment I—"

"I mean, are you married?"

"No." He paused. "Until recently, I was seeing someone, but we were going nowhere. Her office was relocated just before this tour, actually, and we agreed it was a good time to make a clean break of it."

"Ah."

"You?"

"No." She smiled like a front-row student who is the first to notice that the teacher's pen is leaking all over his shirt.

"OK," Wood said calmly, "so a guy looks at a woman and says to himself, *What's a goddess like this doing in the army?* And if he knows her the little bit I do, he figures, *Well, she's there in tribute to her father's memory.* But clearly neither she nor any of her relatives whom he knows about was or is a hard-line Zionist. She's recently attended some sort of desert-warfare convention and probably could take down Arnold Schwarzenegger with a flick of the wrist. And by a casual glance or two he has determined that her allegiance to army life has little to do with gourmet dining. Logic suggests that she might feel more at home in California. So, he feels compelled to ask—"

"Don't," she said coldly. "I have told you way too much already."

Wood's smile disappeared, and he looked at her as though he had just run over her kitten. The fierce jaw seemed suddenly hidden behind a veil. He knew he had revisited a nerve and that more words would not help. He turned and faced the front.

In a few miles, they arrived at the second performance. Corporal Arad pulled in abruptly and stopped in a cloud of dust inches behind the black sedan.

Wood looked at her. "Anat, I'm—"

"Forget it," she said, jumping out.

Wood waited for Lederman and Fatool to emerge before heading toward the building. He fell in behind them, walked a short distance, and felt a gentle touch on the back of his arm.

"Aaron," she whispered. "Are you OK?"

He smiled. "Now I am."

16

RACHEL PERLMAN WOKE at dawn to the sound of light knocking. She looked at the clock, cursed, and lay back down. Her eyes were just drifting shut again when the knocking resumed. Slowly she eased out of the covers and slipped on her bathrobe. She padded to the door and looked through the peephole. *Some drunk; he'll go away.* As she turned aside, the knocking resumed.

"Miss Perlman?" came a low voice.

She froze.

"Miss Perlman? Please, I must speak with you."

She stared silently through the aperture.

"Please," the voice persisted. "It's about Corporal Arad."

Perlman stepped back sharply and looked around the room. Then she remembered and went to the pantry. She opened a drawer, removed the pistol, and tucked it under her robe before padding back to the door. The knocking resumed.

"Miss Perlman? Please, I must—"

"What about Corporal Arad?" she said quietly through the door.

"Ah, good. Please let me in; I must speak with you."

"What about Corporal Arad? Who are you?"

"I am a friend of hers. Please, this is urgent."

"Has something happened?"

"Please, Miss Perlman," said the voice more quietly. "I

cannot talk out here."

She released the deadbolt and opened the door until the chain caught it. Without appearing, she whispered, "What about Corporal Arad?"

"Please let me in, Miss Perlman. I will not harm you."

Perlman closed the door. She removed the chain and stepped back a few paces as she tightened her grip on the gun she held against her skin. "It's open," she said trembling.

A dark serious man she had never seen entered and flashed a quick smile before regaining his lugubrious frown. "Thank you, Miss Perlman."

"Who are you?" she insisted.

"I am an old friend of Corporal Arad's. A former teacher, actually. I came into town last evening, thought I would look her up, and was told where to find her. But she was not there, and I was wondering—"

"If you did not find her, how did you find me?"

"Well, she had mentioned you in a letter, and—"

"That's a lie. Who are you?"

"Why would I lie to you, Miss Perlman? Anat— Corporal Arad—was one of my prize pupils, a very promising young musician. I had heard she was stationed at the security office near the American embassy, but she was not there, and—"

"I'm afraid you've come to the wrong place," Perlman said firmly, surveying the man's disheveled clothing and retreating from his odor.

"No, I'm sure she mentioned you. That's why—"

"Sir, Anat's last music lesson was long before she met me, and a teacher does not look for his forgotten students at this hour. I must ask you to—"

"Miss Perlman," he said more loudly, taking a step forward, "you do not understand. This is family business. It's about Anat's mother."

Perlman stiffened and decided that the man was not going to get any farther into the room. "Sir, I will be glad to convey your message to Anat if I see her. Meanwhile, I must ask you to leave."

The man began to step toward her again when he saw the momentary parting of silk, the flash of pink skin, the bulk of black steel held instantly aloft in two hands. "Miss Perlman!" he said just above a whisper. "I assure you there is no need for—"

"Get out of here. Now."

"Miss Perlman—"

"Now!" she shouted. "Or I will call the police!"

The man smiled briefly, scanned the outline of her body as the dawn sun filtered into the room, and put up his hand. "Very well, Miss Perlman. Perhaps you are correct: I have come to the wrong place. I am sorry." He looked at her once more before turning and exiting.

Immediately Perlman locked the door and ran to the kitchen telephone. She put the gun on the counter, looked in her book, and dialed. The line rang several times without an answer. "Come on, come on." Finally she heard a click.

"H—ello?"

"Mrs. Arad? Oh, thank God. This is Rachel Perlman."

"Who? Do you know what time—"

"Yes, I'm sorry, Mrs. Arad. This is Rachel Perlman. Anat and I were bunkmates, remember?"

"Oh, yes. Of course, dear. But—"

"Mrs. Arad, listen to me. I'm afraid something may be terribly wrong. A disgusting man was just here at my place looking for Ani. He was no soldier. He claimed to be an old piano teacher of hers, but—"

"That's nonsense. Ani's teacher in America died years ago, and even if he hadn't—"

"Exactly. The man said Ani is supposed to be stationed near the U.S. embassy and that he had tried to find her there."

"Well, that's where she is, as far as I know; we spoke about a week ago. Listen, Rachel, it's probably nothing. Please try to be calm. My son, Muhammad—do you know him?"

"Ani talked about him—"

"He has been in touch with Ani just in the last day or two. Give me your number. Let me call him, and I'll call you back."

Perlman hung up and leaned against the counter. She could not stop shaking. She picked up the gun, went to the refrigerator, took out a bottle of milk, drank long from it, and sat down at the dinette by the phone. After several minutes, it rang.

"Rachel? Mirim Arad. Muhammad suspects you may be right. He just got in, and he himself was going up to meet with Ani. If this man who visited you is the man Muhammad thinks he is, it probably is true that Ani is not where she is supposed to be—and that she may be in danger. Muhammad refuses to tell me any details. But if he is correct, the man is next headed here. For that reason, Muhammad insists on staying with me for now. He says you should go to the security office and calmly ask for Anat. You are a native Israeli with an honorable discharge; they have no reason to deceive you. Find out where she is, and call us back. Please be careful, child—you may be followed—but do not delay."

Perlman sat frozen for a few moments, trying to stop her tears. She ran to the bathroom, showered quickly, dressed in a burgundy silk blouse and well-fitting tan slacks, and arranged her thick auburn hair about her shoulders. She slipped the gun into her purse and locked the door behind her.

No one seemed to have tailed her as she wound her way through rush-hour traffic. A block from the building, she lifted the pistol out and slid it under the seat. She walked crisply to the gate and flashed her old military ID at the guard and smiled. He did not admit her.

"Please, sir, I'm here to see an old friend. I only just now heard she was here."

"*She?*" he smirked. "You must mean Arad." *Miss Congeniality*.

"Yes. We were bunkmates a while back."

"Oh?" He looked her up and down.

"Yes. Please, sir, I'd really like to see her."

"It's a bit early for a social call, isn't it? Perhaps I could tell her you were here."

"Please, sir," Perlman repeated, trying to maintain her smile.

The young man made a vague gesture. "Go on in. Up the stairs."

"Thank you, sir. Very much."

"Don't mention it," he sneered. "But she's not there."

Perlman felt the sweat in the small of her back as she walked away from him. She breathed slowly and counted.

At the top of the stairs, she approached a young blond-haired man seated at a desk. He rose and went into the office, and in a few moments he ushered her in and returned to his desk.

Major Goldstein listened and then looked at his watch. "You missed her by almost exactly twenty-four hours, Ms. Perlman. Right now she should be preparing to depart Haifa for a couple of kibbutzim on her way to Tiberias. I assigned her to escort a visiting American musician who is performing here this week."

Perlman pleaded with Goldstein to dispatch someone immediately to protect Corporal Arad.

"Please try to relax, Ms. Perlman. This man you describe does not sound like any of the smiling civil servants we are used to seeing around here. Once my adjutant has taken your statement, we will circulate the description and launch a proper investigation. Meanwhile, you and I both know that Corporal Arad is extremely sharp; furthermore, she is traveling with two U.S. government officials. And since your suspect knows even less of her whereabouts than you did five minutes ago, it's unlikely he would figure it out on his own."

"Where in Tiberias is she headed?" Perlman insisted.

"This pianist—Aaron Wood is his name—is playing tonight at the jazz festival there. Tomorrow they return briefly to Tel Aviv before driving down toward Sunday's festival in Eilat. Why don't I call you when she gets—"

"Thank you, sir," Perlman replied, turning toward the door.

"Ms. Perlman," Goldstein called as he rose from his desk. "I can see that Corporal Arad means something to you. Please know that she means much to me as well—and at the moment she is my responsibility, not yours. I must ask you not to do anything foolish. Do not follow her to Tiberias or anywhere else until we know more about this man. If he is indeed dangerous, you will only lead him straight to Corporal Arad. As long as he is casting about unawares, he is likely to make another mistake: he was stupid enough to tip you off, and we will be waiting for him. OK? So please, Ms. Perlman, go about your routine and leave this to us. I will put you and your home on round-the-clock surveillance."

Perlman cringed at this last sentence but smiled. "Thank you, sir. Anat is indeed precious to me. We were very close, and then—" Perlman's voice faltered. "—well, I feel very badly about the way we parted. How ironic that I might never again have heard her name if not for that dreadful man this morning."

"Well," winked Goldstein, "with you and me on her side, she is in good hands, yes? Just try to behave normally, and I will keep you informed."

Perlman thanked him again, went out, and delivered her statement. When she was finished, she asked the adjutant for a private telephone line.

"You may use the one downstairs, next to the kitchen," he replied.

Perlman descended the stairs, aware of at least one pair of blue eyes and of the certainty that all the phones there were tapped. With that in mind, she merely called her office and explained that she was running late.

She walked back to the car, got in, and retrieved the gun. Looking around, she reemerged and walked swiftly through the early beach crowd strolling along Hayarkon Street, turned a corner, and slipped into the Ami Hotel to use a pay phone.

"Mrs. Arad? Rachel. Ani is safe. I know where she is, but I must not tell you, and Muhammad must not go looking for her. The army is watching me and my flat, so my knowledge is useless. Her commander has promised a full investigation; he thinks this man will resurface soon. Meanwhile, you two should sit tight."

"But Rachel—" the older woman began unsteadily.

"Please, Mrs. Arad. You must trust me. The less you know, the better. Keep Muhammad at your side. I'll be in touch."

Perlman hurried out of the hotel and took a different route back to her car. She drove toward work and began to relax. She was the only motorist stopped at the light three blocks from her office when it happened.

Plain of Sharon, Israel

AGAIN AARON WOOD PERFORMED, felt her eyes, and answered questions. After he had walked through the sea of outstretched hands to the back wall and looked at her, she again had taken on the dark intensity that by now had burned itself into him. In her wet black eyes he saw everything, and why was it this way? Why here? Why now?

They drove the short distance to that day's final destination looking forward to checking in, bathing, and sitting down to a quiet meal before the evening concert at Haifa Auditorium.

As the four stepped away from the registration desk, Wood watched Lederman and Fatool head toward the elevator before he touched Arad's shoulder.

She turned to him, glanced at their companions as they looked back, watched Wood motion them on, and smiled. Her forehead wore the dark glow of exercise, and light sand had settled in her black hair and among her long lashes. Her drab uniform hung as it was designed to do, and her boots shifted from side to side as she felt him looking at her after their long first day in and out of the sun.

They stood in the lobby of a breezy hotel with a magnificent sea view and the quiet humming of Western tourists who tomorrow would sleep in before beginning their carefree day in Akko or Nazareth.

"Anat," he said softly, "do you think it would be out of

line for you and me to dine alone this evening?"

"Out of line?" she smiled. "Well, I hope so!"

"You know what I mean. I'm feeling a little guilty, not only about deserting my official hosts, but also about any inappropriate signals we may be sending. On the other hand, I hate the thought of sacrificing a single min—"

"I know." She paused. "So, Aaron Wood, are you asking me for a date?"

"I suppose I am, Anat Arad."

"What if I told you that all I have with me to wear is another military uniform?"

"I'd say you look smashing."

"The pinnacle of good taste, yes?"

"Absolutely. Don't ever wear anything else."

"Wouldn't you get tired of fatigues, as it were?"

"I don't think I could take the impact of seeing you in something that fits properly."

Arad slugged him not too gently on the arm, raising a small cloud of dust and joyous laughter on both sides. "Then fasten your seat belt, pal."

On the way to his room, Wood stopped by Lederman and Fatool's.

"Hi, Aaron. How's it going?"

"Hi, Bernie, Idris. I don't know how to say this, but if I've been breaking any rules by talking with Corporal Arad I ap—"

"Don't be silly, Aaron," replied Lederman. "Besides, we think it's cute."

"Yeah, I was sensing you might."

Lederman and Fatool let him dangle.

"She's very bright," Wood offered, "and has quite an

interesting background."

The two responded only with sincerely raised eyebrows and smiles.

Wood looked down. "So anyway, I was wondering if you guys would mind if she and I had dinner—"

"Relax, man," Fatool said. "She knows where not to wander in these parts. Hell, you're in better hands with her than you'd be with either of us."

"It is an interesting feeling," Wood reflected, "being with a woman who could save your life as automatically as we answer the phone."

Lederman and Fatool showed no trace of envy.

"Well," Wood said, moving toward the door, "I'd better hop in the shower. See you."

"Have a good time, Aaron," Fatool said.

"Thanks, Idris."

"By the way," the young man called, "you play wicked piano."

"We too noticed," Lederman added.

"Thanks, guys."

Wood strode down the hall, bathed, and dressed.

When he called for Corporal Arad at her door, there was a momentary hesitation. Then she emerged, resplendent in her crisp, figure-hugging dress whites. She stood in the doorway smiling regally.

"My word. Corporal. I'm speechless."

"That's a new twist, isn't it?"

Wood viewed her as he would a Rodin. "God, you're lovely." He cleared his throat. "Well. Why don't we go downstairs?"

Arad dropped her key into a small black purse and

walked beside him to the elevator. He made every effort not to look at her, both out of respect and in self-defense. He walked no closer to her than he had all day. Once aboard the elevator, he sensed a trace of clean perfume and allowed himself the luxury of noticing that she seemed not to be wearing the slightest touch of makeup.

She smiled back. "Do you think the guys—"

"I had a word with them, actually. Everything is fine."

"Ah. Good. That's good."

"They think we're cute."

"Damn. I knew it."

"Maybe we are."

"You're cute. I'm—" Suddenly she blushed and covered her mouth.

"Do you really think so, Corporal?" he smiled.

She looked down shyly. "Yes."

"Only one of us gets to be beautiful?"

"I didn't think men wanted to be beautiful."

"This is the nineties, Anat. Everyone is beautiful, right?"

She looked at him seriously. "No. Not everyone is. But you are."

Wood reached down and took her hand softly. As the elevator doors opened, he released her into the astonished lobby.

The formal evening concert was a spectacular success. Afterward, Corporal Arad stood to the side with Lederman and Fatool and watched proudly as Wood was feted by the press, politicians, and a large gathering of autograph-seekers.

The four had arrived together in the black sedan.

When they slipped out the back of the hall, they encountered another group of enthusiastic young people, mostly female, holding out pens, paper, and gifts.

"Gee, Aaron, I think they like you," Lederman smiled from the front seat as they pulled slowly away.

"It's great fun when it goes well, yes," Wood responded.

Corporal Arad sat at a dignified distance beside him.

A smaller group of fans awaited them at the hotel, so they pulled around to the side entrance. Lederman stepped out and opened Wood's door as Fatool opened Arad's.

"Thanks, gentlemen," Wood said as the four smiled widely at one another.

Lederman shook his hand and looked across at Arad. "Now, you take good care of our star here," he said. "Uncle will be on the phone bright and early as usual."

Wood and Arad stepped toward the door as Lederman and Fatool got back in the car.

The fans from outside the hotel had moved into the lobby.

Wood had hoped to diffuse any anxiety on Arad's part or the appearance of presumptuousness on his by visiting the bar, but it was obvious they would have no peace there. And he had sent their unfinished bottle of dinner wine to his room.

They smiled at each other and took the side stairs.

As they rounded the second-floor baluster, Arad placed her hand gently in Wood's. "You were wonderful."

"Thank you," he said.

"I'm so pleased for you."

"Thank you, Anat. I felt you there. I've been feeling you there all day."

"Yes." She paused. "It's been *one day*. I feel I've known you forever. This is crazy, isn't it?"

He lightly massaged her hand.

When they reached their floor, Arad stopped and put her free hand on the door. "Wait here," she said, gently pushing him toward the wall. Then she opened the door and disappeared into the hallway. In a few moments, she returned. "Coast is clear," she smiled. "Come on, star."

They walked hand in hand toward their rooms.

They paused at Wood's door. He leaned against the jamb as Arad turned to him and he took both of her hands. "Listen. I'm sure you're tired. Tomorrow is an even longer day. Perhaps I should walk you to your door."

She tightened her fingers slightly around his.

"On the other hand, tomorrows are in short supply."

"Yes."

"That wine won't be fit to drink tomorrow."

"No," she smiled.

"What if you began giving away state secrets?"

"I don't know any. Besides, we're allies, remember?"

"Yes, we are. And we've established that your own secrets are more interesting."

"Much. And that a glass of wine won't release them without my permission."

Wood stopped smiling and lifted her hands to his lapels. "Anat. All silliness aside: I don't know what your experience with men has been like, but I've rather got the impression it hasn't been all that good. I just want you to know that your permission, welfare, and happiness, none of which I would ever have sought to take from you regardless of the manner of our meeting, have in these few hours grown very dear to me. Besides, I've never dated a woman who carried a gun."

"And I've never dated a m— a musician."

"Well, we get a lot of bad press, you know. Most of us are relatively harmless."

"Then open your door, Aaron Wood, before I change my mind."

Once inside the room, each of them stiffened as though they had just come before a firing squad. Each avoided looking at the bed.

Wood reached for a hanger.

Arad looked out the window.

While Wood poured the wine, Arad moved silently about the room, estimating her arrival at his side in time not only to receive her glass but also to steal a glance at the neatly edited manuscript sitting on the desk.

Wood lifted his glass. "To beautiful surprises," he said.

"To beautiful surprises." She drank, turned to the stack of paper, and turned back to Wood.

"It's just an article for a music-history journal. The deadline's coming up."

"May I?" she smiled, glancing again at the title page.

"Sure, if you want to. It's not the most riveting sub—"

"Oh, God, Aaron: Monteverdi is one of my favorites." She grew serious and read the first few pages as though they were water from a canteen.

Wood moved a step away.

"Aaron, this is very good." She read a few more pages, smiling with admiration. Without looking up, she asked,

"Is there anything you don't do well?"

He shifted uncomfortably. "Well, I'm very bad with artillery." He removed his tie.

Anat Arad turned from the desk, put down her glass, and faced him.

Aaron Wood put his glass beside hers, stepped forward, took her chin gently in his fingers, lifted her stunning face to him, and kissed her lightly on the lips. It was the shortest, softest, most peace-giving kiss he had ever known. He drew back, and she opened her inescapable eyes. Without touching her anywhere else, he leaned forward and kissed her again, as softly and briefly as before. He moved up and kissed her forehead, each soft eyebrow, the tip of her nose, each cheek, each trembling eyelid, each jaw line, under each tiny chocolate ear, and each side of her neck before returning to her full and now slightly parted lips. Suddenly he was pierced with realization, and he kissed her more urgently until he felt her tears on his hands.

He pulled back, brought her to his shoulder, and bowed his head.

Slowly Arad brought her arms up around him and held him to her. He could feel that her hands were not open but were formed into tight fists. She stood shaking in his arms.

He guided her over to the bed and sat down beside her. "Wait." He went into the bathroom, brought back a soft towel, and placed it in her hands.

She took it without speaking and fell back against him crying.

He stroked her tightly bound hair and her hard shoulders. The two sat in silence for many minutes before

Arad regained her composure and sat up a little. He softly massaged her neck.

"This isn't as easy as I had thought it would be," she said softly.

He said nothing.

"Aaron." She looked down at her hands. "Oh, God. Aaron. I am so horrible. I haven't been entirely honest with you. I have not been at all honest with you, and I have used you to discover something about myself. From the moment we met, I felt you, knew you, knew that if it could be anyone it could be you. Do you remember when you thought I was going to ask you whether you believed in fate? Well, that wasn't what I was going to ask. *I love you,* Aaron. I'm in love with you. Christ, Aaron, I've known you less than twenty-four hours, and I shudder at the thought of your leaving me. You are so gentle and right, and what you do is everything I have ever thought love is. Your hands on me sing like your music, and your mouth makes me weak and hungry. I want you more than I have ever wanted anything in my life. These things are crazy and impulsive and careless, but they are not wrong. They are not selfish and frightened of the vicious passage of so little time. And I cannot bear to stay here another minute and feel you burning into my shame." She started to rise.

"Anat," he whispered, gently pulling on her shoulder. "You can't go like this. Whatever it is, it goes back long before today. Release it. Give it to me."

"I cannot tell you how it rips me apart to think that I can only disappoint you."

"Look at me, Anat. You cannot disappoint me except by continuing to wear your pain where I can't try to heal it."

"Hold me, Aaron. Don't make me look at you when I tell you this."

He wrapped her in his arms and stroked her fragrant hair.

"Aaron." She took a deep breath. "I have never been with a man."

He was silent a few moments. "Never?"

"Never."

"You are a virgin?"

"I am what is called a virgin." She paused. "Aaron Wood, I am a lesbian."

He held her closer. "God. Are you being unfaithful to someone right now?"

"No."

"As of how recently?"

"I've been on my own about a year."

"Have you always known this about yourself?"

"Since childhood. It has more than a little to do with Father's murder and with the brutality I saw in so many— well, most men."

"This must feel very unnatural to you, Anat."

"No." She paused. "But it's the moment of truth."

He held her in silence for a while. "Speaking of which, please don't feel you've deceived or manipulated me. First, whatever becomes of us, I'm honored that you chose me, even by mistake, or even if it was only because you knew that in a few days you might never have to look at me again. And second, I had no right today to encourage you to discuss your family and your politics. The knowledge you gave helped me understand your people and consequently is helping me do the job I came over here to do."

She embraced him tightly. "I knew, and you know I knew. God, you feel good."

"Yes, your behavior has not been especially homosexual. What prompted this experiment?"

"I'm so glad you're not angry with me. Well, it's the oddest thing: As I said, my lifestyle has had more to do with environment than chemistry. Most of my relationships have begun as friendships that moved on to something more. I turned to girls and women because they were all the things you said today—and because when they hurt you it was only on the inside. Eventually I learned that women can be just as crude and thoughtless as men. And then just recently, just in the last few weeks, I've developed this alien stirring. One day I found myself— you're going to think this is so warped—staring into the mirror and fantasizing that I was a man, that I was making love to a man who was my reflection. Now, let me tell you what's even stranger than that—and don't you dare laugh—"

"Dear, you haven't told a good joke yet."

"I just don't want you to think I'm going all weird on you here."

"You've laid out some very heavy information today, Corporal. Weird at this point might be just the thing."

"Well, I think this fantasy was a vision, a visitation. I think I felt you coming to me, Aaron, that something was going to happen to change my life. I just didn't have any appropriate model to go by, so I made one up."

"Well, as a matter of fact, I too have been feeling a

certain order in the timing of my recent breakup and in various fantasies that all seemed to make sense this morning in Goldstein's office. I've never felt anything like what I've been feeling for you today. If it's the stars or God's will, I'm glad to read the literature, my delicious Palestinian Catholic lesbian friend."

"Have you ever had such a vision of androgyny? You're not rough like other men."

"I'm not afraid of myself, if that's what you mean."

"What about gay fantasies? Am I embarrassing you?"

"I've been propositioned often enough. I guess with me it *is* chemical. And while we're traveling the back roads here, let me assure you that I'm not expecting to convert you to some righteous new highway. I would have no trouble sharing you with a woman—assuming the feeling were mutual and it didn't lead to more pain."

"I hope I can do you justice."

"You already have."

"May I ask you something?"

"Anything."

"Does my past turn you on?"

He smiled. "Sure. There's the beautiful imagery, the challenge, the gossamer unknown world—the whole idea of a society of women is sexy and wonderful—"

"The possibilities—"

"To be honest, I think we could do a lot worse than to spend a little time concentrating on each other."

"I agree. Now come here, Aaron Wood, and kiss me."

18

Tel Aviv

THE LEFT HAND WAS ROUGH, and it stank of tobacco as it darted in and closed hard across Rachel Perlman's mouth, snapping her against the headrest. She gasped as she felt metal being pressed against the side of her head. She tried to look to her left, but the callused hand and the painful steel held her fast. A morass of greasy flesh, body odor, and foul breath swept into the window. Wet lips squirmed in her ear.

"Step on any pedal and you will die," said the low voice. "Make any sound or any unnatural motion and you will die." Suddenly the hand jerked around and unsnapped the back-door lock, and in the next instant he was behind her. "Smile like a good girl, Miss Perlman."

Perlman sat stiffly and looked straight ahead. As the light turned green and she eased forward, she became aware once again of the sweat running down her back.

"Before we have a misunderstanding such as my associate described, Miss Perlman, please hand your purse back to me. There is no reason for further unpleasantness."

Perlman glanced into the mirror and did as commanded.

"Thank you, Miss Perlman. I have no intention of harming you. Please turn right at the next light and continue to the end of the street."

Perlman tried to breathe.

"You're not smiling, Miss Perlman. You're so pretty when you smile."

"Where are you taking me?" she asked quietly.

"Now, I didn't ask you to speak, did I? I asked you merely to smile. That's right. We're just going for a little private talk. After our talk, I will bid you farewell and you may go about your day. Everyone needs a break in the routine now and then."

They drove many blocks in silence.

"Ah, good: turn left here and then immediately right into the parking lot. Go to the far end and pull around behind the building. There's really no need for tears, Miss Perlman. I'm certain you are eager to show me the good manners you would have displayed earlier to my partner had you not been sleepy and confused. Here, this is fine. Please turn off the engine and hand the keys back to me. Thank you. Now step out and stand still."

Perlman steadied herself against the side of the car. In a moment, the foul smell was washing over her from behind and the hard metal was pressing the wet blouse against her spine.

"Through that door, please."

She felt the hand on her backside as the probe knocked against her vertebrae. With her knees on the verge of collapse, she made her way over a small pile of broken concrete and steel reinforcement wire and into a large empty warehouse illuminated by three broken plastic skylights.

"Straight to the far left corner, please, Miss Perlman."

She walked, her stomach churning.

"Here we are, Miss Perlman. Step into my office, if you

245

would, please."

She was pushed abruptly into a small windowless, unpainted room furnished only with a gray metal desk, an old oak swivel chair, and a clothes tree. The desk, chair, and floor were covered in a thin layer of sandy dust.

"Please forgive the slight untidiness, Miss Perlman. I must have a word with the staff." The man reached into a drawer and pulled out a soiled white hand towel. "Please be so kind, Miss Perlman," he said smiling as he motioned toward the furniture.

"I am comfortable standing," she said.

"Oh, no, Miss Perlman. Please, I insist."

Perlman turned and dusted the chair.

"Thank you, Miss Perlman. Now the desk, please, if you don't mind."

She complied, feeling his eyes as his smell permeated the little room.

"Thank you, Miss Perlman. Please: have a seat," he said.

After she had placed herself stiffly, the man leaned forward, put his big yellowed hands on the arms of the creaking chair, and pushed it hard against the desk. "There, now."

"Please, sir. I don't know what it is you want to know. Please let me go."

"Now, see, there you go again: bad form. You've already injected a negative tone into our discourse. How can you possibly be certain you don't know the answer to whatever innocuous question your host may ask you?"

"Please, sir." She lowered her head.

"As a matter of fact, I do have a question for you. And I

think you do indeed know the answer to my question. I think it's quite possible that you were telling my associate the truth when you said you did not know the answer. But I feel quite confident that after your little chat with Major Goldstein and your gay promenade along the seashore you are virtually brimming with helpful new insights, yes?"

"I asked Goldstein, but he wouldn't tell me."

"Wouldn't tell you, Miss Perlman? Wouldn't tell the concerned former bunkmate who carries in her purse a most charming photo of two, shall we say, extremely close girlfriends?"

Perlman struggled to contain herself as the man paced slowly back and forth in front of her gesticulating with a large pistol equipped with a silencer.

"I'm most surprised, Miss Perlman. Major Goldstein's reputation for compassion must be overstated. I find it difficult to believe he would withhold from Corporal Arad's pretty concubine—oh, but I suppose Goldstein knows only that the two of you are old pals—such an innocent piece of information."

"Well, he did. Sir. Please, I don't know where she is."

As he paced before her, the man began occasionally brushing the barrel of the silencer against the front of his dark-gray polyester trousers. Perlman averted her eyes.

"Fortunately, Miss Perlman, I'm not in a hurry. We have all day, really, to get acquainted. Please relax and take your time."

"I tell you, I do not know where she is."

The man stopped pacing, stood directly in front of her, and continued stroking himself with the silencer. The large acrid left hand grabbed her chin and made her face

247

forward. "Think very clearly, Miss Perlman."

Perlman closed her eyes and tried to turn away.

"Please, Miss Perlman. There is no need to be upset." He paused. "Speaking of bad manners, I must apologize on behalf of our friend here. He seems to have a mind of his own, yes?"

She did not answer.

"Since our friend has inserted himself into the conversation, we may as well show him the courtesy of acknowledgment, don't you agree?"

Perlman opened her eyes briefly and closed them again. Then she felt the metal tapping her left temple. She reopened her eyes and fixed them on the front of the man's trousers.

"Good," the man said. "And now, it is only proper that the two of you should be formally introduced." The man spread his legs, stepped forward, and closed his knees hard on the outside of Perlman's thighs.

Perlman trembled and wept softly. When she shut her eyes, the silencer tapped her on the side of the head. She glanced up at the grinning face and considered her options.

"I think you've got his attention, Miss Perlman. In fact, I'd say he's eager to come out and say hello."

"Please, sir. I cannot help you. Goldstein has me under surveillance. Any second now—"

"Oh, yes, you must mean the robust young Mossad gentleman who accompanied you at some distance on your promenade. Well, he too appeared wanting in proper etiquette: seems he was rather brazenly admiring your derriere as you walked. Alas, before I could have an admonishing word with him, he met with a most unfortunate accident."

Perlman bowed her head.

"Perhaps you noticed your automobile was running a bit heavily just now—I'm surprised you didn't mention it, inasmuch as your military domain was the motor pool."

Perlman's mind raced.

"Oh, now look, Miss Perlman," sighed the man, "this digression seems to have left our friend looking somewhat downcast. On the other hand, in his present state he may be easier to coax into the light."

Perlman took a deep breath, silently shifting her feet to clear away some of the dust on the floor. She opened the man's fly, fighting down the sudden lurch in her gut.

"There. That wasn't so difficult, was it, you two?" He smiled politely. "Miss Rachel Perlman, it is my pleasure to introduce you to my dear young friend Corporal Anatoliy Aradkin."

Perlman winced.

"Tell me, Miss Perlman: have you had breakfast?"

She did not answer.

"Well, I'm happy to tell you we've arranged a special treat for you this morning: a full three-course presentation. And if you're a good girl, you'll even get dessert. You'd like something warm and sweet, wouldn't you, Miss Perlman?"

She trembled. "Please, sir. I cannot tell you what you want to know. Why can't you, please, why can't you let me go?"

"Let you go? Without a good solid breakfast? I wouldn't think of such a thing. First, our appetizer."

Tears ran down her face and onto her blouse.

"Open your mouth, please, Miss Perlman."

She looked at the gun and closed her eyes.

"Wider, please, Miss Perlman. Yes, that's nice. Thank you."

She started to vomit.

"I'm so sorry, Miss Perlman," the man said. "Someone of Corporal Aradkin's commanding presence must be most careful."

Perlman gagged again.

"That's right. I'm beginning to think the two of you are going to get on just splendidly."

Sweat began running from her scalp. Suddenly the man pulled back.

"Well, that was delightful, don't you think? Now it's time for our entrée. Stand up, please, Miss Perlman."

The man stepped back.

"Please, sir!" she cried.

"Oh, now, there's no need for humility, Miss Perlman. You've clearly earned this lovely entrée. Stand up, please."

Perlman rose slowly and stood bracing herself against the arms of the chair.

"Good. Now take off your clothes, Miss Perlman."

"Please!"

"Miss Perlman, I must tell you these crocodile tears of yours are growing tiresome. Take off your clothes. Please." He brushed the outline of her breasts with the silencer.

Perlman looked at the clothes tree and measured the distance. She undressed and hung her things on the tree.

"Very lovely indeed, Miss Perlman. Your photograph hardly does you justice. Now sit on the desk, please."

"Sir, I—"

"Miss Perlman, please just sit on the desk facing me."

She did as commanded.

"Very nice. Now lean back on your elbows, please, and raise your legs," he said as he pushed her shoulder. "Open your eyes." He jabbed the silencer into her left breast.

She stared at the sweating face and did not realize she had cried out. The dripping skin and acrid odor swam around her head, the rough left hand pushed hard against her right knee, the silencer trembled and dug into the skin between her ribs, and her pain, humiliation, astonishment, and hatred were so intense that she felt nothing. When she saw traces of her blood she thought nothing, and eventually she heard nothing. She thought only of Ani, saw, heard, smelled, and tasted only Ani, knew that if this was to be the end it was for Ani that she had lived and for Ani that she had died.

Then suddenly he stopped.

She looked up at the distorted animal face and nearly laughed.

"Well, I—must—say, Corporal Aradkin certainly is— having a lovely morning. And now, as promised, since you've shown such exemplary table manners, it's time for dessert." The man stepped back and replaced the chair. "Get up, please, and take your seat."

She stepped down onto the floor and sat in the chair.

"I must ask you one more time: is there nothing you would like to tell me this morning?"

She did not answer.

"Nothing at all?" he asked as he lightly stroked himself. "You know, Miss Perlman, time has a way of slipping by so fast that we hardly notice before it is too late. I would hate to think that we have overlooked any detail that could have made your stay more enjoyable."

She did not answer.

"Well, then."

The man stepped forward and held her thighs as before, and she did not delay or resist. She watched the gun and the man's jerking body. Finally she positioned her feet and waited for the moment when her life would reenter her body and demand that she reclaim or relinquish it.

At that moment, Rachel Perlman grabbed the gun barrel and thrust it up and over the man's thumb. As she heard a bone snap, she drove her right fist with all her might. As he began to double forward she bit him as viciously as she could. Leaning back hard against the desk, she recoiled her right leg and kicked the man's nose into his brain. Before his reeling body could hit the floor, she seized the gun and fired it into his face and everywhere below. She watched him career backward staring with monstrous widened eyes and piglike nostrils. He slammed into the wall and collapsed in a seated position. She looked at him for several minutes as the rivulets flowing from his body slowly became pools. Finally she walked across the room, bent down, and put her lips close to his ear. "She just left Haifa. Sir."

19

Gaza

MUHAMMAD KADIR SPRINTED across the courtyard and took the old stone steps two at a time, cursing himself for still not having installed the railing that leaned against the building at street level. He tapped twice and used his key.

His mother was seated by the telephone knitting another pullover that both knew he would never wear. Her eyes had the misty glaze of one who has been looking long out to sea.

"Any news?" he asked.

"Only that she is *safe,* whatever that means," his mother replied softly.

"But she's not at the security office?"

"Apparently not. Rachel was about as forthcoming as you've been." She waited. "What's going on, Muhammad?"

"Nothing's going on. It's just that this guy is a madman, and the less you know of him, and him of you, the better."

"What on earth would he want with me, Muhammad? And since when do you associate with madmen?"

"This is no time for questions. We must get you out of here for a while. Where's a little suitcase?"

"What have you got yourself involved in?"

"I'm sorry. I can't tell you. I'm not even sure it's he. But if it is, neither of us wants to be anywhere near him. He surely assumes I know where Ani is. He managed to find Rachel, and in his search for me he'd have little trouble finding you. I cannot let that happen. Now, get up and pack a small bag, and be quick about it."

"This is insane, Muhammad. I'm not going any—"

"Yes it is, Mother, I'm terribly sorry about it, and, God willing, I will put a stop to it. Meanwhile, though, you're coming with me right now whether you like it or not. I'm only going to settle you in with some friends for a few days."

"What friends?"

"Faculty. People I can trust. You'll be fine, and soon this thing will be in the past."

"And you will tell me what in God's name is going on?"

"Mother, that I cannot. Believe me, in this case, the truth is worse than a lie. Please. Look, I made a stupid mistake, fell in with this person and his lunatic ideas—and since he found both Ani and me at the same time, she too is up to here in it. There is still time, but we must take action. You must get up, *now*."

Mirim Arad looked at her grown son and wrestled simultaneously with her urge to slap him and with her unforgettable guilt at having given him up and then having regained him only through tragedy. She looked back at the sea and lamented the peacelessness of her life and of all the lives she had known in this land that was not hers. She looked around at her small flat and at her things and tried to believe that they were no more hers than was the agitated young man standing by the door begging to save her from a foolish unnecessary peril whose nature and reason were not hers to know. She set the yarn and the trembling needles aside and rose from the chair.

"Good. Thank you," Kadir said gently.

She did not answer as she walked slowly to the bedroom.

Kadir shuffled over to the chair and stood by the window. When his mother emerged with her old overnight bag, he held out the yarn. "I hope you saved room for this," he said.

After settling her in across town, Kadir went out and sat in his rusty subcompact. If al-Malik was still in the dark and was headed his way, in which case he would arrive within the hour, Kadir could confront or ambush him there in Gaza and the whole thing would be over. But al-Malik had many sources in Tel Aviv; Perlman may have been but his easy first choice. Kadir felt confident that his mother was in a place al-Malik would have no reason to seek her. Kadir decided he had only one choice: to go to Tel Aviv and try to gain an audience with Goldstein. The officer had not hesitated to inform Rachel, whose only connection to Arad was a bit of compulsory service; surely he would agree to see Arad's own brother. Maybe Goldstein did not even know Kadir was a Palestinian. Maybe he would not care if he did know. And there was always the chance that Kadir would intercept al-Malik on the highway and have the pleasure of leaving him for the jackals.

But Muhammad Kadir's drive north to Tel Aviv was notable only in that it reminded him of various neglected automotive details, and in that the barren landscape and the shimmering sea looked particularly beautiful on this last day before Jerusalem.

He began to sense imbalance as he wound his way

along Hayarkon toward the embassy. The beach crowds were standing rather than strolling, and they were not facing the water. Motor and even foot traffic came to a standstill a few blocks from the building. All parking space was occupied, and a glance into the mirror confirmed that the whole area was about to crystallize. Kadir pulled as close as he could to the line of parked cars, got out, and started running until he could only walk and walked until he could only push his way apologizing through the dense crowd. He saw the smoke from a block away.

He got as far as the guardhouse before he realized his was one among many faces huddled together outside the courtyard, staring up at a shattered window on the second floor. An ambulance and a fire engine were pulled up halfway onto the sidewalk, but their lights had been turned off. A few grim-faced young men in uniform were standing near the door.

He watched until the paramedics came through the door with the body bag. He searched the faces, and he knew that the lives of a thousand horrified civilians meant no more to al-Malik than the life of one kind old soldier who could have retired years ago. And he knew that somewhere out there beyond the faces was Ani, that somewhere perhaps nearer was Rachel, who knew where Ani was, and that all he knew of this Rachel was a telephone number scribbled on a scrap in his pocket. As he began to move away, he overheard a few more words from the guardhouse.

"I never saw him drink anything but Kentucky bourbon."

"I was in the commissary this morning, and Edelman

showed me the requisition: a full case of the best cabernet he could lay his hands on."

"I'll be damned."

"I told Edelman to sign for it anyway: we'll drink it in the old guy's honor."

20

Galilee

THEY RODE IN SILENCE FOR SEVERAL minutes holding hands and smiling at each other like teenagers. Water and trees that the day before had been only beautiful now took on the quality of a dream.

"Do you suppose they fell for the wake-up call?" she smiled playfully.

"I doubt it," he answered. "But you must understand that the State Department is the closest thing we have to the samurai code of *Bushido:* saving face is everything."

"Yes," she said mistily. "In your face I see everything."

"I love you, Anat Arad."

"And I love you, Aaron Wood."

He smiled exuberantly. "You know, I don't feel much like playing the piano today: why don't we just keep driving?"

"That's a lovely idea."

"Yes."

"Of course, we'd have to pass through Syria and perhaps be blown to tiny little bits." She took a deep breath. "You'll be fine," she said. "Won't you?"

"Sure," Wood answered. "*And now, ladies and gentlemen, Corporal Arad and I will demonstrate a few uses for the piano that Signor Cristofori perhaps failed to imagine—*"

"Was I really OK?" she asked seriously.

He gave her the same look of disbelief she had elicited

with similar questions the day before.

Eventually they reached the day's first performance, the lunch table, and the second performance. On each occasion, Anat Arad and Aaron Wood carried out their duties, and their composure only increased their desire for each other. Corporal Arad stood in the wings that night in Tiberias and suppressed tears as Wood bowed to a long ovation and received a bouquet of red roses.

Wood strode off stage and placed the bouquet in Arad's arms.

Since on this night Tiberias was teeming with jazz connoisseurs, Wood and Arad lingered undisturbed at a lakeside table with cups of tea, the easy air, and the low murmur of voices.

"Aaron, I'm so proud of you."

"As I am of you."

"How so? All you've seen me do is drive the jeep."

"Corporal, I don't know the local terminology, but that's not exactly what I would call last night."

"No," she giggled. "But you made it so easy." Arad grew serious and bowed her head. "Aaron? If, I mean, if somehow we could, would you ever teach me the piano?"

"It would be my honor."

"Really?"

"Remember Robert and Clara Schumann."

"True. Of course, he ended up in the loony bin. God, I love you."

"And I love you."

"What the hell are we going to do?"

He looked around. "What we're going to do right now is get up from this table and go inside before we make the front page of tomorrow's paper."

They went to their room, and he took down her long black hair.

21

Tel Aviv

RACHEL PERLMAN'S BLEEDING seemed to have stopped. She stood by the door and did not look back at the man, the chair, or the desk. As for the agent in the trunk of her car, she would simply have to dump him along the road to Tiberias. Perlman acknowledged what she was thinking on behalf of a girl who wanted nothing to do with her. She reached into her purse, pulled out the gun, and walked painfully but swiftly out of the building.

She climbed into her sunbaked car and suddenly doubled forward. While she was still reasonably certain she could drive, she started the engine and wound slowly out of the industrial park. She was somewhere near the north railway station, so she felt her way west over to Weizmann Street and pulled into the lot at Ichilov Hospital.

She took a deep breath and winced. Feeling faint, she held the purse before her and nearly made it to the desk before collapsing in the arms of a young nurse who had seen her come in.

"I've been—" Perlman began almost inaudibly as the woman eased her into a wheelchair.

"Yes."

Perlman was in and out of consciousness during the examination, but she came around when the nurse told her it was all right to shower. She emerged, gathered on a soft robe, and was ushered into the quiet room where she would rejoin her nurse and face a counselor and a young female police officer.

"And Major Goldstein?" the officer asked when Perlman was finished. "When did you last talk with him?"

"As I told you," Perlman answered, weighted by fatigue, "the first and last time I ever talked with him was this morning in his office. Why?"

"Ms. Perlman, what time did you leave Major Goldstein's office?"

"I don't know—nine, nine-thirty, by the time they were through interviewing me."

"Ms. Perlman, are you aware that Major Hiram Goldstein was killed this morning?"

"What!"

"Yes. By a package bomb. Our people are still over there mopping up."

"Oh! God! No!"

The officer studied her. "It happened not long after you were there with him, Ms. Perlman. Unfortunately, the timer was destroyed, as were any prints. So determining who delivered the package, and when, will take some time." She paused. "More unfortunate, perhaps, is the fact that no one remembers his receiving any visitor this morning except you."

Perlman was stunned. "Officer," she began unsteadily, "I don't know what you are getting at, but any of the men who watched me walk in and out of that building can tell you I carried nothing with me."

"They all distinctly remember your large expensive purse there."

"My God!" Perlman cried to the other two women, "I

went to Major Goldstein for help, and he most graciously provided it." She swallowed air. "The beast that raped me is the one who killed Goldstein's man—a man I never saw and on whom I assure you my fingerprints will not be found—and stuffed him into my car. Now, if we are fin—"

"No one is trying to get at anything, Ms. Perlman, except the truth. We have to follow every—"

"Well, I've told you the truth, I've just been through the most horrible experience of my life, my best friend is somewhere out there being pursued by murderers, the man who was trying to save her is now dead, and you're sitting there—" Perlman broke down against the nurse's shoulder.

The officer leaned forward. "Ms. Perlman, I'm very—"

"I think there's been enough of this," the nurse said softly as she stroked Perlman's hair.

The cop rose and placed her hand on Perlman's shoulder. "Rachel. It's been a horrible morning for us all."

Perlman nodded slightly, and the other two women looked toward the door.

"I'm going to need your car keys," the officer continued softly.

Perlman pointed to her purse on the tray. The other two women watched the cop reach in, lift out the ring, detach the car keys, and replace the others.

She touched Perlman's shoulder again and walked to the door. "When you're ready, I'll take you home."

After the cop left, Perlman talked briefly with the counselor and the nurse. They kept Perlman's clothes as evidence and gave her some things to wear home.

When the three women came out of the room, the

officer smiled apologetically at them. She took Perlman's arm and escorted her down the hall and out of the building.

"When will I get my car back?" Perlman asked as the officer helped her into the cruiser.

"Soon," she replied gently. "You never saw the Mossad agent?"

"No. The Arab told me about him only to intimidate me."

The officer was quiet as she settled into her seat but glanced a few times at her passenger. "You know, Rachel," she smiled as they pulled away, "what you did this morning took courage." The young cop then faced forward and gripped the wheel. "It happened to me once."

Perlman looked at her.

"Nothing nearly so awful as what you went through. But it was against my will, just the same. Captain of the debate team, popular guy—our first date. No one believed my side of it. Today, he's one of the most successful lawyers in Tel Aviv. Guess what he specializes in."

The two women looked at each other and burst out laughing.

"I wish I'd had those nails of yours: he'd be down at Mann starring in *Aida*." She grew quiet and serious. "It's why I joined the force."

Perlman looked around and welcomed the sight of her fashionable building. "Thank you, Officer—" She glanced at the nametag.

"Menuhin. Please call me Nora."

"Thank you."

"Look, about the questions: Goldstein and my dad

served together. Hiram was practically an uncle."

"I'm sorry," Perlman said, shifting slightly.

"Here, I'll walk you in."

Menuhin helped Perlman out of the car and accompanied her inside. Both smiled discreetly at the plainclothesman pacing the hall on Perlman's floor. Menuhin insisted on opening the door and going in first. For a moment, they faced each other awkwardly in the living room before Menuhin extended her hand.

"Get some rest, Rachel," she smiled warmly. "And here: call me anytime. I mean it."

"Thank you." She held open the door and watched Menuhin walk down the hall. Then she looked in the other direction to confirm that the plainclothesman was still there, and she locked her door.

Suddenly Perlman remembered the time. As she started to dial her office, she found she had a message:

"Rachel: This is Muhammad Kadir, Anat's brother. I've been trying to reach you all morning. Sorry, I don't know where you work. Please call me as soon as you can."

She wrote down the number and erased the message. As she did so, she thought about the recorded voice and how it rose and fell in a familiar manner. She badly needed sleep, but she figured Kadir probably had not slept much lately himself.

"Shalom. Picasso." There was restaurant background noise.

"This is Ms. Perlman returning Mr. Kadir's call."

"One moment, please."

In a few moments, the kind young voice came on the

line sounding distracted.

"Muhammad? This is Rachel Perlman."

"Thanks. Listen, this place is nuts. Is there somewhere quiet we can meet?"

"Why don't you come over to my place?"

"Is it safe?"

"Big Brother is watching me."

"That beats what's watching me. Have you had lunch?"

Perlman realized she was starving. "No."

"I'll bring something from here."

Perlman set down the receiver and smiled at the music in his voice. She limped back and changed her clothes.

Muhammad Kadir shuffled down the hall about twenty minutes later. When he stopped at Perlman's door, the plainclothesman approached him and peered into his bag.

"Sorry, this is for the lady," Kadir smiled.

The man looked him over, frisked him briefly, and waited with him by the door.

Perlman had already decided to make a prudent show of greeting Kadir as an old friend, but the startling resemblance made it too easy. "It's all right, sir," she beamed as she opened her door wide.

Once they were inside, Perlman raised a finger to her lips, walked Kadir into the middle of the room, and extended her hand. Kadir laughed softly, shifted his bag, and shook the hand. They stood smiling at each other for a moment.

"Here, let me take that," Perlman said. "Thank you so much for doing this," she said as she walked the bag stiffly into the kitchen.

"I'm grateful for the change of venue."

Perlman smiled back at him as the aroma of breakfast began to fill the air.

"The special," he said. "Comes with the room at the Aviv."

"Perfect," she replied. "Glass of milk?"

"Do you mind if I use your—"

"Down the hall to the left."

When he returned, she was already at the table.

"I hope you don't mind," she said, as her fork and a chunk of bread jockeyed back and forth like a catcher and a third baseman who know the series is theirs to lose.

"Not at all." He tried not to watch her. "You have a lovely place, Rachel."

"Thank you," she said between bites, looking around comfortably.

"What do you do?"

"I run an ad agency."

"I should shut up and let you eat."

"No, no," she mumbled with her mouth half full and the tiebreaker wearing fast. "You?"

"I teach college English."

"That's right: Ani said you would be on sabbatical in the States."

"Yeah, at UCLA this past year. I stayed with a friend we grew up with."

"Ah."

He gazed out the window. "So, you were bunkmates."

"Yes, for a while."

Kadir put his curiosity on hold. "Well. Why don't you tell me where she is, so we can keep her away from this piano teacher."

Perlman drained her glass. She quickly erased her white mustache and smiled. "God, that was good. Thank you so much, Muhammad. Dinner's on me, OK?"

"As long as it isn't eggs and coffee."

"You have my word."

Kadir tugged at his sea-green golf shirt. "I'm not exactly prepared for fine dining."

She played with the stem of her glass. "I'll fix us something here."

He could see her eyes getting sleepy. "So, you took the day off?" he asked.

"Uh, yeah. That guy showed up at dawn and scared the hell out of me, I went down and saw Goldstein, and—"

"You know about Goldstein?"

"Yeah. I heard it on the radio. I called here and got your message, so—"

"I think the guy who visited you this morning iced Goldstein, as punishment for reassigning Ani. Where he slipped up was in letting you find out where she is." He looked at her seriously. "I'm surprised you weren't followed."

"I was—" Perlman stiffened and looked away.

"Did you get a look at him? Was it the same guy?"

"No, I don't know. I guess Mossad scared him off. We can't go anywhere without drawing a crowd, and what I really need right now—oh, I'm sorry. You came all the way up here for information, and I'm falling apart on you."

"No, it's all right. Why don't you go back and catch some sleep?"

"Are you sure?"

"Absolutely. I've been eyeing your sofa since I walked in here."

"I guess right now we're not much good to Ani or anyone el—" Suddenly her eyes widened. "Muhammad, where's your mother?"

Kadir touched her hand and smiled. "She's safe, with friends of mine. She went under protest, of course." He paused. "I just wish I knew where al-Malik is."

"Who?"

"Your visitor. Go to bed, Rachel. I'll guard the living room. If I snore, just call in the hall monitor."

"I won't hear you," she yawned as she floated down the hall.

Tel Aviv

KHALED AL-MALIK PARKED SEVERAL blocks back, walked into the industrial park, and was about to round the corner of the building when he saw flashing blue light reflecting off the sun-bleached wall of the building next door. He had decided to go on to Jerusalem and set up for Plan B, but he had waited an extra hour hoping to hear from Abdullah. Either he too had jumped ship or al-Malik had grossly underestimated willowy Rachel Perlman. He walked around the opposite side, jumped up from the loading dock to the fire escape, and tiptoed across the roof to the skylight closest to the little room Abdullah seriously called his office. Al-Malik was familiar with the place, having once enjoyed an arrangement with Abdullah, a freelance film crew, and a dozen teenage girls who had actually believed they were auditioning for French modeling agencies. From his present vantage point, al-Malik could see that a more prosaic form of photography was taking place; but he could not see the subject. Only after the door was opened wide enough for the stretcher did he catch a glimpse of the splayed black shoes and dusty charcoal cuffs.

Al-Malik did not want his anger over the growing number of people he should long ago have killed to diffuse his concentration on the one person he had planned all along to kill, with or without the teammates he had once considered his students but who apparently had decided to skip commencement. *I will deliver their diplomas personally,* he thought as he watched the paramedics struggle with the big corpse.

Why had his flock lost the faith? Had he not made perfect sense? You simply assassinate each Israeli premier, regardless of whatever artificial olive branch he extends when things are quiet or whatever belligerent stance he assumes when a few hot-blooded kids take to the streets, regardless of which side is in power. You do it cleanly and professionally, with a deft combination of inside and outside help, preferably early in the term for maximum publicity. Eventually the government will be so weakened and demoralized that the disparate Arab states will see their opening and unite long enough to obliterate the Zionists once and for all. With enough strength and surprise, they could be recycling Knesset letterhead before the lights went on in the White House.

And what *about* the great Phallus of Freedom? Would it not welcome the gentle fingertips of Sister Palestine with the same self-righteous pulsation that eventually greets every other fait accompli? If Saddam Hussein suddenly started behaving like a good German, would not the next day find him glad-handing in the Rose Garden and chatting with Barbara Walters?

Khaled al-Malik simply could not understand where his believers had gone wrong.

He slipped quietly over the edge, down to the ground, and out to the street before the ambulance doors were closed. He walked back to his car, watched the sad little procession drive by, checked his gas gauge, and set out for Jerusalem.

On the way, he summed up the situation.

Perlman had got to Goldstein, but Goldstein had put her and surely anyone else she contacted under surveillance. Al-Malik had taken care of Goldstein, so Perlman's visit probably had sent out relatively few ripples. And if Abdullah had done his job with his usual flair before Perlman somehow got away from him, she probably had bled to death in some alley or was lying in a bed over at Ichilov with cops at the door.

Kadir had proved more slippery than expected, but news travels fast: he probably was down in Gaza whimpering in his mother's apron strings—and he had the wrong itinerary. Al-Malik regretted every minute he had invested in the likable young fool.

Xenakis was himself a loose cannon, on board only because of the kids. And his hatred for al-Malik was strong—but far more predictable was his old constitution. If Nick were still alive when al-Malik returned to Cairo, it would be a special pleasure to walk in and eliminate him in front of a shop full of midday customers.

The one great imponderable, though, was Anat. *Anatoliy.* He loved pushing her buttons by calling her that. He had especially enjoyed imparting the name game to Abdullah to use against Perlman—he wished he could have seen the redhead's face when Abdullah produced his mighty warrior. For as long as al-Malik could remember, he had missed no chance to dream up a new male name for Anat, since apparently she had started showing the signs of her perverseness a good while before he had spotted the striking twins running laps. He had watched them for several weeks before approaching them. He had noted that, as often as the girl would vanquish her brother at whatever game they played, there were times when it seemed the boy would let her win just because he knew it meant so much to her. Muhammad was kind, no doubt about it. But Anat was perfect, full of anger and single-minded determination—and gorgeous. With the proper encouragement, she could grow into the most effective ice woman in history. So what had happened? How could Goldstein have let her slip away? And where the hell was Bloch during all this? Did he not sit right outside the old Jew's door? Ah, but all the others were small change. Anat was his fierce one-woman war. He had cultivated her with paternal attention, made her introductions, taught her how to infiltrate and to lie so convincingly and with such heartfelt passion and with such a devastating smile that no one in the world could have anticipated her bullet. Up to now, she had known only the adolescent thrill of shredded paper and vaporized melons. She was the only good one of the lot, including the dispensable thugs who drifted in and out from street gangs and detention centers—Abdullah having distinguished himself by virtue of an attribute only God can bestow. And much as he would have liked to, al-Malik had never placed a hand on her. Never had he even discussed such things with her before that night in Paris— because he had wanted to keep her pure. Her hatred of men was her most useful weapon. How easy al-Malik had found it to whip up Anat's ire by pointing out public behaviors that illustrated man's primeval need to subjugate woman and keep her cowering at his feet. Anat had been his one supreme sacrifice. To preserve her for the cause, he had planted in her only those seeds that would guarantee her loyalty. And now this: even she had defected, had learned by some biological time-release her brother's pathetic weakness, had been softened by the strains of some alien voice. Whatever had happened, she had known the last of his kindness. When Khaled al-Malik next saw Corporal Anatoliy Aradkin, her final solution would be the daylong culmination of a decade's ascetic devotion. Al-Malik pictured Anatoliy leather-bound to four corners writhing, flexing her perfect musculature, receiving him in every gentle and cruel way until she would long for the moment of her death with a fervor matching his own lust for the instant he had lived hundreds of times alone in his bed. Then he embraced a new fantasy, one that had insinuated itself only in the days following Anatoliy's disappearance: the opportunity to explore her for as long as she remained warm after fellating his black silencer.

Khaled al-Malik eased into a feeling of pleasant satisfaction.

Tiberias

ANAT ARAD WOKE JUST BEFORE DAWN still in Aaron Wood's left arm, with her head on his chest and her left leg draped across his thighs. She looked at the clock and smiled at the realization that she had nearly thirty minutes to lie there and think.

She had much to think about this day. She would drop Wood off in Tel Aviv, make her excuse, and go to Jerusalem. She would find her spot, and she would direct her faultless eye. She no longer looked forward to the moment. But she knew that she was the best shot, that she had the best opportunity, and that, even if he spotted her, al-Malik would expect her bullet least of anyone's. Wherever Kadir and Xenakis were, Corporal Arad knew where she would be, and that she would be the one to end the madness. She was assigned to the prime minister's auxiliary guard detail and in discovering and eliminating a lone Arab sniper would only be doing her job. What pierced her heart was the thought of spending that much time away from Wood. She would lie to him and hate it, and perhaps she would never tell him the horrible truth of a job for which she had spent her life preparing and from which she now could not wait to escape. Already she rehearsed in her mind the glorious return to his arms and to a future she no longer was willing to imagine without him.

She looked at the clock again. Wood had not stirred.

Without moving any part of her except her left arm, she drew the covers down. Nature took her cue even as Wood continued sleeping peacefully. After a slow crescendo Arad sensed his tide and the dreamlike sound of her name.

She stayed in place until his body had resolved. She treasured the cradle of his arm, and she lay still.

"Good morning, Corporal," he whispered.

"Good morning, Mr. Wood," she replied softly against his skin. "The artist-relations committee is wondering how you are enjoying your tour so far."

He kissed the crown of her hair.

They lay quietly for several more minutes before Wood glanced at the clock. There was an episode of giggling and a brief wrestling match before she was trembling, moaning, and running strong fingers through his hair, arching her back, burying her face into the pillow, and muffling her cries of joy. Finally she laughed and let her arms collapse at her sides. "God, how do you do that?"

He could not resist one more soft kiss.

"Jesus, man!" She cupped her hands over his shoulders and gently pushed him away. He rose to one knee just as the telephone rang.

Aaron Wood was accustomed to various distractions while trying to talk on the phone, but he was hard pressed to ignore those that greeted him when he worked his way toward the nightstand and lifted the receiver.

The two showered quickly and met Lederman and Fatool in the lobby.

The embassy officials were not smiling. Lederman waited for Wood and Arad's bright expressions to dissipate before he held out a copy of that morning's *Jerusalem*

Post.

"Oh, no!" Corporal Arad exclaimed as she found the small headline in the lower right-hand corner of the front page just above Goldstein's photo.

Wood read over her shoulder and winced.

Instinctively, Arad pressed her face against Wood's shoulder and cried.

Lederman and Fatool stepped away as Wood wrapped her in his arms.

"I'm so sorry, Anat," he whispered. "God. Why?"

By the type of explosive described, Arad knew not only why but who. *The gutless bastard,* she thought as her trip to Jerusalem took on more purpose.

At Lederman's cue, the four slipped into the coffee shop and found a booth in the far corner where Arad could collect herself and where they could make sense of what little they knew.

"I talked with Reiger a few minutes ago," Lederman began. "Every indication points to a random act of terrorism. It doesn't seem to have been directed at the embassy. It appears to have been aimed specifically at—" He lowered his head as Arad's crying intensified.

"But why?" Wood repeated.

"No one needs a reason," Lederman shot back as he looked at the table. "Not here. Usually it's in the name of God."

Arad's weeping slowly subsided, and she averted her eyes. "I'm sorry, gentlemen." She moved yet closer to Wood's side. "There was just something about him, a decency—" She drifted into melancholy silence.

"I realize no one's much in the mood," Lederman said,

"but we should eat something before the drive back."

The four opened their menus.

The waitress noticed Arad's inflamed eyes and viewed the men suspiciously until she saw Arad gently stroking her partner's hand.

Another long silence ensued.

Lederman glanced around the table at the three downcast faces and then looked seriously at Arad. In a few moments, he propped the folded newspaper against the wall as if putting it out of his way.

As the waitress brought their coffee, Arad extended her hand. "May I see this?"

Lederman continued viewing Arad at intervals as she turned pages to find the continuation of Goldstein's story and as the four of them busied themselves with the comforting sound of spoons.

Arad did not react visibly when she reached the paragraph near the end of the article describing the young woman who had visited the security office early the previous morning seeking a missing friend who was thought to be stationed there. Such information would not have been mentioned except that the woman had been the major's only visitor. Arad showed no relief as she read that the woman had been questioned briefly and dismissed. As their food arrived, Arad looked up briefly, met Lederman's eyes, and closed the newspaper.

After breakfast, the four checked out and headed to the parking lot. They exchanged brief quiet words and repaired to their separate vehicles.

At the left side of the jeep, Wood touched Arad's shoulder. "Why don't you let me drive today?"

She smiled softly. "Are you sure? It's not allowed, you know."

"It'll be good for us both."

She squeezed his hand as he walked her around to the passenger side.

They pulled out of the lot, out of Tiberias, and onto the road south. They spoke only now and then, resorting for the first time to trite phrases about the scenery.

"There's something I should tell you," Wood said finally.

Arad looked at him as though he had discovered a wedding ring among her keys.

"I promised I wouldn't, but now I think you should know."

Arad turned toward him.

"After Major Goldstein introduced us, he closed the door and told me a little bit about you. Nothing personal, of course, but enough to indicate he knew you were unhappy there. I had met him, Bernie, and Idris two nights before, at a well-lubricated little dinner. The major and I got to talking, and that morning in his office he sort of gave me his blessing to draw you out. It was just as you said, a genuine concern for your well-being."

Arad smiled and dabbed at her eyes.

"He said the greatest thing in the world to him would be someday to see a smile on your face. We bet a bottle of wine on it."

Arad reached for Wood's hand and cried softly. "I love you so much, Aaron."

They rode mostly in silent reflection until they reached the outskirts of Tel Aviv, where Wood signaled ahead and pulled over. "I guess it would look better if you guided us into port," he said.

Arad was still dazed but had lost none of the disarming luster with which she had captured him just north of this neighborhood only two and a half days before.

"Certainly," she smiled crisply. "Thank you again."

As they wound their way through town, the two were seized simultaneously by the same fear.

"God, what if—" Wood began. "I feel terrible for saying this, but what if Goldstein's replacement sees no reason for your being with me and separates us?"

Arad looked at him seriously. "I won't let it happen."

They rode and stole quietly desperate looks at each other as they neared the embassy.

Finally Arad spoke up. "There is an errand I must run today that will keep us apart for just a little while."

Wood knew that a little time away from Arad might not be so unhealthy. But he had never been in love like this. The most foolish mistakes of his past would pale by comparison if he were to let Anat Arad slip through his hands. He looked at her as if she were the personification of life itself.

"Oh, Aaron."

"I'm sorry," he began. "I swore I wouldn't do this."

"I did too."

"I was thinking, after we know more about what happened, of renting a car and just being a tourist for a little while."

"That's wonderful," she said. "Just check in with Al or someone. I won't be gone all that long, just a few hours."

"I've been curious to check out a few places I remember."

"So we'll have a bit of catching up to do."

He smiled. "Yes, Corporal, we will."

Tel Aviv

IT WAS JUST AFTER SUNDOWN when he heard the screams. Muhammad Kadir opened his eyes, peered into the gray half-light, and remembered where he was. In the next instant, he was in the kitchen silently lifting a large knife from its holder. A few seconds later, he was bursting into Rachel Perlman's bedroom.

She was alone. She had kicked off the covers and now lay on her back furiously kicking as her cries filled the room: "No! Please! Oh, God, no!"

Kadir dropped the knife and ran to her. She was naked, and he could see red marks that would soon turn black and blue. He replaced the covers over her before he sat on the edge of the bed and softly rocked her shoulder. "Rachel," he whispered. "It's all right. Rachel."

Perlman froze and opened her eyes. She saw the man sitting on her bed and began to scream.

"Shsh," he said softly. "It's me: Muhammad. You're all right. You were having a nightmare."

She burst into tears.

Kadir located a box of tissues. "Shsh." He patted her through the covers.

Suddenly Perlman sat up and buried her head into his shoulder.

Kadir held the covers around her as she grasped at his back. He stroked her hair and rocked her gently back and forth.

After several minutes, Perlman began to relax. The gathering darkness was consoling. "I'm sorry, Muhammad," she whispered.

"Shsh," he repeated.

"Do you think he heard me out in the hall?"

"We'd know by now if he had."

Perlman thought about what she was not wearing and how thoroughly Kadir had wrapped her up. She knew from Arad's few words about her brother that he was no stranger to darkened rooms and young women; yet she sensed in his arms the same undemanding care she had known in his sister's. "Thank you," she whispered to the ceiling.

They held each other in silence until Perlman's breathing and heartbeat were calm and the room was nearly lightless.

Kadir eased Perlman back down to the pillow.

"Whew," she whispered. "What a day, yeah?"

"Yeah."

They looked at each other, both knowing that, of the many truths and falsehoods hanging in the air, the only essential truths were those Perlman had regarding Arad.

She looked over at the alarm clock. "I suppose right now she's in Tiberias," she said softly.

"Tiberias?"

"Yes, at the jazz festival there."

"Jazz?" he mused. "Ani?"

"Goldstein had assigned her to escort an American musician who is here on a State Department tour." She giggled. "Nuts, isn't it? Goldstein thought he was just being nice, getting her out of there for a while because she was climbing the walls—but, God: it saved her life."

"And cost Goldstein his."

She shivered.

Kadir brushed Perlman's tousled dark hair away from her face.

She smiled. "Wow. Talk about climbing the walls. I don't know what I'd do right now if you weren't here."

He looked briefly at the outline of the bed and imagined Perlman and his sister here together. He thought about how some monster, maybe even al-Malik himself, had put those marks on Perlman.

She slipped her hand out of the covers and cupped it over Kadir's. She brought it warmly against her head and listened as the ocean sang in his palm.

Kadir could see her eyes were glistening. "Why don't you tell me where else our Ani will be on this crazy tour."

"Yes." She stretched. "Meanwhile, I promised you dinner." Perlman removed her moist hand.

Kadir withdrew and stood up. "I'll set the table."

"Thank you, Muhammad." She looked at his silhouette. "In the lower part of the credenza out there is a nice merlot. I think we both could use a drink."

He laughed softly. "Maybe so."

Rachel Perlman lay quietly for a few minutes and listened as Muhammad Kadir moved about her home. Finally, she drew back the covers. She rose slowly and walked around the dark room a while before stepping into the shower. When finished, she switched on the bathroom light, wincing as she dried off.

When Perlman emerged in jeans and a T-shirt, Kadir had not only set the table but had spared the dining-room lamp in favor of candles, had poured the wine, and now was nestled in a corner of the sofa with a magazine.

He looked up and smiled warmly.

"Not much light to read by," she grinned.

After a brief silence, he jumped up and flipped on the kitchen light.

Perlman floated through the dining room and flashed Kadir a knowing smile. "It looks very nice."

They were quiet for a few minutes as Perlman busied herself at the counter.

"May I help?" he asked.

"No, no." Perlman smiled again.

He stepped forward and gently touched her shoulder. After a moment, he returned to the sofa with his *Mademoiselle*.

"There's other stuff to read, you know," she called.

From his position, Kadir could see only one part of Perlman. "But this is fascinating."

She glanced around the corner and smiled. "Really!" Again she mostly disappeared. "Well, unless there's been a publishing revolution in the last week or two, I'd say you're reading about either how to avoid food or how to make love to your man."

He glanced at her and winced. "Actually, I was studying my horoscope."

"Uh-huh. What's it say?"

"That some evening in the near future I will make a fool of myself in a strange woman's very nice flat."

She giggled. "Ah. Well, let me know if it comes true."

He looked up briefly.

"What's mine say?" she grinned.

"What are you?"

"Guess."

"Um, Pisces."

"No way!"

"I was kidding. Scorpio."

"Ani told you!"

"Nope."

"Hmm. OK, what's it say?"

"That there is more to you than meets the eye."

"Think so?"

"Come see for yourself."

"I just might."

There was a long silence as Perlman continued working.

Kadir glanced toward the kitchen. "Smells good."

"It will be."

He smiled to himself, put the magazine aside, and picked up an old copy of *Time*.

Perlman closed the oven, padded out onto the carpet, and set a tray of hors d'oeuvres on the coffee table. "Dinner will be ready within the hour."

"Beautiful," Kadir said to the tray before he watched Perlman walk to the table and return with their wine glasses. "Very creative."

"One has to be in my field," she smiled as she sat down in the opposite corner of the sofa. "I did the tourism insert in that issue, by the way." She blushed. "Actually, I rarely get a chance to cook for someone."

"This is wonderful, Rachel." He lifted his glass. "To teamwork."

They clinked and drank.

Perlman held hers aloft. "To our Ani."

They sat in silence for a few moments. Both were relieved when Perlman picked up the rest of the tour story and they made plans to find Arad when she returned to Tel Aviv the next day.

"She won't want to see me," Perlman admitted. "She disappeared after we broke up—well, after I did a stupid thing and she rightly told me to go to hell. To think that that disgusting man this morning—what did you call him?—"

"Khaled al-Malik," Kadir pronounced as if swallowing rotten meat.

"—to think that it was he who found her, by not finding her." She shivered and took a drink. "Of course, I could have tracked her down if I had thought it would repair us. But when this al-Malik said she was in danger—"

"Only from him."

Perlman's brow regained its tension, and she took another long sip.

Kadir reached over and touched her hand. "Listen: tomorrow Ani is involved in a secret mission that will take care of this whole thing. That sounds melodramatic, but for national-security reasons she was vague about it. Remember: she works with the best in the business. Just know that you will not hear from Khaled al-Malik again." He smiled and cast a softly disapproving look at Perlman's nearly empty glass.

Perlman sat back gracefully. "I don't know why she doesn't quit. She could be doing something much more fulfilling—and a lot less perilous." She looked at Kadir and grinned. "Hey: if you knew where she would be tomorrow, why did you rush up here today?"

"Because, until you told me of this innocuous jazz-festival business, I was afraid al-Malik might have got to her. She could have been kidnapped, or killed."

Perlman turned toward him. "I didn't think it was safe to discuss on the phone."

"Oh, I understood that. I thought we could help her by working together." Kadir refilled Perlman's glass.

She smiled loosely. "Are you trying to get me drunk, Muhammad?"

"Of course not," he smiled.

"Ani told me about you."

"What do you mean?"

"That you have a way."

He smiled bashfully. "That's nonsense."

"Right."

"Besides—"

"*Besides,* what?"

"Well, I didn't think you, um, did men."

She giggled mischievously.

"Wrong?"

"I'm not quite as dedicated as your lovely twin, Muhammad."

"Ah."

"But I haven't dated anyone, male or female, since Ani." She looked down. "It was a little straight fling that broke us up."

"Are you still in love with her?" he asked, then immediately looked away. "I'm sorry. That's none of my—"

"Don't be silly."

Kadir turned toward her.

"I don't deserve to be in love with her, so whether I am doesn't matter."

"Maybe there was more to it."

"Well, as I said, I handled it very poorly. I even invited her to try a ménage à trois. She regarded it as a betrayal, not only of her but of our gender."

Kadir looked reflectively at Perlman. He regretted having invaded their world, and he remembered his sister's disturbing revelation in Paris. "Well, I came up here knowing practically nothing about you, and I wouldn't presume to speak for Ani even if I could." He paused. "I do know we all could use some peace."

She leaned over and touched his hand. "Yes."

In a little while, Perlman presented Kadir with the most delicious meal he had enjoyed in memory, each of them luxuriating in its tension-melting effect and in the ritual of nonchalance.

As they cleared the table, Perlman's stiffness began showing more in her movements and eventually in her face. Kadir pretended not to notice as he took things from her hands and loaded the dishwasher. Finally, Kadir reentered the living room to find Perlman leaning over a chair with her long hair falling forward.

He cupped his hands around her shoulders.

"I need to lie down," she said unsteadily.

Kadir guided her over to the sofa.

"No, I'd better go in there," she pointed weakly.

He walked her down the hall and sat her on the bed. He lifted her feet as she lay back slowly, on her elbows first before collapsing onto the pillow. Gradually her pained expression resolved to heavy exhaustion.

"Do you want to get under the covers?" he asked, as he subdued his instinct to unbutton her tight jeans.

"No, I just needed to get off my feet," Perlman whispered with some difficulty.

Kadir sat down next to her and guided her hair away from her face.

Perlman looked away. "I think you figured this out some time ago," she whispered, "but I was attacked this morning."

Kadir nodded gently.

"A despicable goon sent by al-Malik." She looked at him seriously. "How do you know this guy, anyway?"

Kadir thought a moment. "Originally, Ani and I knew him because he was our high-school soccer coach. Later, he started feeding us appealing but half-baked political ideas and eventually recruited us into this little guerrilla band. He'd take a bunch of us out to the desert or into abandoned buildings and teach us how to use various weapons, some homemade, most stolen. At first, we went along because it was naughty fun. When Ani joined the army, he kept tabs on her and pumped her for news about raids on Palestinian neighborhoods and so on—not that she was privy to anything classified. Then, recently, al-Malik seized on an absurd plan to pull off some serious terrorism. We started avoiding him like the plague: their association could have got her court-martialed, or worse. And if it weren't for Ani and Mom, I'd be back in L.A. by now. I can't wait for this madness to be over."

Perlman stiffened, moved away, and looked at Kadir with incredulous anger. "Do you mean to tell me I was brutally raped and spent half the day with doctors and cops so that you and your sister could play war games?"

Kadir's eyes welled. "Oh, God, please don't do this. There's much more to it than that. Al-Malik got out of control, got close to too many dangerous people. He's planned something terrible that would have international repercussions. I'm sorry I can't tell you more. But I promise you that tomorrow it will end."

Perlman pushed Kadir's hand away and turned onto her side with her back to him. "I want you to get out of here, Muhammad. Get out of here, and don't ever return." She doubled forward.

"Rachel, please!" he cried. "You don't know how deeply Ani and I regret having met al-Malik, and how I feel about your being dragged into it." He started to touch her shoulder but withdrew. "Rachel, if I could do anything in the world to erase this day from your memory, I would do it. Please: after tomorrow—"

"After tomorrow I will be one day closer to forgetting I ever knew either of you," she cried. "Now leave."

"Rachel—" he began softly.

She turned over suddenly and faced him seething. "*Now!*"

Kadir rose. He took a deep breath and closed his eyes. "Rachel," he whispered, "you can't possibly understand, based on what I've told you, how an Israeli soldier and her expatriate brother got involved in a stupid Palestinian plot. But I think you do understand that I wouldn't be here if I didn't care about you and—"

"You're here because I had information about the little bitch. Well, now you have your information. And you didn't even have to screw me for it, so get out."

"Rachel—"

"Muhammad, I'm warning you—"

"I don't think you should be alone right now," he said softly.

"*Alone?*" she screamed. "Oh, I am hardly alone. I have my friend out there in the corridor. I have some whining young cop who thinks *she* knows what it's like. I have pictures of my ass posted all over city hall. You want alone, Muhammad? Alone was sitting there this morning while that stinking Arab—" She broke down and pounded her fist on the mattress.

Kadir sat back down on the bed and tried to embrace her.

After a momentary hesitation, she recoiled and crouched in the far corner of the bed.

He stood up. "I am so sorry."

She looked at him with fierce green eyes and pointed to the door.

He leaned down and set the tissue box on the bed close to her.

Muhammad Kadir turned and left Rachel Perlman's bedroom. He paused in the living room and looked at the sofa and the table, and he went over and turned off the kitchen light. He walked out the door and out of the building and into the night before Jerusalem.

Tel Aviv

IN JUST OVER TWENTY-FOUR HOURS, the crowd of bystanders had devolved to intermittent waves. Drivers and pedestrians would slow down and look with brief resignation at the charred window covered with plastic that fluttered softly in the ocean breeze.

The plan was for Lederman and Fatool to drop Wood at his hotel before returning the black sedan to the embassy and for Corporal Arad to return to her post around the corner. But without having exchanged a word on the matter, the four drove directly to the ribboned intersection and paused beneath the window before pulling into the embassy lot.

Lederman and Fatool parked and walked back to the jeep.

"We'll meet you inside when you're ready, Aaron," Lederman said. "Corporal Arad." He paused. "Again, please accept our condolences."

Arad shook their hands.

Fatool nodded, and Lederman touched Arad's shoulder as the two men stepped away and entered the building.

Wood and Arad sat looking into each other's eyes for a while without speaking.

Arad turned and stared through the windshield into the distance. "So strange. They train you to handle weapons, to survive in the wilderness, to steel yourself against death. And then, the first time it happens to someone you served with, it's like this, a harmless old man, in downtown Tel Aviv, with kids strolling by with their ice-cream cones like extras in a Hollywood movie."

Wood reached for her hand.

Both of them knew that whoever might be looking absently out an embassy window could be less discreet than Lederman and Fatool.

Arad buried a laugh and patted her thighs with nervous energy. "Well. So where will you go today in your rented car?"

"I'm curious to try to find our old house. There isn't time to go everywhere I'd like. But I'd regret not revisiting Jerusalem."

Arad started.

"Anat?"

Her face clarified, and she turned slightly. "Aaron. Today is not a good day to see Jerusalem."

"Oh?"

"I guess no one had any reason to tell you, but this evening, Prime Minister Rabin is delivering a speech at the Damascus Gate—a speech on Israeli-Palestinian relations. The event will be telecast live throughout Israel and the neighboring Arab states. As you can imagine, the security operation will be monumental. There will be roadblocks and checkpoints everywhere."

Wood thought for a moment. "Well, that may not be so bad: State warned me not to go there without an escort, so with the increased security—"

"Aaron, please listen to me," she insisted. "The prime minister of Israel is going to set himself up in a place of great historical importance to Christians, Jews, and Muslims and tell them of a way they can learn to get along. Assuming he is still alive by the end of his speech, he is likely to be greeted by derision or riots. I do not want you anywhere near Jerusalem today. Do you understand me, Aaron?"

He looked at her with admiration. "That's what your errand is today, isn't it? Guarding Rabin?"

She burned her black eyes into him. "Yes, it is."

"Goldstein told me you were the best markswoman he'd ever met."

She flinched and smiled weakly. "Please don't worry, Aaron. I'll be part of an auxiliary detail, posted on the perimeter, and I'll be surrounded by experts. Any fool who makes a move on the premier's entourage will be history before anyone knows he ever existed."

"And you are one of the potential history-makers."

"If I discover my commander in chief to be in trouble, yes. I wasn't even going to tell you. For me, theoretically, it will be another day at the office." Again she struggled to produce a smile. "My gig, as you would call it, does not normally involve chauffeuring gorgeous piano players."

His response was similarly unconvincing.

"I am an extremely competent soldier, Aaron. I probably can kick more butt than any guy you know."

"That's most comforting."

Arad could no longer restrain herself. "Look at me. This time tomorrow, you and I will be sitting right here in this jeep driving south to the festival in Eilat. You'll meet Nick and my crazy brother, and we'll have a blast. And when I get you alone in that room with the Red Sea shining outside our window, I will make you forget you ever heard of a place called Jerusalem. This I promise you, Aaron Wood, on my father's grave."

26

Tel Aviv

ANAT ARAD PULLED INTO THE LOT and parked the jeep. She hopped out and walked around to the front entrance. She did not look toward the guardhouse.

"Hey, Arad!"

She turned to see Kornberg motioning. She managed a faint loosening of the jaw and walked over to him.

"It's a bitch, isn't it?" he said, pointing to the window.

She said nothing.

"Listen, Arad: some chick came by here yesterday morning, looking for you."

"Did this chick have a name?"

He smirked. "I was too busy to read her ID. I can tell you she's come a long way since that mug shot."

"Very helpful, Kornberg. It's good to know our citizens are getting their money's worth from you. What did she look like?"

"A little taller than you, slender, reddish-brown hair, nice ass."

Arad appeared bored.

"She was shouldering a very chic black leather bag. Big enough for a couple of vibrators. Or a bomb. Guess I should've looked in it."

Arad turned and walked to the building.

Once inside, she was greeted by the usual sour grapes, their acid tempered only slightly by the funereal atmosphere. She mounted the stairs. The upper reception desk was unoccupied. Goldstein's door was taped over, and a plainclothesman sat outside skimming a magazine. Arad turned and went back downstairs. "Where's Bloch?" she asked two men leaning against the wall.

One of them pointed back toward the kitchen. As Arad passed, he called, "How's our little holiday?"

Without turning, she replied, "Most refreshing, till just now." She rounded the corner to vague obscenities.

Bloch looked up from his coffee and newspaper. "Ah, it's Annie Oakley, back from the range." He took a sip and looked back down.

Arad stood at the table. "Kornberg says I had a visitor yesterday."

Bloch did not look up. "Yes. A very pretty one."

"That seems to be the consensus. Did you happen to catch her name, Bloch?"

"I took a written statement from her, actually, which I submitted for Goldstein's signature." He paused. "I'm afraid there's not much left of anything in there now."

Arad winced.

"The cops questioned her briefly," Bloch added. "She shouldn't be hard to find."

"A statement?"

"Seems that some smelly Arab had knocked on her door about dawn. Looking for you." Bloch smiled at the paper.

"And I don't suppose you remember that name, either."

"Sadly, he neglected to leave it."

Arad decided not to ask any more questions. She turned for the door.

Bloch swallowed quickly. "You babysitting in Jerusalem tonight?"

She paused in the doorway. "I'll steal you some biscuits." Impulsively, she struck a provocative pose and blew him a kiss. In the hall, she smiled to herself as she heard his cup make an emergency landing.

Corporal Arad went around to her quarters and lay on her bunk.

So al-Malik had been resourceful enough to find Perlman. And now Perlman knew how to find Arad. But this whole situation was temporary, and at any rate al-Malik would not have wasted time on Perlman when his moment of eternal glory was just around the corner. He had always made it clear that the team's participation was optional.

The team: she frowned with disbelief at the very notion. Xenakis had come along grudgingly to maintain his once-famous hiking skills. Something was not right between him and al-Malik, but she did not know what. As for Kadir, the only real teammate she had ever known, he had been in, just as now he was out, because he loved his sister more than he had ever loved anyone else on earth.

She thought of Rachel—Sister Rachel, who in the last few days had nearly ceased to exist. Before Arad could visualize her, she had to accept Kornberg's too-apt description. Nice ass indeed. A bit too nice, apparently, to confine to one flat. Arad knew even in the rapture of her new love that someday she might once again be able to fantasize about Perlman and thereby to reposition her in that shining firmament of old lovers whose faults and cruelties have receded into pleasant denial and whose ageless perfection is available with a closing of the eyes. But Perlman's poignant reappearance was not reason enough to reopen that wound. Arad knew that if she saw Perlman again, the hunger would return.

Wood had already said he could share her with a woman. But would Perlman, who once had suggested such an arrangement at a time when Arad could have regarded it only as abhorrent, be so unselfish? The plain truth was that thinking of Perlman hurt, whereas thinking of Wood felt like prayer.

Anat Arad opened her eyes, looked around, and took a deep breath. She gathered her things, went to the jeep, and drove to the base to join the others. She would, as always, hate riding in the back of a truck full of leering men, but at least these guys were professionals. As she pulled into the gate, she looked down at her long-range rifle and shivered.

27

Tel Aviv

AARON WOOD SHOOK HIS COMPANIONS' hands and started to climb out of the sedan. "I wish I knew how to thank you guys," he said holding onto the door handle.

Lederman smiled back at him. "It's beginning to look like more than a fling, Aaron."

He looked around. "I know it's insane."

Fatool smiled. "Tel Aviv and Washington are very far apart."

Wood looked wistfully out the window. "I suppose we could wake up next week and discover it was just a mirage."

"Or," Fatool continued, "with your luck, you could meet someone in Egypt who makes Anat look like Golda Meir."

There was a skeptical silence.

"Well, whatever happens," Lederman concluded, "we wish you the best."

"So this day is R and R?" Fatool grinned as Wood made a second play for the door.

"I might check out a few of the old places."

"Just remember what Reiger said: save Jerusalem for another day."

"Thanks again, guys. I'll see you tomorrow."

Wood closed the door and entered the hotel. He welcomed his day of solitude, but he would gladly have sacrificed it for five minutes in Arad's arms. He smiled incongruously at everyone in the lobby and went up to his room.

He spent a few minutes looking out over the sea, thinking about her, trying not to worry. The morning was all but gone. He went to the telephone book to find a rental agency and noticed the message light.

"Yes, Mr. Wood. You have a call from your embassy."

He took down the number and dialed. His hands were shaking.

"Mr. Wood? Thank you for getting back to me. This is Barbara Middleton, Al Reiger's assistant. I'm sorry to bother you, but a young woman called here a little while ago, hoping to speak with you. She wouldn't leave her name. She sounded a bit agitated, and I didn't want to give out your number."

"Thank you. I don't know anyone here except you, Al, and the folks I've been traveling with."

"Yes. I heard you made quite a splash two nights ago in Haifa," she chimed, "and I thought this young lady might be a fan, or a reporter. If she calls back, I'll press her for a number—if you want to follow it up."

Wood considered Middleton's speculations. Right now there was only one woman in the world, and all Wood had to do was get through a single day of sightseeing in a land he had spent decades thinking he would never revisit and there she would be. Wood arranged for a car, changed into comfortable clothes, and had started for the door when the telephone rang.

"Aaron Wood." He cursed his automatic response.

"Mr. Wood? Please don't hang up. You don't know me, but I must see you at once."

"How do you know me?"

"I know you're touring here this week. I called your embassy. They wouldn't give me your number, so I started combing likely hotels."

"Guess I'd better have a word with the desk clerk."

"I'm sorry, Mr. Wood. I'm not a groupie. I know this sounds crazy, but please agree to see me. It's important. I'll be in the lobby in fifteen minutes."

"And if I decline your invitation and enjoy my one day off?"

"Please, Mr. Wood. I need only a few minutes of your time in a neutral place."

"You're not a journalist?"

"No. Just a friend, I hope."

The hotel lobby was as neutral as it gets. If the woman were a nut, he could use a prearranged signal to have her escorted out. He did not think he had said anything during his stay to invoke the wrath of terrorists, and they generally did not make appointments. Maybe she was the daughter of one of his father's old colleagues—but why the intrigue? He looked at his watch. "All right, I'll give you ten minutes. How will I know you?"

"I'm wearing a yellow blouse and white slacks, and I have long auburn hair."

"Sounds visible," he mused.

The voice smiled.

He put down the receiver and returned to the window. He felt suddenly dirty, as though he had been unfaithful to Arad. What if she had solicited a friend to test him? An unseemly discovery like that would shatter everything. Probably it had nothing to do with Arad. He grabbed the room key and went downstairs.

He arranged for security and posted himself in one of two prominent armchairs in the middle of the floor.

Exactly fifteen minutes after his strange phone call, the yellow blouse, white slacks, and auburn hair floated through the door. The woman scanned the room and responded to Wood's discreet wave. The house detective nodded as Wood rose. Watching the woman approach, Wood fought off images he recalled from films, where the assassin was the beautiful one with the benign smile. He shifted uneasily as she came within reach and extended a soft white hand. He felt well-groomed nails encircling his fingers.

"Thank you for meeting me, Mr. Wood," she said pleasantly. "My name is Rachel Perlman." She seemed to wait for a reaction.

Wood motioned to the chair opposite him and sat uncomfortably in his.

"First of all," she said, "I suppose you're wondering how I knew you were here in Israel. I learned that from Major—the late Major Goldstein. Did you meet him?"

"Yes." She had the synthetic smile of a saleswoman. He looked away and thought of Goldstein and all the trouble the officer's kindness had summoned.

"I'm here, Mr. Wood, as a friend of Corporal Anat Arad." The woman paused. "She has been escorting your party, yes?"

He made no effort to mask his suspicion. "Yes."

"I served with Corporal Arad some time ago." Again she paused. "I don't know whether you've had a chance to speak with her—"

Wood continued viewing the woman carefully.

"—but I have reason to believe she may be in trouble."

Wood sat stiffly upright.

"Dangerous trouble, really."

Wood studied the glamorous face. In Arad's line of work, she probably ran into unstable people every day.

"Have you had a chance to speak with Corporal Arad?" the woman insisted.

"A bit. Look, Ms. Perlman, I think you should be telling this to Corporal Arad's commanding officer."

"I did, and look what happened. Now I'm being watched night and day by government agents."

"Ms. Perlman, I came over here to play the piano." He took a deep breath and looked at her seriously. "What makes you think Corporal Arad is in danger?"

"It's a long story, but let's just say—Mr. Wood, do you know about Corporal Arad's brother, Muhammad?"

He shook his head vaguely.

"Well, I myself just met him yesterday. He told me of this trouble, which at one time involved him too. I got terribly upset and ordered Muhammad to leave. When I called him this morning to apologize, he had disappeared."

"Disappeared?"

"Well, he had checked out of his hotel. Had he gone home, he would be there by now. But there's no answer. He was concerned enough to move their mother in temporarily with some friends of his, but he didn't tell me where."

"Ms. Perlman, can you be more specific about this trouble?" Realizing his hands had become moist fists, he opened them slowly around the soft arms of his chair.

"No, I'm sorry, I can't. I don't know much about it, really," the woman said unsteadily. "I thought, you know, a musician, sensitive person, cruising up and down the coast with her for two days, maybe you had struck up a conversation."

"And if we had?"

"I know," she said softly. "I was just thinking maybe you could—mention that her friends are worried about her."

Wood saw that the woman's eyes were wet. He started to rise as she reached into her purse.

"I'm sorry, Mr. Wood. This is crazy. I'm probably overreacting as usual. Muhammad even assured me everything would be taken care of today. I just—"

"And what does that mean?"

The woman lowered her head. "I don't know, exactly. I just know something big could happen today, and Muhammad is counting on Anat to put a stop to it. I think Muhammad may not really have divorced himself from the affair as he wanted me to believe."

"Muhammad is not a soldier, correct?"

"Correct."

Wood struggled with his inclination to buy the woman's performance and his reluctance to reveal anything he knew about Arad and her background. Ms. Perlman, if that were her real name, could be anyone: an army spy, a Palestinian double agent, a dime-store novelist, a talk-show host—maybe even a former lover. Whatever she was, he could not help smiling kindly at her.

"Ani's well-being means a great deal to me, Mr. Wood."

"I can see that, Ms. Perlman." He leaned forward slightly. "Look, I'm sorry if I've come off a bit cold here, but you have to admit—"

"I know," she said, smiling shyly and reaching for a fresh tissue, "and I know that if this trouble is real, there's nothing you or I can do to keep her from it. Ani is the best, she serves with the best, and there isn't an enemy in the world they can't put down if they know where it is." She took a deep breath. "I was afraid to revisit the army; they might suspect Ani of wrongdoing."

"But you don't think—"

"Oh, no. I think that as kids she and Muhammad got hooked up with some bad elements and that things got out of control. But Muhammad said it would all be over today," she continued, breaking down again, "and tomorrow, she will be back on your tour, and perhaps you can mention—"

"You know about the rest of my tour?"

Perlman dabbed at her face and looked at him intelligently. "Goldstein told me. Just to make me stop fretting."

Wood attempted a light smile. "I wish I could get this kind of representation back home."

She giggled.

"Am I to keep this meeting secret, Ms. Perlman?"

"How do you mean?"

"Well, obviously, I'm not going to speak to anyone official if it might get Anat—Corporal Arad—in hot water. But should I convey this concern in your name, or do you just want her to know that her *friends* are looking out for her?"

Perlman looked down and smiled, as her cream-white forehead turned pink. "I'll leave that up to you."

They sat facing for a moment.

"Thank you again for seeing me, Mr. Wood."

"Please: call me Aaron," he smiled. "I promise to give your regards to, um, Ani."

"The woman at your embassy was understandably evasive."

"Only three people need know of this conversation, Rachel. Well, four, including Scotland Yard over there."

Perlman arched one eyebrow and flashed Wood an attractively indignant smile.

"And Barbara did think you were just a groupie."

The two laughed softly and sighed with relief. Not that they had accomplished anything but raise more fears and questions—but at least they now had them in common.

Perlman rose and extended her hand. "Aaron. Here's my card. Please call me if you hear anything. And enjoy the rest of your day off."

"Thanks. I'll try."

Perlman hesitated. "Perhaps I'll see you again."

"Perhaps."

She gave him a last curious grin and turned.

Male instinct had Wood watching her as she floated across the lobby and out the door, but he no longer felt dirty. He had a feeling this Rachel was all right.

Wood nodded cordially to the detective and went back upstairs.

He stood for a while at his window and tried to convince himself that the new questions were only slightly uglier than those he had wrestled with before Perlman's call. So Arad and her brother had been mischievous teenagers. Who hadn't?

The thing he could not shake was the feeling that he had spent the last two nights making love to a woman who knew she was going to Jerusalem today to blow somebody's brains out.

Jerusalem

NICK XENAKIS PULLED INTO THE SMALL semicircular lot and parked facing the front door. He viewed the fan-shaped corner building and its position between two smooth walls that opened onto the square: the embossed facade was just like an architectural speaker cone. His little plan was silly, but it would buy enough time, a second or two, for Arad to do what had to be done—and it could be blamed on a simple short circuit. Xenakis got out, went into the studio, and said hello to the receptionist.

"Go on back, Nick," she said. "He's just running a power test."

"Hi, Ned," Xenakis called to the little man kneeling by the wall. "How's our groovemeister this week?"

"Oy, don't ask," Greenberg replied without looking up from his meter. "If I had one solid piece of songwriting for every pathetic demo that came through here, I'd be piloting my own Bertram right now."

Xenakis gave his low guffaw. "Well, Ned, meanwhile, you know you are welcome aboard anytime. In fact, when this is over, we should all take a year off and sail the Cape of Good Hope."

The pale engineer went over to a cabinet and pulled out two heavy-duty extension cords and a work lamp. "Here you go, Nick. Have fun," he smiled.

Xenakis leaned down and laid a plug on the floor

beneath an outlet, then plugged the other cord and the lamp into an outlet on the opposite wall. Xenakis ran the three cords out under the door and to the front of the van. He hummed placidly to himself as he opened the hood, hung the lamp, and ran the extension cords through the engine compartment toward the little opening under the floor mat. He went around, opened the passenger's door, produced his toolbox, placed it on the sidewalk in front of the van, and laid out a few tools. Then he went back and pulled the extension cords through, hooked one to each amplifier, and checked the volume settings. He returned to the front and looked analytically at the engine for a few moments, made a quick survey of the area, and slipped around to the sliding door. Once inside the van, he checked his connections and smiled.

He considered his other connections, the accumulated benefits of music retailing that had put him in touch with imperturbable sound engineers and lighting designers who seemed always to have an odd piece of castoff equipment that could be had for an Elvis complete works or a few bottles of anisette. He crouched within the small dark city of gear and understood the feeling of power a teenager enjoys when strapping on a guitar in front of a six-foot stack of these things. Even with the doors closed, old Nick had come to this party ready to jam. He checked the CD player and the remote, went back out to the front, and worked ostensibly on his engine. Periodically, he went inside to chat with Ned and Ofra, to eat, to watch the video monitor, and to wait.

Jerusalem

MUHAMMAD KADIR TIPTOED down the hall, hoping to surprise al-Malik still in his room. That would have been the neatest way of all. Al-Malik thought he had sole possession of the correct itinerary. Kadir's heart raced at the vision of bursting through the door and blowing the bastard away before he could stand up. But when the young man made his adrenaline-pumping entrance a moment later, the room was empty.

He was about to back out of the room when something on the nightstand caught his eye. He stood and shivered with coiled rage. It was a teenage photograph of his sister in a bathing suit.

Jerusalem

ANAT ARAD TOOK UP HER POSITION, checked the radio on her belt, and looked around. Her teammates were as invisible as she, an eerie realization made palatable only by the radio's companionship.

She looked out at the spot where she knew al-Malik would be. She tested her ground and sighted the spot periodically. To keep from stiffening up, she moved about and practiced her stretching routines. She looked at her watch.

The crowd had begun forming in the square. Corporal Arad viewed the podium, loosened her jaw, and flexed her fingers.

If thoughts of Wood floated into her mind, she chased them away as if he had walked in on her in the bathroom. She might get only one perfect moment, and, for everyone's sake, that moment must be hers alone.

It was nearly six o'clock. She swung her head from side to side and sighted her spot.

Finally, he was there.

Corporal Arad's body trembled briefly. She measured her distance and calculated her moves as if she had not done so a hundred times in the last five minutes. He was early. He had been early—and the wrong person—in Paris. But she could not have asked for a better opportunity. The crowd was still slightly fluid. In one graceful gesture, she would rid the world of a poisonous insect. She cleared her mind of all reality, fantasy, right, and wrong, and she raised the rifle to her shoulder. She leaned in toward the scope and brought her hands gently to bear in their familiar places. She subdued another chill as she centered the crosshairs on the back of al-Malik's head. She had just started to press the trigger when her target shifted. In the instant she needed to relax and refocus, she failed to hear the faint click at her side as the radio was switched off. Before the event had registered, the rifle had been jerked upward and a hand had swung around and clasped hard across her mouth. Her instinctive motion to gain control of her opponent was not a second old when she felt metal pressing against the back of her neck. Corporal Arad froze.

"To the shore, comrade," whispered the voice close to her left ear.

Another hand reached in, removed the radio, and tossed it into a clump of tall weeds growing through the parched concrete.

"Lower the rifle slowly and quietly to the ground, please, Corporal. Good. Let's go."

Immediately she was wheeled around and guided down the old stone steps, through the narrow alley, and into the backseat of a faded silver sedan.

"Lie down, please, Corporal."

She had heard the voice before. She did as commanded. The hand, the probe, and the weight of a small man followed her down to the seat. Many minutes of stop-and-go driving passed before the car began to maintain highway speed.

A few minutes later, the voice whispered, "We have a little way to go, Corporal. There is no reason why you should not sit up now and be comfortable. Please understand, however, that if you speak or move I will not hesitate to kill you."

The weight receded. Corporal Arad sat up and glanced briefly to her right.

It was Bloch.

The driver was a big Arab man she had never seen.

When they reached the outskirts of Tel Aviv, Bloch motioned to her. She lay back down on the seat. Bloch and his silencer followed. After a while, she began hearing faint railroad noises. The car slowed, turned, and wound through a bumpy area, and she could hear the tires laboring over rocks and ringing metal objects. Eventually, the car turned again and stopped.

"You may rise again now, Corporal. I must remind you not to speak, and to move only as instructed."

She sat up and saw that they were parked in an alley between what appeared to be two large warehouses.

"Please step out now, Corporal, and stand still."

She did, and an instant later Bloch was behind her.

The driver stayed in the car.

As Bloch guided Arad toward a door, the car backed out of the alley and could be heard driving away. Arad was pushed through the door into a large room illuminated by three broken plastic skylights.

"To the left rear corner, please, Corporal," Bloch whispered, close to her ear.

She was guided toward a door at the far end of the room. Arranged along the left wall were a dusty gray desk and an oak swivel chair. Lying on its side nearby was an oak clothes tree. The desk and chair bore brown stains under a layer of dust. Two large photographic floodlights on tripods stood in the corner, next to a battery pack.

"The door, please, Corporal."

She was pushed into a tiny airless room that smelled like sun-ripened garbage. The room was empty except for an old chipped white hospital bed with a stained mattress and four black-leather straps affixed to the railings at the corners. The walls and floor were heavily stained and smeared. The only sounds were her breathing and the buzzing of flies. She stood still. If she could get past the gun, she could snap Bloch like a twig.

Suddenly he pushed her toward the bed. "Please have a seat, Corporal." He smiled. "We have a reasonably short wait, and then Khaled has planned a little celebration. Please don't look so serious, Corporal. This is a great day for Palestine." Bloch backed against the wall alongside the bed and pointed the silencer at Corporal Arad's calm face.

Jerusalem

MUHAMMAD KADIR SPOTTED al-Malik about ten after six. Kadir was lucky to have got this far into the square with his shoulder piece, but he would have to get much closer. The crowd was nearly impenetrable, and he was aware of the many unseen rifles pointed into the square. His only consolation was that one of those rifles belonged to his sister. He kept his eye on the back of al-Malik's head. Any second now, it should flare up red and disappear from view. There would be panic, and the entourage would be hustled away. The television networks would scramble for something to program while news updates filtered in. Aside from these inconveniences, the world would be a cleaner place. Kadir watched and waited.

At six-twenty, he began to worry. Arad should have made her move by now. Perhaps from her angle someone was in the way. Perhaps an inattentive teammate had picked up her weapon by mistake, and she was making do with an unfamiliar one—but Arad would never have let that happen. Something was wrong. Khaled al-Malik was still standing there, thinking that Kadir was off schedule and that the last person in the world Arad would point her gun at was the visionary coach. Something was terribly wrong.

At six-twenty-five, nothing had changed except that the podium had been bathed in white television light. Al-Malik was still in position. He almost looked like a legitimate news cameraman. If only the folks at home knew what was built into that tripod. Kadir thought about his young mother with al-Malik/Goodman, about al-Malik staring like an animal at his sister's photograph, about al-Malik standing in Perlman's doorway, and about the mutant that al-Malik had sent to torture Perlman. He thought of the scars these women would wear for the rest of their lives. He looked at the unchanged back of al-Malik's head.

Kadir raised his left hand, waved to no one, smiled brightly with feigned surprise, called out a name, and pretended not to have been heard. Then he turned to his neighbor, took on a mischievous grin, placed his finger to his lips, crouched down, and began moving forward through the crowd. When someone protested, he raised his finger and whispered in English, "I'm going to surprise an old friend." In his American clothes, he looked like a tourist.

Kadir was almost within infallible range when the announcement was made and the prime minister and his party made their way to the stage. Al-Malik had not moved. The activity of applause and shuffling feet allowed Kadir to reach for his pistol. Rabin took the podium and the crowd suddenly died down. Al-Malik made a subtle move toward his tripod. Hoping al-Malik's motion would finally attract the bullet from Arad's weapon, Kadir hesitated. Rabin opened his text and smiled.

Just as the first word left the prime minister's mouth, a huge white flash was seen from a side street off the square. A second later, a deafening metallic din echoed through the alley and out into the square. It was the classic ten-piece recording of Thelonious Monk's "Epistrophy."

Before Kadir's automatic smile could signal his recognition not only of the prank but also of the perpetrator, the secret police rushed forward and tackled the premier. The crowd erupted in screams and laughter as the stage was instantaneously cleared. Kadir gasped and looked back toward his target.

Al-Malik was gone.

Kadir searched through the bobbing heads but could not see the one he sought. He pushed his way back through the crowd and exited the square by the least likely direction. Then he crossed through an alley and made his way toward al-Malik's room.

Again he hoped to surprise his target in the hall or after breaking in his door, and again he was disappointed. He waited several minutes inside the bathroom thinking of the moment when al-Malik would walk in and Kadir would empty his weapon, but the moment never came. Finally, Kadir stepped back out into the room and looked at his sister's photograph. And he knew.

Tel Aviv

"HELLO?"

"Rachel. Muhammad here. He got away. Do you—"

"Oh, my God!"

"Listen! Do you remember the place where you were assaulted?"

Perlman burst loudly into tears.

"Rachel! Listen to me! Ani's life is at stake! Could you find that place again?"

"Oh, God, I don't—I think so, maybe. It was near the north rail station."

"Good. I'm on the edge of town. Meet me at the station as soon as you can. But first go out and tell that guard what's going on; take him with you."

Perlman ran to the door.

The plainclothesman was not there.

Swell. I'm no longer a menace to society.

She looked out her living-room window.

The man who had been posted down at the street had likewise disappeared.

She ran to the pantry, then remembered that her gun should still be under the seat of her car. She envisioned the few steps between her door and the garage. She reached over and pulled out the big knife. She looked at the telephone. A false alarm was better than dying. She clawed through her purse and found the card.

"Officer Menuhin, please."

"Officer Menuhin is on vacation through next week. May I help you?"

Perlman looked at her watch. The cops knew exactly where she had been attacked and could be there before anyone else. "This is Rachel Perlman. I was raped two days ago in a warehouse near the north train station. I have reason to believe another attack is going on there now. Please send—"

"Who? Miss, please, you'll have to slow—"

"Perlman! Rachel Perlman! Please get someone over there now!"

"Perlman. Rachel. Did you get a look at him? When did you say—"

"Oh, for God's sake! Look it up!" She slammed the receiver down and ran out the door.

Tel Aviv

ANAT ARAD HAD NOT MOVED. Nor had she taken her eyes off Bloch's face. He similarly had remained motionless against the wall with the gun pointed at Arad. He had spoken a few times. She sat hugging her knees with her lower back against the head railing. She had calculated the weight of the bed.

She heard a distant crunching noise and a single car door. Still no movement.

She would need a diversion, a chance to turn the two against each other. She knew she probably would need a miracle. Footsteps approached.

Khaled al-Malik entered the little room and flashed his patronizing smile. "Hello, Anatoliy. Sorry to interrupt your little soirée, but tonight we have some partying of our own to do."

I should have blown you away in Paris.

"I see your manners have taken a turn for the better, Anatoliy. That's most encouraging. I hate uncivilized parties, don't you?"

She remained silent but stared at him with immovable black eyes.

"Well, now, reticence can be just as rude as volubility. Can't it, Comrade Bloch?"

Bloch smiled. "Corporal Arad is just being a good girl, Comrade al-Malik. I asked her nicely not to speak, and she has been most cooperative."

"Yes. Very good, Bloch. But you mustn't refer to Corporal Arad as a girl. She is wholly unlike the chattering females she could have grown up with. She was a woman before her time. Yet she's not really a woman at all. Are you, Anatoliy?"

She glanced at Bloch's silencer and at his ice-blue eyes.

Al-Malik laid a small black case on the foot on the bed and opened it. He pulled out a black pistol. "Well," he said. "It's time to begin. Lights, please."

Bloch pushed away from the wall and left the room.

Al-Malik smiled at Arad.

Bloch returned carrying the two floodlights and set them down near the corners of the bed aimed at Arad's face. Then he left and returned with the battery pack.

Al-Malik reached into his black case and produced a pair of long scissors.

Suddenly the room was washed in hot light. Arad blinked but did not change her expression as she viewed the two silhouettes. Al-Malik motioned toward the bed, and Bloch quickly moved in and grabbed her left arm. She started to struggle, but al-Malik came forward and pressed his silencer against her forehead.

"You don't want to spoil our party, now, do you, Anatoliy?"

She looked at the sweating face and said nothing.

"Good. Now, Bloch, if you would, please."

Bloch fastened the buckle around her wrist.

"Test it well, comrade. She's left-handed, you know."

Bloch pulled hard on the belt, digging into Arad's soft skin.

She gave no reaction.

323

"Very well. Now, Anatoliy, if you would be so kind, please take off your uniform. Don't worry about that left sleeve; it will have a nice effect."

She said nothing and did not move.

Al-Malik smiled pleasantly as sweat dripped from his face. "Comrade Bloch, I think perhaps you've inhibited our guest. Please assure her that it's perfectly all right to speak now that we're all here."

Bloch touched the side of her head.

She did not react.

"Well, Anatoliy," al-Malik said, "I think that as the evening wears on you may eventually find your tongue. Meanwhile, I will ask you once again politely: please take off your clothes."

Arad smiled. "I'd rather die," she said.

The two men laughed softly.

Arad looked at al-Malik's wet face.

Al-Malik picked up the scissors. "You know, Anatoliy, your government paid a handsome sum for that special uniform—not that anyone else could wear it quite the way you do."

Arad said nothing.

Al-Malik opened and closed the scissors a few times. "One way or another, Anatoliy, your uniform is coming off. The choice is yours." He snapped the scissors closed.

On the one hand, it would be helpful to have intact clothing when she made her escape. On the other hand, the tedious process of cutting through the thick fabric might provide the diversion she needed. Of course, the choice was *not* hers.

"Very well, Anatoliy," smiled al-Malik. "If you would,

please, Comrade Bloch."

Bloch moved in and secured the left ankle, the right ankle, and finally the right wrist.

Arad fought but did not change her expression.

Al-Malik removed his jacket and folded it over the foot railing. His shirt was drenched. "First her boots, please, Comrade Bloch."

Bloch untied Arad's boots, smiling up at her occasionally before he yanked them off and let them drop one by one to the dusty floor. He peeled off her socks.

Arad kept her penetrating eyes on al-Malik.

Al-Malik stepped back and smiled. "Very pretty feet, wouldn't you say, Bloch?"

Bloch smiled at her. "Yes. Very pretty indeed."

"Good. That will be all, Comrade Bloch."

Bloch's smile evaporated, and he started to turn quizzically toward his partner.

Al-Malik wheeled to his right, pressed his silencer against the side of Bloch's head, and fired.

The little body shuddered. Before it could collapse where it stood, al-Malik threw his shoulder into Bloch's chest and heaved the dead man back against the far wall. Bloch landed in the corner. For a few moments, there was the sound of his blood spattering on the floor.

Al-Malik straightened up and looked at Corporal Arad.

Arad was smiling.

"Well, good," al-Malik responded. "You're more relaxed already. Now it's just the two of us, Anatoliy. The way it was always meant to be."

Arad's best hope was that Kadir had followed al-Malik here. And Xenakis was out there somewhere. Maybe they would arrive together. But that was not likely. Al-Malik was right: it was now just the two of them. And the only thing Arad could be sure of at this point was that Khaled al-Malik was utterly insane. She remembered all the times he had bent down behind her to show her how to hold a weapon or how to set a charge, without the slightest intimation of sexuality. She remembered the shock and humiliation she had felt in Paris when, for the first time, he had dared to speak to her of such things. She tried to compare al-Malik's collapsed sense of discipline to her own horrible epiphany in Paris and its wonderful aftermath. She thought of Wood—*Oh, God, Aaron, if I get out of this*—and of the innumerable twists of the human mind. But she knew there could be no logic here, not now. There could be only time. Time is all anyone has, Kadir had said. With enough time, anything was possible.

Al-Malik held the gun in his left hand and the scissors in his right.

Arad smiled and sighed. "Khaled," she said softly. "Something very strange has happened. Something I want to try to understand."

Al-Malik paused and cocked his head to the side.

"Before you do something very unlike you, tell me: What happened to the man, the kind, gentle man who could recognize potential and nurture it? What happened to the young man of action who believed in human rights, justice, sovereignty, and in the inalienable destiny of his people? What happened to the skillful man who taught me about survival, self-defense, and the righteous use of force? The *righteous* use of force, Khaled? This is I! Anat! Your loyal comrade who vowed to use your example to avenge her father's death and to serve a common heritage. What happened that drove you to take this action against one who has lived in your image like a daughter?"

Al-Malik smiled. "Tender sentiments, Anatoliy. Very tender indeed. But since when does a daughter point a rifle at her father's head?"

Arad looked astonished. "What on earth are you talking about?"

"You know precisely what I am talking about. I appeared in the square several minutes early specifically to confirm that you would seize the opportunity."

"Khaled, I don't know how you got this horrible idea."

"The late Comrade Bloch there seemed to believe otherwise, Anatoliy."

Arad sneered at the lifeless form crumpled in the corner. "I am the only one who has never let you down, Khaled. You know that."

"I know that you will never again let me down, Anatoliy." Al-Malik made a move toward the bed.

Tel Aviv

MUHAMMAD KADIR SPOTTED Rachel Perlman when she was still many steps from the station door. He walked quickly out to her.

Each saw in the other's eyes a thousand unnecessary words. They fell into a desperate embrace. Perlman was shaking.

Kadir stroked her hair. "Let's take my car." As they walked away from the building, Kadir leaned in: "Where's our hall monitor?"

"They called off the surveillance, Muhammad."

"Oh, great. Do you have a weapon?"

Perlman angled her open purse to reveal the pistol and the blade. They walked briskly to Kadir's car.

"I did call the police," she continued. "They should be there before we are."

The two wound their way slowly through the area in the twilight. It was several minutes before Perlman recognized anything. Finally, she saw the alley and gasped.

Kadir touched her shoulder.

"I don't know if I can go in there again," she said.

He massaged her neck as he drove on a few blocks and parked on an unlit corner. "You won't have to. Wait here. Stay down and keep the doors locked. Here are the keys." He paused. "I may be totally wrong about this." He looked seriously at her and smiled. He wiped away her tears, leaned over, and kissed her lightly on the forehead. Then he touched his holster and reached for the door handle.

Perlman grabbed his arm. "Wait," she whispered, fixing him with deep-green eyes. "Do that again."

Kadir smiled and leaned toward her.

Perlman kissed him full on the mouth and held his face to her.

Kadir slowly pulled back.

"Muhammad. Please be careful."

In an instant, he was gone, except for the fading shuffle of his sneakers.

Kadir tiptoed to the end of the alley and turned. Suddenly light spilled onto a wall. He slipped alongside the near building and watched shapes move back and forth through the vertical rectangle of light. He was about to step through the door when he heard a click. He jerked his head into the space in time to see a man's body being thrown backward across the entrance to a room at the far left corner of the building. After his initial shock, he swallowed with relief. He waited a moment, hoping next to see his sister walk out of the room. Instead, he began hearing reverberations of distant voices. He slipped quietly into the big outer room and began creeping along the left-hand wall. He was a few yards from the dark outlines of some furniture when he recognized the voices. He gripped the pistol with both hands.

He saw a weak circle of light outside dancing on the debris-strewn alleyway. The circle stopped a few feet from the outside door and disappeared.

A policeman looked in and faced the brightly lit inner room.

Kadir froze.

The officer began slipping silently along the wall.

Kadir weighed his chances: the cop had backup, whereas he had only love and hatred. He quietly holstered his gun and hoped the man inching toward him was not disposed toward snap judgment. Kadir slowly raised his hands above his head.

The cop spotted him backed against the wall from several yards away and aimed his pistol at him.

Kadir shook his head and tipped it toward the inner room.

Without lowering his weapon, the policeman crept up alongside Kadir.

Kadir whispered: "My sister is being attacked in there."

The officer looked suspiciously at Kadir for a moment, until the young man's desperate eyes convinced him. "Stay right where you are," he whispered.

After the cop had passed and was positioned with his back against the wall outside the inner door, Kadir reached in and wrapped his fingers around the handle of his gun.

A moment later, the cop burst into the room and shouted, "Freeze!"

Kadir heard another click, and the cop jerked backward onto the floor. Kadir drew his weapon and charged into the room. He wheeled to his left and heard Arad gasp. He pointed his gun at al-Malik's forehead and pressed the trigger. Nothing happened.

In the instant before Kadir could pull off the second attempt, Khaled al-Malik smiled sympathetically and fired two shots.

Kadir's body plunged backward across the dead cop's

chest.

"Muhammad!" Arad screamed. "Oh, God, no! Muhammad, *Muhammad!*"

Al-Malik stood for several seconds watching.

Arad seethed at him. "Kill me! *Kill me,* you worthless bastard!"

Al-Malik smiled. "Forget the fool, Anatoliy. He earned those bullets long ago. You, on the other hand, are still my little jewel. And the night is young, Anatoliy." He smiled as Arad shook and screamed. Then he stepped to the bedside. "You know, Anatoliy," he said softly, "I'm sorry you had to witness this unfortunate turn of events. But every couple knows that lovemaking serves not just as an expression of desire but also of consolation. And so, let us this evening resolve to join together not merely to satisfy our own longing but also in honor of our dear departed Muhammad, who martyred himself for you with the same lovable stupidity he applied to all his endeavors."

Arad suddenly stopped weeping and regained the calm implacable eyes. "You will have to kill me first. You will have to shoot me in the head, strip my dead body, and realize your pathetic boy's fantasy while my eyes burn themselves into your brain. You will wear my body and my eyes for the rest of your horrible unknown existence. Come on, al-Malik. Fuck me."

Al-Malik smiled. "You see, Anatoliy, this is a perfect example of how you differ from poor Muhammad there: always thinking ahead. You will abandon this curious death wish of yours once you discover how it feels to make love properly: with a man."

Finally that day, she concentrated on Wood. The

source of her greatest and now only joy was actually just blocks away. She would visualize him, hear his voice, bathe in his music, taste his kiss, and surrender to the whirlpool of their union. He must never know what she was about to do to save herself for him. If it had been Muhammad for whom she would have died, it was Aaron for whom she would live.

As al-Malik began cutting away Arad's trousers, there was a faint sound from the outer room. Al-Malik stopped and walked out the door. Arad heard three shots and the sound of a body hitting the concrete.

A moment later, Rachel Perlman entered the room holding a pistol in two hands.

"Rachel!"

"Oh, God, Ani!" Perlman dropped the gun, rushed to the bed, and embraced Arad with all her strength.

For several long seconds Arad shook with emotion. "For Christ's sake, girl, untie me!"

Perlman complied as quickly as possible, both women screaming and laughing as she struggled with the belts.

When she was free, Arad wrapped her arms and legs around Perlman and wept violently in her fragrant hair.

Perlman rocked her back and forth, sharing her grief, horror, and deliverance.

In a few minutes, the outer room was flooded with portable lamplight and the sound of astonished voices. When a pair of patrolmen burst into the little room with weapons drawn, only Perlman looked up and managed a weak smile while her friend cried against her breast. As the officers gently approached, Perlman craned her neck and whispered in the first one's ear. "Don't let her see anything."

When Arad's crying had subsided, the cop gathered her in his arms. The four left the room with Perlman covering her friend's face. The women were ushered into the back of a police car and were taken downtown.

"And you had not seen this guy since high-school gym?" Detective Slonimsky insisted one more time before closing the folder.

Arad lowered her head. "No. Apparently he had harbored this gruesome fantasy all these years and tracked me down when I was assigned here temporarily." She repeated the last word to herself.

Slonimsky viewed the young soldier. Something was familiar about al-Malik. It probably was some other sex crime years ago. Perlman had saved the state enough money to irrigate another acre of the Negev. Slonimsky worried about the armed Palestinian brother. He worried more about the sandy-haired adjutant: Why was Major Goldstein's office boy there? Were he and this demented Arab competing for Arad's affections? Was Bloch a mole? Had Arad and her protective brother got sucked into one of these dim-witted Palestinian splinter groups? Whatever it was, it could wait. Slonimsky had seen his fill of inexplicable death for one evening. He called Perlman in from the hallway. "You two go home and get some rest. I'll have someone drop you off."

Perlman thought of Kadir's car parked back on the street and of her own at the train station. She looked into Slonimsky's eyes. The air in this sad little office was filled with minor omissions. She patted Arad on the back and helped her up.

The officer who had carried Arad out of the warehouse met them at the front door and walked them back to his car. "Where to, ladies?" he smiled softly.

Anat Arad looked up immediately and recited Rachel Perlman's address.

Tel Aviv

AARON WOOD CLOSED THE DOOR behind him, walked to the window, and looked out over the moonlit sea. He thought of the places he had been that day and of how things can look so small to an adult. But the eucalyptus had grown according to his imagination. It had warmed his heart to see how trees and bushes had cast their shadows over and beyond the worn red-tile roof. Here, at least, nature seemed to be gaining rather than losing ground. Their little village lane had been widened, there were more modern homes surrounding the monastic little estate, and the nestled diplomatic community of Herzliya had conceded too much ground to Miami-style monoliths. But he had expected all this and more. He thought of the old trees here guarding a piece of his childhood and of the slightly younger trees back in Virginia. He reached into his pocket and withdrew the handful of seeds he had collected that afternoon at the edge of the property: maybe they would take root in his red clay, maybe not.

He looked at the glimmering water and dragged himself back from the distant future, to the wrenching farewell they would enact three mornings from now in Eilat, when they would spill to each other their wild hopes and unformed plans. He could live here, easily. Or could Arad endure Washington? Maybe she would enjoy the temperate change. The only two homes she had ever known, Israel and Southern California, were nearly identical environments, give or take a few thousand years of human frailty. True, a woman who looked like Arad was wasted in D.C. Yet there was that fierce contempt for commercial success: he could see her outfitted not in Hollywood chic but in K Street riot gear, marching the halls of the Dirksen Building, bursting in on recalcitrant senators, drilling her inescapable eyes into their fat bloodshot faces, and converting them one by one to the righteous fait accompli of Palestinian autonomy. But all of this was pointless conjecture. They had found each other, here and now. The rest was just so much paperwork.

He looked at his watch. The prime minister's speech would be on the news. *Christ, it's nearly eleven o'clock.*

He went over to decipher the television schedule. He had just picked up the remote when the phone rang.

"Aaron Wood."

"Hi."

"God, I love you."

"It's me. Ani."

"Of course it's you!"

The line was silent a moment.

She had called herself *Ani.* He had not heard this heavy tone in her voice. "Anat. Are you all right?" He could hear her fighting back tears. "Where are you?"

"I'm downstairs. In the lobby."

"I'll be right there."

"Aaron."

"Yes?"

"Something terrible has happened." She broke down.

He shuddered. "I'll be right down."

"Aaron."

"Shsh."

"You know I love you."

He breathed in. "Yes."

"I'm not alone."

He grabbed the key and ran to the elevator.

When the doors opened, Arad was slumped in the corner of a sofa. She looked exhausted. She was dressed in baggy civilian clothes. Rachel Perlman sat close at her side, holding her hand.

The two women smiled as Wood approached. Perlman's smile was a good deal more convincing than Arad's, and the taller woman blushed as she dropped her friend's hand and patted it a couple of times. Finally, Arad rose weakly. Perlman followed and provided support.

Wood arrived in time for Arad to melt into his arms. He took in her scent and kissed her hair as she clung to him weeping. Wood saw Perlman standing just behind Arad and to his right. He smiled into her wet emerald eyes.

Perlman tentatively lifted her right hand and placed it over Wood's.

He turned and brought Perlman in, and the three wrapped one another up. They thought of all there was to hear and to tell and wondered how many more nights they could go like this if only they had them to spend.

Perlman squeezed their shoulders firmly and whispered in Wood's ear: "Let's go upstairs."

Perlman and Wood guided Arad into the room and laid her on the bed. They stood looking at her like worried parents. After a few self-conscious moments, they brought two chairs over beside the bed.

Perlman set her purse on the nightstand and smiled

demurely at the two of them as she reached into the big leather bag. "We might need this," she said softly as she produced a half-full bottle of whiskey. She sat and regained Arad's left hand.

Arad turned on her side and offered Wood her right hand.

He kissed the hand, noting the red marks around Arad's wrists. He sat slowly.

Perlman took the first sip directly from the bottle, shook off the jolt, and handed the bottle to Wood.

Wood offered it to Arad.

Perlman smiled loosely and pushed the bottle back. "She's a few ahead of us, Aaron."

Arad smiled dreamily and stretched.

Wood took a polite sip.

Perlman did most of the talking, with only occasional amplification from her sedated partner. When Perlman was finished, the three of them were in tears, wishing that life's gifts were not so often wrapped in cruelty.

Wood looked at his watch and at the women. Arad had several times drifted in and out of sleep, and Perlman was in no condition to drive. He got up, lifted Perlman by the shoulders, and guided her onto the bed next to Arad, where she immediately turned toward her friend and closed her eyes. He covered the two with a blanket. He watched them for a few moments, checked the alarm, and slipped into bed on the other side of Arad.

When Wood woke at dawn, Perlman was standing beside the bed smiling plaintively at them. She reached into her purse and produced a set of keys.

Wood rose and tucked the blanket around Arad, who

was sound asleep.

Perlman motioned toward the bathroom.

Wood followed her, smoothing his clothes and pushing his long hair out of his face.

Perlman steadied herself against the sink. "I'll take the bus over to my car." She handed Wood the keys. "Muhammad's is parked across the street. You can take it to Ani's quarters and retrieve the jeep." She looked at the keys in Wood's hand. "It's time she owned a car."

Wood considered the triviality of his Middle East mission, compared with what the two women had been through.

Perlman looked knowingly back at him. "Finishing your tour will be the best thing for her. We spoke with her new commander last evening. His name is Sergeant Major Ariel Edelman. Ani told me where she thinks Muhammad hid their mom. I'm supposed to go there this afternoon with one of Slonimsky's men, to tell her, and to help arrange for—" She lowered her head. "And I'll call Nick, their friend," she wept.

Wood stepped forward and embraced her softly. "I'm so sorry, Rachel." He stroked her hair. Arad would have to carry on in Muhammad's name, and Wood worried about her burdens in the days ahead. "Do you really think this al-Malik affair is behind everyone?" he whispered.

"Slonimsky feels Ani has suffered enough. Whatever foolishness she and her brother had got into died with al-Malik. If this Sheikh Hadid is smart, he's abandoned the mail-order guerrilla trade. Slonimsky doesn't even know about Nick, and there's no reason he should."

They smiled privately at the image of the mischievous

patriarch waking up at this hour in Cairo, and they thought of the son Xenakis never had.

Perlman squeezed Wood's shoulders. "Take good care of her."

Wood hugged her in return. "And you. After Eilat."

"Shsh."

"You've been strong enough for all three of us."

"So have you, whether you know it or not." She pulled back and smiled. Her face was flushed. "We had a beautiful conversation about you." She looked away and embraced him again firmly. "Don't you worry about after Eilat," she whispered.

"Will we see you there?" he asked.

"I wouldn't miss it." She glanced over his shoulder to her watch. "I'd better get out of here." She smiled, kissed him softly on the cheek, and floated out the door.

Tel Aviv

AARON WOOD WATCHED HER SLEEP for several moments, then knelt beside the bed and stroked her beautiful black hair. He leaned forward and kissed her forehead.

She smiled but did not open her eyes.

He hated to disturb her almost as much as he feared the moment when she would remember.

The moment came, and the tears. He cradled her head in his fingers as she curled tighter into herself, shaking with grief. For several minutes, he knelt beside her and rocked her gently.

Finally, she extended unsteady hands and embraced him.

"Are you sure you're up to this?" he whispered, unable to imagine her springing into the jeep for seventy-two hours' undistinguished duty through the Negev.

She hugged him as hard as she could. "Don't—leave—me, Aaron," she gasped.

He kissed her hair.

After her crying subsided, she caressed his neck and shoulders. "Aaron," she whispered.

He was silent.

"Aaron. Make love to me."

He held her and looked at the clock.

"Please. I need you."

He kissed her and pushed gently on her shoulder.

She turned on her back and opened her eyes.

He pulled aside the blanket and sat beside her. He unbuckled her borrowed belt, unzipped the loose jeans, slipped them off, and laid them on the bed.

"Am I awful?"

"Shsh." He raised her knees, pulled her gently toward the foot of the bed, knelt, and touched his tongue to her.

She arched her back and pulled his pillow to her face.

As she began to descend, Wood became aware of an uncustomary scent on her skin. Then he remembered the friendly kiss in the bathroom a few minutes before and smiled to himself. He gathered their girl in his arms and played to her the one form of music that, so far as he knew, was not in his new colleague's repertoire.

Afterward, Arad lay wrapped around him holding on as though this were their last moment together.

Wood explained the plan Perlman had described, certain that Arad already knew it but less certain of how much liquor she had consumed the night before. He looked at the clock and headed for the shower. At the door, he turned to find her watching him.

She smiled provocatively. "So tell me: how did it feel just now, taking off Rachel's pants?"

"I beg your—"

"Come on."

He smiled. "I suppose I could ask you the same thing, Corporal."

"I've had more practice than you."

"Yes." He grinned and disappeared behind the curtain.

On the road south later that morning, both of them struggled to remind themselves that they could not undo yesterday's horrific events and that after Eilat there would be more than enough time for heartbreak and loneliness. Both considered that Arad's loss was permanent and tragic, the most permanent loss in a life filled with tragedy. Still, Arad was not proud that she would still have Perlman, whereas Wood would return home only to memories and dreams.

"Are you sure you don't want me to drive?" he asked for the second time as he looked at her glazed expression.

"Yes." She forced a smile.

He reached out and massaged her neck. "*Ani.*"

She blossomed.

"I like calling you that. Do you mind?"

"Of course not."

"It would look sensational on the cover of *Vogue.*"

She smiled warmly through the windshield.

"At the very least, you could use a long vacation."

She sighed. "Yes."

"I know this is not the time to talk about any of these things, but they won't get any easier to deal with once we're separated by thousands of miles." He looked away and fell silent. Finally he looked back at her. "I wish I could have known him."

She nodded. "Let's just pretend," she said, wiping her eyes. "For these three days, let's just pretend, OK? It's the only way I'm going to get through this." She steeled her jaw. Then suddenly she pounded her fist on the dashboard. "Oh, God! *Muhammad!*"

Wood touched her shoulder softly.

They rode quietly for several miles.

"Aaron," she said in a low voice.

He impulsively kissed her cheek.

She smiled. "I owe you an apology. I should have known you wouldn't be angry about Rachel. You said as much in Haifa. But then it was just hypothesis. I thought I'd never see her again. I didn't call you because I couldn't bear for you to know about those horrible hours—"

"Shsh," he whispered. "Ani, she saved your life." He thought of Perlman's long separation from Arad and wondered if he would emerge from his own with nearly so much poise.

Arad smiled. "She's happy for us."

"Yes. As I am for the two of you."

"Are you sure?"

"Absolutely. You're beautiful together."

They rode on a while.

"She likes you," Arad said clearly.

Wood blushed and looked away. "Because you do."

"No, she said she liked you immediately. She has very good instincts."

"Well, she certainly has good taste in women."

Arad grew more serious. "I have no experience at this, of course: a triangle."

"She strikes me as volatile but kind."

"Exactly. And sometimes she's the one who needs the shoulder."

He reflected in amazement. "God knows she can rise to the occasion."

Arad filled her lungs with pride.

Wood looked out the window for a while. "You know, I've been thinking I'd like to write about all this one day. Would you mind?"

"*Mind?* I'd be honored!"

"Maybe I should just dive in when I get back, keep my mind occupied."

She reached for his hand. After a long silence, she smiled mischievously. "And how will your story introduce Rachel?"

"What do you mean?"

"What do you think of her, really?"

"Well, at first, I thought she was a troublemaker. But she so clearly shared my concern for you that I soon felt a kind of partnership."

"Yeah? Do you think she's sexy?"

"You know, Corporal, I'm—"

"Do you?"

He shifted. "Well, of course she's sexy. I'd notice her on the street. Until I knew how she felt about you, though, she seemed a bit artificial."

"I thought so too, at first."

He looked aside. "If you don't mind my saying it, she's no Anat Arad."

She smiled. "Thank you, Mr. Wood. I'll keep that observation to myself."

"She probably said the same thing about me."

Arad looked at him skeptically. "Not quite."

"Oh? Apples and oranges?"

"More like bananas and orchids, wouldn't you say?" She giggled and covered her mouth. "No, she thinks you're hot."

"Well, that's very sweet. But her assignment for me was to take good care of you."

"Yes." She struggled momentarily and fell pensive and

345

silent.

They rode on, thinking of the inescapable things they had vowed not to discuss. They dragged themselves back periodically from the horizon. They energized themselves with thoughts of Eilat, and of a bon voyage the three of them would never forget.

37

Eilat

AARON WOOD TOOK HIS LAST BOW, smiled at the sea of tanned faces, and savored for a moment the sound of their unconditional love—a love that seemed too easily earned in a world where personal love depended alternately on miracles and hard work, and in a part of the world where love of any kind was in painfully short supply. He looked out at the Israeli people, celebrating and forgetting for now that their cooperative neighbors just to the south had not so long ago been as intolerant of them as their eastern and northern neighbors were now. He thought of the emerald beauties he had seen during this short week in the land of his childhood. He forgave Israel's paranoia and his own country's myopia, and he wished his audience well. As always, he had only his musician's wonderland for retreat as he considered the possibility that peace might never come to this place, and that history's oldest conflicts might indeed be its last. He looked out at the moonlit Red Sea and thought about those few things he knew for certain. He turned and walked off the stage.

Anat Arad and Rachel Perlman were awaiting him at the foot of the stairs, beaming proudly and looking like small children in the bearlike arms of a big jocular Greek with a few vestiges of gray hair about the ears, a Miles Davis T-shirt, and a pair of twinkling affirmative eyes that gave only the slightest indication that they had in three days shed more than their share of tears.

"Aaron Wood," Arad announced, "this is our dear friend Nick Xenakis."

"It's a pleasure to meet you, sir," Wood said.

Xenakis returned his arm around Arad and pulled her into his ample frame. "Beautiful playing, Mr. Wood. Just beautiful."

"Thank you, sir." He basked in their exuberance for as long as he could stand it, as Xenakis's parental aura made more difficult the task of avoiding the hungry eyes of Arad and her dangerous girlfriend.

"Let me buy you kids a drink," Xenakis sang. He wheeled around still holding onto the women.

The three resembled a Gothic cathedral that suddenly had set out across the countryside. For a moment, Wood lingered in their wake.

Xenakis let go of Perlman to carve a slightly narrower swath into the crowd as he made his way toward the little café about half a mile from the stage.

As Xenakis and Arad talked and hugged, Perlman fell back and strolled beside Wood. She smiled at him for several moments without saying anything. Suddenly she kissed him on the cheek and draped a long elegant arm around his shoulder.

They were exactly the same height.

"You're wonderful," Perlman said brightly. Then she whispered in his ear: "Ani said you had amazing hands."

Wood laughed.

Arad looked back, smiled at them, and faced forward.

Wood casually found Perlman's waist, pecked her cheek, and smiled into worldly green eyes. "Thank you. So are you."

Perlman laughed. "How do you know?"

"I know what you've been doing for her."

They walked on a few steps.

Wood whispered in Perlman's ear. "How's Mrs. Arad holding up?"

"About as well as one might expect, I'm afraid," she said, unconsciously brushing aside Wood's hair as if it were her own. "We decided she's better off where she is for a day or two, until Ani can be with her." She squeezed his shoulder. "Try not to worry about anything tonight," she whispered.

Arad looked back again.

Wood and Perlman smiled to themselves.

"God, she's beautiful," he said.

"Yes, she is." She looked at him. "You know, I owe all this to you."

He thought of all he owed Perlman.

"If you hadn't come over here, Ani would never have been assigned to watch over you, and I'd never have learned where she was. You know how proud she is. Someday I'll tell you about it. Meanwhile, thank you." She kissed him on the mouth and laughed her bright persuasive laugh.

Wood loosened his grip on her and watched Xenakis and Arad, who had begun to pull ahead of them.

Perlman squeezed his shoulder. "You think I'm too forward, don't you?"

He patted her waist.

"Maybe I am. I'm certainly less inhibited than our little angel there. I'm sorry if I've made you uncomfortable." She paused. "I can assure you, Ani doesn't mind—which definitely would not have been the case a year ago!" She laughed nervously. "I think after everything we've been through, what you two have discovered together, and what she and I have rediscovered—" She pulled Wood closer. "—and the fact that tonight is, well, goodbye for a while, we all need closeness and openness more than usual."

"Yes." He looked at her curiously. "How about you? I mean, have you ever—" He pointed to Arad, to Perlman, and to himself.

"A threesome?" she smiled. "No. I wanted to once, but it wasn't the right time, or the right person. It cost me Ani." She looked down.

He smiled. "Well, neither of us regards you as a threat. I hope you'll feel the same about me."

"I already do." She kissed him again and laughed.

"Maybe you ought to stop doing that, at least until I don't feel like I'm cheating on her."

"OK," she smiled, "I'll behave. But no one is cheating on anyone—got that?"

As Xenakis and Arad found a table and the other two began to catch up, Perlman gently brushed her fingers through the back of Wood's hair and relished the resultant dreamy look on his face.

"Got it," he said. "Nice nails."

"Variety is a wonderful thing, yes?"

"Indeed." He looked at Arad, still out of earshot, then back at Perlman. "Who found whom, or was it—"

"—love at first sight, like you two?" she smiled. "Well, as you know, we were bunkmates. Of course, we're quite different in some ways. One night she asked me to show her—it sounds cute, she's such an ascetic—how to apply makeup, of all things. She hated the experience, and afterward we just kind of felt playful. It was interesting. I made the first move, as usual. But she was a declared lesbian, whereas I had no idea I was bisexual. In fact, I'm not sure I really am, except where Ani is concerned. She was and is my first and only woman. I had no fear or embarrassment." She paused. "This really doesn't bother you?"

"No. We're on the same team. We just bring different offerings to the table." He gave her a discreet but thorough scrutinizing. "Don't we, Ms. Perlman?"

She laughed loudly.

"Just checking," he said. "I'm not sure how many more surprises I can handle this week."

They sat down across from a pair of smiles wide enough to conceal the deepest pain.

"Ani tells me you're going on from here into Egypt," Xenakis said.

"Yes."

"If you get time, you must come by my shop in Cairo." He handed Wood a card. "Had I known, I'd have set up an in-store and helped you move a little product."

"Maybe next time," Wood smiled to him and to Arad.

"You know," Xenakis confessed, "my niece, Olympia, is a fine jazz singer."

Wood looked interested and tried not to notice Arad's disrespectful grin.

"In fact, I have a few copies of her new CD with me; remind me to leave one with you."

"Certainly!" Arad's toe under Wood's cuff did not distress him nearly so much as Perlman's fingertips on his thigh.

"Finding decent jazz musicians in Cairo is not easy, as you can imagine," Xenakis continued. "Perhaps you'll drop by the hotel some evening and sit in."

"Sure, I'd like to meet her." He seized Perlman's roving hand and retreated into the drink menu.

Arad and Perlman simultaneously giggled as Xenakis gave each of them a brief puzzled look.

A few rounds later, the three rose to say their separate goodbyes to Xenakis.

After Perlman stepped back, the old man entertained Wood with more musical chat and then looked over at Arad, now moving toward Perlman, and he gently pulled Wood to the side.

"Mr. Wood?"

"Aaron, please."

"Aaron. I assume that as a musician you know the story of Orpheus and Eurydice."

"Of course." He smiled as he felt the card in his pocket.

"Well, Aaron, Ani has told me about your magical week together. And I must tell you that, despite all the horror she has known, throughout her life, I have never seen her so happy. Just as you reached all these people tonight, you have won Ani's heart in a way I did not think possible. Now, you two have asked each other some questions for which there will not soon be answers. But she is strong. And if you are as strong as the music I have heard you play, there is a love here such as comes but once in a lifetime. It is easy to want a thing too much. Ani has just lost the only man she ever had a chance to love. Well, she has me, but after she and Muhammad were grown—" He looked down. "Ani has had so little to count on—that is why she has stayed so long in the army—and now, suddenly, she has the opportunity not only to know lasting love but also to blossom into the bright creature she was destined to be. If you find that you truly love her, Aaron, she will come to you. Set her free in America. We know that a man needs laughably little to be happy. A woman, though, deserves more than will ever be available to her here. Take some time, Aaron. Be sure. You both know how you feel today; you will know soon enough whether you cannot live apart." He paused and fixed Wood with penetrating dark eyes. "Her beauty is more powerful than you yet know. You will see her in your dreams and carry her image with you wherever you are, and still when you see her again, her actual beauty will surpass the limits of your imagination. She has cast her spell on you just as unconsciously as the sun gives life to the earth—she cannot help it. She has chosen you above all others on whom to shine her light. Be not dazzled by her beauty, Aaron. When you walk away from Ani tomorrow, do it with your head up and your eyes facing south into Egypt. Go strongly from her. She will feel your strength and add it to her own. She will come to you. Do not return for her."

Wood smiled. "I have considered these things, Nick. But I wonder why you think Pluto's fatal decree applies now in our unpoetic age?"

Xenakis looked out toward the sea and smiled wistfully. "A long time ago, I was in love with an impossibly beautiful woman. She loved me as an equal. I could have married her. But I was a poor historian in a museum, and I felt unworthy of her. I refused to accept that a woman so beautiful would have had me without riches or fine clothes. I did not believe enough in myself to fight for her. And so one day she quit her internship and returned to her homeland. Shortly thereafter, she married a man who had even less than I: a soldier. She and I remained friends. To this day, I have loved her and have looked after those she loves; and I have wept for her losses. I mourn the death of her son. It is my hope that one day you, Aaron, may marry her daughter."

Wood smiled through tears. "Does Ani know about this?"

"No."

"Promise you'll both be there, and that you will give away the bride."

Xenakis smiled warmly. "If God will have it so."

The two men shook hands.

Wood stepped away and looked at Arad. He watched her approach Xenakis trying to mask her sadness, and he watched Xenakis blessing her. He felt Perlman moving next to him and placing her hand in his. He thought of the people he had met during this week of weeks and of the profound sacrifices most of them had made in the name of love. He thought of Xenakis and of his lost dream, of Arad's father and his fatal devotion, of Arad's mother alone in Gaza, of Xenakis alone in Cairo, of tragic Muhammad Kadir, and of his own dead parents and their long inexplicable marriage. For the first time in his life, Aaron Wood felt commissioned to something loftier than an ephemeral piece of music.

Perlman turned him by the shoulders and forced him to look at her. "One of the things a salesperson learns to do is to carry on one conversation while listening to another. Tomorrow we all will need your strength." She smiled and kissed him softly on the cheek. "Tonight is Eilat."

Eilat

THE DESK CLERK LOOKED UP BRIEFLY as the trio walked by arm in arm and got on the elevator.

As they rode up, Aaron Wood got out his room key.

Rachel Perlman turned to Anat Arad and said, "Give me yours."

Arad and Wood looked at her inquisitively.

Perlman touched their shoulders. "You two should wake up alone together." As they neared Wood's room, Perlman maintained her selling smile.

Wood opened his door.

Once inside, the three shuffled about nervously.

Wood hung up his jacket. "I'm going to take a quick shower. Those lights were brutal." He started to unbutton his shirt, then felt both conspicuous and slightly unwelcome. He smiled at the women, slipped into the bathroom, and closed the door. He undressed and enjoyed the muffled sounds of giggling and of jewelry being spilled onto wood. As he reached to turn on the water, he heard Perlman's voice just outside the door.

"Wouldn't you just die if we joined you?" she laughed.

He looked at the door handle. "Isn't water conservation one of your religions over here?"

The women laughed, but their attention was now directed elsewhere.

As he dried off, Wood heard more sounds. He waited until they had subsided. He withdrew the curtain and looked in the mirror. Wrapped in a towel, he took a deep breath and opened the door.

The women were sitting far apart in the bed, wearing girlish grins on flushed faces. Arad's breasts were peering over the covers. Perlman's were not. Hair in general was untended. Wood thought of the brevity of his shower and admired their efficiency. "Will you allow me the courtesy of a dignified entrance?"

Arad giggled.

"Oh, no," laughed Perlman, "we never order dessert without first viewing the whole selection."

Arad shot an admonishing look at her friend, who feigned embarrassment.

Wood climbed into the middle of the bed, got under the covers, and drew out the towel.

Perlman placed the towel on her nightstand.

Wood looked at Arad, across the room at Arad's clothes folded neatly over one chair, at Perlman's draped haphazardly over another, at Perlman, and straight ahead. He laughed when he saw their unrelenting smiles bearing down on him from the mirror. He put his left arm around Arad and his right around Perlman, leaned back, and looked at the ceiling. "I have no idea how many men in real life ever find themselves in this situation," he said, "but, all delusions aside, I just want you two to know—" Suddenly he felt their fingertips and gasped.

"Shut up and lie down, Aaron." The voice was Perlman's.

He obeyed.

"Close your eyes."

He did not need to see anything as he felt the covers

being drawn down and then their hands, breath, hair, lips, tongues, and mouths. He heard their gentle words for each other as they shared him, and eventually he discerned they were taking turns. As one pair of hands concentrated, another medley of fingers or nails moved up and down his body. Then it was the one more familiar mouth as their voices grew more urgent and the skipping nails more impatient. Finally, as he caressed the soft trembling waist to his left, he felt the nails dance up his chest to his neck and encircle his head. He felt the abundant hair, heard the excited voice, tasted the new lips. As Arad's magic reached its apex, he accepted Perlman's generosity and welcomed her to the shuddering deep oneness that both understood they could know only with Arad.

As Wood began to descend, Perlman kissed him more gently and eventually moved back down his body.

They continued their gentle attentions until every muscle had resolved.

He lay silently for several minutes. He still had not opened his eyes, out of respect for Perlman, and in homage to Arad. He felt a final kiss and the gentle laying on of warm palms, and he sensed their smiling up at him.

"Aaron?" she whispered.

Ani.

"Aaron?" again, in stereo.

He felt the mischievous nails. "Ladies. That was wonderful. Thank you."

Perlman slapped him lightly on the thigh. "Don't get too comfortable, pal."

They all laughed.

"May I open my eyes now?" he asked.

There was a moment of silence and then the sound of shifting. "Sure," Perlman said.

He looked at the ceiling a moment. Then he lifted his head, pulled a second pillow under him, looked down, and smiled. Arad was sitting cross-legged at his left holding his hand and smiling with deep satisfaction. He looked a long time into her misty eyes. Feeling suddenly rude, he looked over at Perlman.

Twice.

He was not surprised to find her more dramatically posed, sitting on her calves with her legs together, leaning back on her left hand while she smiled demurely. Her bruises were not as bad as he had expected. Her long neck, flexed arm, and shoulder muscles announced tastefully ample breasts and a torso even trimmer than the neatly cut clothes had implied. He smiled at her matching gold navel ring and squeezed Arad's hand. Someday he would ask about their adventures. Her long milky thighs were scarcely less edible than his intended's. Perlman looked sensational. His smile was not the only indication of his approval.

Perlman giggled. "Thank you."

Wood got up on his elbows and asked Perlman for the towel.

Instead of handing it to him, she used it to wipe the sweat from his brow, face, neck, and everywhere below, while Wood and Arad smiled at each other.

When Perlman was finished, he took back the towel, got up, walked to the bathroom, and returned with fresh towel. He set it aside, knelt on the bed, took Perlman gently by the shoulders, and guided her down to his former place in the middle.

For the first time since their initial meeting, Perlman seemed vulnerable. She looked seriously between the two of them and finally at Arad.

Arad and Wood knelt on either side of her, stroked her hair, and gently caressed her neck and shoulders. Wood did not touch her intimately. Only after Perlman took a deep breath did Arad's fingertips begin tiptoeing down between her breasts and slowly around each pink nipple. Wood continued smiling at Perlman and stole occasional glances at Arad's placid face as her dark hands moved slowly over her lover's white body. When Arad bent forward, he held back her hair. Arad showed a trace of self-consciousness and then gradually moved down.

Wood lay on his left elbow and continued stroking Perlman's hair.

Perlman finally smiled at him, just as Arad's tongue found its mark. She closed her eyes and arched her back.

Wood leaned down and kissed Perlman's forehead, the tip of her nose, her cheeks, and her lips.

Her excitement grew quickly. As Wood began to kiss her neck, she cradled him and whispered in his ear: "I wish I could have you inside me."

When his lips arrived on her right nipple and his fingertips on her left, a watchful Arad increased her pressure.

Perlman soared.

Suddenly Wood felt Perlman's right hand wrap around him. He started to take it away, but he saw the left was clenched just as desperately in Arad's hair. Interpreting the gesture as security more than provocation, he tried to ignore it. An instant later, Perlman threw her left arm around him and shuddered violently against his neck. He massaged her shoulders as she began to release her tension, her spine eased closer to the bed, and her flushed face regained its former state of repose.

They lay in a long silence.

Wood reached back for the dry towel and touched Perlman softly with it. He ran his fingers through Arad's long hair and watched her kissing Perlman's thighs. He turned back to see the magnificent redhead smiling through grateful tears. He knew, and Perlman's conspiratorial glance confirmed, that their Ani had earned the orgasm of her dreams.

Eilat

"NOT BAD FOR BEGINNERS," Perlman said an hour later.

Arad and Wood moaned in agreement.

"God," Arad said breathlessly, "I panicked when you guys grabbed my arms, and then—" She nudged Perlman. "—you! Christ Jesus! Give me a break already!"

They laughed, then lay quietly. No one had looked at a clock since entering the room.

Perlman began to stir.

Arad and Wood pulled her back.

"How can we just—" Perlman began.

They stroked her hair and squeezed her shoulders.

Arad smiled. "You two will have to get used to seeing me in civvies."

"Except when we get you alone like this," Wood whispered.

"Yeah," Perlman concurred. "We'll strip you down to just holster and boots."

Wood pressed against Arad. "I have the feeling you two rather enjoyed your hitch in the army," he smiled.

Arad smiled wistfully.

"Well," Perlman clarified, "the accessories are one thing. The life is another." She looked at Arad. "I'm glad to hear this one's finally had enough of it."

Arad hugged them. "Until now, I didn't have anything outside the life strong enough to support me."

Perlman got up on her elbow, worked her neck, and issued a satisfied yawn. "Well, then," she said. "It's all settled. Somehow we're going to get through a period of excruciating grief and uncertainty, somehow we're all going to be together somewhere, and, meanwhile, we're not to worry about it." She patted the mattress a couple of times.

There was an uncomfortable silence as Wood looked into the mirror at the three of them.

Perlman's eyes misted over. "I talk too much." She sat up. "And I promised you a little privacy." She rose and reached for her clothes.

When Arad saw that Perlman was ready to go, she lay back.

Wood got up and walked Perlman to the door.

Arad smiled as they embraced.

"Will we see you before I go?" he whispered.

Perlman held him harder and shook her head.

They stood a moment in silence.

"Thank you, Rachel," he whispered.

"Thank *you*. Aaron." Perlman pulled back, fixed him with wet green eyes, and kissed him hard on the mouth. She made a funny face to Arad over his shoulder, turned, and left the room.

Wood closed the door, looked back at Arad, and smiled. He slid the chain across and returned to her.

Chantilly, Virginia

AARON WOOD WALKED OUT of the terminal and into the Virginia summer. The reminder of lush greenery did him little good. He crossed the parking lot toward his dusty convertible feeling the deep sweat of his homeland. He took in a chestful of humid air and thought of the good things. He had in his life known solitude, had welcomed and protected it, but he had had little experience with loneliness. He recalled Arad's devastated voice the day before on the crackling telephone. He could see the tears in her beautiful eyes, smell her clean skin, hear the bitter yearning as she wrestled with their schism and with her own crushing responsibilities. He recalled talking briefly with Perlman the night before, and he thought of the delicious tone of Arad's voice then as Perlman fulfilled her assignment with customary devotion. He opened the car doors and stood back as the searing cloud of heat rushed out. He thought of the perfumed evening air of Tiberias, heard lapping water, saw hungry eyes looking into him from across the table. He got in, started the engine, and turned on the air conditioner. He sat for a moment in the rushing wind. He looked across at the empty passenger seat and saw her there riding back from Tiberias, fighting her fierce jaw as he told her of Goldstein's wager. He closed his eyes and thought of how they had courted each other with politics and music, of how much they had learned in one week, of how much they had left unsaid. He leaned back and remembered the chronology of their astonishing first sight of each other, first words, first touch, first kiss, Arad's revelation, and their first aching streams of moonlight. He opened his eyes, looked at the parked cars glistening in waves, and calculated the inches, feet, yards, miles, and hours between himself and the grace to which his spirit called. The figures were as cruel as the numberless lights in the black heavens were beautiful. He eased the car into reverse.

As he wound slowly out of the airport and onto the forty minutes of lost farmland and malignant suburbia between there and his home, he thought of their last morning, of how fraternally Lederman and Fatool had behaved as he struggled with himself like a condemned prisoner, of how he had stood melded with Arad, each trying to memorize every nuance of the other's presence, of how right she had felt in his arms, of how beautiful she had been as they took in their last desperate sight of each other.

He slowed down and remembered Xenakis's Plutonian decree. As he sat waiting for a light to change, he snapped open his briefcase, found the card, and looked closely at the eyes of Eurydice shimmering in the distance. He knew that when he had the honor of meeting Mirim Arad he would recognize those eyes and would see in them the impossible beauty poor Xenakis had passed down to him.

He could not help smiling as he drove up his quiet cul-de-sac and saw the towering black walnut, and he imagined he could hear it inhaling before dropping its thumping hail of green fruit. The scorched midsummer grass had hardly grown in two weeks. An outside light had burned out, and the reliable ivy had insinuated a few swollen arteries into the carport. Otherwise the property appeared to have fared perfectly well without his assistance.

He took in his things and opened all the windows. He went to the telephone and listened to his messages. All but three of them were the predictable stuff of business and society. Third from the end was the senatorial voice of Arnie Vogel. Wood wondered how Vogel would react if one day Wood and Arad were to appear in his office doorway and shower him with gratitude. The penultimate phone message commanded more attention. Such words as there were tended toward monosyllabic repetition. Whether the two women were actually having sex or just playing mattered less than the joy they were sharing with him. He smiled at their crescendo. The final entry was the one he had been waiting for.

"Aaron. This is Ani.

"Rachel and I were not acting, by the way.

"I want you to know that she has my blessing to love you and you to love her. And whereas we have tasted Rachel's faults, we also have seen the depth and courage of her love. When she is selfish or cruel, we must remember that her fiery nature does not always speak for her heart. And when she opens her mouth once too often, we simply will have to put something wonderful in it, yes?

"Why am I going on about Rachel after I have finally gotten you alone? Well, it is true that she is here, and I am leaning hard on her. But until you left, I had not fully understood Rachel's own developing love for you. She

feels as uneasy about that as you did in Eilat.

"*All this is new and frightening. I understand harems are little tolerated in the West. But you are so precious to me, Aaron. And whereas I had written Rachel out of my life, she reentered it so profoundly that if I do not get all this out in the open, I will die of guilt. You must understand that I could be happy beyond my wildest dreams loving only you. But I have had to admit that I love you both. It will be years before we come to terms with the amazing events of our week and with how the two of us and then the three of us were brought together. Meanwhile, my heart aches to be sure that you know how gloriously and chemically and spiritually and permanently I love you, Aaron Wood.*"

The line was quiet a few moments.

"*God, how can I say goodbye? It will never be goodbye. Call me, write me, think of me, dream of me, and love me, Aaron, forever love me.*"

She started to cry.

"*Oh, Aaron. Au revoir.*"

Falls Church, Virginia

THEY SAT ON THE BACK PATIO in the weightless May breeze, leaned back in their green hardwood chaises, and stared up into the big silver maple that loomed close to the low stone patio wall.

Suddenly Anat Arad covered her mouth and laughed.

Aaron Wood smiled and looked absently back at his newspaper.

"What happened there?" she asked, laughing softly.

"Lightning. A long time ago." He casually turned a page.

Arad softened the focus of her eyes. "Doesn't it look like something to you, something rather particular?" she asked as she stretched at full length.

"I'm not sure what you're talking about, Corporal Arad."

"That's *Citizen* Arad to you, man." Again her eyes narrowed. "No, really, you don't see it?"

"See what?" he smiled.

"You know precisely what," she laughed as she slugged him on the arm.

"I have no idea what you mean."

Arad yanked off her running shorts.

Wood looked around as though he did not know they were concealed by dense foliage. He grinned but said nothing.

"Recognize it now?" she insisted.

"I believe you may be on to something."

She laughed. "And if you're not onto it in the next five seconds, it's coming over there after you."

He looked around again. "Here?"

Arad planted her calves on the arms of her chaise.

Some minutes later, as he knelt on the cool flagstones, he saw her misted eyes redirected up into the tree.

"You can't tell me you never noticed the resemblance."

He kissed her thigh. "Until now, I thought I was the only one who had."

They embraced in silence.

"*Here,*" she whispered against his neck. "I really am here." She looked around at the azaleas, the beautiful yellow rain, the dogwoods and gentle redbuds, the deep-green ivy. "And it is so beautiful."

"Yes, it is," he smiled. "August will be very humid— unlike anything you knew in the desert."

"Sounds wonderful." She wrapped herself tightly around him.

He glanced over at the magnolia, with its clean perfume and its falling train of creamy petals. For the first time in over a year, he experienced a warm vision of Elise. As Anat Arad smiled at him, he finally consigned his teenager to that bright firmament of old flames whose innocent miscalculations have receded with dignity into the reliable past.

Arad lazily stroked Wood's tanned wrist. "What time do you think it is?"

"Feels elevenish."

"Her flight gets in just before two," she said.

He noted the slightly longer but unpainted nails and

369

smiled. "I'll shower after you."

"Rachel will insist on a thorough inspection."

"You're not going to become one of those sartorial reformers, are you?"

"We both know she will step off that plane dressed to kill. We might as well humor her."

"I suppose."

Arad smiled. "You have to admit: it's more fun to disrobe someone who looks like a million dollars."

"True. Personally, I thought Rachel in T-shirt and jeans was pure poetry."

"You'd say that about any chick with a figure like that."

"So would you, angel."

She kissed him, stood, and took up a handful of dishes.

He watched her go and listened to her bare feet on the stairs. Then he followed her inside. At the top of the kitchen stairs, he embraced her from behind.

"Save something for our guest, dear." Arad turned around.

He lifted her and carried her laughing to the shower. With some difficulty, they avoided a relapse and dried each other.

Wood took a deep breath. "So this interview Monday should be a breeze?"

Arad loosened her neck and stopped kneading his head. "I'd say so. She was downplaying it, of course, but her friend at *Time* said it was all but locked up." She gasped and laughed. "Would you please stop doing that?"

He smiled and stood up. "Well, if anyone can spruce up your government's tarnished image, it's Rachel."

"Yes."

They smiled proudly into the mirror.

"And what of your options?" he asked. "Might you design paramilitary fitness wear? I already have a name for your line: *Anatomie.* Or does our humorless capital reveal some other promise to you?"

"Well, since two of the three of us seem to have put down roots here, since I'm in a unique position—damn you, stop it—culturally speaking, and since I've checked out the scholarships, I'm considering a degree in International Studies at American University."

"Perfect."

"I have a live-in grammarian."

"At the moment, your punctuation is exquisite," he whispered, ducking out of the way.

"I insist on paying for my piano lessons."

"I'm merciless about practice."

"Have I ever let you down in that regard, Herr Schumann?"

He looked at the two of them in the mirror and smiled. "Absolutely not. You are my foremost interpreter."

Arad and Wood went to their bedroom and dressed. She turned around before the vanity, set down her grandmother's mirror, and smiled at him. He yearned to ask for her hand. But he would not deny their friend the only symbol of acceptance the world had seen fit to bestow on love. He had learned enough *Bushido* to know that whereas Rachel Perlman would hardly begrudge Mirim Arad and Nick Xenakis the ceremonial fulfillment of their abandoned promise, the elders would decide for themselves how to observe the gossamer society of women. So Aaron Wood looked into Anat Arad's beautiful black eyes and led her back out through the garden.

Four years later, beside the placid Wye River in the neighboring state of Maryland, Madame Israel, Sister Palestine, and their worried Uncle Sam sat down to another sunny breakfast that would grow cold while they discussed which one of them should say grace.

Thank you for reading.
Please review this book. Reviews help others find
Absolutely Amazing eBooks and inspire us to keep
providing these marvelous tales.

If you would like to be put on our email list to receive
updates on new releases, contests, and promotions, please
go to AbsolutelyAmazingEbooks.com and sign up.

ABOUT THE AUTHOR

Hal Howland is the author of *After Jerusalem: A Story and Two Novellas, Cities & Women: Short Fiction, The Human Drummer: Thoughts on the Life Percussive,* and *Landini Cadence and Other Stories,* a finalist in the 2011 Next Generation Indie Book Awards and a recipient of the 2012 Eric Hoffer Award for excellence in independent publishing. *Cities & Women* earned an honorable mention in the 2014 Lorian Hemingway Short Story Competition. Howland has released three award-winning, critically acclaimed jazz recordings, *The Howland Ensemble, Reiko,* and *10 Years in 5 Days,* and has received a jazz fellowship from the National Endowment for the Arts. Born in Washington, D.C., and raised in Virginia, Europe, and the Middle East, Howland lives in Key West, Florida.

Praise for *After Jerusalem*

"'Murder in the Percussion Section' [is] a gourmet trip through the percussion kitchen—accessories and all!"
   -**Fred Begun,** principal timpanist emeritus, National Symphony Orchestra

"Hal Howland is a great observer of human nature. He has an uncanny ability to get right to the heart of matters with a dry and subtle wit."
   -**Andrea Comstock,** executive director, Key West Art Center

"Entertaining!"
   -**Peter Erskine,** jazz drummer

"One hell of a read! A real page-turner, enriched by Howland's wry sense of humor and twisted imagination. Characters [are] vividly drawn, [with] possibly the most considerate episodes of sexual congress ever recorded: warm and real and attractive. Hard-hitting action, suspense, and sweeping local color aplenty. Howland's voice is strong, gripping, and laugh-out-loud funny. After Jerusalem is a trip: pick it up and buckle your seat belt."
   -**Constance Gilbert,** *Solares Hill*

"Hal Howland weaves a tale that is reminiscent of when short stories flourished in magazines and publishers fought each other for writers' stories. Howland brings the

Key West I know so well to life and captures the essence of the characters that call the end of the road home. Howland's weaving of his knowledge of music through the stories is masterful. I not only enjoyed the stories, but closed the book having learned something too."

-**Michael Haskins,** author of *Chasin' the Wind*

"Hal Howland mixes musical mystery, sexual mayhem, and foreign intrigue into a literary treat of symphonic proportions. Bravo!"

-**Michael Suib,** author and former *Miami Herald* columnist

Praise for *Landini Cadence*

"It's great! It kept me guessing till the end."

-**Larry Erskine,** Key West city attorney

"Just started reading Hal Howland's Landini Cadence, *and it is easy to see this is another runaway Key West hit for him! His Rich Castillo, the homicide detective who moonlights as a drummer, is a winner. Loved his conversation with the racist, holier-than-thou Pastor Pilcher after the murder of his two church members. Howland paints that area of the Lower Keys exactly as it is. Can't wait to read the rest of the book!"*

-**Peg Gregory,** author of *Starfish*

"What a fun book! A great example of the inspiration of love."

-**Michael Larson,** St. Peter Catholic Church choir director

"I love it! It grabs the reader from the first page and doesn't let go. Read it twice!"

-**Howard Livingston,** singer-songwriter

"Howland's best piece of fiction yet! On its surface the novel is a well-structured work that fits cozily into the niche of crime fiction, a pitch-perfect poolside read that's amply disturbing and compelling. What sets it apart is its most unexpected gift: an unflinching look at the politics and customs at work in our sunny island chain."

Praise for *The Human Drummer*

"Bravissimo! What a wonderful achievement. This is a great contribution to what we are all about."

-Fred Begun, principal timpanist emeritus, National Symphony Orchestra

"Really enjoyed it very much! Hal has obviously done his homework. Great reading, understandable, and should be in every musician's library."

-Hal Blaine, studio drummer

"Hal must be congratulated! He offers much wisdom into the performer's life and the realities of the business. Young drummers would find it inspiring."

-Tony Cirone, principal percussionist, San Francisco Symphony Orchestra

"Opens the drummer's world to everyone!"

-Britt Conley, Washington drummer-photographer

"Very interesting! Glad to know that my name is mentioned among such notables."

-Andrew Cyrille, avant-garde jazz drummer

"Fills a niche! Says many things of interest to both drummers and laypersons, entertaining, explains the everyday world of the working musician, substantial—there is an interested readership out there for this book."

-Peter Erskine, drummer and leader

"I couldn't put it down! It just blows me away."
        - **Roger "Hurricane" Wilson,** blues guitarist

"A masterpiece! I love it. As a teacher, I need to know this."
    -**Ginger Zyskowski,** owner, Professional Drum School,
                                     Hutchinson, Kansas

The New
Atlantian Library

NewAtlantianLibrary.com
or AbsolutelyAmazingeBooks.com
or AA-eBooks.com

www.ingramcontent.com/pod-product-compliance
Lightning Source LLC
Chambersburg PA
CBHW060813030726
47503CB00002B/476